CLOVIS

a novel

Annie Dike

To my Mom,

whose strength, tenacity,
and notorious butthole mouth
made this author possible

PROLOGUE

DIRTCASTLES

In every cracked cow patty memory from my childhood, Jude looks like he doesn't fit there. Like a dewy rose in the desert, an angelic Michelangelo at a yard sale. We're in the "sandbox" by Dad's trailer, although it's more ground dry clay than "sand"—orangish-red and too fine on top to build with. Like all dirt in Clovis, New Mexico, it's too dry for dreams to grow. The "box" is formed by two half-buried railroad ties cornered by two cinder block walls, one broken like a jagged smile. There are spoons and sticks in the dirt. A pail. A half-burnt, bent castle mold. Its once-pink hue is now a streaky brown. I'm all dirt knees, pig braids, with tortilla from our bologna lunch rollups still in my teeth. Freckles. Scabs. A runny nose. Then there's Jude. Slender, thick-haired, long-lashed. The golden hazel of his eyes set off by his creamy white skin. He's so aware, always thinking, seeing a different reality than I do.

Jude grabbed one of the big, plastic Allsups Tallsips cups from the cupboard in Dad's trailer and filled it with water to take to the sandbox. Although I asked a million times during the short walk if he was going to dump it on me, Jude kept rolling his eyes but not answering. So I keep my eyes on the water. Although if he threw it on me, it wouldn't really matter. It's not like I was dressed up. Around Dad's, I pretty much wore the same jeans three days in a row and my favorite *My*

Little Ponies t-shirt, feeling proud that I knew p-o-n-y became p-o-n-i-e-s when plural, because Jude was teaching me. We'd been going page by page through the garage sale Encyclopedia set Mom got us back at her house.

At the sandbox, I take the kitchen spoon and butter knife I'd shoved in my grimy back pocket from Dad's trailer, and hand one to Jude, so we can start digging. While I start filling my dented castle mold, Jude digs a big divot the size of a mixing bowl and uses a scrap of black tarp to make a pool. There are always pieces of that tarp blown up against fences or caught in tumbleweeds around here as people lay it under their rock yards to stop weeds from growing. Jude starts mixing clay-sand and water, adding it from his Tallsips cup into the pool, until he has created a wet, almost sandy mixture. Then he starts to drizzle.

I stop making my behemoth castle to watch him, dazzled as I always am watching Jude create. Jude takes handful after handful and continues to drizzle his sandy mixture, dribble upon dribble, until his structure starts to erect itself up toward the sky. Jude's creation is a good foot taller than my squat building when he drizzles the last graceful touches, bringing the structure to a fine sandy point, straight up, like a mystical pencil. Jude sits back on his heels and cocks his heart-shaped face to the side, admiring his creation. I smash some extra dirt on the top of my brute structure, trying to improve it, as if it's an insult to Jude's.

"It's a skyscraper," Jude says. "Like in New York City," he tells me, and the words feel like marbles in my mouth. So foreign. I look at it. This gloopy, fine spire almost as tall as our belly buttons. Then I look at him, fascinated but also frustrated, thinking what I always think. How is it we—Jude and I—could come from the same place, the same genes, and yet, I can never do or be what he is? But, somehow, miraculously, I am his and he has chosen me, bologna teeth and all.

"It's pretty cool," I say, in consolation, then start filling another castle mold to form another ugly mound that I know I will just smash, to hide the weird boil of emotions roiling inside me as Jude creates a little toothpick path and fence around his New York skyscraper. When we see the first big dollop of rain spatter onto the dry clay, we grab our kitchen spoons and Tallsips cups. Jude takes one look back at the box before we jog back to the trailer in the building, in the rain. His lashes are so long I see raindrops collect on them. He turns his head briefly back toward the sandbox as if imprinting what he's seeing in his memory. I do the same with his silhouette against the grey sky as his voice seeps through like a dream.

"C'mon, Callie!" Jude says with a spark in his eye, his gaze a ray of light that illuminates me.

One rainy game of *Monopoly* later—even starting me with the extra $100 bills we made out of construction paper, Jude always wins—he and I walk back to the sandbox to see what became of our creations. My mud monster is still pretty much recognizable, the two squat bases still standing, although some of the edges and little carved-out windows I'd added have been worn off. But Jude's. Jude's lofty concept is completely gone. The spindly skyscraper he'd erected has been erased entirely, washed down to a sad lump, with toothpicks strewn about as if they were simply dropped there. Every bit of his fanciful spire, his elegant creation, is gone, without a trace. If I hadn't seen it myself, I almost wouldn't have believed it was ever there.

It's my most vivid memory from my early childhood. It's crisp and clay red, smells like rain, and it haunts me. I'm only six. How is it I already know?

Contents

CHAPTER ONE
JOLT

I blink into the blinding white, confused. *What am I seeing?* The packed dirt is gone. A sea of white fluff blanketed it overnight. Suddenly, the dusty flatlands around Janessa's trailer are pretty—beautiful even. But, unrecognizable. Where is her lava rock yard? Ugly like Mars. Where are the round green cow patties? The horseshoes she and Jude had been threatening to throw at me yesterday? How could a simple dusting of brilliant white powder turn a clay-colored New Mexico cattle farm into a land so sparkling that Queen Frostine from Candy Land could live here?

I rub my little six-year-old fists into my eyes, thinking it might be a trick. This day can't exist—a whole Saturday. No school. And this frosty playground to roll around in all day? I want to bolt out the door in my *Peter Pan* flannel nightgown, the one that sparks when I rub my tummy really fast under my covers at night. It's my favorite nightgown, but it's getting a little small because I've had it since I was four. I want to see if it will spark in the snow. I want to feel that white fluff on my skin. To smear it on my face like old lady cream. To eat it.

I'm about to run right out in my nightgown and bare feet when Jude jumps in front of me and hip-bumps me into the wall by the door of Janessa's trailer. I don't love when we hang out with Janessa because she's closer in age to Jude and always tries to sidle up next to him, thinking she can then tell *me* what to do. But she lives right across the highway from Dad's, and Dad needs a place to chuck us sometimes when he makes long cattle hauls in his big rig, Blackie, a huge, shiny Peterbilt that I'm in love with. I fall clumsily onto the musty pile of shoes everyone leaves by the door and scrunch my angry little face up at Jude.

"You'll freeze, dummy," he says, shoving me again, playfully. "Calm down. Janessa's getting the snow stuff. We're gonna go out in just a minute. And build a huge snowman!" his arms fly out in a circle. We. *All of us*, I think—Jude and I and stupid Janessa. I beam at Jude. And pee a little. It's all so exciting. The first time I've ever seen snow.

Janessa comes from the back of the trailer, her arms stuffed with old ski pants, mismatched jackets, several pairs of rubber mud boots we use when we help her scoop cow patties, and a wadded-up handful of men's tube socks, better known to us as mittens, or puppets—depending on the occasion. Janessa lords over the pile, doling out each piece to us with dramatic flair so she remains in charge. She hands one sock delicately to Jude, watching him slide it up his slender milk arm. She's hoisting the others up in the air so I have to jump and snatch at them as she hands Jude a toboggan and watches him put it on.

I've got a long white men's sock on my left arm with three rings at the top, two blue, one red, that bunches under my armpit, and a two blue-ringed number on my right that fits much better around my elbow. They're cinched under a scuffed yellow puff jacket with my nightgown tucked into a pair of oversized camo pants. I'm ready! I'm clapping my sock-clad hands together as Jude pushes the trailer door open, then I see it. A glistening sea of white. All the dirt and clay and cow patties have been transformed into a cottony white ocean. I blink. It's so bright I can't see. Jude grabs my hand and says the words I always love to hear, the words that make me feel like I'm his and only his.

"Come on, Lil Bit," he whispers, and we tear off toward the pasture.

—

"Let's build him here," Janessa says, scraping her too-big rubber galoshes to make a big X.

Janessa and I are rolling up the middle section when Jude comes back from the trailer with a few charcoals from the clamp-on grill on Janessa's back porch, a couple pieces of gnarly wood, and a stomped-on trucker's hat that's been living under the tire by the telephone pole for as long as I can remember. My brain blinks an image of our Mr. Potato Head at Mom's into my mind as I realize what Jude has found. *Face stuff!*

"You're not making the mouth right," Janessa whines, moving anything Jude puts on the snowman and getting charcoal remnants everywhere, until Jude finally gives me that *Uggh, Janessa* look and concedes.

"All right," Jude says. "The charcoal can be the buttons," as he's packing white snow back on the snowman's face to hide the nasty charcoal smudges Janessa created, so Mr. StayPuft no longer looks like some strung-out actress when they cry in the movies. Janessa gives me a *"See?"* look, like I'm on her side. I force my eyes not to roll as I turn my head back to Jude, who is carving a pretty cool hole where the snowman's mouth should be. He lines the edges with branches to make lips, and plunges a big weed into the snowman's mouth that hangs out like he's chewing on it, then steps back. Magically, it's even better than a charcoal mouth, and I am once again reminded. It doesn't matter how many times you reject Jude or try to press him down. He just comes back reinvented, somehow impossibly better, like he's too slippery for oppression.

Shoulders back, I turn to Janessa and give her a *"See?"* look, but I see she's trying to whisper something in Jude's ear. Jude is leaning far away from her, craning his neck and pleading to me with his eyes. I know why. Janessa has really bad breath. So bad it's become the "Breath of Death" in some of mine and Jude's darker LEGOs and Pony plots. I pinch my nose like I'm smelling something stinky and begin pulling off one of my sopping wet tube socks to try to warm my frigid, blistered-pink hands.

I swing the long, wet sock into the air to drape it over the electric fence around Janessa's cattle pasture. Right before it touches, I hear the little pop of the fence and something in my brain emits a reciprocal click, but it's too late. It happens. The minute my wet sock connects, my body is momentarily paralyzed. My eyes bulge. Or maybe it's my sockets that bulge, not my eyes. I'm not sure. But something physical moves around my eyeballs, pushing them out of the way, as it ejects out of my eye sockets. I'm being shocked. The feeling of electricity leaving my body through my eyeballs is unnerving. Other worldly. I feel injured and empowered at the same time, like a superhero.

I hear another beep as the jolt from my dream awakens me. It's the monitor by my bed. Groggily, I open my eyes. My hospital bed. Still here. My body is still wounded. Beep. Janessa and the snowman have vanished. Beep. Jude is gone. Beep.

CHAPTER TWO
LITTLE WARRIOR

Confined to the bed, I control my breathing and slowly pan the room, still not believing I am actually here. In a hospital room, with sickly cream walls, a TV in the corner with electrical tape around its wires, and plastic blinds that turn with a rod. I am here. I look at the monitor beside my bed that's showing my blood pressure, heart rate, and other vitals, and it confirms it right there at the top.

CALLIOPE ANN POTTS

You are here.

But I notice the admit date is two days ago … I think. I blink and focus on it again, but it remains the same: July 12, 2012. That's two, no three days ago? What's today? Then it all crashes into my mind, sounding like a pyramid of Solo cups tumbling. July 12th was a Thursday. I had a mediation that went late into the afternoon. That afternoon, I met Braden at the coffee shop to talk. After we spoke, I walked. And after I walked, I went to Nick's.

I turn my hands around in front of me, trying to gather clues from anything. I see some dirt and what looks like—*is that blood?*—under my right forefinger and thumbnails. My vision is swimming a little, and my eyes feel gummy, the light painful, so I close them. Seeing the remnants of blood on my hands takes me immediately back. To ugly swirls on a linoleum floor. To my eight-year-old hands, smashing toilet paper onto my bleeding foot. To the smell of cigarettes and gin. Back, back, back. To Mom's.

———

I'd be hard-pressed to say which place is better, Mom's or Dad's. Dad's trailer is pretty falling apart. In certain places you step, the floor will go soft. The plywood cabinets in the kitchen are swollen and never really shut properly. The one toilet, which often backs up, is slowly sinking into the floor. But Dad's trailer is close to the stockyards and has a sandbox and a sack swing Jude and I had hung from the big oak behind the neighbor's doublewide. There's that.

Mom's is an actual house, a flat one with rocks on the roof, if that ranks higher than a trailer. We don't have central heat or AC in the house, just an electric wall heater in the hallway for winter and open windows and fans for summer. The kitchen has this thin, greasy red carpet, while the rest of the house is shag. But we do have a decent backyard with a cinderblock fence that Jude and I can walk on top of, yard to yard, like bridges to new places.

Mom and Dad are divorced, since I was tiny, like two years old. I have no memory of them ever being in the same room together, but something tells me it wouldn't go well. Jude was a little older. Five, maybe? He says he's got some memories of their "knock-down, drag-outs", he calls them. But just a few. Jude tells me they only come in flashes, mostly of sounds—chairs scraping the floor, doors being slammed, shouting, but, in his memories, he can see Mom and Dad's arms flailing and knees and hands hitting the floor as he looks down to avert his eyes from their conflict. The sounds alone, as he describes them, tell me I don't want those memories.

Mom remarried a few years back. We call our Stepdad "Steve," and he's good to us. He's a mechanic. Works on tractors for Ford.

Means he can pretty much fix or assemble anything, which I think makes him really cool. He doesn't have the song and dance flair of Dad, but not nearly as much of a temper either, and he doesn't fight back. I'll bet that's what Mom likes the most about him because she's basically a single mom. Any privileges Jude or I have or punishments to be doled out begin and end with her word. That's why Jude and I always tried to hide our shenanigans from Mom. Secrecy was better than her scrutiny, which begins with Mom's "butthole" mouth. When she's pissed and scrunches it up, tight as a frog's ass, that's when we really know we've done it.

Like the time I fell about twenty feet down out of the tree in the backyard, climbing higher than I was supposed to. Jude scooped up my scraped-up body and shoved it through the window of his bedroom to the bathroom so Mom wouldn't see. There he wound a toilet paper roll around and around and around my Care-Bear tummy, mummy-style, before dinner so Mom wouldn't know what had happened. I'll never forget his squinched-up face as he had his arms ram-rod straight going around my oozing torso to avoid the bloody goo. "Jesus, that's grody," he'd said. I was sure the whole kitchen smelled like iron from my bleeding body as we all sat awkwardly through dinner. Jude kept eyeing me harshly from his spot at the table as the blood started to seep through my Starbrite t-shirt.

Back then, we never tried to figure out the *why*. I just felt like Jude and I knew not to whine about pain. Or much of anything for that matter. Whining led to whoopings, that's what I'd learned. So ingrained, it became instinct. Like knowing a stove is hot. The more Mom drank, the hotter she got. This night was no different.

I'm eight and sitting on the toilet in our only bathroom, staring at the stupid pattern on the yellow linoleum floor, trying to lose myself in the gaudy swirls, trying to see faces in them, give them expressions, trying to do anything to distract me from what I know is coming. Mom is coming.

Mom and Steve had invited some friends over for beer and a Cowboys game. I'd been watching Mom closely. She was usually the life of the party at these get-togethers. Telling the best jokes, spinning wild tales, and getting people up to dance. When she gets that first happy sheen, she's vibrant and animated, but—as it always does—that seesaw begins to tip the other way. As the after-dinner drinks continued, Mom became louder and more slurred. Even as a kid, I could tell she was talking over the others and interrupting everyone to tell stories that made no sense.

Jude and I had picked up our sloppy joe plates from the table on the back porch to take into the kitchen, hoping we could retreat to the safety of our rooms before she set her sights on us. That's not what happened. On my way in, one plate slid off the top of my stack, hit the wall in the hallway, and shattered with a splitting crack on the floor. The laughter and chatter from out back died instantly. The music was turned down. I heard chairs scooting across the concrete slab of our porch. I dropped to my knees and began scooping and snatching ceramic plate pieces off the floor, hoping I could clean most of it up before they reached me. *She* reached me. I had collected most of them, so I jumped up quickly to take my carnage to the kitchen. But when I did, I stepped down hard, with all my weight, on a big shard, and it immediately cut into the tender underbelly of my bare foot.

The unexpected pain of it had shot through my nerves and made me drop my handful of shards, which clattered even louder now in the silence and only broke into further pieces. "Dammit!" I shouted in pain before my brain could stop me. As I stared, paralyzed for a moment, at the shards on the floor, I knew I'd done it. I'd broken things Mom 'works very hard to buy.' I'd 'made a mess.' I'd 'banged myself up.' And, to top all that stupidness off, I'd just 'spoken like trailer trash.' I was so deep I started to cry far more out of fear than pain. And anger. Hot seething anger.

As I sit on the toilet and mash more red wads onto my zombie foot, I am infuriated with myself. Staring at the dumb swirls on the yellow floor, I now only see angry faces. Eyebrows pitched down. Gnarled teeth. Mom eventually pushes the bathroom door open and slumps onto the door frame.

She is a thin waif of a woman, her skin leathered from weekend afternoons spent sitting in a tri-fold lawn chair in the back yard, oiling herself up with one hand, beer in the other. Her once-beautiful face is now marred with cracks and wrinkles from a lifetime of smoking and drinking. Her stringy, dyed hair spills out of a messy clip on top of her head, and her mascara is smudged under her eyes, but it only seems to make them more piercing.

Mom leans back and lets her head hit the door of the bathroom with a thump. When she takes it off, it's swimming slightly on her shoulders.

"I'm sorry, Mom, I … I," I stammer, then sniff. I don't look at the cut. Just mash harder. I already know the words that are going to come out of her mouth. Their stupid simplicity is making me even madder. Just because something makes sense doesn't make it easy to do.

"Stop. Yer. Crying," Mom draws out. *Those are the words.* "What's crying gonna do?" *That is the question.* I know the answer, but that's why my tears are embarrassing. I smack the back of my empty hand at my face, swatting my stupid tears away, not knowing I have created a little Indian red warrior streak under each eye. I look at Mom with all my anger and steam and little-kid fury. She looks back at me and we hold this stand-off for a quiet, painful minute or two. I swear her eyes start to clear a little. These weird moments where I feel like I understand Mom a little, and maybe she understands me, unnerve me. Makes me feel like a bundle of twigs that's come unstrung.

Mom lips her cigarette, opens the medicine cabinet, and raises her eyebrows, nodding her head toward it. Looks inside. Looks at me, and I know. I put my wadded-up foot down as she blows a big plume of smoke out. I pad over and pull out the old brown and white bottle of hydrogen peroxide and some gauze and tape. I pad back over to the tub, dump a little puddle of peroxide in it by the drain, and straddle the edge. I clench my jaw tight and don't make a sound as I splash my foot around in the liquid, and the bubbles burn into my cut.

"When you're bandaged, clean the floor in here. Then the hall. Then the kitchen." A long pause. "Then yourself," as Mom finishes her glass, eyes still on me. I see her mouth tug ever so slightly at the corners. *Is that a smile?* She shoves some rough hairs out of her face with the heel of her hand, then pushes around on her nose like she does when she wants another drink. "Then go to bed," she says.

Mom pulls the bathroom door closed. I lift my foot up to see the gash beneath. It's really not that bad. About an inch. Not too deep. A clean cut, not jagged like many others I've inflicted on my little kid body. With Neosporin, it'll heal quick. I hear Mom making another drink in the kitchen as I push gauze onto the bottom of my foot and wrap tape around a couple of times. After I rinse the blood and peroxide down the drain of our mustard yellow tub, I hear her back out on the concrete porch in the backyard—the scrape of her metal lawn chair, the clink of her glass ashtray being pulled across the rickety table as she eases in to sit out there for a while alone before bed, as it seems everyone cleared out while I was cleaning up. I'm sitting in the bathroom, not fifteen feet from her—through walls—feeling content alone as well, wondering if she and I are more alike than we think. I don't try to pretend I know why Mom likes to be alone so much, or why she likes to drink so much, but a part of me understands the solace I assume she feels when she does.

But I'm still curious. *Why did she smile?*

CHAPTER THREE
HAPHAZARD HERO

When Jude and I were younger, and Dad was a long-haul cattle truck driver, he would sometimes come pick us up near Mom's neighborhood in his big shiny Peterbilt, Blackie. Dad would lay on the jack brakes when he came up Gidding Street and give us one loud honk to let us know he was parked at the nearby Allsups where we always met him. At the sound of his honk, Mom would toss our bags out on the lawn, two stained, blue, and khaki duffel bags, the ones that actually said "Duffel" on them that were stuffed full of ratty t-shirts and shorts for the trip, and a little quart Ziplock for our toiletries. Jude and I were somewhere in the range of six and nine when Dad had to hang up his rodeo boots and spurs to start doing long-hauls.

As soon as we would round the corner to the gas station, Dad would let his herding dog, Pepper—smart as a whip—out, and she would run toward us, the little nub of her tail wagging. Pepper was just as her name said it—sprinkled all over like someone had shaken salt and pepper all over her, with some bigger black spots, and a few honey brown spots thrown in, especially one right around her left eye that looked like a patch. Jude and I would climb into Blackie behind Pepper to start setting up our "fort" in the sleeper of Dad's truck. Jude liked to hang "curtains" (a sheet with holes cut in it) with little shower curtain clips on a bungee, essentially making a doorway between Dad's truck cab and our fort, and tie them back with shoestrings done up in bows.

The squeak of the plastic hospital mattress under me now reminds me of the little three-inch plastic pad Dad had in the sleeper of Blackie, if that thing could qualify as a mattress. Looking around this cream room with its blinking, beeping machines, I find tears brimming in my eyes at the aching need I feel for my brother Jude to be here, to explain everything that has happened and assure me it will all be okay. Or for my dad to blow the ceiling off of this cell of a room with his booming voice. I want him to sing some silly song, kiss my wounds, and—as only dads can do—make it all better. Knowing neither of them will, my brain seems to stop asking questions, stop worrying altogether. It wraps its feathery wings around me once again and takes me back to a time when I felt I still had guardian angels.

———

I believe I was around six on this particular trip, and Dad had pulled over on the shoulder of the road so we could all "do our business," which was an errand we were very used to. The boys headed toward one clump of bushes, and I, ever the "lady," headed to another, toilet paper in hand. I don't know how Pepper knew we were both "ladies", or maybe she sensed I was the younger one and needed more protection. For whatever reason, Pepper always came with me on this particular business errand.

On the way back to the truck, I managed to step in some kind of heaping hornet's nest or buried beehive or something because I had, in my mind, a swarm of monstrous, vicious, alien-like wasps swarming me on the way back. I was running and flailing and screaming and swatting them with the toilet paper, and had just about cleared them when I felt something on my eye. I reached up out of instinct and smacked at it and must have smashed that stinger right into the lid of my eye because I instantly felt the venom—or whatever putrid, seething substance those alien wasps were carrying—singe into my skin. I howled, and Pepper, on instinct, howled with me, then she took off toward the boys as fast as her incredible legs could carry her.

Jude heard me first and flew from Dad's rig toward me in a full sprint, sensing my lung-rattling scream was not for fun or kicks. He seemed to have a finely tuned radar when I was in actual pain, which I was with my eye puffing up to the size of a ping pong ball. Dad was quick behind him. He did a roadside assessment of me, which ended with an *"Awww … hell"*, and started to rummage around the passenger floorboard of his truck as Pepper circled me, whimpering in concern.

Dad was a long-time Copenhagen connoisseur. He always had a big hunk of chaw packed down below the gums of his bottom teeth. I came to love the smell of it as I associated it with Dad and found myself strangely attracted to some pretty hideous redneck deadbeats in college because of it. But, I now know that tobacco is more than a sticky, cancer-causing, sickening habit. It can work wonders when you've been stung by alien wasps.

My Dad hooked his finger in his mouth and pulled the big, wet wad of tobacco out from his bottom lip and slapped that sticky mess on my eye. And, as soon as he did, I could feel the alien wasp venom leaving my body. The tobacco wad was cool and wet and incredibly soothing. And, I even liked the smell. I'm sure I was smiling from the instant relief, caring not about the stray tobacco juice that was leaking down my cheek and onto the shoulder of my faded Care Bears shirt. Dad had fixed it!

He held the wad to my head while he kept rummaging around the floor of the cab for something to keep the wad on my face and contain the mess. And, as it seemed he always did, Dad found the perfect thing: a big, thick Maxi pad—with wings, mind you! At the time, I had no idea why Dad had a Maxi pad in the cab of his truck. I'm sure he had many a lady-friend join him on a haul or two, or just the night, and she clearly left some remnants of her womanhood behind. Or, perhaps Dad just kept a pack of them around for some highly useful purpose on the truck, to contain a small oil spill, or patch a leak. I have no idea, but I was grateful that day that he did.

Jude's eyes popped wide when he saw my bandage contraption. He closed his mouth and shook his head.

"That's just … no," he said in a near whisper.

But whether Jude thought I was presentable or not didn't matter. I was his only partner out there. Stinky or tobacco-ey or slapped to the hilt with a Maxi pad, we were an inseparable duo. When we stopped up the road at a Love's so Dad could "doctor me up more," I had no idea I was running around the store with a woman's menstrual device slapped to my face and sticky, stinky tobacco juice crusted up all over me. I probably wouldn't have cared anyway, as *my* favorite part of these truck trips with Dad was not the fort-building in Blackie like Jude, it was the gleaming Wonka-esque coffee machine that spat out hot water and added a steaming stream of brown to make hot chocolate. When Jude first squirted a swirly mountain of whipped cream on mine, to the point of toppling, and deemed it a "kapperchino" with one pinkie in the air holding his identical toppling cup, I fell in love.

As Jude and I made our way up to the kapperchino machine and began making our masterpieces, I was starting to elicit some stares. I didn't know what all the hub-bub was about, so I tried to behave as much as possible—*"Yes, ma'am. Excuse me. The small cup, please. Thank you."* But, despite the polite act, a bulbous woman who smelled like Aqua Net got me in her clutches. She turned me around by the shoulders and said with a tone, "Little girl, do you need help?" Both Jude and I knew something was up. But we both knew instinctively, the last thing we wanted was any *help* from Aqua Net.

For reasons unbeknownst to us, a ruckus was definitely afoot. "No ma'am, I …" I started to respond, but lost my train of thought when I saw Dad come into the store. Jude and I both hung our heads and dug our toes in the ground, thinking a spanking would certainly be forth-coming. Aqua Net repeated her inquiry even louder as Dad pushed through a few folks, glared back at some old country biddies who were giving me a solid stare, and answered Aqua Net for me with a "No, she don't need no help." He then scooped me up and hoisted me onto his hip and said, "Come here, Babes. Let me fix it."

———

I find I'm smiling, as I scoot around in my plastic-coated hospital bed, making the same sound both Dad's sleeper mattress and that maxi pad did as Dad gently tugged it off my gummy, saliva-slathered face in the men's room and doctored me up right. I'm twiddling with the coarse white blanket the hospital staff has laid over me, shuffling through a dozen other memories where Dad did that. Swooped in several times a year, turned the ordinariness of our dusty lives in Clovis into some kind of new adventure, and even imparted nuggets of poignant cowboy wisdom when it was needed most.

There was the song Dad made up for Jude that always brought Jude out of a funk, no matter how deep. "Jude Boy, Jude Boy, Where Ya Been?" he'd ring out in his strong tenor, humor and spark in his voice. If that wasn't enough to prompt Jude to sing the second verse, Dad would take it over himself. "Round the world. I'm going again!" which usually would at least be enough to have Jude trying hard not to smile at that point, so that Dad would continue. "What are you gonna do when you get back?" He would eye Jude gently. "Take a little walk down the railroad track," Jude would say softly, which would prompt Dad's big finish, in which I always joined: "JUDE BOY!" Even my slight jealousy that Dad had made a song just for Jude, not for me, could be overshadowed by that grand finish. Dad and I had excellent jazz hands.

There were the unforgettable stories Dad would tell about him and his high school buddies, particularly the scrawniest of them: Runt. "One time," Dad would start, "we launched Runt clean across Smith Lake by wadding him up into a young pine and bending it back like a catapult." Dad would stand ramrod straight then, lean way over—like that signature Michael Jackson move—jut his chin out and plant a firm salute to his forehead. "And he held the salute, just like that, until he hit the water! Bawoosh!" Dad would make a big splash sound, then clutch his sides from the laughing pains. Runt stories were my favorite.

Then there were the little thimbles of wisdom that could magically dry my tears when Dad would lean down to inspect whatever cut or scrape I'd just endured, wipe the dirt and blood off of it with his bare hands, and tell me, "Aww, that's nothing. I'm pretty sure you're gonna live, Babes. Scars make good stories." Suddenly, I forgot how to cry when he said that. I would turn and pet Pepper and tell her, too, to make sure I truly believed it. "Scars make good stories," I'd tell that beautiful spotted face.

These memories are mingled with others, not so bright. The time I saw Dad holding a lighter under a spoon in the back bedroom of his trailer, at, unfortunately, an age that I knew exactly what he was doing.

The handful of girlfriends Dad exposed me and Jude to—Mundi, Sissy, Peg, Krystal (with a "K")—each of them strung out on their own unique form of self-medication, self-loathing, insecurity, and insanity. Krystal, with a K, once tried to grab me from the bed she was wailing and wallowing around in and pull me toward her. I've never gnashed and fought a snatching so hard in my life. Thankfully, Pepper had my back, barking and snapping behind me, which finally prompted Krystal to let go.

The haunting rumble of slamming fists, thrown furniture, muffled shouts, and skin slapping I would sometimes hear while sleeping on the couch in the living room at Dad's—even through the pillow I was jamming onto both mine and Pepper's ears—from the bedroom in the back of the trailer when he and whatever girlfriend he was with at the time got in a fight.

Dad was a lot of things: a rowdy, fun-loving cowboy, a healer of horses, skinned knees, and broken hearts, a fantastic singer, an incredible story- and joke-teller. A great dog owner. But he was also a failure at many things. He missed many of our birthdays and school events. Dad never got a college degree or held down a steady job. He never owned his own home. He used, mangled, and abused his poor cowboy body. But his smile, his snicker, his melodic baritone outshone all of that—even Mom's cold discipline.

"I know it hurts to say bye for a bit, Babes," Dad would say, his right hand—the one with the thumb he almost ripped off roping—snaked back behind the driver's seat to me on our way back to Clovis, back to Mom, his eyes still on the road. "But you know what?" he'd say, perking up his voice a little. "We can't know joy," he'd squeeze my hand, waiting for me to answer. I'd snuffle and swallow all that snot and mucus and get my froggy voice in gear.

"Without pain," I'd say.

My mind shuffles through a catalog of images as I pick at the rough cotton of my hospital blanket, not even really seeing it. Instead, I see Jude's hands on ponies. Blood on a torn-open patch of my elastic-waisted little-kid jeans. The smoke of Mom's cigarette wafted beautifully up. Cinder blocks in our backyard. The sandbox at Dad's trailer park. Pepper herding cows, happiest when she's working. Hiding under a blanket by Jude while we both tuned out the violent noises around us. Kip's hair blowing in the breeze. A Biscuit Donut sizzling in grease. I hear the voice from the *Dream Phone*. I smell Mariah's cast. As I lie here, it's as if I'm feeling and reliving my childhood all over again. *Why?*

Am I supposed to understand something I didn't previously? Uncover a secret? Forgive someone? With everything that has happened in my life recently—the bomb that detonated two months ago essentially eviscerating my world—I cannot possibly believe my past, as troubled as it might seem, could have prepared me for the colossal volumes of loss and confusion that form my present.

I flinch at the thought of the person I may be supposed to forgive. *Not her. Not yet.*

Even laying here, calmly unpacking it, I wholeheartedly believe nothing in my past can explain why Mom picked the one fight with me that I could never forgive her for. Why had she been so blinded with rage that she was hellbent on denying Jude the one ounce of dignity and autonomy he had left? *What happened to her that cut so deeply?*

The more I spend time trying to unravel all the darkness and pain I see behind so many of the sunlit, cowpatty memories of my childhood, the more I believe I will never understand her—my own mother. So, I do what I have always done. I give up trying, and I put another brick in the wall I've built between her and me.

CHAPTER FOUR
THE ACCIDENT

I'm twisting my hospital bracelet around my wrist—reading and re-reading my name, date of birth, and blood type on it—trying to remember how and where the hospital staff got this information. I have no recollection of even coming through the doors of the Emergency Room, assuming that's how I got into this godforsaken building. My first memories after the accident were waking up in the middle of the night with beeps and buzzers and low lights. Lots of whispering and movement about me, but no one is talking *to* me. The whole scene looks and sounds like it's underwater. I'm not sure why I didn't scream or demand to know why I was there. Was I too scared to find out? Incapable of moving or speaking? A visceral memory without any accompanying thoughts or realization of even being there can be terrifying. I learned later that I had been intubated that night and sedated and prepped for surgery to relieve swelling in my brain from bleeding.

The first nurse who sat with me in the ICU before I was subsequently transferred to the floor—was it Clara? I couldn't remember—was soothing and empathetic. She told me I had been in a very bad car accident, although she couldn't tell me what type of car, where the accident had happened, if anyone was with me in the car, whether my car had been struck by another car, or had struck something. Nurse Clara could, however, and did tell me a good deal about my medical condition. When I was admitted, unconscious, the trauma to my head had been their top priority. I'd suffered a depressed skull fracture and concussion. Thankfully, they had been able to drain the blood around my brain and stop the bleeding. The doctors put the skull pieces back in place and stapled the wound. I could still feel the shaved spot on the back of my head. The rigid, rough edges of the staples still baffle me. They also inserted a needle into my spine to drain the excess cerebrospinal fluid.

After managing my head trauma, the medical team turned to my far less life-threatening mangled limbs and broken ribs, which seared like hell anytime I lifted my torso or breathed in deeply. I was terrified of coughing or sneezing the first two days, but that pain had eventually begun to ease. Aside from the healing wounds, bruises, contusions, and sprains, I was going to live. "Be fine," Nurse Clara had actually said. I was going to 'be fine.' But I wasn't sure I would be.

What bothers me even more than the bills I know I am constantly generating, while simultaneously keeping me out of work, is that I cannot remember anything after going to the bar. Nick's. It's such a shithole. Not a place I'd spent a lot of time. I just knew it as a place where you could drink and disappear. As long as you didn't draw attention to yourself, you could sit at the bar for hours and drown yourself, and no one would care. Hell, no one would notice. I did remember why I had wanted to drink myself to drowning. I hadn't forgotten that. Who could?

Also, I had *driven* to Nick's. I remembered that. Other than plopping down at the bar—depressed and disheveled, in my work suit, pantyhose, and slicked-back bun, albeit paired with muddy sneakers—and ordering up my second gin and tonic, double, I couldn't remember anything much after that. I wonder briefly about my car, which I'm hopeful I can still drive, once I find out what kind of shape it's in.

My car, Jesus! What the fuck happened?

None of the people I used to turn to are here now to comfort me or help me answer these terrifying questions. Memories of that little girl—dirt-streaked cheeks, grimy teeth, crystal blue curious eyes— flood me. *Am I still her?*

I find more than my husband—even more than my brother—there is another man I miss the most right now. His humor, his laugh, his tobacco scent. His silly songs. I let tears fall onto my blanket as I hear a knock on the door of my room, and I hear faintly somewhere in the distance him singing in the backdrop of my memory: "Who's that knocking at my door …"

The knock comes again, and I realize it's a real knock. Someone is actually here, about to enter my sad circus of memories. I swat at my face trying to wipe away evidence of the tears, and I sniff up a huge glob of snot and swallow.

"Come in," I rasp.

And there she is. Not my dad. It's Mom. I immediately hear the words *Stop yer' crying* the minute she walks in. She looks thinner, more gaunt than I remember. But I guess I do, too. It's been one hell of a summer for us both. Her eyes are more piercing. They seem more crystal blue than the last time I saw her a couple of months ago. Her frail hair is swept back in a clip with wisps sticking out on both sides. She's got an old jersey on for the San Francisco 49ers, a team or sport none of us ever followed, paired with leggings and slouched down gym socks jammed into grey hiking boots.

Stupidly, my head scrolls through the blazers, pantsuits, and blouses that now fill my closet, that I stress over pairing together— every morning in the dark—to try and look like I fit into my professional legal world. Some huge chunk of me longs for the ease of my past, when I could wear jeans under a dress, a Play Inc. sweatshirt with shorts and jellies, a 49ers jersey with leggings and hiking boots. Suddenly, I ache for the fact that it never mattered what we wore back home. Our entire wardrobe was grungies, and I'm overwhelmed by a nostalgia for every single grimy piece. I snap back at the sound of her shutting the door to my room, leaving us with the beeps of my equipment and the buzz of the overhead fluorescent lights.

"What?" she asks me, and I realize my face must have registered surprise when she came in. I shrug my shoulders and shake my head, realizing she did make the seven-hour drive over from Clovis. Again.

"I am still your next of kin," Mom says. "After your Dad and Jude," she has to add.

I turn away at the sound of his name. I don't like it on her lips. We haven't talked since the blowup, when the world opened up between us and created a chasm I thought could never be bridged. My feelings toward her are so mixed I don't know whether I want to crumple into her sinewy arms or push her away so fiercely she'll never come back to me. I am a tug-of-war of need and repulsion: gratitude and anger.

We stare at each other, and I'm overwhelmed by the possibility that she may be feeling the exact same things.

A nurse comes in and breaks our stalemate. Is it Clara?

"I gave her some pain medication about fifteen minutes ago," the nurse tells Mom. "It may put her to sleep pretty soon," she says to Mom, then turns to me and starts checking my machines, tapping my IV, fluffing my pillow. I meet Mom's eyes, standing by the door, wringing her hands together as if she wants to do something with them but can't.

"I just wanted you to know," Mom starts, but I start to feel the backs of my eyeballs get thick and fuzzy, and I know a sedative is kicking in. My shoulders sink into the bed, and I can feel my muscles all over relaxing. Mom's voice sounds like it's coming to me through a tunnel.

"There's a detective out there trying to question you," I believe she says, although I'm fading. "About the accident, you know … 'cause you was drinking," she adds as I start slipping away. My tired brain tries for a moment to put those pieces together, to try and flip the right switches to create panic and fear, but the little guy in there is getting too sleepy.

Instead, he just sits on a stool and slumps over as a comforting darkness starts to grow around the edges of my vision. My eyes close on their own, and the last thing I hear is Mom telling me:

"But you rest, Callie, 'cause I won't let him."

CHAPTER FIVE
OUR LITTLE PONIES

"Cherries doesn't talk like that," Jude huffs, laying down my Cherries Jubilee pony. She's the one I've had the longest. Dad got her for me at a Wal-Mart somewhere in Texas when I was little because it was the only thing that seemed to stop my tears at the time. Now she's scuffed, parts of her features worn from mine and Jude's years of handling her, and—apparently—not talking right.

"Sorry," my knee-jerk reaction to a Jude scolding. "I was just thinking," I say in a mousy voice, not yet confident defending myself to Jude's face. "What if Cherries was young this time. Like if we played out a scene from her teenage years. Maybe show why she never trusts the high school crowd and why she's afraid to start something with Brian." Jude had named him. He's our only male pony, a lanky white horse with flowing orange hair. Brian's shaped differently than all the other ponies, who are shorter and have broader shoulders and rounder butts.

Jude lifts Brian—our unspoken cue for a break from the action—and begins twisting his plastic pony hair around his finger, thinking, then sets him back down with a snap.

"Come on, Cherries," Jude—in Brian's higher-pitched soft voice—says, moving Brian's whole body side to side, an imitation of a shaking head. "I'm being serious. I want you to go to prom with me because I like you, I really do." And just like that, Jude and I hatch an incredibly twisted plot where Brian and the other ponies decide to have a vat of pig guts and blood spill on Cherries at the Pony Prom. Jude and I convince ourselves that it is a completely unique plot, never tried before. "This is going to be wicked," Jude says with a gleam in his eyes.

It's the summer before my sixth-grade year, and Jude and I are spending our summer days how we often do—watching *Price is Right* reruns all morning while making and eating half a loaf of cinnamon toast or, when Jude gets in the right mood, Biscuit Donuts. Jude pops a can of biscuits, usually in my face because he knows it freaks me out, and mashes holes in the center of each doughy puck to make a doughnut. He then throws them in the Fry Daddy Mom keeps on the stovetop, acting like a French pastry chef with a honking accent, so we can scoop them out and dip them—hot from the grease—into sugar, butter, sometimes syrup. These mornings form the bulk of my childhood memories.

On this day, the Pony Prom, Jude and I raid the kitchen for pig guts ingredients and come up with a goopy mess of mayo, ketchup, and canned peas, half-mashed, that looks pretty disgusting, which makes it pretty freaking perfect for pig guts. "Uggh, grody. I would not eat this," Jude says with a scrunched-up face.

"It's perfect," I breathe out in awe as Jude mixes the ingredients in a bowl and begins picking up the spoon to let the pinkish-red guts drop down into the bowl. Jude and I spend the next two hours building a prom stage on our encyclopedias out of LEGOS and planning the drama. It pains me a little—when we spill the goopy pink mess and Cherries is covered in pig innards—to know no one else will witness the theatre magic Jude and I have just created. As with so many poignant memories from my past, I find it a tragedy that there was only Jude and me there to witness them.

The arc of blood that flew from my mouth when Jude decided to pull my loose tooth out by tying it to the doorknob of his room and slamming the door shut. My tooth launched into space, not to be found for several days. I was so mesmerized by the sight, I choked on the blood in my mouth and spit up more. He and I scrubbed the shag carpet for an hour and hand-washed the towels afterwards in hopes Mom wouldn't find out. Thank God Mom never found out.

The dark black Sharpie streak Jude accidentally put in my hair that we had to cut out. We'd been playing "School" again, where Jude would teach me by writing in Sharpie on the glass screen of the little TV in his room that no longer worked. It always rubbed right off with glass cleaner. Even in those early years, Jude and I talked often about our plan to get the heck out of Clovis. Knowing that would require good grades and college, Jude had started teaching me early on. This "pretty cursive" lesson had somehow devolved into a Sharpie fight. After a half hour with me laying over the side of our tub and Jude scrubbing at the back of my head, to no avail, he eventually just cut it out—a quarter-sized amount, shorn just behind my ear, that I hid for weeks with an awkward side pony and braids. Thank God Mom never found out.

That Saturday morning, Jude and I decided to draw stupid penises on our new cousin, Jay's, face the first time he slept over. When Jay's deadbeat mom, Debbie, decided to move to Texas with her new boyfriend, she also decided to leave Jay with his Grandma Peggy— Steve's mom—who lived a couple of blocks over from us at Mom's. This meant Jay was over at our house more than I would like, although I did like Jay. He was timid, but funny, wicked good at making up voices and doing impersonations, and the best gin rummy player I've ever met. But he gravitated more toward Jude even though he and I were closer, just a year apart in age.

Whether it was because they were both boys, or Jude was older and our natural leader, I didn't know, but I hated it when Jude sometimes chose Jay's idea over mine, or gave him a much better role in our imagined escapades. "Callie, you be the lookout. Jay, you're the robber." *Excuse me?* Trying to exert whatever jealous kid sister authority I felt I still possessed, I had selfishly pestered Jude into the penis drawing. Jay couldn't see how wildly laughable he looked when he woke up and started talking to us like he was normal. Jude and I had tears spilling out laughing so hard at him, but Jay was pissed, and rightfully so. It took some serious scrubbing to try to get all those misshapen, anatomically incorrect penises off. Without telling Mom, we even tried Comet from underneath the bathroom sink. Poor Jay was scraped red raw by the time we were done with him, almost a worse outcome than the penises!

An hour or so after we end the Pony Prom saga—having decided last-minute to have all the ponies dance around in the pink goo, forgetting it was pig guts—Jude and I are washing the goop off of the ponies in the tub before Mom and Steve come home for lunch, deciding we'll just tell Mom we decided to have a pony carwash in the tub. We knew she'd be fine with it if we scrubbed the tub to a shine after. As I hold Cherries under the faucet and watch the pink run off of her, I'm brought back to the summer Dad bought her for me.

———

I don't have as crisp a memory of it as Jude does, although we've only talked about it once. But, when I was somewhere around six, Jude nine, maybe, Mom lost her shit. Jude and I had been staying with Dad for the summer. That year, he'd been renting a trailer in Lubbock, Texas, with his girlfriend at the time, Sissy. Dad had been gone for a few days, which wasn't too strange. As a truck driver, he was often gone for several days—a week, or even sometimes—making a cattle run cross-country. When he was gone, we often stayed with Janessa if he was living in Clovis, or his girlfriend at the time, whoever that was, and her kids, whoever they were. Thankfully, Sissy didn't have her pack of five snot-nosed, barefoot kids with her this time. Neither Jude nor I knew why, and we didn't ask. We enjoyed the peace. And, Sissy was funny and let us get the real cereals with tigers and toucans and such on the boxes.

When Dad got back, though, we knew something was wrong.

He was kind of wild-eyed and grabbing some of our things that were strewn around the trailer and throwing them into a garbage bag—our occasional version of packing a suitcase. Pepper was circling him and whimpering. "Your mom's coming," he said, which stopped Jude and me cold. Jude hadn't seen Mom and Dad in the same room in years; I had never seen it. The thought of Mom driving hours across Texas to come within firing range of Dad, at Sissy's, nonetheless, was just terrifying. Jude and I set off running toward Dad's truck, trying to get out of there before Mom got there. I didn't even grab my ponies.

We didn't make it. I heard gravel crunch and spit out as Mom skidded her beat-up Oldsmobile into Sissy's driveway. She turned the wheel hard until her car made a half turn and stopped suddenly as she threw the gear shift into park and flew out of the driver's side, leaving the long boat door hanging open.

"You son of a bitch!" Mom hollered at Dad. She was not drunk, I could tell. Her eyes were fire, but they were sharp, as was her tongue. Her seething, piercing focus on Dad was steady. "You think you can threaten *me*?! I told you I was, and now I am. I'm taking 'em for good. You'll never see these kids again," she said to him, her voice steely and hot. Mom terrified me. I hated her in that moment. Pepper, Jude, and I sat huddled on the gravel driveway and were scared and quiet.

Mom got to Jude first and yanked the shoulder of his shirt so hard he fell backwards on his hands and backside. His eyes were wide with fear, unblinking. He scrambled back, stunned. Pepper whimpered as I realized I was gripping her fur too tightly.

"Get in," Mom pointed to the open door of her car behind him without looking at Jude. Her eyes never left Dad's.

"Charlene," Dad said. It sounded like a warning. Even in that moment, I thought he must not know what to do. The four of us had never been together in the same spot in all of our lives. I don't think any of us really knew how to act or what was going to happen. I thought the world might blow up. The sky might rip open, and some bright light would singe us all. *Psst. Zap. Poof. Done.*

"Charlene, *what?*" Mom hissed, taking a step closer to Dad. I heard the screen door of Sissy's trailer slam behind me, and I closed my eyes tight, praying—this time—Sissy would be smart enough to keep her redneck mouth out of this. She didn't say anything, but I felt her back there. Probably as terrified as we all were of Mom.

"I warned you," Mom's voice sounded like metal on metal. Like a knife sharpening. "You ever even so much as hint you ain't bringing 'em back when you say, and I told you, you would never see them again."

Dad wiped a raw hand down his face. I could hear his calloused hands scrape across his stubble. Mom stepped to him then. Her back was ramrod straight. Her butthole mouth pinched tight. Dad's chest was heaving up and down.

"Callie!" she shouted, her eyes still on Dad. She snatched forward so fast I didn't have time to retreat. Mom had snared my little wrist in her hot hand, her grip a vice. Dad leaped forward with equal speed. I don't know if it was to protect me, or just to fight Mom's impulse to take from him, hurt Dad however she could. Either way, I was stretched between the two of them, both of their hands locked like steel on my wrists. I looked to Jude, who was huddled with Pepper near Mom's Oldsmobile, crying into the scruff of her neck. His eyes darted from Mom to Dad to me and back again. He didn't have an answer. I looked at Mom with eyes full of rage, my anger taking over my fear.

"I DON'T WANT TO GO WITH YOU!" I spit at her, my eyes suddenly spilling over with tears I didn't know had formed. "I want to stay with Dad!" I wriggled against her grip, trying to break free from her.

Mom's eyes finally locked on mine. Something dark and roiling flashed over them, quick and instant, then they went back to their usual ice blue. "Fine," she said as she flung my arm as hard as she could, like it was a snake on her, using such force that it swung back and struck my side with a thud that still hurts my feelings when I think about it. I was only six.

Mom pulled Jude to his feet by his shirt and pushed his dusty, scraped limbs into the car, forcing him across the bench seat to the passenger side. She pushed Pepper back with her heel. The realization of what was happening then set in, and Jude started screaming, a murderous, painful wail. In my head, it sounded like a chorus because I didn't realize I was screaming, too, my throat tearing with the sound, equally loud, equally murderous.

"Shut up!" I heard Mom yell at Jude. "Stop yer' crying!"

Dad still had his hand locked on my wrist. I looked up at him, my face contorted with confusion and horror, wanting him to stop whatever madness was happening. I yanked on his arm as hard as I could, over and over, shrieking Jude's name. Dad's mouth was open, his jaw hanging slack, as he watched Mom back her Oldsmobile up at full speed, slamming into Sissy's chicken wire fence and not giving a damn. She backed up harder, crushing it further, and flipped Dad off before she peeled out of the driveway to make the drive back to New Mexico, back to Clovis. I could see Jude's body flopped over the bench seat, reaching back toward the rear windshield, his reddened cheeks wet, his mouth an open black hole.

Dad let go of my arm gently. And it seemed like he was coming out of a haze. "Babes," he said to me. His nickname for me, which usually made me feel incredibly special and took away all pain. Today, it did nothing. Jude was gone. Mom had taken him away. "Babes," he said again. "Your mom's," he started, then stalled. "She's just. Being a mom has been hard for her," Dad said. I heard the words, but they didn't make sense to me. *That didn't look like it was hard for her,* I wrestled in my mind.

Dad tried to scoop me up, but I just crumpled to the ground, landing with a thump and cloud of dust on Sissy's driveway with Pepper Army-crawling on her belly toward me. I would learn later that Mom and Dad both knew this wouldn't last. That it had just been a battle of wills, a tactical play made in their decade-long anger game. They knew mine and Jude's separation would never remain permanent.

But Jude and I didn't know that.

We weren't adult enough to know the stupid, childish games adults play, the deeply hurtful, scarring things parents at battle sometimes do out of anger and revenge. Things that have nothing to do with the kids but everything to do with the jagged, confusing memories they leave behind.

I twisted my dirty hands into the dirt of the driveway, trying to dig my nails off to create a pain greater than that of losing Jude. I didn't know I would see him again. I didn't know it would just be a few days while Mom and Dad stewed, but then they came to their senses and Dad eventually drove me back to Clovis. I thought I had lost the only person who knew everything about me, who carried all my memories because he had helped me make them, the only one in the world who would write pony plots and blow up LEGOS with me. I had lost the best and only real friend I'd ever had. That's what I believed and felt, under a baking sun on a dirt driveway in Texas.

The one time Jude and I talked about it, years later, Jude told me Mom was pissed because Dad had been arrested. For drugs, likely. Or possession of it. Something like that. That's the real reason he'd been gone for a bit, and we'd been staying alone with Sissy. He hadn't been on a cattle run this time. It had just been a few nights in jail, a fine, and community service. But it was a final straw for Mom, and it had set her off. She threatened Dad, saying she would take Jude and me away from him forever, which, in turn, had set Dad off, and he'd threatened to basically kidnap us and never come back—real mature stuff.

What Mom hadn't planned on, though, was me pulling back and choosing Dad. And Dad didn't know that having Jude ripped away from me would cause me to implode. He didn't know my heart physically hurt, my mouth tasted like copper, my body turned nauseous in rebellion. My tummy grumbled weirdly and cramped at times. My eyes dried into sore cotton balls from the millions of tears I'd cried. After days trying to soothe Zombie Callie, Dad finally packed up my little Coleman duffel bag and stuffed me into his truck. He didn't tell me where we were going, and Zombie Callie didn't care. I just buckled up, stared out the windshield, and held my hand on Pepper's back in the bench seat between us to keep me tethered to this world.

Dad stopped at a Wal-Mart and took me to the *My Little Ponies* section. "Pick whichever one you'd like, Babes," he said, his voice solemn, his hand on my shoulder heavy. It was a nice gesture that should have made me happy, but happiness had escaped me. It seemed impossible without Jude. I didn't even know if I would ever play ponies again. *Who would play with me?* I thought. Then Dad said the words that turned my world around.

"I'm taking you back to your Mom's. Back to Jude." I looked up at Dad, my eyes wet, my vision bleary, begging him to confirm this was true. He really was taking me to Jude. Dad nodded. I wiped a grimy hand across my eyes, trying to dry them, my lashes all globbed together. The minute I saw her, I knew which pony I would choose. Cherries Jubilee. Two gorgeous shades of pink, her coat and glossy mane. These green eyes look like they're asking you a question. Her head cocked slightly, a hitch in her stride, a pose that told me she would stop and listen to whatever I might want to tell her. She's just beautiful. Cherries looks like she'd be a good friend. Having spent the week without mine, I felt I needed her.

As the water of the faucet pours over Cherries, washing her clean, the memory of that terrible dusty day in Texas washes down the drain, and I look over at Jude. We're both on our knees, bent over the tub. He's scrubbing Brian, his favorite pony, in the milky pink water. Jude feels me looking at him, my eyes probing, my hands holding Cherries in a way that tells him I've been cradling a painful memory.

"Stop it, goober," Jude says, teasingly. He drops eye contact and nudges me playfully with his shoulder, buoying me up. "I'm not going anywhere."

CHAPTER SIX
I DON'T MATTER

"I'm not going anywhere," I hear from somewhere far away, like a person is trying to talk to me through a door. The backs of my eyelids feel so incredibly heavy; I feel there is no way I will ever lift them. I can barely make my eyeballs move at all; they feel stuck in place. I realize the voice I heard was a man's, but it was so muffled I can't be sure. I feel a hand stroking mine, but my hand feels like it's been stuffed into a big Carhart glove, my senses and dexterity dulled. I try to lift my eyelids, but they are massive gates, locked at the bottom.

I try to will my hands out of the pink, murky water, back through time to the present. To this hospital bed and the rough, white cotton blanket I've been rubbing like rosary beads for days. But, I find I can't. My senses are torn between the vivid, visceral scenes of my childhood and my bleak, blinding present. They are striving to feel, hear, and taste both. My eyelids, however, refuse to open, like they've vetoed the very idea of consciousness.

I hear the muffled male voice again—"I'm not going anywhere"— and I'm struck by familiarity as I realize I know that voice. I know who owns that voice! But, my exhausted, strung-out brain can only snatch this voice from the present and drag it back down to the depths of my mangled past, where it seems destined to dwell while I heal.

Back again. I'm twelve and my hands are on LEGOS.

"Why are you doing it that way?" he asks. It's Jay's voice. He was often asking Jude and me how or why we did things because Jude and I had been operating as a silent, well-oiled team since we could crawl. I hated to admit it, but sometimes the growing pains we were feeling trying to work Jay, this come-lately cousin-in-law, into our duo were rubbing off on me. When they did, I would try to remind myself that Jay's "bedroom" at Grandma Peggy's is really a converted utility closet, not much bigger than a bathroom—if you were to put a bed where the tub would go. Our first year with Jay was the first time I could remember the feeling that, between me and a peer, *I* had more. But, when it came to Jay, surprisingly, Jude and I did.

I take a breath.

"You have to think about the windows and doors at the very beginning, when you're building the first layer," I explain to Jay, who was botching things trying to retrofit a window into his misshapen LEGO house.

"But if I'm gunna pahk my cahr here," he says in his primo Boston accent, "I'll want a winduh so's I can shoot anyone tries to steal it, see?" Jay is bobbing his shoulders all the while because, for some unfounded reason, we think Bostonians talk with their shoulders.

I roll my eyes and take a LEGO out of his hand. "See, if you try to put a window in later, it can break down the whole structure," I say as I show Jay how the interlocking bricks would refuse his eleventh-hour architectural plans.

I break it down and build in a window all proper like Jude taught me, but we're interrupted by some strange scuffling and muffled shouts coming from what sounds like our baked front lawn. As latchkey kids, the three of us often ended up together after school, doing our homework or playing with LEGOs while watching Full House or Family Matters. Although Jude—who was in junior high where Jay and I were still in elementary—often came home later, he didn't usually come with a noisy entourage.

Jay and I immediately drop our LEGOs and bolt up. Through the kitchen windows on our tiptoes, we can see three boys ganged together near our lawn, pushing Jude's shoulders, forcing him off the sidewalk into the grass. Jude's hands are up in defense. I can't hear exactly what the boys are saying. "Pussy" this. "Pretty boy", that. They have Jude backed up to the porch when the main scumbag throws his backpack down.

I feel my blood start to pop and spittle. *That's my brother.* But Jay is bigger and faster. He beats me to it. Bursting out of the house, he slams his hands so hard into the boy's chest that the boy falls backwards, landing hard on his hands and butt in our dried dusty yard. Jay and I hadn't wrestled in a while, and I guess I hadn't realized Jay—now thirteen—had been quietly growing, getting taller and stronger.

"Shit," one of the two boys standing says, hushed and low, like he didn't mean to say it. It just slipped out. They seemed stunned, not sure how to proceed. Scrabbling to regain my role as Jude's guardian, I decide to use Jay's element of surprise.

I slam the door open and yell "Moooo-oommm!" hoping the numbnuts will believe our mom is home and will be coming out soon. Even at that age, most kids still freaked out at a threat of "I'm telling Mom!" I pray it will work as I hold our rickety screen door open, looking back inside, as if Mom is in the house somewhere, stamping out her cigarette and getting ready to come out and strike fear in these stupid boys. It feels silly, but I realize there's nothing more I want in this moment than for my mean Mom to come out and unleash on these idiots. She would have them running with her narrowed eyes and butthole mouth. And, if they didn't, I imagine her putting out her cigarette on their cheek. The imaginary singe and shrieks I hear bring me great joy. *Sometimes it can be nice having a mean mom,* I decide.

"Come on, Tyler," one of the two punks behind the guy on the ground says, who I now know is Tyler. *I will murder you, Tyler.*

Tyler stands up, wiping his dirty hands on his pants, his eyes darting between me, Jay, and Jude. His two minions are now out of the yard, on the sidewalk, indicating their retreat. Tyler is outnumbered now. He'd have to pummel both Jude and Jay and a little girl—*a goddamn scrappy one at that*, I think—all before her mom came out to get away with whatever he's trying to accomplish here, which remains a mystery. Those aren't good odds. Tyler's feet begin to shuffle backwards. But Jay won't let him off that easily. He shoves Tyler again, not as hard this time, and points his finger in his face.

"My Dad's a cop. Come back again. Mess with Jude one more time. Find out what happens." Jay's words slide out through gritted teeth.

I try to keep my face straight so I won't betray Jay's lie. *Jay doesn't know who his dad is.* He'd never met his father. Jay's dad had been out of the picture since forever, since Jay was born, as far as Jude and I knew. But Jay had thrown him and his imaginary occupation out in that moment with such conviction that it felt true. Hell, it could be. Who was to say?

Standing in our yard, his fists balled, Jay looks taller than I remembered. As tall as Jude. *When had that happened?* He plays football at school a lot and has more muscle than Jude, who has always been more spindly and lean, like I wish I could be. I'm built more like Jay, like a beefy version of a little girl. I don't know whether Jay is actually bigger than Jude, or whether the confidence and fire he's just unleashed somehow expanded him. Jude and I stare at Jay, seeming to both notice the change for the first time. *When had Jay grown up?*

Tyler picks up his backpack, then he and his dufus bodyguards run down the street. Jay watches them until they round the corner before he turns around to face Jude and me. Jude swallows audibly.

"I," Jude starts, sounding sheepish. "I was …," Jude rolls his tongue over his teeth to fill the silence. "Thanks," he says to Jay before re-shouldering his backpack and heading inside. *Thanks. To Jay?* I fume. I was there, too. I did … something. But, the truth—I know—is Jay did what really mattered, and that burns me up.

"A cop?" I ask after Jude makes his way inside, trying to do what I'm not sure of. Pick at Jay, who just saved us?

Jay finally takes his eyes off Jude's back and looks at me. He shrugs slowly. "If I don't know him, he can be anything I need him to be, right?" Jay throws a shoulder and an eyebrow up, suggesting it could be true.

I'm slammed again by this weird feeling of *more*-ness that I have with only Jay. Because I do, in fact, have a dad. He's not around all the time, and Mom hates him, but when he pulls up in his big shiny Peterbilt, sunshine coats my life.

I don't know what to say to Jay.

"And that mom bit," Jay says with an odd chuckle, changing the subject. "You know there are no cars in the driveway, right?" he teases. I look at the empty driveway, an absence that would tell anyone who knew our little family that no adults are home. Thankfully, Tyler hadn't put that together. I throw a shoulder and eyebrow up, mimicking Jay's recent concession, unsure what kind of standoff we are having here.

"Maybe she takes the bus," I say, realizing how much Jay and Jude and I know about each other, how much time we've spent together over the last few years. But something is still bothering me about the whole scene, about Jay's role in it. I can't let it go.

"I was going to get my bat next, you know," I tell Jay, not really sure why.

"I'm sure you were, Callie." Jay looks at me for a long moment, takes a breath in, and finishes with "I knew you would."

I nod at that comment, somewhat satisfied. But then, there's something else.

"Jay, did we make it worse for Jude?" I ask, knowing it was code among guys that if a girl had to fight your battles, you were a total pussy, which is what I'd heard them call Jude. *Was this about me?* I wondered.

"Maybe," Jay answers honestly, pushing his hands into his pockets.

"What about you? What if they …" I trail off, not wanting to finish the question aloud that didn't need finishing.

He shrugs. "I don't matter," Jay says, which stings me, but I can't come up with the right words—genuine words—in the moment to dispel that. And a selfish snake slithers up my spine as I button my mouth, thinking *Not as much as Jude, you're right.*

"I'm gonna go home," Jay mumbles before I can get my thoughts together. He turns quickly and starts toward the sidewalk. I watch him walk the same path the three bozos who'd been picking on Jude just ran down and around the corner toward his home, Grandma Peggy's house. It's like I'm seeing Jay for one of the first times, for exactly what he must feel he is—a mismatched patch that's been poorly glued onto our family, not sticking well and threatening at any minute to be peeled off. Something grinds inside me. A handle snaps off. Feeling responsible somehow, I start to lurch toward Jay, but it feels like my feet have been nailed to the porch and I'm sinking down into the earth.

———

I have that same sinking feeling when I open my eyes and realize I'm back in the hospital. There's the twirling blinds, the taped-up TV, the chair with the bottle cap under one foot. Nothing has changed here, although I feel like I've been on a journey and come back. I look around the room and see him crumpled into a chair by my bed, sleeping.

It's Jay. He's here at the hospital with me, and I'm now confident his was the voice I heard, however long ago—*several hours, a day*—before I slipped away again. Jay appears uninjured. There's no hospital band on his wrist, and he's not in a gown. He is disheveled, but I'm sure that's from sitting and sleeping in various chairs and benches all over the hospital. I'm grateful to know he wasn't in the accident with me, as that whole segment of my memory is still gone. After the second drink at the bar, I believe I ordered a third, although I'm not sure. I had been drinking a good bit the last two months, after the earth I had been standing on disintegrated beneath me, and I often snapped into a new form of functioning that I'd begun calling "autopilot," where I appear alarmingly coherent and functional, but Callie is really nowhere in sight.

Although I feel like I never want to have a drink again, I know why I was drinking my mind away then. The sight of Jay brings it all back. No accident could erase that, especially when he's sitting right here in front of me.

But I do notice, for the first time, a cluster of photos on the windowsill of my hospital room. They're the same photos I have taken with me from my college dorm, to rental houses thereafter, to my home where I live now. I smile at the photo of me and Jude in front of Mom's old grey Oldsmobile. The one where he's sporting a smile at me that tells me I'm the only thing that matters in Jude's world. That picture of me and Jude sat on my little dorm room desk all during my first year of undergrad, right next to the one of me and Dad on Little Man and Kip, with Pepper in the frame, that I always propped the belt buckle Dad had given me up against.

I wonder briefly how these photos got here. Only a handful of people—Braden, Jay, Jude … my mind drifts—who would know what these photos mean to me, enough to bring them to my hospital room and prop them up here for me to see.

I slide my eyes over again to Jay sleeping in the corner. *Had to be,* I tell myself. I watch him silently with a weary eye, wondering why— against the odds—he's even here, sitting by my bed. I haven't said a word to, or even seen, him in over two months, although a brief silence would do nothing to erase our long, colored history. I move my mouth around to unstick it from my gums, feeling suddenly self-conscious of my breath and hair. *How long has it been since I showered?* I make the mistake of scooching myself up on my bed, and the plastic mattress lets out a tattling squeak.

Jay rouses.

My heart picks up. I start sweating.

"Hey," he says. Jay's eyes are soft, concerned. The scar on his cheek has a slight red tint from being mashed into his hand while he was sleeping.

"Hey," I say, awkwardly pushing some hair back from my face.

"You're awake," Jay starts timidly.

I just shrug. I'm not trying to make this harder on him; I just don't know where we stand. Does a near-death accident nullify a fight? *Who should apologize here?* I find I am groping around, unable to find the anger I once held for him because he is here, by my side, when no one else but Mom is.

I want to ask Jay where Braden is, but I decide against it. It's embarrassing and hurtful to face the fact that my own husband is not here with me. Sensing my struggle, Jay stands. He turns round to grab some things on the little counter by my bed before I can see them and whips back around to face me with his hands behind his back. Despite it all, a little game brings me a slight thrill.

"We don't have to talk," Jay says. "I don't know what the right thing is to say either," he adds, meeting my eyes. My shoulders relax.

"I brought things for you." He is wiggling his shoulders now, and I try to stop a smile that is spreading on my face because I believe he may strike up a Boston accent if he keeps it up.

"I can see that," I say as I tip my chin at the photos on the windowsill. Jay smiles. *It was him.*

"Something else," he sashays, one elbow toward me, then the

other. I look at his right elbow and back to his eyes, enjoying our silent communication.

"Ahh, good choice," Jay says, whipping out a stack of flashy gossip magazines, the kind that make a big showing of celebrities' cellulite, as well as their recent fallouts, fashion faux pas, and flings. It's a great choice for the hospital. I smile, and Jay nods and lets out a breath I didn't realize he'd been holding. I take the magazines from him.

"And, now?" he wiggles the other elbow. I look at his left elbow and then back to his eyes.

"Good choice, too," Jay says, sporting a loopy grin as he pulls his left hand out from behind his back. It's a LEGO kit. A little castle and a dragon to be put together, even a little block-headed dragon slayer. "All they sell nowadays are these stupid kits," Jay says—a hint of mock irritation in his voice. "Where's the creativity?" he scoffs as he turns the box around for me to see all sides. "But I liked this guy," Jay points to the little dragon slayer—dressed smartly in chain metal armor with a helmet and sword—and picks up in an Irish accent. "I'll spear ye trew yer' evil beat'n heart, Drago. Ye bastuhd!" I laugh. I can't help it. Jay's voices are the best. I stick my hands out like a child. *Gimme.*

Jay starts to make his way toward my bed, holding the box in his outstretched arm. I take the box in my hands, dazzled by the colors and shine and the promise that it can distract me from the hell that is my current situation, if for only just a minute. Jay starts to ease down on the bed with me, and I gasp aloud when he does.

Out of habit, I had tried to pull my left leg up toward my body— and out of his way—so Jay could sit down, but the sudden movement had brought me pain along with a jolting realization.

The lower half of my leg—from below my knee down—is gone. Missing.

No matter how many times I've seen the stump or the nurses mention my amputation or check the wound, I cannot seem to instinctively remember it yet. Attempting to jerk my ghost limb away from danger, my brain refuses this new reality. But there it is.

The lower half of my left leg is, and will forever be, gone.

I remind myself again: *You are an amputee.*

CHAPTER SEVEN
DAIRY QUEEN

"Why is she such a snot to you?" I ask Jude the next day as we're walking past the Dairy Queen after school. "I hate her," I add. Jude rolls his eyes. Janessa had just passed us by on Main Street in the passenger seat of her mom's faded purple Cadillac. As the car passed by, Janessa had rolled the window down, yelled Jude's name, and flipped him off, and giggled as she passed. I had secretly hoped Janessa's mom would pop her in the mouth for that one, and that I could have seen it and giggled back. *Janessa.* Even her name sounds like snot.

"You don't hate her, Callie. You don't care enough about her to hate her," Jude tells me matter-of-factly, as if I'll understand that. But he's wrong. I do. I hate Janessa, and that's the whole point. If you hate someone, you don't have to care about them. You can shove that person off a cliff. *I hate you, bye!* and not give it a second thought. That's the whole point of hating. My brow is knitted up trying to figure out Jude's weird ways. We're walking home from school—me from elementary. Jude from junior high. We met up at the Dairy Queen on Main Street like we always do—about eight blocks or so from Mom's house. Jay used to walk with us, but he'd started playing baseball most days after school, a pick-up game at Stanley Field.

But I was okay with that because I'd made a new friend, too, whom I had been hanging out with more after school—Mariah Avalero, who had been in my third-period Earth Science class last year. Mariah was a pretty, petite Italian-looking girl with thick black hair and gorgeous skin. Mariah and I both sat pretty close to the front of the class and—like me—Mariah always did her homework and always knew the answers to Mr. Gibson's questions like I did. After a few weeks of talking in class, our friendship had evolved into me going over to Mariah's house often after school. She had a massive basement, completely detached from the adults, that was the coolest kind of labyrinth with a pantry that leads to a bathroom that leads back out to the living area. In other words, the perfect setting for Lights Out Hide Out and an easy choice over my lackluster, one-level house.

To me, that seemed a very easy difference. I liked Mariah. I hated Janessa.

"You wouldn't understand," Jude says as we walk. He slips his slender arm easily into his jeans pocket. Jude's wearing the one pair of stone-washed jeans he owns, which he wears three times a week because stone-washed is super cool right now, with a yellow and blue tie-dye shirt tucked in at the front. Much cooler than my Wranglers and hand-me-down Hulk t-shirt hanging down to my thighs.

Jude pushes a lush lock of brown hair away from his eyes and tucks it behind his ear. He's started wearing his hair in this glossy helmet-looking thing that a lot of the older boys are doing now. I think he must have Dad's hair, which is short but thick, because Mom's is thin and stringy. "Janessa likes me, Callie. It's a ..." Jude fumbles for the word. "A teenager thing," I scrunch my face up because the implication that I'm too young to understand 'teenager things' irks me, and it doesn't make sense.

"But if she likes you, she would be nice to you," I say in my little girl wisdom. Jude's eyes fly away again, back into his head, and I notice his long lashes. I can tell he doesn't like talking about him and Janessa, though. He changes the players.

"It's like flirting. Don't you have a boy or two in your class that

… pulls your hair, or sticks his finger in your food or something?" Jude asks.

"Gross, no," I immediately reply. *Fingers in my food*, I think. *I'd punch him.*

"Janessa wants to get a reaction from me because she wants my attention. Does that make sense?" I'm silent, trying to figure it out. An idea comes to Jude. "It's like, remember that time Sissy took us to that zoo in Lubbock?"

Of course, I remembered. She'd forgotten our shoes, and Jude and I had walked all the asphalt paths barefoot, getting stares and a lifelong case of Wal-Mart feet. The nice thing about Sissy was that when she got drunk, she got loopy and sweet and did nice things. Not like Mom. Or Dad. Barefoot or not, though, that was the first time I'd seen animals so foreign to me: a lion, otters, a cheetah, and that white tiger.

"You remember the white tiger you loved?" How had Jude read my mind? I shake my head in agreement, focusing intensely on Jude's face. He just gets me.

"Remember, you kept clanging your Coke bottle on the bars of his cage so he would look at you?" Jude reminded me. *I did.* "You did that because you liked him. You wanted him to look at you." With that, Jude cocks his chin to one side as if he's just explained gravity to me. But I get it. Janessa wants Jude to look at her. New gears in my head start to turn, dropping little bits of brain rust down as we round the corner to Mom's. Jude and I both stop walking, breathing even, when our house comes into view.

It can't be five o'clock yet, but there's Mom's car. Jude and I look sharply at each other, thinking the same thing. *Why is she home?* Jude and I immediately straighten up. I tuck in my grimy Hulk shirt. Jude smooths his hair back. These actions are just instinct, as we worry, we should be home doing our homework, cleaning our rooms, or doing something other than just casually walking through the door.

———

Jude and I come into the house quietly, careful not to let the screen door slam. As soon as we step inside, we both sense it. Mom—angry—gives off this staticky feel in the air and makes my mouth taste like I've been sucking on a copper penny. I don't like it.

"Mom?" Jude says tentatively. She's not in the living room. Not in the kitchen. We hear that exceptionally unique sound of the scrape of one of our metal porch chairs on the rough concrete slab that makes up our back porch. Jude and I turn to each other, knowing exactly where Mom is—the place where she does most of her smoking and drinking.

Jude and I make our way tentatively to the back yard and step gingerly onto the porch. "Hey, Mom," Jude says. She's changed out of her work clothes into her 'grungies' she calls them, a threadbare plaid button-down, a few sizes too big, with the sleeves cut off, and some grey sweat pants, cut to shorts. Her back is facing us as she pulls a long drag on her cigarette. I can hear the paper burning. There are three Coors beer cans on the diamond-pattern iron table, the fresh one dripping onto the concrete.

"Where have you two been?" Mom snaps. She finally turns to face us, and her eyes are steely. Her stare is so severe that Jude and I both avert our eyes.

"Walking home," Jude says, his eyes to the ground. I look over to read any cues he can give me, but his glossy brown locks hide his face from me. I hear Mom snubbing her cigarette out in the old glass ashtray that lives on the back patio table. An awkward moment passes.

"Grandma Peggy passed away today," Mom says it so bluntly, I'm not sure I heard her right. My head pops up in disbelief. Jude's too. "What?" we both grunt out together. Mom sits there, leans back in her chair, one hand draped on her beer can, her eyes moving from Jude to me then back to Jude, almost as if she's conducting some kind of emotional experiment, intensely curious how we'll respond.

"I've been on the phone for an hour. It was a heart attack. You know her … circulation problems," Mom waves her cigarette hand and takes a pull of beer. Jude and I meet eyes quickly, searching each other for what's right in this situation. We find no answers there.

"It was sudden," Mom interrupts our silent exchange. "She went quick." I feel a weird thickness in my throat. I'd never been close to Grandma Peggy. She was just an adult in our lives. She was old and smelled kind of like onions or something. She was always ironing clothes for money, but Grandma Peggy had never been mean to us or anything. She gave us cookies now and then. It feels weird to think she could just be dead all of a sudden, which makes me suddenly think of *him*.

"Jay," I blurt out. It's a question, but it sounds more like a statement, a dumb utterance. But his words—*"I don't matter"*—had somehow wafted through the air. Mom blinks at me. She's no help. "Does he? Was he …" I trail off. My troubled mind imagines Jay hunched over a slain Grandma Peggy, trying to shake her back to … *what?* Back to life? Back to normal?

The scrape of Mom's metal chair as she scoots it back across the concrete is abrasive, disrupting my panic. She rises and comes over to Jude and me. She kneels down in front of us—a rare position for her. The strangeness of it makes Jude grab my arm. Mom looks up at us. Her eyes are softer now. She acts like she's going to take our hands, but then thinks better of it and puts her hands awkwardly on the backs of our pants near the knees.

"Jay wasn't there," she says to me. "He was at school. Grandma Peggy must have known what was happening. She called 911 herself, but they didn't make it in time. Steve went and got Jay from school. They're at the hospital now. Saying …" Mom blinks something back. "Goodbye."

"Goodbye?" I blurt again. "But she's dead?" I don't know why I'm saying these things that make no sense. All I know is my chest feels tight, and air will not come in.

"I know," Mom says harshly to me, giving me a look I can't figure out. "But, Debbie's here now," she says. Jay's mom. "They'll figure it out." *They*, I think. Last we heard, Debbie had been living with a boyfriend in Portales, a city about twenty miles away, not really caring where Jay went or what he did. Ever. I swallow hard.

Jude pipes in, and I realize I've almost forgotten I'm standing on our back porch with him and Mom. "Should we … go see her too?" he asks, as Mom hasn't really explained to us what's going to happen, what we're supposed to do. Maybe she doesn't really know either.

Mom stands up in front of us. "No. She's gone," Mom says. She squeezes our shoulders kind of oddly. "Debbie and Steve will handle the funeral and all. You'll get to see her …" Mom fumbles. "Jay. You'll get to see Jay then." Mom gives our shoulders a little shake. "Hey," she says to get our attention. Jude and I both turn our faces up at her.

"This kind of stuff happens," Mom says. "People." She looks at each of us. "Pass." Jude's arm slips off mine. I barely feel it. My skin feels gone. "Tears won't bring them back," Mom says. I bite my lip hard, wanting this torturous moment to end. Jude and I know people die. We're not stupid. I can't figure out what Mom is trying to say, or trying to teach us.

"You just. Life isn't easy. Loving people," she pauses. "Losing people. It can hurt. It will hurt. You just have to suck it up. And be strong. But never forget that …" Mom trails off for a moment, and my mouth starts talking before my mind can think better of it.

"Forget? Forget what?! That Debbie doesn't really care about Jay, and she's going to treat him like garbage. That only Grandma Peggy really took care of him. She took him in. He lived at her house. She made him dinner and bought him pencils and clothes and stuff," I'm half-crazed trying to defend this injustice to my mom, trying more so to convince myself that my growing resentment of Jay did not cause this.

I march blindly on, despite Jude's fist tugging at the back of my shirt. "Debbie never. She's not gonna … " I heave in a great gulp of air and say the stupidest thing. "Jay lost the only person who had been willing to take care of him. Who provided him a home. You can't just *forget* when your only family abandons you or doesn't care about you. You can't just 'suck it up and be strong,'" I say mockingly, "about *that.*"

The second it flies out of my mouth and hits Mom in the face, I see it. Her jaw tightens. Her eyes cloud over. A storm brews there. Ice forms in her irises, making her look like a real-life Dairy Queen. *What was I thinking?* I chastise myself. I've stabbed too deeply. I feel Jude unfist my shirt and see him drop his head as we both realize the acrid, treacherous ground I just stomped and spit on.

Mom's past.

——

Mom's dad died when she was twelve, just about the age Jay is now. While a grandma is a bit more removed, Jay doesn't have a dad, so the comparison still works as he's lost the only person who cared for him. When Mom was twelve, her dad was an electrician. They lived in Hagerman, New Mexico. The few times Mom talked about her dad, she described him as tall as a tree, stout, with a big, thick neck, biceps she couldn't wrap her little girl's hands all the way around, a huge laugh, silly, sly jokes he would make behind her mom's back that made Mom giggle. He liked to sing and tell elaborate, grandiose stories. He sounded jolly. A lot like Dad. He also had five kids. Mom was the oldest by two years. He had a wife, a home, a perfect little family. Then he went to work one day and never came home. He was electrocuted on the job and died instantly. He was thirty-two.

But that's not the worst part. In the face of that insurmountable loss, my mom's mother left her and her siblings. She just vanished.

Mom tried to keep it all together. Waking her four younger brothers and sisters in the mornings, making them put on clothes for school, feeding them what was left in the kitchen, wiping the muck and dirt off their faces with her shirt sleeve, and stealing bread and peanut butter from the school cafeteria to feed them at night. But she couldn't keep the appearance up. Calls from the school started to mount, and eventually, social services stepped in and broke all the kids up.

I have a recurring dream sometimes about Mom during that time. She's trying to get her brothers and sisters cleaned and fed, but her arms are torn off at the elbows, both of them. They are bloody, pussy stumps that leak and drip all over the front of her dress and onto the floor. Mom tries to use her oozing stumps to pick up things and wipe her siblings' faces, but she just leaves blood and slime everywhere, making everything worse. In the dream, I can smell the putrid scent of her decaying arms. It's acrid and visceral. I hate that dream. I've never told Mom about it. Only Jude knows. He has one about Mom's mom, even though we've never met her. Jude's nightmare is worse than mine. Much worse.

———

I look Mom in the eyes, taking her in. Her wispy grey hairs. The wrinkles around her mouth. The mascara smudged a little under her bottom lids. She looks weary, and I know she is. I've only stabbed at her childhood wound, but there are so many more. To start, Jude is not Mom's firstborn. That's another topic we just know never to talk about.

Mom scrapes her chair across the patio with her foot and slams the back door on her way into the house. We hear a couple of kitchen cabinets bang inside as she's preparing to do … something.

I snap my face to Jude's. *To apologize?* I know I've set her off. But what will be the result, neither of us can guess. Jude looks at me with an expression that says *Why, Callie?* I cringe.

"Get the bowl!" Mom hollers from inside, breaking our attention.

Jude and I spook like scared horses and turn to make our way inside. Inside, something feels electric. Stuffy. As we turn into the kitchen, I feel it prickle down my spine. It's Mom's anger. I fear that if I touch her, it will zap me like the electric fence at Janessa's. I feel it in my mouth when I lick my teeth. Copper.

Jude turns to me with a terrified look on his face and brings his hands up to his head as if to hide his hair. He knows. So do I. I touch my bangs out of instinct. Jude and I both hate it when Mom cuts our hair. She literally puts a dinged-up metal salad bowl on my head and cuts bangs that are always way too thick and short.

"And the clippers!" Mom shouts, grunting our one big bar stool, that we use for cutting hair, out the back door. But Mom hasn't buzzed Jude's hair in years. Since he started working—mopping aisles at Stansell's—Jude's been able to pay for his own haircuts at SmartCuts. And, the last couple of years, he's really been growing it out. Jude has amazing, thick, chestnut hair that waves and falls around his face like he can control it with his mind. I've always been jealous, as my knotted-up blonde mess just blows around and gets in my mouth. Just then, Jude's panic sinks into me as if by osmosis. I don't grab the clippers. It feels like a betrayal. But I grab my old little-kid stars and comets sheet and salad bowl that Mom left on the kitchen table and march slowly out back.

Out back, Mom's got the chair sitting in the yard, just outside the porch. She's got some scissors laying on the old railroad tie that serves as our porch bench. I set the bowl and sheet by the scissors. Jude comes out behind me. He doesn't have the clippers. Mom sees it, too, and I feel fear tighten my throat.

She pulls a long drag on her cigarette, eyeing Jude intensely. "Get. The. Clippers," she says. "I need you brats to be put together for the funeral. You know… *for Jay,*" she cuts her steely blue eyes to me. "Who lost everything," she says while holding my stare. Mom blows out a thick shaft of smoke. "We're not going to look like white trash at the service."

"Mom," Jude starts. His voice is thin and wavering. "I don't want a buzz cut," he says weakly. "It's not. Not." I know what Jude wants to say, even as a clueless elementary kid, I know it. *It's not cool,* I think right as he says it. "It's not cool."

That was not the right word to use. Jude and I both sense it. Mom's face says *Cool?!* as if it were a curse word. "Your dad's mom dies and all your selfish ass can think about is being *fucking* cool?" Mom fires off. *Dad.* She didn't usually call Steve our dad because he isn't. He's our stepdad, but not our dad. I'm so confused, but my terror has taken over. She's going to cut the crap out of my hair, too, and I know it. To spite us both.

"It's …" Jude tries but fails.

"It's …" Mom pauses just like Jude did. I feel like she's mocking him, and I almost pipe up to defend Jude. Almost. "It's what you do when family dies. You pay your respects. You clean your filthy face. You comb and cut your hair. And you sure as shit do what your mom tells you because you're lucky to have one," Mom spits out, then flings her spent cigarette out into the dry yellow grass.

I can't look at her. Mom's mean as a snake when she's like this. I fear, though, if I look up, I will see her arms as bloody, pussy, dripping stumps, and I just can't.

Mom grabs Jude by the arm and yanks him down into the chair. Her mouth is pinched up into that puckered, pissed little line that strikes fear in us—her butthole mouth—although right now there is nothing funny about it.

Mom stomps into the house and comes back out with the clippers in hand. I risk bringing my eyes up just to get a peek at Jude. Tears are falling down his reddened cheeks. He and I both know there's no fighting this. Mom pops the sheet viciously, then lays it over his body and clips it behind his neck with a rusty clothespin. She clicks the clippers on. At the buzzing sound, Jude loses it.

"Mom, no!" he shouts through tears. I see strings of saliva bridging his top teeth to his bottom. "NO! NO!" Jude yells, his voice snotty and wet, to no one who can help him. I still can't look at Mom. I don't know how she's holding the clippers with those pussy stumps for arms. I don't allow my eyes to go higher than the top of Jude's head. I'm just standing there like a dumb person, breathing through my mouth, seeing fuzzy shapes and brown clumps of hair fall in my periphery.

The next few minutes are a hazy blur as Jude gets out of the chair without Mom saying a word and walks inside. I watch his tennis shoes shuffle through clumps of brown hair on the ground. I approach the chair and sit like a zombie while Mom plops the salad bowl on my head and starts cutting. I hate her breath. I hate the snippy crunch sound the scissors make. I hate the itchy, unbearable feeling of my shorn hair on my face, but I hate—*more*—the thought of her blowing it away with her horrible cigarette breath.

"Don't," I tell her when she pulls a big breath in and prepares to blow on my face. Mom stops. Her blue eyes are clawing into mine. To my surprise, she doesn't blow. She lets her puffed-out cheeks drop as she holds my stare. I let the itchy feeling on my face burn in, relishing the annoyance and tinge of pain it causes me. I want more of it to sear into me, so that she can see what I can endure. I try to convey to her in that stare. *I can endure you,* my stare says, because I hate this chair. I hate this yard. I even hate my own hair for being visible enough to be the object of her fury. I try to think I hate her. I think it is as hard as I can.

CHAPTER EIGHT
MOM

God dammit, that little girl burns me up. Callie. She's all spit and fire and gumption. I thought she was starting to resent Jay being around all the time, the way I've seen her pick and bicker with him, but here she goes defending him against me. Like I have no idea what it takes to raise a young man, like I ain't got a son of my own and *I* haven't done anything for Jay?! I haven't let him become a fixture here, eating meals with us, getting Jude's hand-me-downs, having Steve around to fix his bike, and whatnot. But, with Callie. And Jude, for that matter. It seems no matter what the hell I do, I am always the enemy, always the force to unite against.

But damn if I'll let that stop me from raising them right. I'd rather be here for them—in ways they believe they hate—than not here at all. Having a mom who thinks you and your brothers and sisters aren't good enough to stick around for is a feeling I live with and see in the mirror every day. I will never let Callie or Jude feel that pain.

I remember watching the two of them at Grandma Peggy's funeral. Jude was fidgeting awkwardly around his neck, overly self-conscious about his buzz cut, although it looked better anyhow. I couldn't stand that messy brown mop he was constantly pushing out of his face and sweeping behind his ears. I only wanted Jude to stand up straight, show his handsome face, and swap those ridiculous stone-washed jeans for crisp pants and a belt so the world could see what a smart, capable young man he has become. But Jude always walked a different path, like he was looking past our shoulders at something bigger, trying to figure it out. It's not the same with Callie, though. Those crystal blue eyes are dead set on her future, which I'm sure she feels requires climbing over, or through, me. I don't know if Callie will ever have kids, but—probably every mother feels this way—selfishly, I hope she does, so she might finally, one day, understand. Then cut me some damn slack.

I remember her standing behind Jude with the other mourners at the funeral, following him the way she always did. No matter how jealous I get of those two—and their super glue bond—I will never regret that they are a pair. They have one another, unlike my brothers, sisters, and I, who were ripped apart before we even got to know one another. We were spat out like a shotgun to different foster homes across the state, only to spend our childhoods entirely alone. I know Callie would be fine without Jude. She came out fighting—wiggling her way out of clothes, diapers, even her crib. She was born forged for a fight. But, having Jude around to teach and guide her in her younger years, shield her where I couldn't, will soften her in ways I never could, and I'm grateful for that.

I can see the young woman she is becoming because of it. At the funeral, I saw her friend Mariah come bicycling up, looking clean and put together in a simple black dress, all by herself. Her parents were nowhere in sight. Mariah walked right up to Callie and squeezed her hand, stunning me where I sat uncomfortably—in my wrinkled black dress on a plastic chair, craving a goddam smoke. To have made a friend like that so early. I didn't have friends like that growing up. I haven't even had friends like that as an adult, which tells me Callie is different.

I also saw her give Jay something at the funeral, something she'd been clutching tightly in her hand from the minute we left the house that morning, the four of us looking strange and ill-fitted in our back-of-the-closet clothes. I noticed it was one of her and Jude's favorite little

LEGO people, they're always leaving them strewn around the house for Steve and me to step on—the little astronaut one they call Arnie Armstrong.

Jude and Callie think I'm so callous and tuned out when they are playing, but I'm often listening, amazed at the crazy little plots they build up. I knew that little plastic person was important to Callie. So, seeing her give it to Jay on that day, I felt my heart tear a little, seeing Jay's reaction. He ran away crying. But, especially knowing what I knew. Debbie was about to cart Jay off to Portales, come hell or high water, because she learned she could get food stamps more easily with a dependent. Steve and I had offered to let Jay stay with us—tight as we were, we felt we could make it work—but Debbie was hellbent on using him like a pawn. What could I do?

Callie didn't know Jay was about to be crudely ripped out of her little world. Seeing her, though, my daughter, trying to offer comfort and help to people she considers family, told me I might be doing something right. But the minute any mom thinks that, the next hour she'll feel she's completely botched the job and there's no salvaging the wreckage. I never thought I could worry this much.

I don't know what happens when she and Jude go and stay with their dad. I don't have to think very hard to imagine it, but I know Jude will do everything he can to protect Callie from Bill's darker sides—his drugs and drinking. Just as I do, when that reckless cowboy takes their feelings—and stuffs them in a Duffel he slings onto the side of the road every time he leaves town for months and misses their little birthdays and Christmases—I'm the one who has to pick it up, wipe their dusty tears away, and reassure my kids not all parents will leave you.

And, Callie's still young. Only twelve. Right or wrong, I harbor some flimsy hope that I can still strengthen her more, reinforce her backbone for what's coming. I can make sure she knows how hard life is going to be, how nothing will be handed to her—but that she can achieve and be anything she wants, anything her and Jude dream up together. If I can just keep her clothed, healthy, and her grades up until she can graduate and get on to college, then it's on her. Whatever relationships she may form or break along the way, the people she may hurt or who might hurt her, I can't control. All I can do is make Callie strong, as Jude has already made her wise. And be sure she knows I will always have her back. Mean or not, this snake is in her corner.

But Jude. He's fifteen now. I don't know how the hell he came to be so smart, but he did. He can pass any class or subject handed to him, but he's failing most of them. A fact I'm confident Callie does not know. Jude is slipping down a road much like his dad's that I'm not sure he'll ever be able to turn off. Drugs. Drinking. But there's something deeper, more dangerous, brewing in Jude. Small towns like Clovis—where folks don't have as many resources or goals or good role models—can sometimes breed generation after generation of deadbeats. Although I know my kids are capable of far more, and they know I won't put up with any whining or excuses, something dark's got Jude in its grip, and I'm scared of it. I fear it more than a child of mine contracting some rare disease, getting mangled in a car accident, or—I hate to even say it, but—dying on life support right in front of my eyes, which I've witnessed before.

But I don't want to talk about her today.

Jude won't talk to me about what he's working through. He's not even talking to Callie about this, I believe. This is a battle Jude is fighting all alone. He and Callie think I am so callous and unaware, but I'm not blind, and I am his mother. I can feel anger and confusion pulsing off of Jude. He needs a friend, but I cannot be that for him.

I am the mother.

I provide the roof and enforce the rules, which Jude is breaking. And, I can't stand by and let him believe there aren't consequences when one of the most important things I've spent the last fifteen years trying to teach my kids is that there are consequences for their actions, good and bad. That's why you have choices and you have to own them.

As much as Callie is going to hate me—even more—for this, I have to draw and hold this line. I am the only one who will.

CHAPTER NINE
CRACK

It reverberated like lightning in the house, pulling me out of my sleep and into the hall where I could watch them pacing and snarling in the kitchen. Jude's hand to his cheek, the red welt that was already forming, and the clicking of his jaw as he moved it around told me what I already knew. Mom had just slapped Jude.

"I am beyond disappointed in you!" Mom's voice thundered through the house. "But what the hell does it matter? You don't give a damn what I think. You don't care about all the work and bullshit that Steve and I go through just to give you a roof over your fucking crack head!" she yelled.

My hand instantly flew to my mouth. *Crack? No. No,* I thought. *Not Jude.* My hands gripped the edge of the wall, trying to keep myself grounded, where I was hiding behind the corner, listening to Mom and Jude unleash into the worst fight between them I'd ever seen. This wasn't happening. From my vantage point in the hall, I could see— through the window in Mom and Steve's room—a car on the sidewalk, its headlights still on in the dark. It had struck our cheap metal mailbox and knocked it down. My eyes darted back to Jude and Mom.

Jude's eyes seemed wild. He was pacing in front of Mom. Shaking his head 'no.' Wringing his hands and popping his knuckles. His hair looked greasy, dirty. His shirt was untucked, and he was barefoot. He looked so different, so unlike Jude. It scared me. My heart pounded in my throat. In the pads of my fingers on the wall. I felt sweat drip down from my armpits into the waistband of my sweatpants. I didn't dare move, as it felt this had been a long time coming.

Something between Mom and Jude had turned sour, rancid, the last time she forced Jude into a buzz cut before Grandma Peggy's funeral. Afterwards, Jude grew his hair out longer than his chin. He shaved the underside, which looked stupid to me, but lots of people at school were doing that, even girls. He started dressing like a grunge band member and hanging out with a lot of high school girls who looked like trailer trash—dirty, cracked teeth, slutty clothes, one even had a baby that she put in daycare during school hours. "The skanky girls", Mariah and I had started calling them, because it fit.

Jude had turned sixteen, and we didn't even have a little party at Mom's house: no cake or anything. I gave him a card I had made, but it was kind of an awkward exchange, as Jude and I had just drifted apart a bit. Jay had been out of the picture since Grandma Peggy's funeral, and I had started hanging out with Mariah more while Jude stewed and roiled in his teenage angst. I'd heard Jude and Mom argue often, usually when Jude would come home late, after, or during dinner, or when the school had called to report his absence. I was in AP classes at the time—focused on mine and Jude's plan to get the hell out of Clovis—so I often tried to tune them out. When Jude and Mom rumbled, I turned my headphones up and kept to my studies.

I peered around the corner to see. There was something on the round linoleum table Mom kept pointing at, next to her drained tumbler and full ashtray. It looked like a pencil box with gauze and stuff in it. Like a first aid kit, almost. Then, I was struck dumb by the realization that it looked a lot like Dad's little Cocaine box. Suddenly, I was that eight-year-old, watching him through the crack in the door of his bedroom in the trailer, another little layer of my innocence being stripped away.

"Well, that's fucking it," Mom stepped to Jude, turning his chest toward her. They were the same height now. Jude was still slender, and he and Mom were almost the same size. I didn't know what either of them would do. "You hear me?" she stabbed a finger angrily into his chest. "I will not live with an addict again," she said, breathing slower now, letting her tone slide down to something deeper, colder than rage.

"Not to mention the other shit you do," she said. I had no idea what she was talking about. "I am your *mother*, Jude. You think I don't know you through and through?" Jude cocked his head at that. "You're not doing that shit in my house."

Jude caught my eye briefly.

"Callie, go to your room!" Mom didn't even turn to look at me. She just knew I was there. I gave Jude one petrified look before I turned back to my bedroom and closed the door. I heard muffled voices, scooting of chairs in the kitchen, and then Jude's door slammed, and he started rustling around in his room. I could hear garbage bags popping open. The sound of us packing.

I slinked in.

Jude was shoving clothes into the bottom of a big black contractor's bag. I could see he was crying, and there was a hand-shaped red mark on his left cheek.

"Callie, I can't. Not right now. I just … I'm going to Dad's," Jude said. That threw me.

Dad's trailer across town just seemed like a fun camp for the weekend. I couldn't imagine what it might feel like to really *live* there. Do your homework. Get yourself up for school? What would Jude eat for breakfast or dinner? What if someone was in the shower when he needed to get ready? I suddenly realized I didn't even know how Dad got his own clothes washed. A laundromat, I guessed. But I was sure he didn't even have a vacuum or mop at the trailer. I never saw him clean anything or straighten up. With all the sketchy people that came and went around the stockyards, I wasn't even sure it was safe.

"I don't … understand," I started. "Why? What did you do? Drugs?"

Jude's shoulders dropped. He took one big breath in, finished filling his bag, and tied it before standing up to face me. Jude pulled me into his chest. He smelled of smoke and something pungent. I didn't like it.

"I did a lot of things, Callie. A lot of stupid things. But it's going to be okay, you hear me?" I can feel Jude's breath hot on my neck, talking into the crown of my head. He sounds like he's trying to convince himself as much as me.

"I'll just be across town, and I'll see you every time you come to Dad's, okay? Just … come over more," he said as he released me.

Nothing about this felt right. My stomach convulsed at the thought of this room, the one next to mine, where Jude had lived my entire life, being empty. I had already lost Jay to Debbie's snatching him over to Portales, and now Jude was going to move out and live with Dad? I felt like the important pieces of my life were shifting around under my feet.

"But, no. I … no. Mom can't, she wouldn't …" I started to object, but Jude shut me up, slinging the trash bag over his shoulder and opening his door. I didn't want to incur Mom's wrath because I knew she was still out there in the kitchen, seething. I could feel the heat of her anger when he opened his bedroom door.

"It's done, Callie. I gotta go. Keep studying. I'll see you soon," Jude said, and he walked out.

Mom just sits at the kitchen table staring at her ashtray as Jude walks by and out the front door, letting the screen door slam behind him. He throws his big black bag in the back seat of whoever's car he's driving and backs up off the mailbox, the eerie sound of scraping metal piercing the night air, leaving a permanent, painful scratch in my memory. I watched Jude's taillights go down the street, feeling the same overwhelming sadness I felt when Mom tore Jude from me, dragged him into her Oldsmobile at Dad's, and drove off seven years before.

———

I feel all of that thirteen-year-old anger and terror as my eyes start to open, first to the bright display numbers on my monitor, red as Jude's taillights that night. I let out a raspy, useless shout as I pound my sheets, knowing the monitor will only respond with callous beeps: silence and beeps. My screams, internal or external, change nothing. Because here I lay, banished to this God-awful hospital room, missing a leg, missing the last few days from my memory, and petrified by the same thought I had that night: *What has become of Jude?*

The detective came again today. But this time, he made it into my room. Jay had been staying by my side religiously, sometimes sleeping in the uncomfortable-looking chair by my bed. I haven't seen Mom since the first time—maybe a day or so ago, I'm not sure—but I have to imagine she's around, trying to run interference on the detective just like Jay has. But this asshat must have been watching and came in intentionally when Jay or Mom went to get some coffee, or a smoke, because it had been too convenient to be a coincidence.

Fifteen seconds after Jay clicked my door shut after I calmed down and started building the dragon slayer kit, it clicked open, and there he stood. His menacing build and acne-scarred face, smelling of stale cigarettes and mouthwash. Detective Carter. I didn't say anything at first. I didn't remember anything anyway. *What was it he wanted to know?* I wondered as he attempted some small talk in vain. I willed Jay or Mom or anybody back with every fiber of my being. As if smelling my aversion to him, or a ticking clock, Detective Carter dove right into what he had come to find out.

"Callie, there was an exorbitant amount of alcohol in your system the night of the accident." I looked at him with a straight face. That part

I had remembered. I knew I was drunk. I knew I had been operating on autopilot. That was why I had no fucking clue what had happened. Carter's expression told me he knew I wasn't going to respond. One, because he hadn't asked me a question. But two, because I wasn't going to respond to anything he said or asked of me. He marched on.

"I have to ask you, Callie. Do you remember what happened the night of the accident?" Detective Carter asked me point-blank, to which I could not respond even if I wanted to, because I did not know. I couldn't even tell him if I hit a house, a barn, or a person.

Suddenly, the reality of that seared into my brain. I might be looking at a DUI—if I'm lucky—a manslaughter charge or worse if I'm not. A felony at least. *A felony.* The gold-embossed name of my firm appears before my eyes, and I wonder if everything I have worked so hard for is going to be stripped away because of one stupid night, one stupid decision to drink, then get behind the wheel.

Feeling panicked, I start mumbling. "I … I'm …"

"Not talking to you," Jay barks from behind Detective Carter's back. He must have just slipped in. My savior once again. I had stopped counting the number of times he had saved me by then.

"She's not in any condition to give an interview," Jay told Detective Carter sternly. "I told your partner that," he said, an edge to his voice. "I was clear." Jay stepped in between me—laying exposed in the bed, and Detective Carter standing near the foot—and I could not remember ever feeling so grateful to stand behind his cloak.

Detective Carter put his hands in the air, one held a small notepad and a pencil, the other his sunglasses. His face was a mock apology. "I'm sorry," he'd said, without an ounce of sincerity. "Sloan didn't tell me that," which I had been sure was a lie.

"Callie," he leaned over to make eye contact with me over Jay's shoulder. "I'll come back another time." And with that, Detective Carter slipped out.

CHAPTER TEN
DADDY'S GIRL

"Who's that knocking at my door?" I smile at Dad's horse Kip—a glossy, muscular Bay, my favorite of Dad's horses—when I hear Dad coming around the corner of the stall with Kip's saddle, singing one of his typical silly circus songs. "Who's that knooocking at my door?" I've never heard of these songs outside of Dad singing them, not at school, not sung by other kids or adults. They're Dad's and Dad's alone.

"It's Barnum Bill the Sailor!" Dad and I sing the last words together as Dad slings the saddle over the blanket on Kip's wide, gleaming back. I'm so excited I get to ride Kip today. Pepper yips and hops around, sharing in my excitement. I've been riding since I can remember, either with Dad or on my own on ponies, and just recently—after I turned thirteen—on my own on bigger horses, including Kip.

Jude had been living at Dad's for almost a year, but I wasn't getting used to the transition—both Jude's move to Dad's and his slide into the grungy, gaunt, sullen teenager he was apparently becoming. Jude had been holed up in the living room in Dad's trailer, splayed out on a stained bean bag chair with a liter of Mr. Pibb next to him, playing the Nintendo he now keeps at Dad's since he's been living there. Jude is addicted to Sims world-building games, particularly the theme park version. His video games had taken the place of the time we used to spend playing LEGOs and Monopoly, and my *My Little Ponies* had been packed up ages ago into boxes on the top shelf of the musty utility room at Mom's, where Jude hasn't returned in months.

"You coming?" I asked Jude as I'd come in, patting the dust from Kip's coat off my jeans. Jude didn't stop playing. Didn't make a sound. Just threw a shoulder up and shrugged. Kept clicking his buttons.

"I don't think so," he said. This wasn't entirely out of character for Jude, though. While I was usually a sunburnt, grimy mess with brown fingernail tips, chapped lips, greasy hair, and skinned knees, Jude had always preferred the less strenuous, cleaner indoor activities than I did. But I felt bad just walking away. As distant as Jude and I had become over the last year—with my growing relationship with Mariah and devotion to my school activities—I still wanted to include him. I would always want to include him, although I was growing increasingly more aware that Dad wasn't. He and Jude were just different now. Off. It was weird.

"Callie," Jude pauses his game and sets down his controller to look at me. "This isn't about you," he says. "Go. Have fun. It's fine, I promise." He doesn't sound mad at me. He doesn't sound angry at all, really, more like resigned. Or numb. Jude is a weird version of himself these days, but then again, he is sixteen. But something about this candid conversation gives me the courage to ask the thing that's been bothering me since Jude moved in here.

"Jude, what's wrong between you and Dad?" I ask. Jude waits a bit before answering.

"We," Jude pauses, "know secrets about each other." Jude finally concedes.

I wait for a moment, holding his eyes, which don't seem to harbor any hostility towards me. But they are still clouded over. Jude is in this room with me, but he's also not. I don't know what else to say or do, as I know from the way Jude told me, he won't disclose the secrets. We both hear Dad call my name from the pens outside.

"It's fine, Callie. Don't worry about me. Go, have fun," Jude pushes me up. I feel this weird seesaw moment of either staying by Jude's side or going to Dad's, both pulling me equally.

Jude picks his controller back up and puts his focus back on the TV screen, swaying me to the other side.

"Okay," I shrug. "I'll get you another Pibb if we ride by Allsups," I tell him, to which Jude nods and smiles tightly. His words haunt me, though, as I make my way out of the trailer and back to the pens where Dad is.

What secrets? I wonder.

——

"Babes." Dad catches me off guard when I make it back out to the pens where he has both Little Man and Kip saddled. "I got a little sussy for ya." My eyes brighten. None of us—Dad, Jude, or I—had used that word in a long time. It was kind of a little-kid word now, but for whatever reason, in that moment, I didn't care. *Little kid it up, Dad. Let's do it.* My body started bobbing without any input from me. "What? What is it?" I bounce around, then close my eyes and hold out my hands like old times. "Wait?" I stop bouncing and ask through a barely open eye locked on his. "Is it bigger than my hands?" Dad laughs through a big smile. I see and smell the Copenhagen in his teeth, that snaggletooth peeks out that I know so well. *Dad.*

"Close 'em," he instructs. I do, and he drops a silver piece in my hand. "I found it tucked away in an old box in the barn. It's an old buckle I used to wear when I was young. 'Bout your age."

I turn it over in my hand. It's one of those old-style western belt buckles with the little prong that sticks into holes punched into the belt. Smaller than Dad's big daddy roping buckle, made for a youth belt. Fits in the palm of my hand. It's got a little horse, looks like a pony, reared up on his haunches, his mane flying in the wind, all *Black Beauty*-like.

"Thanks, Dad," I say to him, beaming, turning the buckle over and over in my hand. I wrap it up in my saddle soap rag gently and slide it into the bag looped over my saddle horn that has the pliers, clippers, and other tools Dad and I will need for the fence-mending job we're going to tackle today at Doc Malley's and finish lashing Kip's saddle.

Dad kneels down on one knee like he always does when I need a boost to mount horses bigger than ponies. As I straighten my back, proud to be atop Kip and cock my chin up, I see Jude through the window of Dad's trailer. He's not playing his video game anymore. Jude's looking out at Dad and me. I wonder how long he's been there watching us. *Did he see what Dad gave me?* Something weird tugs at me. *But Jude wouldn't have liked this belt buckle. It's too cowboy-ish. Too … Dad?* It comes across as a question in my mind. I try to think of the last non-Christmas or birthday thing Dad gave Jude. I blink a couple of times but can't come up with anything. Jude holds my gaze through the window as if he's heard what I was thinking, which I swear he sometimes does. More often than not he does.

Dad clucks to his horse, Little Man, and turns him around to start our journey. I tug Kip's thick neck and head and turn him away from the window, following behind Dad as we walk our horses toward the power lines.

CHAPTER ELEVEN
DAD

I'll never forget that day with Callie. It's one of the last I can recall us spending the whole day riding horses. After that, she shot off like a rocket, doing all her spelling bee and student government stuff and spending time with that new friend of hers, Mariah, snickering about boys, I'm sure. She didn't have as much time for cowboy things after that, and I didn't blame her for it. I should have been there more during the years she did have time for it. But I'm trying now. I've been taking lots of extra-long hauls recently so I can pay the child support arrears and keep this trailer up to stay near them, Jude and Callie.

I thought about trying to get things renegotiated with the child support when Jude moved in about a year ago, but I don't want anyone from the state coming out to inspect my trailer and all. I'm not sure it would pass muster, although I do my best to keep it tidy for Jude, keep some peanut butter and cereal and things in the cabinets, and take his clothes with mine to the laundromat every couple of weeks. I know it's not a good, safe home for a young boy, but it's all I can provide.

I hate to say it, but it's been tough having Jude around all the time. I don't know what to say to him, what things to talk about most of the time. He's just so into his video games, driving around with his friends, and staying out all hours. He doesn't talk to me about anything, but that's expected for an angry teenager. I don't push him.

When I asked Jude what happened at home—why he was moving in with me—he was pretty tight-lipped about it. Just said Charlene didn't want him at her house anymore. Charlene only said, "I told Jude he could stay at my house as long as he made better choices. Cleaned himself up and stopped bringing that criminal filth into my house. He chose to move in with you instead. But you'll see, Bill. Our boy is on a bad path. You watch him," was all she added. And, as with any conversation with Charlene, shorter is always better, so I just welcomed him in. Best I could.

But Jude never did ride with Callie and me again after he moved in. I don't know if he just outgrew it or never really liked it in the first place, but something inside him just turned a bit rotten. Callie, on the other hand, remained bright-eyed, driven, and eager to please me as always. I have to admit that's a good feeling for a dad, one I took for granted and basked in, even when I knew her admiration wasn't justified, or earned. But I didn't want to shatter her vision of me with the truth. The way Callie looked at me always made me feel like maybe I had done something good with my cowboy life.

But Jude isn't the main reason I remember that day so well. It started with Callie. She sure worried me that day. My little girl, although not so little anymore. When we went riding up near Doc Malley's place to mend his fences, that shady ranch hand of his—Chip—kept hanging around, kicking dirt, doing nothing but eyeing Callie. I didn't like it one bit. A boy is stupid to think a man can't smell those thoughts on him. When I came up on them two in the pasture, Chip approaching her and Callie's knuckles white-gripped on her pliers, Pepper growling behind her, I sent Chip off with a warning so graphic I hope he has nightmares about it.

I kneeled down in front of Callie after Chip had ducked and run and taught her the best trick I knew for a woman to take the upper hand. I explained to her why people—guys mostly—like Chip feel like they're entitled to things. Because they believe, right or wrong—mostly wrong—the world hasn't given them a fair shake. I have no doubt

Callie knew what Chip had been thinking. I could feel it in her fingers, gripped like a vice on the pliers as I peeled each one off.

With my hands on her shoulders, I placed Callie squarely in front of me and showed her how to ball up her fist, with the thumb on the outside. I took a piece of leather from my saddle bag, held it to my throat like some kind of makeshift knee pad, and told her to do it.

"Punch me in the throat, Babes. Hard as you can."

Callie cocked that smart head of hers, asking if she was really allowed to sock her dad.

"I'm telling you to do it, Callie. I want you to know what it feels like. You need to put your full body weight behind it. I'll be fine, I promise," I'd told her. But, heck, if I hadn't thought it through, because that girl would do anything to make me proud. And, my baby girl can sure land a punch.

Callie cocked back like this punch would be her last, and she slammed her fist right into my throat. Exactly like I'd told her. Hard as a bag of bricks. She sent me back on my ass, coughing and sputtering, wondering if I'd damn near made a mistake. But I soon recovered and had to chuckle at Callie slinging her knuckles, pacing around, and eyeing me like a spooked horse.

I told her: "Anyone—especially a man—ever tries to take something from you you aren't willing to give, that's what you do, Babes. You punch that asshole right in the throat."

Guys like Chip are all over, especially in desperate, dusty places like Clovis. I wanted Callie to be ready. Be strong. But I was never able to teach Jude things like that. I don't know if he just never respected me because I got sideways with the law now and then, or if I didn't have a stable job or a stable house like Charlene. My cowboy charm just didn't work on him. Where Callie saw this larger-than-life rodeo mirage, I always felt like Jude just saw me—a struggling man, hiding behind jokes and humor.

But it didn't take long for me to see what Charlene had been seeing. She had been right. She usually was. Our boy was in trouble, and he wasn't going to listen to either of us. Our words or our fists. That night, after Callie went back to Charlene's, I found Jude back in my bedroom. He'd gotten into my stash, which I know is my fault. I shouldn't have been doing that shit, but I took my embarrassment out on him. I shoved him out of the house. And later that night, when I saw things no dad should ever see, I shoved him so hard he fell down the back porch steps. I wasn't even drunk or high, just angry and hurting for him. For the choices he was making. Thankfully, he wasn't hurt, but the look on his face told me he would never forget it, and he would never let me shove him again, which he didn't.

But Jude didn't cave in that moment. Turns out he was stronger than I knew, and a hell of a lot smarter than I am. He stood and bowed up to me right there on the porch and fought back with something far smarter than fists. Jude landed threats—smart, savvy legal ones— that he knew would get me sent back to jail. So, he and I called a truce after that; we were in a stalemate. Cold roommates far more than father and son. I wanted to change it, work on it, salvage whatever I could between us, and I vowed to do so many times. For months, I tried to work up ways to talk to Jude about it. But, Jude up and left before I could fix us.

I curse myself to this day because I can't remember the last thing I said to my son before he left Clovis.

CHAPTER TWELVE
RODDIE

I feel like a broken toy a child has cast off to the back of her bedroom in this putrid hospital bed with my ugly stump. I am no longer worthy of being cast in a central part in any of the elaborate plots Jude and I used to cook up. Now, I can only play the psycho evil villain. The busted war vet. A cooky aunt. Weird Barbie.

I've only looked in the mirror twice. Both times, the gnarly stump beneath my left knee was bandaged so it almost looked like a mirror trick, how a magician fools people on stage. The first time, I had turned away immediately and asked Nurse Clara to cover the mirror with a sheet. She didn't. This is the second time, and I have taken the grey metal hospital cane assigned to me and flipped it handle-side down so I can sweep the crook back and forth under my left leg, like a scythe trying to cut wheat that isn't there. I find I am hypnotized by it, swinging forward then back, forward then back, underneath my bandaged stump where a calf and foot should be.

I find myself lost in memory, trying to recall what scars I had on it. What my toes had looked like. Were there moles on my calf? What would it look like in high heels? Then I find myself equally transfixed by the thought of what the hospital has done with it. Did they throw it in the trash? Bury it? Burn it? Use it for spare parts for injured people?

The image of my dead purple leg crudely stitched to another

person's body does something to me. My eyes roll back in my head. Blackness closes in. I hear a clang—the noise so violent and disruptive it takes me back. Suddenly, I'm fourteen, staring in the dark at a jar of busted pickles. It's the night of the Stupid Fucking Party, but my mind goes back to the beginning: to the day I met him.

My little twelve-year-old heart stops when he walks in. I flush and cough and start wiping sticky hands on my too-big Jude hand-me-down jeans. Mariah hates him, but she's supposed to, at least most of the time. He's her brother. "This is Roddie," she says, offhand, as we walk into her house for the first time, as if he's the family dog, or just a weird sculpture in the living room that needs explaining.

To me, he's the only thing in the room because he has sucked out all of the oxygen. He has thick black hair in waves. Stupid long lashes for a boy. Doe eyes. The typical lithe, sculpted body of a young athlete. He throws a Nerf football at Mariah's face, and I marvel at the mental calculations and accuracy he just displayed, aiming it perfectly. Roddie must be brilliant. Mariah is slow to react, and it lands. Then he smiles. *He smiles.*

"Hey," he says to me, and I stand there dumbfounded. He's gorgeous. He has good aim, chiseled arms, and a great smile. Roddie's in ninth grade, a freshman on the football team at Clovis High School, where Jude goes. He's just a couple of years older than me. Just a little deliciously older. *He's perfect.*

"It's just Roddie. He's stupid," Mariah says, pushing her hair back into place and throwing the football out the window, which makes me chuckle, seeing Roddie's face drop in mock horror when she does. Now he's fit *and* funny. Within days, I'm in love.

"I read somewhere that we—humans—have some caveman, hunter/ the hunted, predator/prey instinct leftover where we can sense another creature's eyes on us," Mariah tells me one day at her house. She's super brainy. Way smarter than me. But, thankfully, I feel just smart enough to keep up. A little slowly this time, though, as it dawns on me seconds later than it should, that her predator/prey bit was because I'm staring at Roddie. Mariah and I haven't spoken about my crush on Roddie, mostly because it feels in violation of some girl code to me, but also because we've been quite busy dissecting Mariah's crush.

Tyler Beck is this super popular, all-American looking guy on the football team that Mariah had been paired with in earth science. He's also the asshole who Jay pushed down in the dirt of our front yard a couple of years back, so I hate him. Tyler is nice enough to Mariah during science because Mariah is carrying his grade along. I hate to tell Mariah, but it's just not going anywhere. Not because she isn't pretty enough. Mariah looks like a fiery Italian with glossy black hair, fair skin, and she's thin, always a plus, with a nice figure coming in. If you can overlook the cast—poor thing broke her arm, then fell in her cast and broke it again, which put her in a cast for almost a year solid. Outside of that setback, though, Mariah's really blossoming.

But she and I just aren't cool. We aren't popular or rich. We wear hand-me-downs, not any recognizable brands. I'm stocky and never tuck my shirts in, and my face is starting to get greasy and break out, which means I have to mash anything threatening to emerge into a bloody crater. Mariah's always hiding behind this shield of hair she sprays up into what Roddie has coined 'The Wall' with enough Aqua Net to put a hole directly above her head in the ozone layer. We're geeky misfits.

Walking to Mariah's house after school one day, we see Tyler and his cool entourage up ahead at the Allsups. Mariah slows, fusses with The Wall, and meets my eyes. She's nervous, and I get it. I would be, too, if Tyler were my Roddie. I fuss around a little too and tuck my oversized Dallas Cowboys t-shirt in, not really knowing what it will do for us. Mariah gets really brave as we walk up, and she waves at Tyler.

"Hey, Tyler," she says. "What'chya doing?"

Tyler seems stunned she has addressed him outside of earth science—like a turtle looked up from the sidewalk and started talking to you. He stands there dumbly, not answering her.

"We're going to Taco Box," Mariah trudges on, although we aren't. We never do. That's the cool after-school place to go, which is why Mariah and I never go there. Mariah and I go to Mariah's and play *Dream Phone* in her basement. We're those cool kids.

The whole group laughs. One of Tyler's friends elbows him and whispers. "Dude, your science girl just asked you out on a date."

"She's not my girl," Tyler immediately corrects, his cheeks on fire. I feel Mariah heat up next to me. It's radiating off of her. Unfortunately, Tyler's friends have left him no choice. He has to do it.

"You know," Tyler takes a step toward us. I gulp. "I don't think I'd go to Taco Box if I were you," he pauses. "That funky arm of yours smells so bad." Tyler picks up Mariah's arm and lets it fall flaccid. "I don't know if they'll let you in." Tyler's friends howl with pleasure, their knuckles go to their teeth, biting back laughter.

Mariah's eyes lift to his. They're brimming. Instantly, I hate him. I hate Tyler. I'm about to open my mouth to say who the hell knows what, when I hear a voice from behind me: rich, golden, confident.

"Hey, Jackass," Roddie slams the convenience store door behind him, having just stepped out and taken in the scene. He throws his Tallsips to the ground with a crash and rushes toward Tyler, grabbing him fiercely by the collar, Tyler's soft blue polo wrinkling in Roddie's clenched fists. Roddie pushes Tyler up against the big glass window. Tyler's friends skitter to either side, giving Roddie, who is easily fifty pounds heavier and a foot taller than each of them, the space he commands.

"You don't talk to my sister. You don't look at her. You don't stand beside her. You don't touch her. And you certainly don't fucking insult her. Or I'll make sure you lose a few teeth so you never forget that. These right here in the front," Roddie says, pushing Tyler's lips back to reveal his teeth. Tyler's eyes pop white. "You hear me? Fuckwad!?" Roddie growls at Tyler and slams him again against the glass. Tyler's sneakers are clawing at the ground as Roddie lifts him up.

Tyler just nods.

Roddie releases Tyler. His fancy shirt is now all wadded and wrinkled up around his neck. He slumps to the ground as Mariah, Roddie, and I start walking home.

"If anyone gets to pick on you for smellin'," Roddie says from behind me and Mariah, but we all keep looking and walking forward. "It'll be me." We walk a bit more. Mariah rubs her nose. I think she's trying to hide a smile.

"Besides," Roddie says, adding a bit of drama. Mariah and I eye each other. "Mom told me this morning they got an appointment with Dr. Parker. You're getting that smelly cast off next week." I slide my eyes, not my head, over to Mariah. Her eyes are darting around. She blinks a couple of times, bites her lip, and pinches the elbow above her cast.

Roddie turns around then—just a few houses shy of Mariah's—and starts walking away from us. He's probably headed off to hang out somewhere way cooler than with thirteen-year-old girls at home. Taco Box or the football field, if I had to guess.

———

Later, at Mariah's, she washes her face in the bathroom in the basement and brushes down her Aqua Net wall, revealing how beautiful she is becoming. I start to wonder what I'm going to look like in the next couple of years. My face is so round, my body so boxy and ungirly. I wonder if Roddie could ever like me *that way*. I wonder if I could get pretty one day, too, like Mariah, and maybe then Roddie wouldn't say things to me like Tyler did to Mariah today?

I decide to answer these questions how I've solved many, many smaller problems over the last few months. Shorts or my pink skirt to the skating rink on Friday? Use my allowance money to buy the Conair curling iron or the Clairol? Write my book report on *Charlotte's Web* or *Matilda*? I place my bet on the *Dream Phone* game. If Mariah figures out her secret admirer first—the "You're right! I really like you." revelation never failing to make us squeal—then I go with my first choice. The way I was originally leaning. Obviously, the pink skirt to the skating rink. *Duh*. The Conair. Naturally. *Matilda* all the way. By putting my secret hopes on Mariah to win, I tell myself I'm being a good human, when the truth is, I don't want to be solely responsible for the bad decision.

But, with this burning question—*Will Roddie ever like me?*—I find I can't determine which way I'm leaning. What if he will never like me back the same way? *"I know where he hangs out. It's not at Callie's."* In my mind, I hear the cheap *Dream Phone* voice burn me. I wipe my clammy hands as Mariah sets up the game, her practiced hands making quick work of it.

I can feel my cheek is burning hot against the stupid pink phone as I make my first call for a clue, realizing for the first time that all the clues are negative. They've always been negative. Mariah and I have spent hours only learning what our secret admirer *doesn't* like to eat, do, or wear. My world feels suddenly upended when I feel *Dream Phone* can't solve my problems. It won't tell me what to wear. What to do. Where to hang out. Who to *be*. Who I already am.

CHAPTER THIRTEEN
THAT STUPID FUCKING PARTY

None of it was Mariah's idea. For her fourteenth birthday, her mom thought it would be a good idea for her to have a "real boy-girl party." She would usually clap excitedly when she said it. That fact alone made it utterly mortifying to Mariah. Plus, even with the cast finally off, she was still painfully shy, wearing it metaphorically. Roddie, on the other hand—sixteen and now a junior at Clovis High where Jude was a senior—was far from it. To my supreme disappointment, I had to watch him flirting with many girls often while we walked home from school or while at Mariah's house as he would breeze in, grab a Coke (never offering me one), and tell Mariah he'd be back before dark with a giggling teenage girl under the crook of his arm.

"So, you know I … how I … you know I like Roddie," I finally just spit it out one day while Mariah and I were playing *Dream Phone.* Mariah tucked in her bottom lip, bit it, and just nodded. "So, if something were to happen. If we play Seven Minutes in Heaven or Spin the Bottle or something at your party," to which Mariah chuckled. I punched her in the shoulder and forged on. "I'm trying to do the right thing here!" it came out almost as a shout, my frustration building. *What was so goddamn funny?*

Mariah put her hand on my shoulder. "And?" she asked.

"If Roddie and I …" I choked out—having never said those words aloud before. "If he happened to … feel differently about me after the party. You'd be alright with that, right?" *Very elegant, Callie.*

"Of course, I would," Mariah said, but her response seemed to dangle at the end. She wasn't finished. "But …" she started.

"But what?" I asked.

"Callie," she inhaled deeply. "Roddie is," Mariah picked at something on her elbow. "He's a good brother to me. He looks out for me and protects me. And, no one knows I do most of his homework as school is just not his thing. Even though he tries. Sitting still and studying doesn't suit him. But Roddie has to keep his grades up to stay on the football team, and he wants to get a scholarship. Keep that between us," Mariah locked eyes with me, sealing the deal. *Done.*

"Part of being the …" Mariah made air quotes "'star football player' is that Roddie has to be cool. He needs to be friends with his fellow teammates, even the coaches, really, to *fit into* that world. In his world, he'll be much more successful if he's liked. His world really revolves around who you know, who you hang out with. Really, who you impress, obviously," Mariah let out that geeky hiccup chuckle she was prone to when laughing at her own jokes, "for that reason, academics will be *my* ticket. Football will be Roddie's. But we hope to go to the same college. University of Texas if we're lucky."

I set the pink *Dream Phone* down, processing for the first time the real relationship Roddie and Mariah had. They were in this together. And, this was the first time I had ever heard anyone—outside of Jude and me—talk as passionately about getting the hell out of Clovis as he and I were. Or had been. Jude and I used to talk about it a lot. That was before. Before Mom kicked him out, and he had to move into Dad's trailer.

I didn't see Jude as often now. Once every couple of weeks, I would spend the weekend with Dad, but he often just stayed holed up in the little middle bedroom of the trailer playing video games or listening to music. Other than that, he was just gone—off with friends, doing whatever high school kids did, I supposed. But Jude's hair was now long and always grimy. His skin had exploded with tons of red, angry pimples on his face. The dollface teenage boy was gone, and a lanky, grungy, irritable guy had taken his place.

When we used to talk about it before he moved out, Jude always said he was going to become an architect and design grand hotels or mega mansions for rich people. He was super good at reconfiguring the pony castle to make it a stage, or amphitheater, or some other exotic setting I would have never dreamed was possible with just walls and roofs. Not to mention his constant world-building. I knew he'd do it. I was going to get straight As and any scholarship I could. Maybe become a lawyer because I admire logic and love to argue even more. Assuming Jude and I still shared our exit plan, one thing I had never thought would be important for us was *cool.*

"Okay, I understand you," I told Mariah.

"Do you?" she asked, but I was too naïve to hear the skepticism in her voice. I nodded with all the feigned confidence I could muster. Bullheaded in my stupidity, I thought Mariah was giving me a roadmap, thinking—as much as I did—that I had a real shot with Roddie. I just needed to act cool until I became cool. I could do that for one night at least.

———

Turns out, I could not do that.

"Oh, Callie, stop," Mariah said, having followed me into the bathroom at the skating rink the night of her party. I had exerted myself like a rodeo clown on the skating rink, trying to impress Roddie and his friends who hadn't even noticed me. My poofy sprayed bangs had deflated, and I was sweating all over. To make matters worse, I'd plopped down on the bench in a huff and sat in something that smelled awful. Piss if I had to guess.

"I look like a dunked frog. Smell like one, too," I said to the mirror, starting to cry.

"Come here," Mariah said, as she turned my back toward the mirror and started running her hands through my gloopy bangs and swiping her finger expertly under my bottom lid to clean away the running mascara. She fussed some more, then swished a little of her strawberry lip gloss on my lips and spun me around to face the mirror.

A surprised gulp rushed out of me at the sight of myself in the mirror. I looked at least two years older, just like that. Mariah had somehow swooped my bangs to the side in an elegant blonde sweep to my ear and tied a little ribbon behind like a headband. *Where did she even get that?* I wondered, but then I turned around and saw that the pretty string that had bordered the collar of her new shirt was gone.

It crashed on me like a thousand bricks. What a crappy friend I was. This was *Mariah's* birthday.

"Come," I started pushing her toward a little bench in the bathroom to sit her down, different from the piss-smelling one I'd plopped on earlier. I pulled out a little mesh jewelry bag. Inside was a friendship bracelet I had made for her. Braided it myself, out of twisted strands of these curtains Mariah used to have in her bedroom. They were sheer with little pink and green seashells on them that I was surprised to see in Mariah's dumpster a few weeks back. Mariah had been really upset when her mom wanted to "update her little girl's room" before the party by replacing her pretty curtains with modern blinds.

Mariah's eyes twinkled as she spun the bracelet before her eyes, turning it this way, then that. "I made it out of your ..." but Mariah cut me off.

"Curtains," she said, soft as a sigh. "I didn't think you'd noticed," Mariah's chest heaved up with a big breath. "How ..." her voice trailed off. Feeling bold and buoyed in the moment, I ran with it.

"Magic," I told her with a wink. "Good friends are like that. Rare and hard to explain, but wondrous all the same," I told her, thinking even to myself how pretty that sounded.

———

After the skating, we'd all caravanned back to Mariah's house and descended the stairs to her basement, for the real "boy-girl" part of the party, my thrumming heart told me. We were a mix of Mariah's friends—me and a few other boys and girls from our junior high—as well as Roddie's high school sophomores and juniors, boys and girls. All night, I had envied Roddie his easy demeanor, cracking jokes and flirting with the girls his age who had come.

Then it was like the earth cracked open and the whole night went askew. Mariah's mom calls down to Roddie, telling him he has another friend that's come. I'm vaguely paying attention—waiting for my turn to play *Jenga*—when I see his shoes, then pants, then his gait as he comes down the stairs. I know immediately who it is.

Jay.

I hadn't seen him in two years. After Jay had shipped off to Portales to live with his mom, Debbie, and whatever flavor-of-the-week she was dating at the time, Jude and I just never heard from him. We didn't have cell phones then. Writing letters didn't cross our young minds. We just lived in separate towns now, and that was that, it had seemed. I had missed Jay, but I got busy with school, Mariah, and trying to get on the drill team and honor roll. And, Mariah and I had big plans for the summer. Although Mom had said her sister Shonna and her husband, Rick, needed help mowing lawns down in Roswell, New Mexico, I had told Mom no. Instead, Mariah and I had planned to get side-by-side jobs at Orange Julius over the summer so we could save up and get our hair permed before high school. Matching perms trumped lawn-mowing any day.

I knew Jay was playing football for Portales High. While I hadn't thought that would mean he knew Roddie, apparently, he did. Jay was so much taller. Head and shoulders above me. It seemed his collarbones had grown outward, as he now had these broad shoulders I hadn't remembered, his arms and chest more filled out.

Jay jogged down the last of the steps and gave Roddie that typical dude handshake/hug thing. In my mind, it was like two polar opposite creatures were meeting in the wild, as if a gorilla had walked up and hugged a kangaroo. Here was my insane crush, Roddie, and my wayward cousin, Jay, whom I hadn't seen in years. *And they're friends?*

I was a jumble of weirdness. I lifted my hand awkwardly in a sort of wave and mouthed "hi" to Jay when he finally looked around the room and saw me, his face conveying the same tie-dye of emotions mine did.

Jay and I gravitated toward each other like magnets from opposite ends of the room.

"I … I didn't know you knew Roddie," I said, kind of dumbly, wondering why I felt nervous around Jay. *It was Jay!*

Jay dug his hands into his pockets and blushed when he looked at me.

"Yeah," Jay finally managed. "We've hung out after Portales games a few times. This is my first time coming to his house. I didn't know …" Jay motions toward Mariah and our circle. Her eyes tell me she's just as confused as I am that Jay is here.

I turned back to Jay. "It's Mariah's party," I said, then corrected myself. "Well, Roddie's, too. Mariah's turning fourteen, Roddie seventeen," I filled the space awkwardly. "But I guess you already knew it was Roddie's birthday."

"Not really," Jay said with a chuckle. "He just said it was a party and I could hang out."

As if on cue, Roddie shouts over to Jay. "Dude! We're playing Street Fighter, get over here! Stop playing with the kids," Roddie says, but with a smile and wink to Mariah. Despite his obvious playful tone, the word stings me, as the whole point of tonight—for *me*—was to graduate from being a kid to a cool girl Roddie could like.

Jay holds up a finger to Roddie and gives him a smile as he lifts his backpack and lets a bottle of vodka peek out of the top. "I'll show you kid stuff," he says, getting Roddie's whole group whooping and nodding.

Something inside me lights fire and singes. I taste ash as I realize I am what I have always been—to Jude and Jay—just a little *kid* they let hang around, an ugly piss-smelling nerd they tolerate while they're getting on with their grungy, grownup drinking and drugs.

My face must convey it as Jay turns back around to me, because his good-time party expression drops immediately. "It's just … part of fitting in, Callie. I didn't mean anything against you," he whispers to me, but I don't believe him. My mouth clamps shut.

"Good to see you," I lie and turn back to my *little kid* group as the teenagers begin topping off the sodas in their solo cups with Jay's vodka.

Roddie's group migrates near the massive pantry, which is my favorite Hide Out hiding spot because it has a secret door that connects to the bathroom. It seems they're going to use the pantry space to play some different kind of game, and I know from experience that they are all getting tipsy. They are talking louder, touching each other more. Their cheeks are flushed, and they think everything—and I mean *everything*—is wildly hilarious. It's pissing me off. I was supposed to be able to finally talk to Roddie tonight. He was supposed to notice me tonight. Then I put together the game they've started—Seven *Minutes in Heaven*.

I watch as Roddie gets up from the circle and starts heading toward the pantry. He smiles and winks at one of the girls in the circle, who giggles furiously and shakes her head no. Roddie just swaggers into the pantry and shuts the door behind him.

Jay's presence—his easy fit into the alcoholic high school crowd—and

Roddie's complete ignorance of me have me feeling off-kilter. I stand up abruptly, telling Mariah I'm going to the bathroom. In there, I turn the knob on the secret door to the pantry area as quietly as I can and stick my head into the dark to make sure it's only Roddie in there. He's alone, leaning against the shelves with his arms behind his back, which makes his chest look amazing. There's a faint glow in the closet from a little night light—perfect for making out, if I knew what that was.

"Hi," I say weakly to Roddie. So nervous, I think I'm going to wet my pants. Again. The realization suddenly makes me terrified that I smell like urine. Roddie cocks his head, confused in the dim light.

"Callie? Get out of here," Roddie says sternly. We're playing an … adult game." Stepping toward me, he puts his hands on my shoulders to try to turn me around and shove me out the way I came from the bathroom, but I push back against him.

Shocked at my own determination, I face him squarely and whisper: "I thought maybe you could play it with me."

Roddie softens for a second, and I think he might be about to bring his face down to mine, but then we both hear a shout from out in the basement.

"Better pop a breath mint in there, Roddie. Gina's a little reluctant," I hear them tease. I watch as Roddie immediately stiffens, and that's when I realize. He would be embarrassed to be seen with me in here.

Embarrassed.

I'm embarrassing him.

My lungs feel like they are crushed against my back. I can't take a breath.

"Callie, no," he says. "You're just a kid. You're thirteen," he continues, slicing me with every word. But he's not done.

"You're my little sister's best friend. That would be …" Roddie searches for a word. "Gross."

Gross.

My little teenage spirit dies right then. My hopes and stupid little dreams. All this time, I was trying to fool myself, but deep down, I knew. I am gross. My family is poor. My Mom's an alcoholic. My Dad's a drug addict. Apparently, my brother and cousin are too, or trending that way. My teeth are yellow and slimy. My dress smells like piss. I'm a flat-chested, smelly little kid who, right now, looks like a dunked frog, only with a bow and lip gloss as a flimsy disguise. I'm so angry at my fate, I snap. I push a big gallon jar of dill pickles off the shelf, and I scream a murderous, shrill screech as it crashes to the floor. I hardly see Roddie through my hot tears as he's backing up toward the door of the pantry that leads out to the basement.

Mortifying light fills the small space as, suddenly, Roddie is out of the pantry and Jay is in, and I'm not even sure how or why it happened. *Did Jay recognize my scream?* I hear Jay shut the door, and I become aware that I'm gulping for air, and salty snot is running down to my lips. All of my fantasies about Roddie have just crashed to the floor like that goddamn pickle jar, and I hate myself for it.

You are gross, Callie. You're a stupid, poor, gross kid from Clovis, New fucking Mexico. What the hell were you thinking? I'm scolding myself as Jay steps toward me, carefully, around the broken jar and mangled pickles on the floor that are starting to stink.

"Callie," Jay says to me gently. I can smell the alcohol on him, but he still seems clear and coherent. "You're so much better than him. You are now, and you especially will be in just a few years. You're smart and funny and strong and ..." Jay seems to be struggling to say things he's been holding onto. "You're going to be so beautiful," he says. At the phrase *going to be* my walls go up. I am so embarrassed and angry at myself that I'm shaking.

"Callie," Jay says soothingly. "Don't let this," he puts one soft hand on my wet, snotty cheek, and I lose it. I have an inexplicable, raging desire to inflict pain. I slap Jay's hand away as my flailing, panicked brain creates a plot to rescue me.

"Yuck, Jay," I say loudly. "I can't believe you would try that," I say even louder, fueling myself with my own rage and shame. I push past Jay, crunching on the broken glass on the floor, and shoving the pantry door open to reveal my snotty little pity party to the whole group. I turn back to Jay in the pantry and shout.

"We're cousins! That's just …" My brain can only grab the singular word that feels etched into the back of my skull with a dull knife. "Gross!" I scream as I slam the door, leaving Jay in the dark. I then turn to Roddie and burn every last bridge left to me.

"And you!" I shout at him, flinging tears out of my eyes. Mariah looks at me in horror, but I block her out. I can't do this anymore. I can't try to pretend I'm like these normal, happy people when I'm not. I'm weird and different and gross and don't fit in here.

"I can't believe I even liked you," I scream at Roddie. Approaching him with shocking confidence, I dig a finger into his stupid, sexy chest. "Someone too stupid to do his own homework. Who has to have his little sister do it for him just to stay on the stupid football team!"

I hear Mariah take a knife-sharp blade of breath in and bring her hand to her mouth. The whole room is silent. I hear a sofa spring creak. One of the prissy high school chicks—probably the reluctant Gina— says, "Roddie, is that true?"

Roddie is as white as a ghost. His mouth is open like a fish. He darts his eyes to Mariah with a look that could slice her. Mariah starts shaking her head fiercely as tears bubble over in her eyes. She starts to walk toward Roddie with her arms outstretched, but he slaps them away and bolts up the stairs and out of the basement.

In that moment, I know. Oh, do I know. I have truly done it now. In that moment, they become *they*, beings completely outside of my existence. I am their dark underside, the belly of the snake that has deceived my way into their lair with only plots to bite them. I don't know how to be anything else in the moment. And, my epiphany is confirmed as I watch Mariah rip off the friendship bracelet I gave her earlier that very night, fling it hatefully to the floor, and run to the basement bathroom, her hands to her face. In my venomous spiral, I think—*Good, Jay's in there. You can have him*, as I storm out of the house.

———

Walking down Mariah's street, I see two figures under the faint glow of a streetlight by the stop sign. One is Roddie, I can tell by the shirt he's wearing. Roddie is waving his hands frantically. His voice, although muffled, is frantic and upset. My focus on them is fractured when I hear footsteps coming from behind and my name. It's Jay trotting toward me.

"Callie, thank God," Jay says when he finally reaches me breathless. I stand facing the stop sign with my back toward him. "You don't need any of those stupid high school people, including Roddie. You're a million times better than all of them."

"Am I?" I snap back cruelly. "Because I think those stupid high school people—all your friends apparently—would all disagree."

Seeing I'm not going to turn around, Jay finally steps in front of me. I wipe the last of the mess off my puffy face and hide it in a shadow.

"You think I give a fuck about them?" Jay asks. "I care about you. If I had known you were going to be here and that we could have hung out, we could have talked. I wouldn't have brought the vodka. I wouldn't even have stayed. The alcohol is … it's just for show, Callie. To … be cool."

The irony of his words burns me. As I keep my gaze focused on Roddie and the other guy, I feel like the entirety of my being blows out of me in a breath.

I recognize the guy Roddie is talking to. The guy he's looking to for solace after I wrecked his and Mariah's fancy little party.

It's Jude.

Roddie is talking to Jude. My world tilts.

"Callie, I've been meaning to talk to you anyway," Jay continues, clueless. My mind has left my body. "Debbie's new boyfriend," he starts, but his words drone out as I watch Jude put an arm around Roddie's shoulder. Jay's words sound like distant car horns to me as he rattles on while I watch Roddie and Jude. After a bit, my hearing comes back with a ringing sound, and Jay's words finally creep around the edges.

"With all that going on, Callie, I was wondering if I could move back in with you. And your Mom and Uncle Steve," I hear Jay ask. "I'm working—doing landscaping—so I can help with bills and food and stuff. But I know you're about to start high school, and one of us would have to share a room, so I wanted to make sure it was okay with you, and then Jude, before I even asked Miss Charlene. I know it's a lot to ask, Callie, but I'm … I'm not doing good in Portales with my mom."

I feel mean. Broken. Entitled to inflict rage. I want to laugh out loud at the irony that Jude is right there. *You can ask him yourself, Jay!* He'll say you can have his room because his bitch of a mom kicked him out. I boil over and sink into the horror that I feel exactly like my mom when I decide to do what I'm about to do.

"I'll ask my mom, Jay, and let you know," I lie to him.

I'm not asking her. I decide *I'm* not letting Jay move in.

He's doing just fine, it seems, with all his high school drinking friends. And, Jude obviously has plenty of friends, including the only one I wanted to make tonight. And, now that I've lost Mariah, I have none. Zero. I'm the one who's *not doing good. Okay, Jay?* I realize with a sickening thud that my summer will now be spent alone mowing lawns in Roswell.

Suddenly, I'm angry at Jay for all of this.

"I don't know if Jude will be up for sharing a room, but I'll see," I lie again to Jay. "And let you know," I add, but it felt flippant, too casual.

Jay's face comes into the streetlight just long enough for me to see a micro expression pass across. Some twitch of something. He drops his head and jams his hands into his pockets.

"Okay, uummm … I understand. Thanks, Callie," Jay says, not meeting my eyes. "Let me walk you …"

"No," I respond curtly and walk away from him toward Mom's house. To complete the absurd cliché, it starts raining.

——

The faucet on my head feels just like the rain that night as Nurse Clara's strong arms support me in the shower stall. The washing feels so good—rinsing both the fresh urine and stale memory of that party—that I just surrender and let them do it. I hold my weight up in the shower, but other than that, I just stand there and let them lift my arms, tilt my head, and move my body and do whatever they need to, without protest. Going back to that night in my mind takes a toll on me, digging up deep regrets that burn and make my heart feel concave now that I've relived them in such detail. I feel sorry for the little girl whose little dreams were crushed in that closet and the young man whose guarantee for a better future I snatched on that street corner.

CHAPTER FOURTEEN
ROSWELL

"Well, well," she said. "Look what the cat dragged to Roswell." I rubbed my eyes to make sure I was seeing things right.

Janessa? Here in Roswell? I couldn't believe it.

I hadn't thought about her since she started at that different junior high across town, and Jude and I never saw her again. But, like an apparition, here she was, walking down the street like she owned it in a short yellow skirt, a baby blue tube top held up by some impressive newly sprouted tits, and a lollipop in her mouth. I got distracted watching her and accidentally ran over a huge clump of dirt that kicked up everywhere. I was sputtering and spitting out dirt when she noticed me and came over, pulling the bright red pop out of her mouth with a loud smack.

"Hey, Callie," Janessa said, her tone a mix of curiosity and disdain. It felt like the perfect time to try out the new persona I had donned for the summer and—I hoped—the rest of my crappy teenage life.

"It's Calliope," I said, trying extremely hard not to avert my eyes to my sneakers. I stood awkwardly before Janessa, trying to muster confidence in front of her as I would in the mirror. "I go by Calliope now."

Janessa snorted. No-shit laughed at me. Her eyes raked me up and down as if considering whether she was going to accept this change. Or, better yet, whether I was worthy of it. I knew exactly what I looked like in my sweaty Coors Light t-shirt and ratty shorts, my dirty hair stuffed under a ball cap, and my legs sporting that dust and grass line around the socks. I held her gaze with an equal level of disdain.

"Okay," she said. "Calliope." The smell of it felt like a time warp back to my youth—the *Breath of Death*. Janessa still had it. I blew a shaft of air secretly out, hoping I didn't take any death breath particles in. Janessa raised one eyebrow. *An offer?* I crossed my arms over my chest and nodded. *An acceptance?* I wasn't sure, but some kind of truce was reached because just like that, Janessa—of all people—became my teacher for the summer.

Staying at Shonna and Rick's was fine. They'd given me my own little twin bed-sized room in the back of their ranch house with dresser drawers. Shonna worked two jobs and didn't hover over me at all. I had a curfew, shelter, and food on the table. All I needed. Rick was quiet. A hard worker during the day and heavy drinker at night, but he was a good guy, and easy, as far as bosses go, as was I, as far as day laborers go.

When I wasn't mowing lawns, which was only the late evenings and Mondays (the only day Rick didn't work), Janessa and I hung out. We'd get slushies at Allsups and go hang out at the strip mall by Janessa's dad's trailer, where Janessa would usually walk away with a new tube of lipstick and some earrings. On weekends, we'd bike up to the library to lie around on the big marble steps all day and taunt kids younger than us. She liked to hang around the Roswell baseball fields when they had games going, so she could flirt with the players and their dads. In a matter of a month, we had become the girls you tried to keep your teenage boys away from.

Janessa taught me many things, but the most important were how to look and act sexy, expertly lift things at stores with no chance of getting caught, look like you were eating while just really pushing food around to stay skinny, how to manipulate adults, how to talk your way out of trouble, how to flirt with boys … and men, and—maybe most importantly—how to give exceptional blowjobs. Janessa had a dildo we actually used for practice. That last one was worth the entire summer, although to this day, anytime something with a slightly rubbery taste gets in my mouth—a rubber band, or balloons, namely—my mind goes back to that summer and Janessa's neon green dildo. I always wondered: *Why green?*

Janessa also taught me the value of secrets and how to smell, uncover, and keep them if I chose.

We talked a bit about folks from Clovis. Not a lot, but a little.

"Your mom?" I'd asked her.

"Still a slut," Janessa had said. "Sent me here on lockdown with my dad for the summer when I found out she was banging Principal Nelson on the side."

My eyes popped wide. Principal Nelson looked like he was in his sixties.

"The man has three kids," Janessa spat. "And she thinks *I'm* the one who needs to work on my 'morals,'" she made little air quotes. "Yours?"

"Still mean as ever," I told her, and Janessa nodded. "She kicked Jude out."

"Jude? That's surprising. I figured she'd kick you out first," Janessa said.

"Me? That's laughable. I'm the good one now—good grades, I follow curfew, and do my chores. I'm getting the hell out. Jude's all into drugs and skanky girls and skipping school. He's so gross looking now, too." I feel kind of bad venting about Jude to Janessa, but I haven't had anyone else to talk to all summer, and his annoying transformation and lack of motivation have apparently been vexing me more than I knew, because I pick up steam. "His hair's long and greasy. His skin's all broken out. I'm not sure he's doing real well living at Dad's."

Janessa cocks her head. "I can't see Jude looking gross, ever. He was always so gorgeous. Pretty almost," she said it like a question.

Pretty? It seemed Janessa hadn't even been listening to all the disgusting things I'd just said about Jude, but the wistful look on her face made me miss that soft-faced friend from my childhood.

"He always said you liked him." It just came out.

"I did," Janessa didn't hesitate.

"Why didn't you two ever ..."

Janessa looked at me for a beat before hopping off the cinderblock fence we'd been sitting on.

"You'll have to ask Jude that one," she said over her shoulder as I hopped off the fence to walk with her.

"What about that other boy y'all were always paired up with. Your cousin. Jay? What's he like now? Is he hot? Tell me he's hot."

"No. Gross. He's my cousin!"

"Oh, please, Calliope. By marriage only. This is New Mexico. Nobody will hold that against you." I was pretending to gag beside her.

"Seriously, though, he goes to Clovis High now, right? Are the three of you still tight?"

Her questions about Jay threw me. I wasn't ready to talk about him yet, but I also wasn't sure if I ever would be after what I'd done.

"No and no," I said. "He goes to Portales. And, we don't really talk anymore," were the only details I was willing to add before shutting the Clovis catch-up session down, feeling stabbed that my last statement applied equally to both Jay and Jude.

———

In addition to a perm, a bikini tan, and a new wardrobe (half bought, half lifted), Janessa also gave me two very important gifts for a newly transformed girl about to dive into high school: sexual experience and birth control.

Although Janessa told me he liked me—this older, gangly bagger at Bailey's Grocery named Sean—I found out later Janessa had actually paid him five dollars to make out with me, and eventually do more. I had to laugh a little when Sean finally spilled the truth, thinking that if I ever did become some big-shot lawyer or CEO of some global corporation, Janessa would have collected one of the best Callie secrets of all: *Gross Lawyer Had to Buy Her First Kiss.* I was actually so grateful for the veil-lifting educational experience that I never called Janessa out for the humiliating prank she pulled.

She also secretly got me on birth control by spinning a lie at the health department that simultaneously shocked and appalled me.

Janessa and I had been stalking the office for a week, trying to decide which counter-front lady was going to be the best target. Janessa had finally settled on this frumpy woman whose hair was shaped around her head like a LEGO helmet, and she had the largest, drooping tits I'd ever seen, almost down to her belly button.

"Okay, Snoopy Tits is alone up there. It's go time," Janessa had tugged me inside.

Once we reached the counter, Janessa leaned suggestively over and whispered conspiratorially to the woman. "Her mom … just passed," Janessa said with a sad face, glancing back at me. I'd pouted.

Snoopy Tits gasped and put a meaty hand to her chest.

"Now she's afraid, without her mom around to protect her." Janessa looked suspiciously around the waiting room. I instinctively made a little scared face as their eyes passed over me, feeling incredibly thankful I didn't have a speaking role in this skit. "That her domineering stepdad will take advantage. We just want to take all precautions," Janessa had added, all proper and adult-like.

It being the first time I'd heard the word: *Domineering* was all I could think of in absolute awe, as Snoopy Tits handed me a year's worth of pills.

CHAPTER FIFTEEN
CALLIOPE

"I want to go by Calliope now," I told Mom, very matter-of-factly, when I got back from Roswell. She'd started to hug me when I got off the bus, and I'd halted her already awkward approach with my announcement. "Not Callie." Mom tucked her lips into her mouth but didn't say a word. Instead, she decided to do what was more natural for her to fill the gaps. She got comfortable in the front seat of her Oldsmobile, opened her jangly silver cigarette pouch, pulled a cigarette out, and started to light it up. I watched her.

"Calliope," she said. It didn't sound quite like a question, but it wasn't quite a statement either. I looked unapologetically at her, liking the sound of being summoned by my full, proper name—my new name. "Do you remember me telling you what your name means?"

My heart thudded against the wall and laid down for a second, curious about my own new persona—wanting to hold it, shape it, admire it in the light.

"Tell me again," I said while keeping my eyes on her as she drove past tumbleweeds, cow pastures, and highway signs. Oddly, it seemed Mom and I found ourselves in this—locked silence—more often than we found ourselves speaking, so it seemed to feel more comfortable than talking.

"Calliope means beautifully voiced," my Mom started, her eyes now staring off in the distance. It was a fact I knew. And while I didn't wholeheartedly agree with it, I did love to sing—on my own, in the shower, while walking down the street. I didn't consider it beautiful, but I did love to use it: my voice.

"*She* never had a voice." Mom was picking at a crack in the baked leather of her armrest—one we all picked at. It was hard not to if you sat in the front seat of her car. It was also the place she had yelled at Jude and me for picking at. And here she was doing it.

"*She* … never got to say a single word," Mom continued. "One week, she was moving and kicking in my belly, the next, I was in labor, and then. She. Was. Lifeless. Then she was gone." Mom ran her tongue over her teeth and pulled a breath so deep in her chest that it heaved up, as she picked a piece of the armrest off and flicked it into the floorboard, not caring where it went. I watched it land near my shoe. "Just gone," she said. "Never to be known. Or heard."

I knew who Mom was talking about. The person—*was she a person?*—we never talked about. My sister, Cadence, whom Jude and I had been told Mom had lost during childbirth. The thought of her stirred this weird mix of emotions in me. I didn't know her. I'd never met her. No one had any good memories or stories to share about Cadence. She had just been here as a child in Mom's belly but had eventually suffered developmental problems during the pregnancy: kidney and lung stuff Jude and I were told. We never really quite understood, and I'm not sure we wanted to. I had always secretly hoped Cadence was such an undeveloped baby that she could never really process her own tragic state in the womb. But Mom could. Mom did. I knew that, even though she never really talked about it. Jude and I just knew Mom had lost a child—her first child—a year and a half before Jude had been born.

Cadence Annalee Potts. The reason our Mom was sad and mean.

Mom took a long drag on her cigarette, clamped her little jingle pouch shut, and turned her head out the window. I wondered if Mom had turned because she was starting to cry, but that was something I could only recall Mom doing once.

When I was five, Mom, Jude, Steve, and I had gone to the Balloon Fiesta in Albuquerque and stayed at a Motel 6. Jude and I had been wrestling, and I didn't know I would break through the wooden railing so easily. We had been four floors up, but somehow—miraculously—after I'd crashed through, I had landed in an open dumpster on a pile of cardboard boxes, slimy takeout containers, and coffee grounds. It was normally something Jude and I would rush to hide from Mom so we wouldn't get in trouble, but she'd heard the cracking of the wood railings and Jude's inhuman shout when I fell, so she'd come running.

Mom had gotten to the balcony just in time to see Jude jump after me and land in the slop right next to me to make sure I was okay. She'd looked down at us with dark mascara streaks already down her cheeks, her hands clawing red lines into her cheeks, with a look of torment—like she hated the fact that any injury we might suffer or our demise could slice her open and turn her completely inside out. She looked enraged that Jude and I were down there, a team, an unbreakable pair, and she was left up there with her … her anger. Jude and I had apologized a thousand times, but I'll never forget seeing Mom's tormented, rageful tears.

Mom wasn't crying now. That or she'd swallowed it down. I didn't hear any cough or a sniffle when she resumed.

"That's why, when I learned what Calliope meant—beautifully voiced—I wanted that name for you because I knew you, unlike Cadence, were going to grow up to be healthy and …" she finally turned toward me, her face a wash of memories and pain but she was forcing a smile "strong-willed," she said, which made me chuckle. "And you would have a voice, a beautiful one, you could use to tell the world what you wanted to say."

I could feel my chest rise and fall in deep, needy breaths. My core temp was rising. It was one of the most penetrating conversations Mom and I had ever had.

"Mom, what happened to Cadence?" I asked boldly.

Mom squared her shoulders back, pushed a wad of sticky hair from her face, and made a decision. I could see it in the way the muscles of her face shifted around. She decided to close that door. Just like I often did. Anytime I decided I was done talking about something.

click Shut. Done.

"She died. That's what happened," Mom said as she put her blinker on to turn onto the highway that would take us back to Clovis.

——

"It's Calliope," I said, almost knee-jerk, out of habit, before I had fully stood to take him in after he'd said the word I don't answer to anymore. *Callie.*

Two months into my freshman year at Clovis High, I had made several things: the JV cheerleading squad, the Student Government Association, the Pop Choir, and twenty fake friends. My goal was to stack on as many extracurricular activities as I could handle because I was not going to give up on mine and Jude's dream to get the hell out of Clovis, although it appeared he had. And—the good news—I found padding my high school resume was so much easier than I thought now that people *liked* me, well, Calliope. I found it wildly surprising how much they seemed to like Calliope when they really didn't know her at all.

But Calliope wasn't liked by everyone. I hadn't yet formed my plan for how to approach or deal with Mariah when the time came. It didn't seem like rekindling our old friendship by apologizing to her and trying to make things right between us fit into my new plan of becoming cool. And, I had been so troubled by the stress of wrestling with those thoughts that I simply hadn't looked for her in my first few weeks of school. In the following few weeks, I started to secretly investigate. I flipped through teachers' rosters when they weren't looking. I checked a stack of attendance records I saw sitting at the front receptionist desk. Nothing pointed to Mariah going to Clovis High School. It was like she had disappeared.

I was on the verge of asking Mom about it one night when I got home after cheerleading practice, but something stopped me. Pride? Privacy? However you approached it, the answer was I didn't want my own mom to know I missed my friend. What I had not expected, however, was to learn about Mariah from an asshole who I thought never liked her.

"Calliope, huh?" he said. And there he was. Eight inches taller than I'd seen him the last time. Eighty pounds more muscle, it seemed. And just one reason why I needed to make him a new friend. He was popular, talented, and cute. Despite it being a direct betrayal of Mariah—and my former self—I was starting to think Tyler might be all Calliope really needed to conquer this high school.

"Tyler Beck," I said to get the jump on him. "As I live and breathe," I added with a slight southern accent, laying an imitation Antebellum hand on his chest, and making eye contact, both intimacies Tyler and I had never shared before, in hopes of throwing him off, Janessa-style. It didn't work.

Tyler took my hand off his chest and turned it around, back and forth, in front of his face. "I don't know," he said, pretending to be perplexed. "This looks like the hand," he paused and let his eyes drift over my entire body, "of a girl I once knew as Callie."

"You didn't know Callie," I challenged, sliding my hand out of his. "But you could *get to know* Calliope." It was an offering.

"Well, Calliope," he started, which I took as acceptance of my offer. "I'm glad you decided to grow up and come to high school here in

Clovis. Not Texas, like that smelly gal that used to be …" he paused before saying my old name, "*Callie's* friend. Mariah."

Mariah? The name caught me off guard. But I practiced my Janessa training, letting out a seemingly nonchalant sigh while lowering into a deep, suggestive stretch of my hamstring. With my head to my knee, my hot breath puffing into my own face, I listened intently until I heard Tyler turn and get back to whatever he needed to do to prepare for the game. I waited. Finally, I heard his cleats grind on the track as he turned around. Tyler put his little paper cup down on the table, clipped on his helmet, and headed back onto the field. Leaving me to my wondering.

Mariah? Texas? I was totally confused by that one. I didn't know Mariah's family had any ties in Texas. But I wasn't going to find any answers on the sidelines of a football game. I pushed the thoughts away. Boxed them up. Put them on a shelf, and kept cheering. We had a game to get through. I had a squad to lead. Good grades to get. Permed hair to style. Boys to tease. I was busy. Mariah was gone. Calliope was here.

CHAPTER SIXTEEN
SISSY

"Calliope?" One of the nurses spooks me by sticking her head in the door and calling me by my full name. I feel like I've been in my childhood bedroom, taking boxes down off the shelf and opening them on the floor, but the boxes aren't filled with the usual: old stuffed animals, photos, mixed tapes. They're filled with memories, and every time I open a box, I'm transported back to the memory as if it's happening in real time. I look up at the nurse as if I've come from a different time, because I feel like I have.

The nurse checks my leg wound, which I've looked at many times. It's healing well. I'm sure they'll take the sutures out within the week. I've pressed on it a time or two—as hard as I can—to see how much it will hurt to put weight on a prosthetic because I know that's coming. Right now it's tingly and painful, so I've decided to let it heal for a while before I try again. I'm feeling jittery and impatient lying in this bed. As much as I know my body needs this time to rest and recover and gather energy for the long road of recovery ahead, I also want, equally badly, to leap out of this bed and run right out of this hospital, or hobble out, whatever I'm able to do.

I would at least like to get out of here before that nasty detective can come back and start asking me more questions I can't answer. Before Mom comes in and we fall back into a fight that's too old to even remember how it got started or why it matters. I'm feeling restless, loopy, and strange here in this bed, like some scientific experiment that people come in and poke and eye oddly every now and then. Poke. Scribble. *"Do you concur, Jim?" "I concur,"* I imagine them saying.

But I am positive this strangeness is only temporary, and that the leaden weight of my reality will begin pressing on me, relentlessly, the minute I'm discharged. While the thought of losing my job at Goldman Carr—if it turns out I was driving during the accident and their PR team decides this fiasco cannot be sufficiently swept under the rug— makes me feel sick, it's not the loss of the job I fear, which baffles even me, considering the time, stress, and money I put into getting it. But, it's not. What makes my blood turn cold is the thought that I may have injured someone else in the accident. *What if I killed someone?*

I shudder at the sound of my hospital room door cracking open, and I see Mom's spindly back fill the gap. She's still sporting that 49ers jersey. It's either the same day or she hasn't changed. Both seem equally likely.

I hear heated voices outside the door. I imagine Mom out there running interference for me, and I'm grateful. Being confined to a hospital bed will certainly make you humble. I'm also really surprised Mom is here, as I said some unbelievably hateful, unforgivable things to her the last time we spoke—more like shouted—ironically in a different hospital room, two months ago. I really thought I had cut the band that connects us for good. Surely at some point, if your daughter is hateful enough to you, you can give up as a mother? Or vice versa. *Right? Can't you?* I glance quickly at the little batch of framed photos Jay brought me; the batch I've taken with me to every home I've lived in since I left Clovis.

With a sickening feeling, I see there's no visible picture of me and Mom there. Surely she has noticed. Only I know, but the photo that Dad gave me of him and Mom in their twenties—smiling in swimwear, blissfully unaware of the wreckage that lies ahead of them—I stashed behind the photo of me and Dad on horseback. I wish I could bring

Mom in here now and have her take it out and see so she will know: *I'm not as heartless as I sometimes seem. I'm just trying to keep it together, and it's hard.* Then something clicks inside, and I wonder if Mom has felt that way toward me and Jude, dozens, hundreds, maybe countless times. Despite it, here she is. Standing guard for me.

I can see through the sliver of open door my Mom's bony arms crossed over her chest, and she's shaking her head 'no,' but I can't see to whom. I lean over just a bit in my bed to see who's standing before her. It's another cop-looking guy with a long cloak jacket and a tie. His hands are on his hips, revealing his badge on his belt. His voice is gruff and stern. He's got one hand up, pointed at Mom's face, but she's not moving. She steps right in front of my doorway and blocks it just as the cop guy—maybe it's that other officer named Sloane—tries to make his way in. I stretch over a bit further to try to see what's going on out there.

Then I see her face. *What is she doing here?*

"No, you most certainly can*not* speak with her," she says, forcefully, to the detective, in a way I've never heard her speak before. "I'm her attorney."

I swallow the sudden realization that the person who may be in legal trouble is me. The person who *needs* an attorney is me.

I gasp and bring my hand to my mouth just as another nurse slips into my room and shuts the door. All I can think about is Detective Carter's stale breath and intense questioning:

"You had an exorbitant amount of alcohol in your system, Callie."

"Do you remember what happened the night of the accident?"

I still can't believe she's here. And, here to represent me.

Mariah.

The nurse who slipped through the door, locked eyes with me, and I knew I was giving her a pained look, begging her for answers she did not have. I slump back down on my bed, knowing this woman knows nothing about me—or what's going on outside my door, likely—so I try to calm myself by watching her, taking her in. She's a bit older than most of the other nurses, in her mid- to late fifties, I think, with dyed blonde hair tossed up into a clip. She's thin and looks like she might have been a really pretty woman in her prime. The lines around her face tell me she's a smoker, probably has been since her teens, but she wears a good bit of makeup to hide her age.

A funny feeling creeps through me as I realize exactly who she reminds me of: Dad's old girlfriend, Sissy. It's eerie how she seems to move just like her, a little frantic, a touch of jitters. But she is quick and dexterous, fueled by her own nervous energy. Watching her, I'm taken back to the last time I saw Sissy, at Dad's trailer.

———

She is hunched over the kitchen table, a piece of leather in one hand, a box knife in the other. Recently, she's gotten into making key chains out of leather, cutting and twisting little four-inch pieces, and punching silver grommets and decorations onto them. I would think it was a pretty cool hobby if she didn't like to do it when she's high as a kite from midnight till three in the morning under a hot lamp clamped to the blinds of the kitchen window. The light shines right onto my bed, currently the pullout sofa in Dad's living room.

The light isn't the issue. I'm pretty sure I could roll over and ignore it. It's the dry, scraping sound of her constantly scratching her arms that I cannot. I'm so attuned to it that I can hear when she hits a scab and razes it. I've started to count the seconds until I hear her suck on the open wound, then smack her lips. It's between two and three. I've never reached three, although I wonder if I'm drawing out the Mississippis in between too long. That is precisely how bored and awake I am lying on the couch.

I had come to stay at Dad's that weekend because we were burying Pepper. She had lived to be thirteen years old, which was pretty damn good for a dog. Pepper was present in so many memories in my childhood. She was the best and smartest dog I'd ever known. We'd buried her that afternoon in a little grave Dad had dug behind the horse pens on his property with a makeshift stick cross and a rock I'd painted on. Although I was sad realizing it was one of the first things Jude, Dad, and I had done together in as long as I could remember. Laying in bed—or the sofa—that night, listening to nasty-ass Sissy pick and suck her wounds, suddenly I find myself overwhelmed with worry for Jude.

Comparing Calliope—the popular, straight-A student, with the SAT and ACT exams right around the corner to seal my college fate—to Jude—the grungy, angry high school senior dropout—I had begun to resent him for not trying harder. Giving up, as I perceived it. He wasn't working nearly as hard as I was to do what we had promised one another we would always do together. Rise from this rubble. Get out of Clovis together. At one point, Jude and I had been an indivisible team. But it didn't feel that way anymore. While I was accelerating in academics and extracurricular activities at Mom's, Jude was sliding into a drug-laced hole of depression and failure at Dad's.

I see light from Jude's video game from under his bedroom door, and I decide to slip in.

—

"Jude?" I ask quietly. He pauses his video game and turns to look at me. He is ghostly white in the light of the TV, but it softens his features, and with his scraggly hair pulled back away from his face, I see he still has that beautiful silhouette. The long lashes, high cheekbones, and pouty pink lips. *Pretty, almost?* Janessa's words surprise me. I shake off the weird feeling they stir.

"Lil Bit," Jude says and pats the bed next to him. Something in my spine softens at that, and I make my way over to curl up next to him.

"You alright?" Jude asks, sensing my unease. I nod.

"Sissy, you know?" I say to him, and Jude starts scratching his arms animatedly and sucking at imaginary wounds, an act so spot-on I have to wad a handful of his covers into my mouth to keep from laughing out loud. But then I find those are grimy too and spit them out.

"You want to know something crazy about Sissy?" Jude starts, immediately drawing me in. I nod vigorously.

"She was Prom Queen," Jude says. I slap the blanket hard, but it only lets out a muffled clomp. My jaw drops as I stare at Jude with this juicy nugget of new information.

"Sissssssseeeeyyyyy?" I hiss at him, and he nods.

"I found an old picture of her in one of Dad's drawers a while back. Sash and crown and all," Jude says while imitating holding a big bunch of roses in one arm and waving like a beauty queen with the other. He wipes a fake tear from his eye, smiles, and nods at his imaginary audience.

"Shut uuupppp!" I punch his shoulder again and realize how brutish I am with him sometimes, this new "me" being far more aware of my old tomboy ways than I had ever felt before. But there is an irony here I have to share with Jude.

"Funnily enough, I'll probably become Prom Queen in a couple of years, the pace I'm at. And, the guy I'm dating, I'm sure you've heard of him—Tyler Beck—he'll probably be Prom King, if you can believe that. And—as much as I really don't like Tyler, deep down—he and I really had no say in the matter. I'm captain of the cheerleading squad. He's the quarterback of the football team. We're a foregone conclusion."

Jude laughs. A genuine, soft chuckle that fills the air and pops like bubbles.

"Oh my gaaawwd, Callie, not that beefy football idiot? The freshman bully. You're dating *him?*"

I had to laugh, because I wouldn't call Tyler taking me around in his truck and buying me a soda he hoped would earn him a blowjob *dating*. However, a BJ was as far as I'd been willing to go with him. Unlike Sean, Tyler gave me this uneasy feeling that he felt entitled to certain things: popularity, authority, handouts, and me.

"I mean. Tyler's handsome, hot," Jude pierces my thoughts. "Whatever. But you two are going to be like the cake toppers at prom? Ahhhh! I can see it now," Jude waves a slow hand in the air above us, making fun of me.

I swat him, and he shakes his head and holds his hands up in defense.

"I only laugh, because Prom Queen—which I know you will get" Jude adjusts an imaginary crown on my head, "is the least exciting thing *you* will become in *your life*, Callie."

I sense a long-overdue Jude lesson coming. I smell Sharpie. I shut up and listen.

"You and Sissy are related in that you both have been, or will be, Prom Queen, but you will be the opposite of her. The yin to her yang," Jude says. I cock my head listening to him, aware—even in the moment—how rare these moments with Jude have been recently and how rare they may continue to be going forward. I try to slow time with my mind as I listen.

"You see," Jude continues. "For Sissy. Prom Queen was her peak. That is the greatest thing she will ever be, and she knows it. But for you, Callie," he pauses to make little air quotes, "Prom Queen is probably the least exciting, or least impressive, of all the amazing things you will be and do, Callie." Jude sets a hand on my knee. "People will not feel sorry for you. They will feel awe, because you, Lil' Bit, have so many more peaks ahead. Challenges, for sure. That's the climb. But, unlike Sissy, you will … ascend."

Like a time warp, the word takes me immediately back to his bedroom at Mom's. I'm sitting on the floor cross-legged, and Jude is writing words—both in print and underneath in 'pretty cursive'—in Sharpie on the screen of his little TV, teaching me, and he has written the word 'ascend,' which I remember means to rise.

I nod, letting Jude know I understand.

"I guess she was popular back in her day, too, then", I say, trying to downplay the compliment and get back to poking fun at Sissy, but it has the opposite effect.

"Now that you mention it. I've been curious. How's all that going for you?" Jude asks.

I take a breath, really letting the question seep in. In all honesty—as this is Jude—I find talking about my seemingly impressive high school resume leaves me with only one emotion. Exhaustion. Some resentment, maybe, that things that really matter very little to me have to be the things that matter the most right now.

Jude interrupts me somewhere between the upcoming election for SGA president and tryouts for the lead choir solo.

"You're rattling these things off like they don't matter?"

I pause, unsure whether that was a question. Jude waits.

"I mean, I guess they do, I …" Jude interrupts again.

"They do," he says briskly. I stop my prattling to listen.

"Callie, I know I've been … a little distant lately, but I've wanted to tell you everyday how proud I am of you. The things you're doing—that I'm *not* doing—all these resume-building college things, they do matter. They're going to help you get into a really good college and get out of here."

I clam up, perplexed by Jude's reference to us as on different tracks. It's a reality I have felt, seen, silently fumed over, but I haven't yet put words to. At least here in Clovis. Hearing them from Jude takes my voice away.

"You're doing all the right things to get out of here and studying hard. Getting great grades. All those extracurricular, flip-dee-do things you do." Jude waves a hand, which does the trick. I laugh.

"You mean, cheerleading?" I ask sarcastically, trying to hide the unease I'm feeling with this focus on me.

"Yeah," Jude says dismissively, chuckling. "All that stuff. That will get you a scholarship, for sure. If not a full ride. It'll be enough to get you started, at least. Get you a foothold. Then there's federal aid, grants, loans, stuff like that. You're looking at the University of Texas in Austin, right? That's a really good school, Callie. If you can get in there, you'll … you'll soar," Jude makes a little rocket motion with his hand, unknowingly searing an image of his hand across the limelight of the TV at 2:00 a.m. that will stick with me for the rest of my life. *You'll soar, Callie.*

While I want to bask in this vision Jude has for me, it feels like it's missing a whole half. I realize half of my worry for Jude is anger at him for dropping the ball, becoming this shell of his former self.

"But, what about *you*, Jude?" I bristle. "You're not doing any of the flip-de-doo things I'm doing to get out of here. You're," I feel anger rise, I didn't know had been simmering inside me, "not doing anything productive. You just hang out with your … slutty girlfriends and skip class and …"

I want to mention other things, but I'm torn between savoring this rare candid conversation with Jude and using it to air my grievances against him. In the silence, I tip.

"Jude, are you still doing drugs?"

Jude is quiet. I breathe in and out twice, hoping he'll fill the silence. He doesn't.

"Are you still trying to get out of here with me?" I ask, a bit scared of how he might answer.

Jude scooches around so we can both prop ourselves up on his little twin bed and face one another.

"I am," Jude says. I meet his eyes, looking for the promise.

You are? my eyes implore.

"I am," he repeats. "I wasn't going to tell you until it was final and all, but I've been saving up. I found this CAD school in Houston that I've been looking at. It's accredited by the National Architectural Accrediting Board, which is perfect. I might be able to stay with this friend I met at school. His cousin's got an apartment in Houston. He waits tables for extra money, which I'll probably do, too, but he offered to rent out some of his extra space to me and my friend for extra money." Jude laughs, which raises my eyebrows.

"Extra space," Jude explains. "More like a sofa for my friend, and a laundry room with a cot for me," he chuckles. "Not much different than here anyhow," Jude waves his arm around his stuffy little closet of a room. "But hey," he stops to look at me. "It's out, right? I'd be on my way."

I count the months in my mind. It's February of my freshman year. Jude is set to graduate in May from Clovis High. At least I assume he is going to graduate. But May is like three months away. *Jude will be gone in three months.*

"I'll be leaving before graduation," Jude says, very matter-of-factly, reading my mind. Like it is equivalent to 'I think I'll catch the morning train.' Like it is nothing, if Jude is leaving before graduation, then he is leaving in *less* than three months.

"How?" I find I am dumbstruck.

"I already got my GED," he says. "Last month. As soon as I turned eighteen." The news subverts me. Jude turned eighteen—a huge milestone—and I'd only given him a handmade card. I wonder what

Dad had done, if anything, because I knew Jude and Mom weren't really speaking. The reality of that made me feel like the inside of my body slipped into a sinkhole.

"But, Houston?" I can't stop myself from sounding like a child. My pace picks up. Worries I didn't realize I had hidden behind my poised Calliope exterior start clattering down like marbles.

"That's like hours away? I won't see or be able to talk to you at all? I don't know exactly where I'm going to go to college yet. Or how I'm going to get loans for it. Or stuff for it, books, a computer? I don't even know what kind of degree I should get or what I'm going to do. I was thinking lawyer, but I'm not entirely sure. I don't have it all figured out yet, Jude," I realize I'm trying to tell Jude I will need him and—like an idiot—I feel like I'm realizing for the first time Jude and I were never going to leave Clovis on the same timeline.

He was always going to go first.

"Lil' Bit," Jude says, snapping me to, his hands on my shoulders. "We will *always* be a team."

I meet his eyes, needing to believe Jude and I will always be a team. His new, dirty, deadbeat persona has not only irritated me, but it has let me down because I feel like I've lost my partner in all of this. I have felt so alone because Jude and I were supposed to be doing all this together. And, a very small, sinister part of me wonders if I still believe this greasy stranger who looks kind of like Jude.

"I will always be there to help you," Jude reinforces. "I'll help you with your college applications. We can choose together where you should go. I'll help you move and decorate your dorm room. I'll work through the scholarship and financial aid applications with you. I'll have already done it all, so I'll be an expert at it," he says with a little smile and a nudge, trying to bring me back.

His assurances bring me comfort, but something I can't put my finger on feels at stake here.

"Promise me, Jude," I play a rare selfish card. "Promise me you'll get out of here, go to college, and you'll help me go, too. Promise me you won't slip down a hole and leave me behind."

Jude looks directly into my eyes, holding them for a meaningful moment.

"Callie, I promise," he says. I see Jude through the grunge, and I believe him.

"You promise," I repeat.

CHAPTER SEVENTEEN
JAY

That's all Potts are good for. Is breaking promises. Wait, no. Making false promises.

I knew Callie was lying. When she stood on that street corner, after Roddie's party, and she told me she'd talk to Mrs. Charlene about me moving in with them. What Callie didn't know is that I knew Mrs. Charlene would take me in, as she'd tried to several times in the years after Grandma Peggy passed, because she knew what Debbie, my piece of shit mom's boyfriends, had been doing to me. But Debbie wouldn't have any of it. I'm just a paycheck to her.

First, there was Gary, who thought the best way to keep a thirteen-year-old boy safe was to lock him in his bedroom all hours outside of school. I finally figured out how to take my bedroom door off the hinges so he couldn't do that anymore. Then he put a shed in the backyard.

Then there was Dirk, who thought a belt was the best way to discipline a fourteen-year-old boy. Honestly, I preferred that brief, embarrassing display to the hours I spent alone thanks to Gary.

The times Debbie spent "single" weren't much better as she became a terror when she's drunk—trashing the house, throwing up on herself, or wrecking the car. She gets irrational and loud. Sometimes I was glad I was locked outside in the shed, hearing her tirades as I could hear them through the shed walls, and I installed my own lock on the inside for just that reason. But I always hated Debbie in the moments I was cleaning up her mess. I was only fifteen. I should have been out having fun. Making mistakes, wrecking my own truck, and sleeping with the wrong people. Lord knows Debbie has. But a normal, safe childhood was something Debbie never cared to provide.

After Dirk, it was Christopher. Not Chris. Or even Mr. Chris. Chris-toph-er. I don't want to talk about what he started doing to me.

But Chris-toph-er was the reason I was willing to take some Potts charity for the next couple of years before I could support myself. While I knew Mrs Charlene would have said yes, I pushed it off, knowing jamming me into the Potts household full-time wouldn't be fair to Jude and Callie. I tried to endure Christopher as long as I could, to make it to eighteen at least, so I could finally get out of Debbie's God-forsaken trailer in Portales, but I couldn't. I couldn't take that one more time.

That's why I asked Callie first. Silly as it sounds, I wanted her blessing on it. Jude and Callie will never know what it meant to me for them to take me in as a kid, letting me into their tight-knit team and treating me as an equal, when hardly anyone had before. I loved them, and I didn't want them to come to hate me because I had been forced on them even worse than before.

Callie's lie, though, cut me in two. I knew I couldn't go through with it after that. Having Jude and Callie both resent me being in their house. Then, when I learned through some fellow high school friends that Jude was living with his dad—a fact Callie obviously hid from me. Knowing that, and realizing she *still* didn't want me there, even in Jude's old, empty bedroom, made Callie's lie feel like a stab.

I distanced myself from her after that. I gave Callie her space in high school to do all the amazing, preppy things she was doing because I knew why she was doing them. To get the hell out of this scorched part of the earth. She and Jude talked about it often, although I never heard an invitation. I only wish I were smart enough to go with her.

I'm just not. That was always clear when Jude, Callie, and I played together.

But I have been keeping up with Callie during her high school years, amazed at the number of things she has accomplished. But not surprised. Not in the least. Callie always pushed herself to get things right, build things perfectly, actually clean and organize them—not in the lazy way, 'cause Mrs. Charlene was always watching—and prove she could keep up with Jude. Although I've always felt Callie was going to surpass Jude. Jude is more intelligent, but he's softer than Callie. Almost too delicate for Clovis.

Even with Callie's shameless lie, I never could shake the feeling of a protective older brother I've always felt for her. She probably never noticed, or wouldn't want to acknowledge, the times Jude and I locked arms to catch her, or dove beneath her to break a fall, or tucked her instinctively behind us when facing trouble, including her mom. Jude and Callie aren't lying when they talk about Mrs. Charlene's butthole mouth. Stupid as it sounds, it terrified me, too. But I respect the hell out of Mrs. Charlene. She was always hard on Jude and Callie—me, too, anytime it was necessary—but she always made sure those two had shelter, food, safety, and support. Every single day of their childhood, Jude and Callie knew someone cared about them. Someone gave a shit. It's more than I can say of Debbie.

But the last time I saw Callie was at her prom in Clovis. I'd been dating this gal Katie who went to Clovis High—though I was going to Portales High School—and she wanted a group of us to go to her prom. I knew Callie would be there. Hell, everyone was sure she would be Prom Queen, so she kind of had to be there. Well, *she.* Calliope, that is. Although no one else really noticed—because Mariah moved to Texas that summer—Callie came back from Roswell a different person. She truly became that "Calliope" character who accomplished all of that glitter and school pride shit so she could get into that fancy University she wanted in Austin. She really did leave all of us behind in the dust bowl and did the very thing she and Jude talked often about as kids. She got out of Clovis. I don't blame her at all for the new identity. Whatever will get the job done. But the secret I know—beyond the shitty lie—was that Calliope did not leave Clovis.

Callie left her there, in a back room behind the gym.

I'd been watching her most of the evening at prom from afar. She had grown into a beautiful young woman, dazzling in this shiny blue number, with even her shoes dyed to match. Her hair was all piled up in curls on her head. She was all tinkling laughter, squeals, and hugs with friends. Hard to look away from. Calliope was so popular. There wasn't a person in the gymnasium who didn't know her name.

And, the real kicker: she had accomplished all of that with Jude gone. I didn't talk to Uncle Steve often, but when I did see him occasionally, I would ask about Jude, and the news was never good. He'd lived with his dad for a couple of years, then left Clovis, headed for Houston, he'd said, and had only sent a handful of two-line postcards since. I felt I might be the only person on earth who could understand the gaping hole a person like Jude could leave in your life. I had a feeling everything *Calliope* had been doing was a mask for Callie's pain, but I couldn't do anything to reach her or change that, especially when she's the one who decided I wasn't valuable enough to be her family.

Despite my resentment of her, I hated that she was dating this complete douchebag, Tyler Beck. Katie and he are like third cousins or something, and Katie told me about some things Tyler had done to girls in the past, even to Mariah. The asshole's got a history. For that reason, I was watching them closely the night of the prom as I could tell Tyler was getting drunk and handsy.

Several of their mutual friends had been peeling off from the prom crowd to go to this utility closet by the bathrooms. I'd seen a pair of them come and go when I went to the restroom. But, as I was coming out a second time, I heard Tyler's voice down the hall. I popped my head around the corner and saw him and Callie, well … *Calliope*, go into that closet.

I didn't think it through. My body just started walking toward them. I guess I wanted to be close in case anything happened. I started stepping quietly down the hall toward the closed closet door. I stopped and ducked into a doorway when I heard some shouts and scuffles from inside the utility room. They were muffled behind the door, but I was sure of what I heard.

"Dammit, Calliope, you owe me!" Tyler shouted, and I started to lunge forward, but then her voice broke through.

"I don't owe you a goddamn thing!" she shouted, and I thrilled at the sound of her voice, solid and strong. I heard a scuffle and then a crash of something metallic sounding. I was about to leap in, but then the door swung open and Calliope burst through. She looked quickly up and down the hall, seeming to weigh her options. Just as I ducked back behind the doorway, Tyler clambered up from whatever pile he had fallen into and thrust forward through the doorway, grabbing her elbow.

Calliope flung her arm down, throwing off Tyler's grasp, and turned around to face him. My heart was pounding and my instinct was to jump in and protect her, but something about her—the woman she had become—was pulsing off of her in waves, quiet but powerful. That's when I knew. That frilly, phony Calliope character was gone, and my badass cousin, Callie, was back. But I would have never guessed in a million years what she was about to do.

"I said no," Callie said, her voice steely. Then she reared back in that pretty blue dress of hers, the slit at her knee ripping clean up to her thigh as she pulled her fist up back near her ear before she let it explode into Tyler's throat.

Right in the throat! *Smack!* Sounding like she'd just punched a piece of steak. Tyler was launched back into that little closet, crashing back down on whatever heap of stuff Callie had shoved him into before. There was a moment of dead silence as Callie was flinging her hand in the hallway, staring at Tyler on the floor, before I heard him take in a huge gasp. I think Callie and I both took in a grateful breath when Tyler started coughing and hacking. At least he was alive.

But, damn, I was proud of Callie. She knocked the crap out of Tyler. But that clown deserved it. Tyler had always been a bully and a predator, like just about every boyfriend Debbie's ever had. I only wish I'd had the balls to have taken him out—like Callie just did. I wanted to high-five her. To hug her. But, before I could do anything, she sprinted past me, her heels clicking all the way down the hall to the red glowing EXIT sign before she burst out into the night.

I ran after her to make sure she was okay, but by the time I got out the door, she had already crossed the parking lot, in a full sprint, splashing through puddles from a recent rain. The scene reminded me so much of the night I chased her after Roddie's party—only to have her turn around and slice me wide open—that the burn of the memory planted my feet to the ground.

I watched Callie run away with a longing I have not felt since. Something between jealousy and love, maybe? I wanted to be running with her—out of the quicksand. Wherever Callie was going—probably all the way to Austin—I wanted to go, too. I *deserved* to go, too.

CHAPTER EIGHTEEN
GREEN MACHINE

No matter how many ways I try to come at it, I find I reach the same conclusion: that's all Potts are good for.

"Breaking promises," I say to myself in the hot cab of Dad's old beat-up Dodge Ram, the Green Machine. This should be a grand, glorious day for me—Move-In Day at Regency Hall at the University of Texas in Austin, which, I was told by a pack of giggly girls during orientation, is both 'a really big deal' and 'a bit of a family affair,' telling me everything I needed to know about it as I wouldn't have any family with me.

I grip the peeling leather of the truck's steering wheel to try to push back my anger. I haven't seen or talked to Jude in over three years, and I've almost come to hate him for it.

Hate. My own brother.

It's not like I couldn't be found. I was living at Mom's until graduation—well, prom, I should say, as I did not walk for graduation. After what went down with Tyler, I was packed up in the Green Machine, ready to hit the road to Austin, when my classmates were smiling for the camera and waving their diplomas across the stage. Although Dad had moved to San Antonio—to take an easier job with the stockyard there and be closer to me during my college years—I left his new San Antonio address, as well as my new address here at this dorm in Austin, at Mom's for Jude to find. If he'd given it just an ounce of effort, there was no excuse Jude could give for not being able to find me.

Whereas Jude, on the other hand, left Clovis headed for Houston— was all he told us—when I was fifteen, just starting high school. He'd only sent a handful of meaningless postcards since. A few from the Houston area, some from cities in California—Sacramento and Los Angeles—saying only that he was doing fine, he loved us, and sending whatever holiday wishes were appropriate.

Yeah, Merry Fucking Christmas to you, too, Jude. Thanks for breaking your promise and leaving me to navigate all of this alone—high school, my resume, college applications and entrance exams, student loan applications, federal funding, my college courses and curriculum. *You promised.*

"We'll decorate your dorm room together," I laugh insanely to myself as I decide—as I do every time I slide into this mood—this is an anger too tired for words, or any more of my energy. My armor goes back up. Those feelings go back on a shelf as I pull into the parking lot of Regency Hall on the UT Campus for the infamous Move-In Day. I've borrowed the Green Machine from Dad and piled it with boxes marked in Sharpie and tied down with orange haybale cords, Beverly Hillbilly-style.

The sight takes my foot off the pedal subconsciously as I ease into the dorm room parking lot. There are people everywhere. Old, young, so many cameras and families posing. Moms are squeezing their daughters. Tears and goodbyes. Dads and older brothers are carrying papasan chairs and bedding. Guess I didn't get the memo about pink-accented zebra being the pattern of the year. I don't see many beat-up Dodge Rams around. It's all new Land Rovers, Nissan Pathfinders, and Mustangs. I didn't get that memo either, apparently. Chatter, laughter, and camera clicks fill the air.

The first inklings of a feeling creep in. *No. No one else. Just you. You don't fit in here, Callie. You're a fraud in rusty Dodge Ram clothing.*

I decide on the stairs to avoid the growing line of chatters building for the elevator and mentally calculate how many trips it will take me to get all my stuff up. I calculate my runs at seven. Seven times up and down to the eighth floor, where I've been assigned to Room 804, with some chick named Danielle. That's all I know.

Just as I'm stacking the last boxes in the corner and sliding the "desk stuff" box under my built-in desk, I hear a squeal down the hall, louder than the other squeals I've been hearing all day. Friends reuniting. Daughters receiving Move-In Day gifts. I learned today *that*, apparently, it's a thing. Immediately after the standout squeal, I hear a high-pitched "Eight. Oh. Four!" *Danielle.*

"Jesus told me we'd be the best of friends," Danielle gushes at me. "I'm Danielle," she says as she wraps her porcelain white arms around me, forcing me into a hug, making me incredibly self-conscious as I try to straighten the sweaty shirt on my back. She smells so clean, like she has literally just stepped out of the shower. *How can she still smell like that in the afternoon?* Her silky frosted hair looks like it has been professionally blown out and curled. Expertly made-up eyes in a Cover Girl face blink at me as she pulls back and holds me at arm's length. Danielle looks like a doll. I'm afraid that if I hug her too hard, she might crack.

"Callie," I say, bluntly. *Jesus didn't tell me anything about you*, I want to say, but don't. I feel naked under a heat lamp with her whole family looking at me and my stack of sad boxes. I see it in their eyes as they put two and two together. *Yes, I'm alone. Yes, I'm poor.*

"We wanted to come see the room first," Danielle says, explaining her lack of boxes. "Then the boys are going to haul it all up here while we girls go to lunch." I see Danielle's eyes dart around my Sharpied cardboard boxes briefly before she adds. "Wanna come?"

"No," bubbles out of me before I can even form the thought. "Than … Thank you," I stutter. "My Dad had to work today." *Why am I explaining my Dad's absence? I don't need him here?* Him or Jude or Mom. None of them ever went to college. I'm the one who's here. Like it or not, I'm doing this alone. I decide that I'm not here to please anyone. Calliope never set foot on this campus. It's only Callie here.

"I gotta get his truck back to him tonight," I explain, noticing my own coldness. "But I'll be back tomorrow," I offer, trying to recover. "I look forward to getting to know you better then." I then shoulder my way past all of them and out the door, secretly rejoicing when I feel the truck keys in my pocket so I can escape. I remind myself this is the odd day—this giggly, family day that will be Danielle's best day. Every other normal college day—where *the girls* wouldn't be here to take you to lunch and *the boys* wouldn't be around to carry the heavy stuff—I will slay.

"Nice to meet you all," I say on the way out, although I hadn't met them at all.

CHAPTER NINETEEN
NOT EVEN JESUS

Turns out I'd been right about Danielle. Move-In Day at Regency Hall was her best day at college. Every day after that, she started to crumble a little more. We tried our hands at being friends at first, but we just didn't have anything in common. Danielle grew up doing beauty pageants. She was super close to her mom and called her every morning, often every night as well. She was super religious, too, and had no problem praying out loud, although it made me feel incredibly weird and self-conscious of any sound I made while she was doing it, like typing on my laptop would be rude while she's talking to Jesus. *Wouldn't it?*

We'd tried grocery shopping together once, her cart filled with expensive health food bars, 100-calorie cookies, pressed juices, Dove chocolates, a baguette two feet tall—*I always wondered who bought those*—and a hunk of some unidentifiable cheese that cost $23.00 while my cart held a square loaf of white bread, a square package of sandwich meat, sugar, and Cream of Wheat, the whole of it not totaling $9.82. Danielle whipped out Daddy's card. I paid in cash. The experience was awkward and clunky and signaled to both of us that there was some undercurrent here, something essential about me, and about Danielle, that made us repel each other.

Soon, we settled into an easy pattern of mutual avoidance. My days started before 6:00 a.m. with a microwaved bowl of Cream of Wheat, followed by classes all day, studying at the library after, shifts at Cracker Barrel five nights a week after, and weekends spent manning the information desk at the Rec Center. Danielle appeared to spend time in bed watching contemporary Christian movies. This pattern continued for the first month or two.

Then I overheard a conversation Danielle was having with her mom one evening when coming back from the community shower. Danielle's voice was thick and gurgled. She was crying and saying how homesick she was, how hard everything here was, and how much she hated her classes. She missed her mom. She missed home. She missed Charlie, whoever that was. I had stood there in the hall, hiding in a door frame, listening, almost in shock, to the complete one-hundred-eighty-degree flip Danielle's conversation with her mom was to the one I'd had with my own mom only a week before.

It was three weeks into my first semester at college, and I was struggling to make ends meet. While my scholarship covered my tuition and board, that left so much untouched: food, clothes, shoes, toiletries, insurance, fuel, and school supplies. The money I had saved waiting tables back in Clovis was dwindling faster than I had anticipated, even though I felt like I was living on white bread and mayonnaise. I hadn't talked to Mom since I'd left Clovis two months prior, as I felt like we had both been craving space from one another when I left Clovis. But when Dad recently told me he still had a year's worth of child support arrears that he was currently paying monthly to Mom, I kind of lost it.

It made me do something I typically would never do. I admitted I needed help.

"I'm really struggling here, Mom. It's hard to cover my food, books, and stuff. I could really use that money," I told her through gritted teeth.

"Well, maybe you shouldn't have decided to move so far away and go to that fancy school you were always talking about," Mom spat out.

"There were good schools here near Clovis," she said. "You could have gotten everything paid for with the state lottery scholarship, but no. You didn't want to do that."

And here we are, I thought. *Finally, at the heart of what we're really fighting about.* Mom was actually doing something she would typically never do, either, in her own way. She was admitting we—Jude and I—had hurt her by both leaving.

"Mom, good God!" I had yelled into the phone, curled around it in the dorm hallway with the cord coming out from under the door. "I've told you a million times. The University of Texas is a better school. It's more highly accredited and has a law school right here on campus. I stand a better chance of getting into law school by going here. I mean, shit! I thought you'd be proud I busted my ass and got accepted to such a … fancy school."

Mom was quiet. I swear I could hear her tongue rolling over her front teeth. "As long as you keep fighting for what you deserve, I'll always be proud," she said.

"Well, I deserve this," I said as I choked back tears and anger. "It's called *child support* for a reason, Mom." The minute I said it, I knew it had landed. What I wasn't sure about was how I felt about it.

The line went quiet. For a minute, I thought Mom had hung up. But then I heard the faint sizzle of her cigarette paper burning back as she pulled slowly on it. I heard her exhale.

"I am aware," she started. "Because who the hell do you think had to pay for your clothes and shoes and all that when your Daddy was too busy snorting your child support up his nose. And it was hard, like you're saying. And I struggled, like you're doing, but I did it. For you. And for Jude. For you kids." I heard her swallow a thick lump in her throat before she picked back up.

"But you're grown now, Callie. And that money is to pay *me* back for the support I gave *you*, support that allowed you to run out of town to follow all your hotshot plans." She took a breath. I was so angry with her, with my situation. I was confused and beaten down, but I was fuming, fueled by my rage. I hated the fact that she made some sense.

"I want you to fight for what you deserve, but realize what you have yet to earn. You won't get your big dreams—or at least you won't appreciate them as much—if parts are just handed to you. If things are made easy for you. Don't be an entitled little shit, Callie. You're stronger than that."

My chest heaved violently up and down as I held the phone to my head so hard it was causing a bruise. I was sweating but cold. I was scared but enraged. I didn't have any more words. I wasn't sure I had any more reason or ground to stand on.

"You made this decision," Mom said. "To go. To create a new life. Now own it. You make it what you want it to be. No one else, Callie. You."

And, with that, she hung up. The click I heard through the line set me off. I screamed into the receiver as loud as I could, not caring whether it interrupted Danielle's quiet movie moment, terrified, happy, warm, rich bitches in their dorm beds, or signified the unraveling of me. My face was hot, red, and tear-streaked. I was sweating down my armpits and into the waist of my ratty sweats. I was alone in Austin. With my life ahead of me, I was fueled by hatred for my mom, my brother, my hometown, and my crappy, poor upbringing that hadn't given me shit.

Then one Sunday, I came back from an afternoon spent studying on the quad to find Danielle's half of the dorm room completely empty and just cleared out, only three months into the semester, not even close to finals. I asked our resident advisor about it, and she said Danielle decided to go home. She had decided she didn't want to "do college" anymore, so she just quit. Just like that. Packed up and went home. I was baffled at first. All that family support, those daily calls with her mom, those beauty pageant good looks—*all that money*—and she couldn't find the willpower to "do college." All of that advantage, and none of it could see her through. Not even Jesus.

CHAPTER TWENTY

THE PAWN

He twirled the small, seemingly benign piece before my eyes for us both to look at.

"It's the pawn, see?" Jude showed me.

As much as I didn't want to, I thought about Jude a lot during my first years of college. Whether it was because of his absence—which made me feel hollow—or the fact that each day reminded me he, and Mom for that matter, had taught and prepared me for this.

My first year of college had proven to be my toughest obstacle yet. I was living off bread and peanut butter, snatching a few books or other supplies from the college bookstore and toiletries from Wal-Mart as needed, thanks to Janessa's light-finger lessons, but otherwise getting by, and excelling in school. I was a strange creature on campus, though. Quiet, oddly dressed, studious, weird.

I remember the fancy French baguette Danielle had left behind when she moved out of our dorm room. (Guess it was too much to carry on top of her monogrammed towels and bedding). I had opened the fridge after she mysteriously moved out and was delighted to see she'd left some of that super pricey soft cheese she was always buying behind, too. I was starving, as usual, so I sat right there cross-legged on her side of the room by the mini-fridge, with a plastic to-go knife, and ate the entire rest of the baguette and the cheese in one sitting, feeling weird and solitary, but free.

My perfect academic record was really the most valuable thing I had. It, coupled with a great LSAT score, could get me into law school at UT. Unlike my peers—the Danielles of the world with new cars they could afford to wreck and jobs they could afford to lose because they could just run back home if they felt they couldn't "do college"— I couldn't take my eyes off the road or let anyone else in the car who would only distract and divert me. Like Jude and Mom predicted, I was the only one who was going to move my piece forward.

"Unlike the fighting pieces, who come out of the box slaying dragons, the pawn is persistent," Jude's lesson frequently came back to me, although I couldn't have been more than ten when he taught me.

"If she stays focused and moves methodically and doggedly forward," Jude said while moving a pawn piece one black and white square at a time across the board, "while the others are distracted and fighting each other," as he slid his dark queen across our mocked-up board to kill a rook. He made a knight do his odd, dog-legged jump to kill a bishop, as he kept moving the little pawn forward.

"Then it is *the pawn* who accomplishes the most incredible transformation that can happen in chess. She then can become the most powerful piece on the board, possibly the whole world," he told me with a wink, replacing my white pawn with the white queen.

Based on Jude's mentoring, that's what I did. I moved my little piece forward to my second year of undergrad, where my new roommates proved to be on par with Danielle when it came to "doing college."

They found me equally odd because I was always studying or working and never went out partying with them, not that they invited me much. I was like a strange dog in the corner, they poked on the way out the door. When one roommate informed us she was going to move back home to Virginia to go to community college, I don't think my reaction helped any.

"But who's going to pay your share of the rent?" was my first and only question.

"My dad will still pay," Fallon—had been her name—said flippantly. As if it really wasn't any of her concern.

"Still *pay?*" I'd asked. My words were not formed by my own brain. They'd just spilled over and fallen out without my thinking about them. "For a place you ain't living?" I'd hissed.

And, in that very moment, I heard it just as well as they did. Like a snake sliding through its leathery egg, too soft and thin to hold it in. *Ain't.* My anger and jealousy had made me sound like trailer trash. Like Sissy. For fear of sounding like her again, I shut my mouth and didn't say another word about Fallon moving out. My other roommate, Chastity—not kidding—followed soon after.

Their rich daddies, however, kept sending rent checks which allowed me to live alone in our dilapidated little rental for the rest of the year, and I *loved* living there alone. It left me free to be my complete, unapologetic self, without attention or judgment. Turned out I liked to sing out loud from room to room, eat peanut butter straight out of the jar, give myself pep talks in the mirror in the mornings—"Let's go, pawn"—and keep everything straightened to absolute perfection. A big night for me, after all my studying was done, was a true crime show paired with a massive bowl of popcorn. Again, I felt weird and solitary, but free.

———

My second year of undergrad became easier because I qualified for in-state tuition and a Pell Grant thanks to Dad. With all his back injuries and wear and tear from his rodeo and trucking days, he had qualified for disability. He'd had to undergo a second back fusion during my second year at college, and he was now walking with a cane and a noticeable limp, but he kept his spirits up. Not long after he moved to San Antonio, Dad had finally met, and fallen in love with, a gal that wasn't such trash as his former tastes: Sissy, Krystal (with a K), Mundi, and the like.

Tammy was gentle, God-fearing, a fantastic cook and homemaker, and she loved my Dad's singing and cutting up just as much as I did. She'd never had kids and had outlived two husbands, which gave her a lot of wisdom and a healthy perspective and probably the most exuberant laugh I've ever encountered.

My only social outings, really, were visits to Dad and Tammy on the occasional weekend, where the three of us would often sit around and play cards or board games in the evening. I was still partial to Monopoly as it was the game Jude and I had played the most together growing up, and Tammy was a little bit ruthless when it came to collecting rent. Dad liked to play poker for M&Ms and Nutter Butters. We would laugh until our bellies ached at Dad's "interpretation" of the rules, always skewed to get him out of trouble. And, Tammy had no mercy on him, which was the right move.

When Tammy learned I didn't really talk to my mom often, she tried to intervene, telling me how much I might regret that if something happened to her. It was sage advice, but—knowing what Tammy did not know about my mom—Dad had stepped in. "She doesn't take well to mothering," was all he'd said, and Tammy had said no more. The only maternal gesture I did allow her was the care package Tammy would stuff in the back of my rundown car before I left her place, headed back to UT—stuffed with peanut butter, bagels, travel toiletries, and socks and underwear. Some months, I only got by because of Tammy's packages.

It was easy to see that Tammy deserved Dad's unfettered love. He'd even created a special song just for Tammy—like he'd done for Jude—that I often found myself singing while on walks or rolling silverware at the Barrel, it was that catchy. Or cheesy. I didn't care either way. It was fun to sing and brought me a smile, just like Dad always did. I can only hear Dad's voice when I sing it, though, to the tune of *Say a Little Prayer for You*:

"I run for my truck, Dear.

While riding, I think of us, Dear (Dad would imitate driving here with his hands at ten and two, maybe an elbow out the window if he was feeling rambunctious).

I say a little thanks for you (both of us point at Tammy here).

At lights, I get clammy (Dad would always shake his hands theatrically here, and I giggle).

Can't wait till I see my Tammy (Tammy usually bites her lips and shakes her head here).

I speed a little bit for you! (His eyebrows go up and wiggle conspiratorially).

Forever and ever, you'll stay in my trailer cause I love you,

Forever and ever, I never will fail her cause she loves me, too,

Together, forever, that's how it must be,

Because life's so much better with Tammm-eeeeeyyeeeeyy!"

Even if Tammy is steaming mad at him—and often rightfully so as Dad is perpetually late, constantly spilling food on himself, and he cannot sit still through a movie to save his life—when Dad starts that up in his smooth baritone—"I run for my truck, Dear"—at first she's all towel-swats and huffs and "that's not gonna work," "not this time," but it never (ever!) fails to eventually melt her and the three of us end up singing the end chorus at belt level, wildly off-key. It's really the only appropriate way to sing it.

One time, I got up the nerve to ask Dad if he'd ever made up a song for Mom because I had sure never heard him sing one about, or for, her. Mom was always an awkward topic for us, and my left-field request made him measure his words carefully before he finally answered.

"Many Babes. I made up a ton of silly stuff for Charlene. But we were different people when we met, so young." Dad looks off into the distance for a beat and heaves a sigh. "Your Mom was different after we lost Cadence. I was, too. We tried to hold it all together for you and Jude, but deep down we blamed each other in ways that can't be forgiven. Said things we can't forget. Life just threw Charlene and me too much at too young an age. You'll just have to believe me on that one, Babes. But, I do have something for you," Dad said then as we sat on the back porch of Tammy's little house, decorated with boots and cow horns everywhere. He pulled out his faded, lopsided leather wallet, dug in deep, and fished out a worn, handheld photo that he handed to me.

It was him and Mom, wet and sunlit like they'd been swimming in the lake behind them in the photo. They were standing on a rock, which looked like they had jumped off of often. Dad was behind Mom with his arms around her, one hand trying to slip under the hip of her bikini bottom. Mom—looking exceptionally sexy—is laughing at the camera, trying to hold Dad's hand back. It is the only candid shot I have ever seen of my Mom and Dad. Every other one I've ever seen of them together is all Olan Mills-type family photos, where everything looks forced and tensions are lying right beneath the surface. But this photo is free of that. It's just an image of two people in love and having fun. They look to be in their early or mid-twenties. Wrinkle-free and in good health. It must feel like a century ago to Dad, I think, and I'm secretly shocked he's kept it so close to him all these years.

"I want you to have it," Dad said. "Remember where you came from. Years ago. It was love."

Bricks I had stacked inside myself ages ago start to slip and crumble. Feeling overwhelmed, I found myself with an unusual lack of words. "Thanks, Dad," was all I could muster.

Dad patted my back. "You'll make your own family someday, trust me, Callie. It'll just happen, even if you try to avoid it," he said, giving me a look with a raised eyebrow that told me he knew how closed off I had become at college.

"People will slip into your stubborn heart, Babes, and love will grow in ways you never dreamed possible. I can only say this because I'm old and have had it surprise me time and again. At your age, I would have never believed the ways my life would tangle, unravel, snarl up, then settle out again. It's incomprehensible from the start, because you just never know what's going to happen. But know that family will hurt, too, Callie. Caring about people, letting people love you, and loving them … invites that, because people are always changing as life is always changing. As amazing as it can be to have people you let into your life, a family you choose, it can also be messy, confusing, even painful, but it's just part of it." Dad lifted my chin then to make sure I was looking at him and listening. "We can't know joy …" he said, nudging my chin to prompt the answer he had drilled into me my entire life.

"Without pain," I said, clutching the photo I knew I would never let go of.

———

Although I tried not to think about my relationship with my past too much as I marched diligently across the board during my first few years of college, Tammy's comment about Mom had found its mark. But I told myself I wasn't asking anything of Mom and Steve. I wasn't begging to borrow money like I knew many of my peers were. I wasn't coming home to crash on the weekends with all my laundry in tow. Hell, I wasn't out getting pregnant (or impregnating others) and then bringing a crying, screaming little mess into their worlds to help raise, like several of my peers had done. I wasn't getting busted for DUIs or drugs or other crimes they would have to deal with, or bail me out of, like I knew other colleagues of mine in college were doing.

I honestly felt like leaving them to their easier, less expensive world with me and Jude gone, and her child support arrears to pay her back, was doing Mom a favor. She could finally have the chapter she felt she *deserved*. And, when I detached my own anger and emotions from that situation, I half-agreed with her. She did deserve it, after everything Mom did for us as practically a single mother. There wasn't much ill will or harsh feelings between us, because there weren't really any feelings at all.

Where my simmering feelings did lie, however, was with Jude. The last postcard I got from him—during the spring of my junior year of undergrad—was from Sacramento, which was just odd as none of us had any ties to any state west of New Mexico. Jude said he'd snagged a better management job at a P.F. Chang's out in California. He claimed to be continuing his college work at night and on the weekends out there. The problem was that his postcard didn't have a return address. Wrestling with these things while my colleagues were frolicking through their days—constantly asking me to pick up their tables, roll their silverware, finish their writing assignments—made me feel like a fraud. Like Cinderella after the pumpkin spell is over. I was only pretending at their game of college ease when I was really a filthy, ravenous wolf hiding in their preppy white clothing.

I'll say this: I never saw pawns traveling across the board in pairs.

The solitary journey suited me, though, as I didn't think anyone but Jude would understand or appreciate my dogged, Cream of Wheat in the dark existence. No one wanted my life. And anyone would only slow it down.

Dad stayed pretty tight-lipped during my undergrad years, although I'm sure he wished he could see me let loose a little and have more fun, but he knew I would hear nothing of it. Knowing my bitter state of mind at the time, I probably would have snapped back with something I would deeply regret along the lines of "What, like *you* did?"

My anger—at Jude for abandoning me, Mom for cutting me off,

the world for dealing me a shit hand—fueled me. I've often wondered during those years, had I been open to it, what Dad's advice to me would have been about my solitary situation. Was I doing it all right, and was he proud? Or did he think I was pushing too hard, passing all the roses by, like I always did? Sadly, I never got to ask him that question.

The day I got my acceptance letter to UT Law was the same day I got the news about Dad.

CHAPTER TWENTY-ONE
WE CAN'T KNOW JOY

"Jay, did you know Mariah was here?" I ask him because I can't help it. As much time as I feel I've spent recently in the past—spinning and skipping through my teenage and college years—seeing her face outside my hospital room door yesterday shocked me. I need to know what I'm facing here. If another tragedy in our family has again summoned Mariah, it's serious.

Jay turns to close the door behind him, giving us privacy. I peek out the door quickly, looking for both Mom's 49ers jersey—although she may be in something different now—and Mariah, if she's still here. I see no one else, and I feel that same uneasy, quavering feeling I've had when I'm alone around Jay since I woke in this sterile bed.

The unavoidable truth is Jay betrayed me. He hurt me deeper than I could have ever hurt him—back when we were just kids, when the stakes weren't so high—I justify to myself. I'm angry with Jay, but happy for him at the same time. It's something between jealousy and love.

I curse the quagmire he and I have fallen into because Jay is the first person I want to ask about Braden, my husband, who is not here. I want to hear his soft, husky voice say: "I need you." I want to push his feather-soft hair back from his forehead. I want to feel his long arms circle around my back and tell me he will absorb whatever I put out. Mostly, I want Braden to still want me enough to be here, but he doesn't. He can't. Or he would be here. But he isn't. I don't want to admit any of that to Jay, though, because my sore heart blames Jay for it.

Jay starts walking toward my bed, and I don't like the fact that he hasn't answered my question. I don't pull my phantom leg up anymore as I'm getting more used to it, but I unapologetically stare at him. Jay stares back. I raise my eyebrows and cross my arms over my chest, because he's a fool to think I have anything better to do. We stay locked like this for about a minute before Jay breaks.

"Okay, Uncle," he says—a throwback to our days spent wrestling as kids when I would not let go of my she-Hulk thigh grip on him until he said those words—and I relish briefly in the tiny victory I have claimed from this debilitating bed.

"I did know she was coming," Jay starts carefully. "But I haven't run into her yet," he evades. I respond with silence because I didn't ask whether he had run into her, and he knows it.

"Callie, Mariah is here because … you need representation. You could be in trouble."

"That's obvious," I snort at him. "I put that much together. Tell me what I don't know. What *kind* of trouble? Did I collide with another car, or hit a pedestrian? Jay, did I hurt someone?" I demand.

"Callie, you …" Jay's head drops, and I lose it.

"Just spit it the fuck out, Jay!" I shout. "I'm sorry, but just tell me goddammit! Did. I. Hurt. Someone?"

"Someone was in the car with you, Callie," Jay says flatly.

Just as Jay finishes the sentence, his phone buzzes, and I hear commotion out in the hall—feet scuffle as Jay rises from my bed, shoving his phone in his back pocket. The door to my room cracks open, and a nurse pops her head in. She catches Jay's eye as quickly as she can. She nods once, and she's out.

"I gotta go right now, Callie, I'm sorry," Jay says, hustling to the door, and I'm infuriated. I'm so sick of everyone around me knowing everything about what's going on with me, but they're not telling me. Jay is almost to the door before I can form thoughts and get words out.

"Wait, Jay! Don't go!" I shout. "Why are you leaving? What's going on?" But Jay is one shoulder out the door, giving me a sympathetic look. He shakes his head 'no' solemnly and bolts out. "Jay, NO!" I holler.

"Who was in the car with me?! Jay! Who was in the car with me?!"

Hot tears spill down my cheeks as I realize I'm shouting to no one in an empty hospital room, and now, in lieu of answers, I have a terrifying new development.

Someone was with me.

My machines are beeping furiously because my blood pressure has skyrocketed with this news. I start gulping air as a nurse swoops in. I smell honeysuckle. The blinds filling my vision become red bricks. I'm staring at Dad's photo on the windowsill, and I swear I can hear his voice in the room. *We can't know joy,* the walls whisper, and I know my troubled mind is taking me back to the last time I felt this panicked.

———

"Tammy. Tammy?" I shouted into my cell phone. "Hang on." It had been Dad's number on my phone, but Tammy was calling. I was walking across campus in the wind, and I thought that's what I'd heard—wind in my ear, not terror in her voice. I slipped around a corner for some wind block and pushed the phone close to my ear. "Hey, Tammy, I'm here. I'm sorry, I was walking in the ..." but she cut me off.

"Callie," she started, and something just didn't sound right. My body tingled and warmed, hairs standing up, internal alarms going off. "Callie, I'm ... I'm..." Tammy trailed off, and I was losing patience. She had me scared. Petrified. My blood pumped in my ears, a raspy, whooshing sound.

"Tammy, what?! What is it?" I begged. "Are you okay? Is Dad?" I couldn't get information out of her fast enough. I remember the grooves in the red brick of the building I was standing under—the smell of honeysuckle on campus. My hair was in a ponytail. I was wearing my Rec Center polo, with the pit stains, and khaki pants. It was March of my final year of undergrad.

"Callie, I'm sorry," Tammy seemed to have finally composed herself. "Your Dad. Bill," she sniffed and let out a forceful huff. "He had a heart attack this morning," Tammy started crying, this deep, sorrowful wail. I felt like I knew, but I had to hear it. My eyes were already flooded. I was sweating. I remember my mouth was so completely dry, like it had never had saliva in it. It made a smacking, dry sound when I tried to speak.

"Tammy, I need you to tell me," I told her flatly. I heard her swallow and take a big breath as the pattern on the brick etched itself into my memory: little divots and crosses, staggered.

"Callie, I'm sorry. Your Dad is gone," she said.

"Gone," I repeated her dumbly, feeling like my brain couldn't catch up with what was happening. What she was telling me. *Heart attack. Gone. My Dad.* Barnum Bill the Sailor. The man who kissed my skinned knees. The deep notch in the thumb he almost lost while roping. His tobacco-scented snicker. Jude Boy, Jude Boy. I see him patting his worn, rough jacket. "I've just been around the campfire, Babes." I start shaking my head.

"Callie. Callie?" I could hear Tammy trying to pull me back from whatever precipice I was about to fall off of. "He loved you so much, Callie. But it's going to be …" I didn't hear what she said after that. My ears clogged, and a ringing sound filled my head. I saw Dad sitting high up on Little Man trotting by. I could see his boots, his Wranglers, his belt buckle. I saw him and Mom in that photo when they were young, both smiling genuine smiles, laughing, and loving one another. He's picking me up in the sunshine when I'm five. He's driving up to

Allsups in Blackie. He's slapping a Maxi pad on my face. Through it all, I'm smiling. Jude and I are standing next to each other, beaming, basking in his blinding glow. *My dad?* The only man in the world who would ever call me Babes. *Gone?*

I felt like my heart was melting, dropping big globs into my stomach, making me sick. With it gone, my chest wrenched inward. I dry heaved and dropped hard to my knees on the rough concrete, my cell phone clattering to my side. I slapped the concrete over and over and wailed at it, refusing to look up as the beautiful sunny day felt like an assault, an insult. Spit in my face. Because how could the world just keep spinning, the sun shining, everyone just carrying on about their goddamn day when the most incredible man I had ever known had just left the earth? "Scars make good stories," I hear his voice. I hear his whistle. His cluck to Little Man. His "ggghnaw" yelling at cows at the stockyard. "We can't know joy." He can't be. Not my Dad. *Gone?*

I don't know how long I stayed like that, crying and slapping the ground, but a nice woman finally came out from the building I was standing in front of and tried to help me. Her presence stunned me back to reality, and I smacked at my tear-streaked face, using the moisture from my tears to smooth my hair back. I stood and wiped the dirt and grit from my hands and knees, picked up my cell phone, and walked away.

I later learned from Tammy that Dad had gone suddenly and quickly. He'd been his usual chipper self that morning, singing and cutting up. He had eaten the eggs and oatmeal that Tammy had made for him and was planning to ride his bicycle—which he had been doing more of recently to help improve his mobility—and paint the fence around Tammy's later that day. But, soon after breakfast, Dad said he was having pain in his chest and upper stomach area. He told Tammy he thought it was indigestion and that he wanted to lie down for a bit to see if it would settle out. However, on his way to the couch, Tammy saw him grab his chest and cringe in pain. He'd slumped against the doorframe and eventually toppled to the living room floor. Tammy had tried to do chest compressions, check his pulse, and she'd called 9-1-1, but it was too late. Within minutes, he had passed. By the time the EMTs got there, all that was left to do was pronounce him.

My dad died on a Thursday.

And Jude was fucking nowhere.

———

I called Mom the day it happened to let her know, having no idea how she would take the news. Stubbornly, I knew I didn't want her to try to comfort me. But, knowing how I would probably react to it, I also knew Mom probably wouldn't try. Comfort wasn't her specialty. What I hadn't expected her to say was:

"I might know how you can get in touch with Jude."

"What the fuck?" I said to her. I think it was the first time I'd so casually cussed at my own mother, but I was taken aback. I didn't think she and Jude had spoken in years. Stupidly, my first reaction was jealousy. *Jude reached out to her first?* I knew it was childish, but it still hurt. Dad was gone, and now Jude and Mom were some newly formed team? I felt like I was losing my footing.

"I haven't spoken with him," Mom said harshly. "And it's probably not good news, but I got some mail recently. Some bills," she corrected. "They call it restitution."

I knew what the word meant. I knew it was payment for a crime committed. *A crime.*

"What? Do you know what for? What did he do? Why did it get sent to you? How long have you had it?" I thundered her with questions faster than she could answer.

"Callie, slow down. It's like any other bill; it can get sent to a collection agency, then they comb public records for any other way to contact you. You know how that goes. Jude must have moved again, or he's ignoring it. I don't know, Callie. I wasn't going to tell you because I knew it would worry you, but you may be able to use it to find him so you can let him know."

I was taken aback by Mom's practicality. Her levelheadedness, because wasn't that usually my role? It felt like all of our character assignments had been rearranged.

"Callie, write this down and start making some calls," Mom said. In a stupor, I grappled around on Tammy's countertop for a pen, knocking over her little boot-shaped salt and pepper shakers in the process. I found an envelope. Not caring at all what it was, I just started writing on the back of it.

"I'm sorry this happened to you, Callie," Mom snapped me out of my tunnel vision on the envelope. "I'm glad you were older and got much more time with your dad than I did with mine."

I see Mom running around Tammy's little kitchen with oozing stumps for arms. I close my eyes.

"He—your dad—was," she paused, "a unique man. Weak to his addictions, but he loved you and Jude. All his singing and jokes and infuriating ways to make you laugh—even when you were really pissed off at him—made him … really special." *Singing? Make you laugh?* Mom had never mentioned Dad doing those things to her before. The only thing she'd ever called him before this day were "your asshole father," "a drug addict," or …

"That stupid cowboy," she said, but this time with a different tone. I heard her sniff, and I just couldn't take it. The softness of her voice unnerved me. Mom couldn't mourn Dad. Mom hated Dad. I was mad at them all for flipping the script on me. But mostly I was burning white hot at Jude—for breaking his promise and leaving me to fend these most difficult chapters alone.

"Try to reach him, Callie," Mom said. "You need to let him know."

I snapped.

"Oh, I do? That's *my* job, huh? To let Jude know his dad, his *father,* whom he hasn't spoken to in six years, just died," I spit out, my anger pulsing in my ears. "When do I get to just check out and disappear?"

"Never is the answer," Mom says flatly. "It's who you are, Callie. Who we are. We do the hard things others can't. The things that have to be done. You need to do this, Callie. At least try."

Undone, I hung up on her and paced in Tammy's kitchen, flinging my hands, a strange roil of emotions.

At least try.

Part of me wanted to take this thread to Jude and use it to hurt him.

Dig into him as he had done me.

I called the collection agency. A nice gal named Tameka provided me with a last known address for Jude in Houston, and I dialed while I was still unsure of what exactly I was doing.

"Hello?" a man answered. He sounded young and friendly. Downright proper. I was hopeful.

"Hi, I'm looking for a Jude Potts. Does he live, or ..." I stumbled, "is he staying there? Do you know him?" I realized I had asked too many questions, and I worried I was going to freak this Mr. Proper guy out. I also stopped feverishly tapping one of Tammy's little boot-shaped salt and pepper shakers when she gave me a look. I mouthed the word *JUDE* to her, and she sat down next to me, stilled.

"I know *a* Jude," Mr. Proper started hesitantly. "His last name isn't Potts, though. It's Cavaletti."

"*Mister* Cavaletti?" I gasped before my brain could stop me.

The minute I'd heard the name, I knew. Jude and I had talked about Mr. Cavaletti often. He was the geometry teacher at Marshall Junior High. Jude had loved him, as had I. He was very neat and proper, sporting suspenders every day that matched his belt and shoes, and a bow tie. Mr. Cavaletti even had a handlebar mustache that he kept meticulously waxed, his appearance and upbeat demeanor a welcome contrast to the other frumpy, unhappy teachers we usually encountered. Jude and I had spent hours in his bedroom—him teaching me geometry, taught to him by Mr. Cavaletti—on his little TV. Jude's lessons had made me a knockout student by the time I got to Mr Cavaletti's class three years after Jude did in eighth grade.

I knew it. In every blood cell in my body, to the marrow of my bones. The name wasn't a coincidence. Jude had changed it, which he'd talked about doing often, though he never told me what new name he had settled on.

The moment I put it together, though, I did not feel relief. I felt betrayal. Again. It seemed that was the only emotion Jude could evoke in me. Because why did this Mr. Proper nobody from Houston know something about my brother, Jude, that Jude hadn't shared with me?

It was also a fact that would make it harder for me to find Jude. And yet Jude had not told me. His sister. *Who the heck was I to Jude anymore?*

"I guess, yes, you can call him *Mister* Cavaletti," Mr. Proper said slowly, almost a question.

"Well, I certainly won't be," I snapped. *Sorry Mom. I'm not who you thought I was.*

"Do you have a message for him?" Mr. Proper asked.

"No, I don't," I lied.

I hung up and set my forehead on the counter. My body was hot. My hands sweaty. My lungs waited a beat, not fully comprehending what I had just decided to do—*refusing to let Jude know Dad died*—before gasping for air. I picked up the envelope and started slapping it into the palm of my left hand as I paced Tammy's kitchen again, trying to justify to myself that Jude didn't deserve to know.

"Oh, you found it. My goodness, I had forgotten!" Tammy's voice spooked me. I gave her a strange look, clueless as to what she was talking about.

"The envelope," Tammy explained. Taking it from my hand, she flipped it over in front of my face, and I read the front. It was addressed to me at Dad and Tammy's place, as I had made it my permanent address for UT. But then I saw the return address.

The University of Texas at Austin School of Law.

"Holy shit!" I shouted in Tammy's kitchen, and immediately recoiled as I knew Tammy didn't like it when Dad and I let a curse word or two slip. "Sorry," I said, looking at her.

She just smiled and chuckled still. "I'll forgive you this one," Tammy said, her eyes sparkling. "Your dad gets the mail every morning and puts it in that basket. We were going to call you later to see if you wanted us to open it up," Tammy was shaking her head now in seeming disbelief. "We both knew you'd say: 'OF COURSE, OPEN IT! NOW, HURRY!'" She said imitating me, which made me laugh again. "But here you are. And …" Tammy placed her warm, plump hand on my forearm. "And, your dad is here in spirit. So, OPEN IT!" She imitated me again.

I flipped the envelope over in my hand one more time. It held the key to my future on its front, and the information for Jude on the back. It felt like a double-edged sword in my hand.

I pulled the paper out, unfolded it, and sent a little message out in the world to Dad.

"Calliope, Congratulations. On behalf of the Admissions Committee at the University of Texas at Austin School of Law, I am pleased to offer you …" I dropped the letter on the counter, started jumping up and down, and screaming at the top of my lungs.

CHAPTER TWENTY-TWO
MURDER AND MARGARITAS

The day of the funeral, I couldn't believe how many times my eyes could well up and dry and puddle again in one day. At times, I would feel resolute and so proud that he had been my Dad. Others, I felt the extreme weight of losing him, and I would sob in selfish fury because no one there had lost their *father*. The man who kissed their scratches and scrapes and sang songs to them when they were little and couldn't fall asleep. Everyone else in the room had lost a friend, a lover, a mentor, but not their dad.

Until he walked in.

I could only see the back of his head in the foyer of the funeral home, talking to other people, nodding, being polite, but I knew the minute I saw him. That chestnut brown hair, his stupid, perfect skin, those shoulders, his stance, everything about him I knew.

It was Jude. I knew the funeral was about to start, and I had remarks to make, but I had to see him face-to-face. To do what, I did not know. But, if he looked perfect, sounded perfect, and walked around like he'd been living his best goddamn life for the last almost seven years, I just might punch him.

I walked as fast as I could, without slipping into a full-on run, toward him. I saw a handsome man standing next to him with a meticulously trimmed beard watching me over Jude's shoulders with eyes widening, but I didn't care. This was my brother. I had rights. Dibs. I spun Jude around and looked him in the eye. Jude was more handsome than I'd ever seen him. His acne was gone. His hair was soft and flowed just below his ears, and it was styled. More styled than mine. His clothes were crisp and ironed. He was trim and tall. When he saw my face, his features softened, and the boy I had grown up with appeared.

"Lil' Bit," he said. He opened his arms to try to hug me, but I started shaking my head and backing up, feeling like I had lost the ability to swallow.

"Callie, I'm sorry. Let me explain," Jude started. The handsome guy next to him cocked his head at the sound of my name and took me in. His honey brown eyes showed true empathy.

Mr. Fucking Proper, I thought. Mr. Knows More About Jude than I do.

"You weren't here. You haven't seen Dad for six years," I said to him, steeled for a fight.

Jude straightened, bit his lip, and reached a hand out to me.

Just then, we heard music for the service to begin. I met Jude's eyes a final time. Those hazel irises I knew so well. I could see the hurt in them that I was causing, and I relished it. Jude deserved this. I clenched my jaw and turned back to the chapel.

I found Tammy and hugged her, deciding in the moment not to tell her about Jude. This was Dad's moment. This day was about him. I wasn't going to let Jude swoop in with all his drama and take this day away from him. I took in the photos Tammy and I had selected to have blown up and placed around the urn sitting on a pedestal in the front of the room. They ranged from Dad's days bullriding and rodeoing, to him with his horses and me and Jude, to a really great one of him and Tammy laughing over a gag gift she'd given him last Christmas. Standing back and taking it in, it seemed like a good life. Full of fun and adventure, and people who loved him.

While I had written many iterations of what I thought I wanted to say when I took the podium that day, the minute I stepped up there and looked out at the sea of faces, mostly from Dad's current life, it struck me that the only people in this room from Clovis were me and Jude. While we had run a small obituary and tried to call folks from Dad's days trucking and rodeoing back in New Mexico, it turned out the drifters, old rodeo hacks, and old girlfriends he hung around with during those years didn't really leave return addresses. Seeing Jude's face in the crowd, angry with him for abandoning Dad just as much as me, I knew I wanted to tell a story of something pretty heroic—or at least clever and funny as hell—that Dad had done that only Jude and I knew about. I stared at Jude as I began.

"I want to share one story that I believe sums up my dad just about perfectly. We were on a long-haul cattle drive once, New Mexico to Oklahoma, my brother, Jude, my dad, Pepper, and me. Dad had pulled Big Blackie off the interstate to let us all do our respective business, when suddenly …"

The big belly laughs, wiped tears, and recovery sighs afterward told me I had made the right choice—alien wasp and Maxi pad and all. I felt Dad would have been proud, as making people laugh had always been his specialty, even posthumously it seemed. I settled back into my spot on the pew by Tammy afterward and felt heartsick over the loss of my Dad. Further into the ceremony, I snatched a look back only to find Jude and Mr. Proper were gone, having left only a note in their pew that I found later.

> I can explain, Callie. Let's talk tonight at the hotel.
> The Town & Country on I-65. Room 204. Come and stay with us.

———

Back at Tammy's that night, the potential reunion with Jude saturates my brain. I am pretty sure I want to ignore him. I want to be the one to let *him* down. Make him see how it feels. And, one word in particular on his note was pushing me in that direction. *Us?* Jude wanted me to join him *and* Mr. Proper? Like some jolly reunion. *Not happening.*

I had told myself I had decided on it when Tammy surprised me again. Stepping into the guest bedroom, Tammy has two envelopes in her hand. She's looking down at them as she makes her way toward me, walking slower than I'd ever seen her move before. I think for a second, perhaps it's life insurance, but I never knew Dad to think that far ahead. It would have really surprised me.

Yet he still did. Tammy hands the two envelopes to me wordlessly, and I immediately recognize Dad's rough scrawl. One letter says "Callie." The other says, "Jude."

"He'd been working on those," Tammy says, but her voice catches. I go to hug her, but she holds up her hands to stop me. "I need to get this out. I don't know what his plans were, Callie. And, I have no idea what these letters say, but I would often find him scratching and rewriting and throwing scribbled drafts away. He just said he wanted to tell you kids things." She raises her head to meet my eyes. "I don't know if, I mean, I didn't know your Dad as long as you and Jude did, but he had something weighing on him, I think. And, I wonder if maybe he somehow … knew his time was coming. Do you think that could be possible?"

Tammy is easily forty years my senior—and she had endured the death of two husbands already before she met Dad—but in that moment, her curious face looks like a child's.

"I think Dad was ready now," I try. "He'd found peace here, for the first time in his life, I think," I tell her because it is the absolute truth. I'd never seen Dad so settled, so calm and happy as he was there with Tammy.

"I know he was there, Callie," Tammy says matter-of-factly. "I recognized him immediately, looking so much like your dad when he was younger."

I wait, surprised by Tammy's quiet awareness.

"You need to give Jude his, Callie."

I look at her then, feeling something reminiscent of what Mom had told me just a few days before. *We do the hard things others can't.* Then I feel it. The clever trick Tammy has just played, finding a way to mother me after all. Or was it Dad and her acting together? Seeing his writing of Jude's name on an envelope tells me everything I need to know. There's no way I will not deliver this. Not for Jude. For Dad. I will do this *for Dad.* I just close my eyes and let my head fall. Tammy gives my forearm a loving squeeze and rises.

"Go talk to him, Callie. And, have fun with those boys," Tammy says, gobsmacking me once again, realizing she must have found Jude's note before I did. I give her a narrow-eyed squint, and she just holds her hands up in defense. Little did Tammy know, though, that she had just coined a term that would thread through the rest of my life.

———

"I'm just here to give you this," I tell Jude as I walk through the hotel lobby doors and see him standing there—looking far too crisp for a funeral—waiting for me. I hold Dad's letter to him outstretched.

"No, you're not. We've got a hell of a lot to say to one another. Me especially. Let's get Mexican," Jude says. "You can murder me there," as he hooks his arm through my elbow, as only Jude can so smoothly do, and walks me back out to my car. As angry as I am, I find I have missed—so impossibly much—his unique sense of humor and the feeling of being with someone who knows me so well, that my boiling anger has cooled.

Just slightly.

Don't get me wrong. Murder is still on the table.

———

As well as margaritas, Jude has the waiter bring us a pitcher to share. We hadn't spoken a word to each other since the hotel lobby, it had almost become a game by the time we'd made it to the restaurant, where I refused to even answer the hostess when she asked: "Table for two?"

"Callie, I know," Jude started after we'd settled into our booth in the corner. "I know all the things you want to say to me. I hurt you. I left. I disappeared. I let you down. I didn't help you. I'm a terrible brother."

I find my anger is holding a steady line as he says all the things that are very, very true, and that he is right, I wanted to say to him. But, they're not all.

"You missed a few. You broke your promise to me. You said we would always be a team. I needed you," I hate to admit, but Jude is the only person I would say that to.

I can feel my core temperature rising as I see myself in all those moments—studying for my college entrance exams alone at Mom's, working shifts at Kripple Creek back in Clovis. The Cracker Barrel in Austin, studying while rolling silverware, going to bed in my dorm room at night hungry because I couldn't afford dinner, watching my haughty roommates look down their noses at me and my basket of ham and bread at the grocery store. I had always known Jude, and I didn't have as much as others, but it had all been bearable when we'd had each other.

In the shadow of Jude's betrayal, his absence, I realized I have forged myself with armor for this solitary path. But, where Dad's passing had already speared right through my chest plate, now Jude's return was causing every other piece of my armor to split at the welds. I didn't think I could stand to let another family member—or any person, for that matter—in only to have him break another promise and cut me clean through all over again. I wouldn't be able to stitch myself back together after that.

I brace for what I know I really need to say to him, now, before I lose my nerve.

"No reason you can give me can make me understand why you left me, Jude. Why I wasn't good enough? Why didn't you love me or care about me enough to find me?"

There. I got it out.

I don't swipe the tears that are dropping down my cheeks. I just let them fall and stare at him. Jude. My beautiful brother. I watch his jaw muscles work, and I know he's fighting back tears, too. I hate that I've done that to him, but I hate what he did to me—to us—more.

"No reason will ever make it right, Callie, but I think, just a few of them, can help you understand. I should have reached out. I know that. And, the reason I didn't has absolutely nothing to do with you, nothing to do with you being good enough, or me not loving you enough. Those were never in question."

I cross my arms over my burning chest and look away.

"I didn't contact you, Callie, because I was," Jude looks up and swallows, trying to keep his throat under control.

"I was ashamed."

Ashamed? This throws me. Coming from the boy who helped me wrap bloody toilet paper around my 'grody' Care Bear Tummy. The brother who knew I often peed my pants and threw the soiled underwear away so Mom wouldn't find out. The teenager whose blackheads I would mash with a fury. *That guy's* ashamed?

"Bullshit," I tell him because I can't comprehend something Jude would be ashamed about around me.

"It's true."

I shake my head.

"It won't justify my absence, I know that," Jude is trying desperately to pull me back. "But, I am apologizing, sincerely, and I promise to spend the rest of my life making it up to you, Callie."

"I don't want any of your false promises. All you do is break them," I huff.

"I'm just asking that you listen," Jude says, resigned. "Let me tell you some things that happened. Okay?"

I don't look at him.

"Will you just listen?"

I uncross my arms but refuse to meet his eyes.

"I was in jail," Jude says.

"I know that. You don't think I've stolen shit? I had to swipe books from the bookstore, shampoo from Walgreens, fucking burritos from the gas station just to get by. You think I don't know what it takes?" I can't stop myself. I have years' worth of Jude resentment built up just to spew at him. "I'm not going to have some pity party for you for getting thrown in jail. You shouldn't have got caught, dumbass."

Out of my periphery, I can see Jude do that thing where he rolls his tongue along the front of his teeth when he's thinking, and it pricks me because I've missed his stupid teeth, his mannerisms, the sound of his voice.

"I got engaged," he tries.

I finally bring my eyes to meet his to see if that's true.

It's true.

I'm listening.

"I have a daughter," Jude says, and the air stops completely still in my lungs.

I look at him now differently, my anger finally softening. I open my mouth to start to speak, but Jude holds up a hand to stop me.

"Callie, I'm gay."

CHAPTER TWENTY-THREE
CHEERS

The minute Jude said it, his fun, cheerful demeanor dissipated, and his eyes blazed into me, looking for ... I didn't know what. *Surprise? Or feigned surprise because I already knew?*

But I hadn't known.

The news hit me so strangely, like something completely out of left field, but at the very same time, like a puzzle piece that had just been waiting to be snapped in. *Click.* A dozen flashbacks cycled through my brain.

Janessa: "You'll have to ask Jude about that."

Jude about Dad: "We knew secrets about each other."

Mom, when she kicked Jude out: "Not to mention the other shit you do," she'd said. "I am your *mother*, Jude. You think I don't know you through and through? I don't want any of it in my house."

Jude's favorite pony, Brian, has a slender body and flowing orange hair.

The boys at school were calling Jude "pussy" and "pretty boy" before Jay had shoved them to the ground.

Jude and I sat in that Mexican restaurant for three hours—eating chips and salsa and drinking two pitchers of margaritas, before we'd said everything that needed saying. Hearing Jude's entire story made me feel almost like a fool. Like I was there, for it all, but in so many ways, I was learning I hadn't really been there at all. Jude kept rattling off facts that blew my mind, each one pulling back another layer of the aware, observant boy he was.

Jude knew something was different about him since he was a child, describing it as the sensation that his "skin didn't fit right."

He often spilled things on any little dress Mom tried to fuss me into because he was jealous. *I knew it!*

Jude often tried to talk deeper or stand straighter around other boys to fit in, but they made fun of him, so he stopped trying.

Janessa had figured it out pretty early on and indicated as much to Jude, but she never divulged his secret, not even to me.

Jay and Jude had kissed once. "We spent a lot of time together, Callie. Boys get curious, too," was all he said. *Jaaayy?*

The bastard kissed Roddie, too. *My* Roddie. "He was no longer curious afterward," Jude had laughed.

But, Jude and Roddie remained close friends until Jude left for Houston, Roddie having confided in him first about him and Mariah's dad getting sick and the family's move to Texas so they could get him the kidney treatments he needed.

Oh, here's a kicker. Mom did *not* kick Jude out of the house. She gave him an ultimatum to "stop doing what he was doing," which Jude said he could have interpreted as the drugs or fooling around with boys, which he was sure Mom had put together years before. Scary as it was—to be a young gay man in Clovis, New Mexico, in 1995—he knew he couldn't change. Furious at her unfair ultimatum, Jude chose to move out to spite her. *Jude chose to move out.* I felt like the Mom tapestry I had woven my entire life, Jude had just unraveled.

Then he grabbed a string on Dad's and began to tug when he told me Dad was the first person to actually catch Jude with another guy, behind the pens near his trailer. Dad collared him and shoved Jude down the stairs. My heart hurt imagining what it must have felt like for Jude to have faced such violence from our dad solely as a reaction to the person he is and will always be.

Jude hadn't told Mom or Dad about getting his GED or his plans to move to Houston so he could study to become an architect. I didn't blame him after hearing all that. He'd just left Dad's on a Tuesday morning, on a bus headed east.

Jude lived in Houston initially, working at a P.F. Chang's, and he had started night classes, where he met Rachel—"a clever, spirited woman" whom he grew close to and shared most of himself—minus the fact that he was gay.

He'd tried not to be. For Rachel. By proposing and agreeing to move out to her mom's place in Sacramento after Rachel found out she was pregnant, unaware of the vibrance of the gay scene out in California. "Everyday felt like looking in the best window display you'd ever seen and wanting everything on the other side," Jude had said. But, when Rachel's mom—who'd been suspicious of Jude from the start—caught him with another man at a coffee shop, she blew everything up and kicked Jude out.

"I spiraled after that," Jude told me. Drugs. Doing and selling and running through carousels of men while stealing, lying, and sleeping on various couches. Until he was arrested after stealing a car.

Jude spent eighteen months in jail. *Eighteen.* Rachel was the only person to visit him. "Just the once," he said. To tell him she'd had the baby, but to make him promise never to look for her or try to contact her child. *Their* child.

Jude agreed but decided in jail he was going to live openly as a gay man and never again try to pretend, or keep that part of himself a secret.

"I will say, being stuck in jail with a bunch of guys is not a terrible place for a gay man," Jude had tried to joke about it.

Weary after Jude's shotgun reveal, I'd covered my face with my hands. "Stop it. This cannot be funny."

"Can't it?" he'd fired back. "I kind of feel like it has to be. I'm the one who was locked up, remember? I get to decide what's funny and what's not."

Jude then told me about Levi. Mr. Proper. Apparently, he'd rented a room from Levi for a time while he was working and going to school in Houston, around the same time he met Rachel.

"Levi was the first man I connected with who was openly, unapologetically gay," Jude told me. "I admired him. I wanted to be him. I thought he had feelings for me—as I knew I had feelings for him—but Rachel and I had just found out she was pregnant when I met Levi. I just couldn't."

Jude also kept his promise to Rachel. When he was released from jail—only four months ago—he did not look for her in Sacramento. Instead, he decided to go back to Levi. A part of me felt vindicated because I had known, sensed, that he and Levi shared something Jude and I had lost. As immature as it sounded, I felt better knowing my jealousy had been well-founded.

"I thought about reaching out to you, Callie, of course. But I knew you were killing it in undergrad at the University of Texas—all on your own, too. I kept tabs on you. And, I knew having me in the strung-out, sorry state I was in, coming crashing into the impressive life you were single-handedly holding together would only derail you. I knew you would bend over backward to help me, and it would … drown you, Callie."

I blushed and stewed at the comment, not knowing whether to thank him or object. *Would I?* I knew the answer was yes. *But, would it have?* I did not know.

"But, I didn't think about the toll it would really take on you,

Callie. Me just exiting stage left of your life," Jude said, sternly. "I didn't … think enough about you. That was selfish, and I'm sorry."

I almost didn't want to change my feelings for Jude because I was so used to being angry with him. I had used it as fuel, and I wasn't sure what would continue to propel me forward without it. *Would I deflate?* While I knew I would never agree that Jude made the right decision *not* turning to me, his sister, for help, I was starting—at least—as Jude had predicted, to understand.

"Levi took me in, Callie. When I was at my worst—broken, missing teeth, missing hair, with no job, no money, literally nothing to show for myself than a trash bag of crap and a raging STD. I don't know what I've done in this life to deserve him, Lil' Bit, but Levi is my person. He is my partner, my lover, my best friend."

I tried not to bristle at the best friend comment, but Jude sensed it anyway.

"Levi brought you and me back together, Callie. He's the reason I'm here, *with* you. And the reason I was able to attend my dad's funeral," Jude gave me a look then that told me he knew what I'd done.

"It's okay. I deserved it," was all he said, and I was grateful for it. It's all that needed to be said.

I think it was that very moment that Jude and I melded back together and became brother and sister again.

"Levi's smart, Callie. He knows everything about me. After that odd phone call from a young woman sounding worried, surprised by the name Cavaletti. I'm sorry … '*Mister* Cavaletti?'" Jude imitates me, and I can't help but laugh. Turns out Mr. Cavaletti was the first person in Clovis Jude believed to be gay and the first to acknowledge it to Jude with their silent code—a knowing nod. It had been a lightning strike moment for Jude as a teen.

"It didn't take much for Levi to put it together that it was you," Jude explained. "After you hung up on him," Jude had given me a look, "he started searching for anything Potts in Austin to try and find you—for me. That's when he came across Dad's obituary."

Jude crumpled his napkin on the table and clenched his throat.

"I hated myself for not trying harder with him. I believe we could have had a conversation about it. I think Dad and I could have found common ground," Jude had looked at me then as if he'd asked me a question.

"I know you would have," I'd told him, laying a hand on Jude's on the table. "This is proof," I'd said as I handed him the envelope containing the letter Dad had written for him, knowing not what it said but knowing my dad well enough to trust his main intent with the letter was likely to give Jude peace of mind, and probably apologize himself. It made me wonder briefly what was in my letter, but I knew I was going to save it for what I didn't know. Some cowboy wisdom when I needed it the most, that was certain.

Jude told me he had started back with his architecture classes in Houston. He was now waiting tables at a posh steak restaurant during the day, and taking classes at night, while Levi was pursuing his English degree at a local college in Houston. They lived together in a little apartment on the west side of town, and Jude hadn't touched drugs since.

"I've sketched my first house," Jude told me with pride as he explained the open floor plan and the second-floor balcony looking over the sunken living room. "There's even a room for you, Callie," he'd said, which touched me in a way he would never know, the fact that he had included me in his beautiful new life. Suddenly, I was five with bologna in my teeth, and the sun was shining on me again. Jude was back.

"You should have seen Levi's face, Callie, when he took me in on his doorstep after almost two years, with my trash bag of stuff. I guess our days shuffling around with Dad and our Duffel bags in his big rig did teach us something. We do pack light," Jude had raised his glass then, indicating I do the same.

"I'm afraid to cheers you now," I'd said hesitantly. "I don't think I can take any more secrets."

Jude laughed. A genuine, warm laugh that tinkled in the air and resonated through me. That or the alcohol did. I wasn't sure, but both felt good. We were winding our epic night down. After I finished catching him up on my first years in college with law school up ahead—the whole of it not nearly as exciting, or lengthy, as Jude's saga—Jude made me a promise I believed, this time, he would keep.

"No more secrets, Callie. I'm sorry I went MIA," he'd said. "I know that worried you, and I hate that I wasn't there for you during what I'm sure were some tough times for you, too. I mean, you moved halfway across Texas and started college entirely on your own. And now you're going to law school. Again, all on your own. I'm not surprised, Callie. I never will be when it comes to your goddamn iron will, but I am impressed. And, proud as hell to call you my sister. To the point that I felt any news from me would just bring you down, depress, and distract you. I mean, how the hell could I tell you all that in a letter? It would sound like a bad country western song."

"Puh-leease," I countered. "No grandmas got run over by reindeer," which made him chuckle. "Sounds like you met someone you really cared for. You started a relationship that was simply never going to work out. Throw a wayward pregnancy in there, some jail time, and a coming out of the closet, and it sounds like a pretty run-of-the-mill teenage angst story to me," I had told him, trying to take some weight off him, as we sat there still holding our glasses up.

"Well, I'm glad because that's it. My big, nasty secret. The reason I went quiet. But now I'm back, and I will never leave your life again, Callie. If you'll have me—please have me—I'll be the best big brother you've ever had, you and Levi, and I can start our own family. A fucking real one, where people don't slap and shove one another around. Where they don't keep hurtful secrets. We won't be broken and desperate and strung out on drugs. We'll laugh and have fun, live in mansions, and support one another. What do you say, Lil' Bit?" Jude's glass was still raised.

I suddenly felt even more proud to call him my brother. This element of him made him even more the resilient, creative, charismatic person that I always knew he was. My gay brother: Jude. I knew it changed nothing for me. I would always love Jude and want him in my life. That was true if he was a purple dragon with one eyeball. If he were a mute. A circus clown. He was still Jude.

"Cheers," I told him, and we clinked on it.

CHAPTER TWENTY-FOUR
JUDE

Callie was the last person in my life I was afraid to tell. Well, let's be clear. After Rachel and Levi, there was no one else in my life at the moment, really, left *to* tell. Callie was the last person left, and I just didn't know how she would take it, exactly. Knowing the person she spent most of her childhood with had—the whole time—been secretly gay, hiding that from her. I had tried to be such a mentor and example for her, but I thought it might ruin what I was to her. Or what I had been to her. Back when we were kids.

Back then, it was only when I was alone with Callie that I was free to be my complete self. Gay tendencies and all. "Honey," this. "Please, child," that. I never told her outright when I figured it out, because she wouldn't have even understood at the time. She was only six. Maybe seven, then. But I was never my fake macho dude persona with her. I bet if I had tried it one day—if I'd gone all "Hey. Sup. That's my bike,"—Callie would have shaken me by the shoulders, asking, "What the heck's wrong with you?" That's probably why I stuck by her as close as I did back then. Being with Callie was like taking my mask off. She was a relief. She was home.

But little kids just don't notice—or fear or ostracize or hate—mannerisms like that until they're taught to. That was one of the reasons I pulled away a bit from Callie once she got into junior high. I was afraid she would figure me out, and she wouldn't be able to keep something that big and huge a secret. I know her too well. Callie would have taken up my cause, championing for me. She would have fought all the bullies of the world for me. And, it would have shaped her identity and changed her agenda. I didn't want that for her. Callie deserved to just grow up like a normal girl—crushes and upsets and all—without having to be the little sister of the only outwardly gay boy in Clovis.

Everything that happened with Mom, Dad, and then Rachel only solidified my choices back then. People think if you're gay, you figure it out early on, commit to it, and that's that. But that's not true at all. It's undeniable, but also terrifying and weird, and you're just trying to fit in. You start relationships with the opposite sex to see where it leads, but you mess things up. You hurt people. You have kids, even. Not that it's perfect now, but it just wasn't that clean and simple for many gay men back then, from my experience. But there was always one clear answer. Every time I came (or was forced) out to someone I loved, it detonated everything.

Being gay is one of the most destructive secrets I've ever known and kept. But not anymore. Thanks to Levi, I am completely out, with nothing more to hide. It makes me feel both elated and terrified. My joy is new and fragile, but I've been trying to don some dazzling shades and fake it till I make it. Of this I'm sure: there is no way I would be the man that I am today—whatever that amounts to—without Levi. When I showed up on his doorstep four months ago, fresh out of the pen, in the worst state I have ever found myself in, I thought he might loan me a little money. Let me sleep on his couch for a few days while I get myself sorted. I would have never guessed he would give me a permanent, loving home.

But more than that. Levi gave me hope. He granted me permission to start over by owning my past—not running from it—the mistakes and tragedies, and building on them. Levi let me talk about everything I felt growing up with Callie, my troubled relationships with Mom and Dad, the trauma my heart went through with Rachel, and the tormenting months I spent in jail. Levi is also the only other person in the world, outside of Callie, who knows I have a daughter out there, although I know he's torn on whether I should break my promise to Rachel and try to find her. I can't help but wonder, though, if enough time has gone by that it would be okay to try to contact her. I think about it every day.

But I also know Levi fears losing me to my daughter, and maybe Rachel, again, and I can understand that. While I would like to sound very brave and upstanding, saying I had not tried to find my daughter only to spare Levi, that's not entirely true. Part of me—most of me—is terrified that she won't want anything to do with a gay dad. I can sit here and say that wouldn't wreck me, but it would be a complete and baseless lie. So, I did what Mom always did when those troublesome feelings started to snake around me. I validate my actions and put those feelings on a shelf.

And, why would I detonate everything when my life looks like a damn Colgate commercial? I got my teeth fixed. My hair's grown back, thick and silky. I live with this Greek Adonis who adores me because I'm impossibly pretty. I've reunited with my incredibly inspiring sister and got to witness the headstrong beast she has become. When I see the bond her and Levi have begun to grow, I am confident these years will be some of the best of my life. While I dreamed many times as a child, then a teenager, of my life as an adult, an honest adult, I often envisioned myself with a man quite like Levi.

And Callie was always there, very much like she is now, sitting around laughing with us, playing a game, the three of us just happy to be together, without any secrets. It all seemed like such a mirage that I sometimes have to pinch myself when I see it has come just as true as I imagined it. I love nothing more than to watch Callie and Levi poking fun at one another, creating inside jokes—calling one another 'Counselor' and 'Professor'—and picking on me in ways that make me feel truly accepted, like being gay is just as natural and silly as having unruly hair, being tall, or terrible at dancing—which for the record, I am not. On the dance floor, I dazzle. But, unlike Mom and Dad, Callie and Levi know it was never a choice for me. It's just who I am.

And, Callie is who she is. I mean, damn. She is killing it at law school. When she comes over to Houston to stay with me and Levi for the weekend, and she tells us what she's up against, I'm always mesmerized. While Callie was a big fish in a little pond in both high school and undergrad—because she's that smart and driven—now she's in the fucking ocean, swimming with sharks. I'm taking little night classes and working toward my architecture design degree, sure, but Callie is really in the ring with all the rich people—the blue bloods we thought we could never mingle with—and she's holding her own. In a top-tier law school! Getting As and Bs, writing briefs, and doing oral arguments.

While I know she doesn't feel like it, Callie's not pretending anymore. She's not a fraud. Callie is the real by-God deal and soaring like I always knew she would. Every time I taught her something new on that little TV we scribbled on for years, she absorbed it like a sponge. And, if she didn't get it right the first time, she would repeat it, and repeat it, and repeat it until she couldn't get it wrong. Frankly, it was a bit unnerving to see such drive coming from a mere child. That's Callie, though. I wish her uppity, old-money counterparts at that law school could see a side-by-side of Callie at age eight to themselves. They would be terrified as they should be.

But I do hate to see her doing all of this, accomplishing all of this badassery, with no one by her side. Those years she spent alone—forging diligently ahead—have hardened her. I know that's partly my fault, and it is the reason she won't let anyone else in. Hell, she barely forgave me, her long-lost fabulous brother. Imagine a Hallmark movie where, in that final "I forgive you; I love you" scene, the main character just clocks the other one—*bam*—and then walks away as heavy metal fades out. That's about where Callie's little stone of a heart is now when it comes to outsiders. Like the Grinch when he stole Christmas. But here's what I know.

It will grow.

Someday, someone is going to start to seep into her topsoil and plant a little seed. Then the massive, beating life force that is Callie's heart will come to life. It's already starting with Levi; I can see it. Callie teaches both of us things from her law school classes—often using whatever game we're playing at the time. Monopoly lends itself well to lessons in contracts and property, not surprisingly. And, Levi likes to tell her about classic literary plots and point them out in movies we all watch together. "Even silly rom-coms are based on the classics. Take the Oedipus complex we have here," he'll say, pointing out some arguably nonexistent metaphor playing out between a gratuitously bare-chested Matthew McConaughey and a scantily clad SJP until Callie and I both throw popcorn and M&Ms at him, telling him to shut up.

But, I know, outside of visiting me and Levi—and Tammy occasionally, whom Levi and I have grown fond of as well—Callie spends ninety percent of her time alone—working or studying. She takes her law school outlines to Cracker Barrel with her to study while rolling silverware. She recites and records them while cleaning her house and plays them back to herself while on the treadmill at the gym. She scrubs and mends thrift store clothes to try to make them look new. She packs lunch everyday and eats it while studying. Callie turns down most social invites because she doesn't want anyone to know she can't afford the tab. She resides on the fringe.

Callie also doesn't know she's beautiful. She's smarter than she gives herself credit for (although I deserve half). And, she's one of the most capable, compassionate humans I have ever met. Nothing can stop her. But, nothing can change her mind right now, either, on letting others in, because she thinks, well, Callie thinks there's no space for it in her world. But mostly, Callie believes her true self isn't worth sharing. I know that because I used to feel the same. My entire life, up until four months ago, I felt the same. Callie and I have both spent so many years trying to hide our poverty, our *less*-ness, so that we could infiltrate the upper half. She doesn't yet know she's better, stronger than all of them. But she will figure that out. Eventually.

I did when I finally opened myself up to Levi—showing him the sad wreck of a man I had been, but also the smart, loving man I knew I could become. And, it was scary as hell doing that. I know that's why Callie's closed off. Just like I was. And, I'm partly to blame. I'd taught her to be like that when we were kids so that I could have her to myself. Also, because it really was she and I against the big unknown. I wish I had known back then and taught Callie that there are people out here worth trusting, who won't disappoint you, hurt you, or shove you down. I want Callie to know there are so many men in the world who would love her *for* her silly quirks, her iron will, and her ocean-sized heart. The world will love her *for* her Clovis roots, not despite them. It will come.

Callie will find her Levi.

But I feel sorry for the bloke because he's going to have to win over these two queens first. Callie deserves someone who will love her even when she's angry and beating up on herself, who can absorb the unbearable pressure she sometimes exerts on her little world, and who will understand and accept the lengths she will go to for those she loves.

I am actually more excited for Callie than I've ever been, because she's finally just given Levi and me the best news we could have ever hoped for from her.

Callie has met someone.

The poor bloke.

CHAPTER TWENTY-FIVE
GIRL TALK

"So, that's who? Your brother?" The nurse asks me. It's the one who looks like Sissy, and I've had a hard time trying not to imagine her in a prom queen sash with a wilted bouquet of roses in her hand, waving as she works on me. She's been eyeing the photos on my windowsill, and I think her curiosity finally got the best of her.

"Yeah, that's Jude," I tell her, indicating the photo of me and Jude in front of Mom's old grey Oldsmobile. I think for a minute to correct myself, but then decide I don't want to have to explain all of that to this nurse, so I just let my answer sit between us.

"Looks like he thinks the world of you," Sissy Nurse says, trying to be nice, but she's pricked me, unknowingly, and I don't want to talk about Jude anymore, so I just nod. A light rap on the door gets my attention. Looking for another topic, I say, "Come in," with a rasp. Realizing how much I tore my throat up shouting at the last person who came here to visit me, I vow to be nice this time.

"Jay?" I ask as I see his soft brown hair peek into the door of my room. I feel like I've been slipping in and out of the present again. I don't know what kind of painkillers they've got me on, but that loopy, exhausted feeling it gives me seems to come and go in waves. I feel overwhelmingly groggy when I come out. I pinch myself to try and wake my brain up so I can stay here, clear, for at least a few hours. Time enough for someone to tell me something real.

"I know you're angry with me," Jay starts. His eyes are searching mine for what, I'm not sure.

"I'm not angry with you," I correct him. "I just want to know what's going on. Why did you run out of here in such a hurry last time? What exactly happened, and what am I facing? If you're going to sit here with me and *not* tell me those things, then, yeah, I'm going to be angry with you."

We stare at one another. Jay finally nods. "I've got Mariah coming to tell you everything."

Although I'm a little confused as to why Mariah needs to tell me, I'm glad she's coming. Mariah and I didn't get to really rekindle our old friendship the last time we were thrown together a couple of months ago, but that was mostly on me. I was drowning in a shit storm. I was a terror to everyone I love, and I know it, which is why I thought I would never see Mariah again. Just like I thought, I might never see Mom again. Hell, I didn't even know if I'd see Jay again, but here we are.

Then it dawns on me.

"Wait, you all want Mariah to talk to me about what happened so everything I say can … remain privileged."

It isn't really a question, but Jay nods.

"But I don't remember anything," I feel tears welling in my throat, and I try to swallow them down. Jay comes over to me immediately and sits next to me on the bed.

"I know, Callie. I know. But don't say anything to me. Mariah is on her way, okay?"

"It's not good, is it, Jay?" is all I ask.

Jay solemnly shakes his head 'no.' "It's not, Callie, but …"

I send a silent prayer up: *Don't you dare tell me 'it's going to be okay.'*

"We'll be right here with you to get you through it," Jay finishes, and I'm grateful. It's not a lie.

Jay pats my good leg and starts to head out of the room as Mariah slips in. She looks tired. I can see light grey bags under her eyes. But her luscious black hair is still shiny and thick and snaking over her shoulder in a luxurious, fat braid. She's slim and sure in her movements. She has dress slacks on, but comfortable shoes and a low-key white blouse tucked in. She sets her notorious woven satchel in the chair by the door as she makes her way over to me.

"We gotta stop meeting like this," Mariah says, which brings me a chuckle.

"What, in hospitals?"

"No, when you're being supervised by professionals, although I do take some comfort in it."

"Double your rate," I tell her, grateful for our easy banter.

"You wouldn't be able to afford me."

"You don't know what I can afford. Hell, what do I need? Can I get some two-for-one family special here?" I'm finding my sense of humor, though, is waning. "Just talk to me, Mariah, please. Tell me everything that's going on," I plead with her.

"I will," she confirms. "I promise," and I realize instantly that I believe her.

"But nothing is going to change in the next fifteen minutes, and I've been running around hospitals now for months, it seems, getting you out of jams, so I call the shots here, got it?" Mariah says curtly.

"Who was in the car with me, Mariah?" I can't help it.

"Okay, don't have it. Still the same ole' Callie. Jesus lady. YOU are in a hospital bed. I am the attorney here to help you pro bono. Can we show a little appreciation?" She gives me a look that shuts me up. *I love this woman*, that's all I can think of.

"I will tell you about the other person in the vehicle—the *alive* person—after we talk." Mariah looks at me solemnly and crosses her arms over her chest—an ultimatum.

"Nothing will change in the next fifteen minutes?" I can't help it.

"Nothing will change," she confirms.

I let out a sigh and pat the bed next to my lady stump, craving more than anything some quality girl talk right now that has nothing to do with hospitals or accidents or my fucked-up life. Mariah's features soften as she trots happily over to my bed and plops down.

"You are the worst client ever, you know that?"

I nod.

"It had been what, thirteen, fourteen years—junior high—since we'd spoken, and last time we collided like two meteors in a shower. Let's just catch up for a hot minute."

I like this plan. I've missed Mariah. She has a quiet wit and a slick sense of humor—her compassion and emotional intelligence. I feel like I've been on the defense—a feral animal backed into a corner—the whole time I've been here, and I know it would be a huge relief to set my worries, my guard, down for just one minute to talk to a friend.

"When they broke the news to me, we were going to move in less than three weeks. Roddie had already enlisted. My dad had his treatments scheduled. It all happened so fast," Mariah says, talking about her family's move to Houston. "Oh, but, Jesus, Callie. I haven't told you what happened in those three weeks," she gives me an intriguing look. "Do you remember Tyler Beck?"

A laugh gurgles out of me. *Do I.*

"So, when you went to Roswell that summer, he started hanging around me more, chatting me up at the Allsups and stuff. I guess since my bodyguard was gone, he felt he could finally make a move," she nudges my good leg.

"But I thought he was really into me this time, ya know?" Mariah explains. I can tell from her tone, though, that he was into something else. "I'd finally gotten my stinky cast off," she waves her left arm around, which is now tan, toned, and beautiful. "And, he asked me if I wanted to get a Coke together, so I said Sure," Mariah tells me they hung out a few times before he kissed her. "I felt so special," she looks at me, then, because I get it.

I one-hundred-percent get it. Attention will do that to a young, geeky, insecure girl. It can also do the opposite when the attention turns mean. Ask me about Roddie and a jar of pickles.

"I didn't love making out with him. He was so aggressive," to which I nod in agreement. I didn't love it either. Tyler was anything but gentle. "But then one day, we were down in my basement. No one was home, and Tyler was putting his hands all over me. I mean, I had just turned fourteen. I wasn't ready to give up my virginity! Much less to that creep," she huffed.

"Sing it, sister," I coax her on.

"I just. I was pretty surprised it was actually happening. Like, he was really going to try it? He was really *that* stupid. Tyler knew I had an older brother who had taught me a thing or two." I can feel a smile start to spread on my face because I am so excited to hear where this is going. Maybe Mariah gave it to Tyler better than I had. A girl could hope.

"I said no like five times. Tyler, the idiot, didn't hear me or didn't care, and he kept at it. So, I grabbed the *Dream Phone*," Mariah pretends to hold that clunky pink thing in her hand. "It was the first thing I could reach with him clutching all over me—and I clocked him with it. Callie, it knocked out a tooth!"

"A tooth?!" I shout incredulously, cackling. I would have never guessed that bulky *Dream Phone* could be that deadly. "WAY TO GO MARIAH!" I put up my hand for a high five, and she slaps it hard, with her left, and I'm overwhelmed by how much I've missed her and missed having a girlfriend.

"Yeah, Roddie must have come home right as it was happening, and he came running down the stairs when he heard me shouting and the commotion. Callie, Tyler was all doubled over, mumbling and fumbling with blood and drool coming out of his mouth." Mariah is imitating him now, clawing stupidly at my hospital blanket, her mouth agape.

"He looked ridiculous, Callie, and he was actually trying to find his tooth in that big fuzzy rug in our basement, which still to this day makes me laugh. From the look of my clothes and our blotchy faces and the bloody *Dream Phone* weapon in my hand, Roddie put it together pretty quickly, and he picked Tyler up by the collar and dragged him up the stairs and out of the house." Mariah is laughing now. "It was a pretty awesome sight. If there was anyone I could have wished was there to just watch it, it would have been you."

I find myself feeling thirteen again, beaming at Roddie's unprecedented heroism and strength. And I think secretly to myself: *Boy, do I have a Tyler story for Mariah.*

"I knew you were killing it in Austin," Mariah snaps me back to focus. "My folks still talk to some people back in Clovis, and they get little updates. Your mom tells everyone about you, Callie, like you're some Olympic gold champion or something. If you came back home, I think they might paint your image on the water tower." This has me laughing. Maybe they'll paint me a gimp, too, with one leg, I think. But Mariah's comment about Mom pierces me. It hurts me to know Mom is proud of me and bragging about me to folks in Clovis when I hardly think about her most days. I pick up on something else to shove the sting aside.

"So, Roddie served in the military?" I ask her, which perks Mariah up.

"Oh yeah. He joined the Marines, Callie. Surprised us all. Did two tours in Iraq. He became an officer!" I can feel the pride she has for her brother. It's palpable. "We were definitely all a little shocked when he told us he was going to get his GED—which Jude helped him with by the way—then enlist, but he had to make a change when … things didn't work out with the football scholarship he was planning to UT," she looks briefly at me, and I cringe.

"Callie, stop worrying about it, seriously," she assures me. "Moving to Houston was the best thing for everyone in my family. I mean that. You really did us all a huge favor."

"Don't ever let me off the hook like that again," I scold her. "What I did was terrible."

"What you did when you were *fourteen*? Jesus, Callie. Our brains weren't fully developed by then. At least yours wasn't, obviously," Mariah chuckles weakly.

"Mariah, just let me apologize for it, okay?" We stare at each other. Mariah blinks. I take it as consent. "I am more sorry than I could ever be. It was a hateful, hurtful thing that I did. And, the worst part about it was I broke your trust," I tell her, swallowing back thick, bitter emotions.

"You did," Mariah admits. "But I forgave you a long time ago. You were young and hurt and mouthed off. Before that moment, you'd been the best friend I'd ever had. And I did miss you. Terribly."

"I missed you more," I tell her quietly. "I have not had a single girl that I would call a real friend in my life since you. Not a one."

"Not surprising," Mariah says, and I flash a look at her. "Moving to Austin on your own. Crushing undergrad. Getting into UT Law. Getting on at Goldman Carr, one of the most prestigious firms in the state. Although they work for the devil—defending insurance companies that deny legitimate claims," Mariah huffs. "Despite that, and the fact that I became a lawyer in Texas, too, I damn sure did not climb that high. You did, Callie Potts."

I'm silent. She just said it all—even the devil's observation, which I had been circling around on my own.

"I'm proud, and that's all I'm saying. Wouldn't want to overly inflate your hospitalized ego," she smacks my whole leg. "But you need friends, you idiot. I also think you haven't yet figured out how to own your accomplishments. Use them to embrace what you care about."

I give her a funny look as that all sounded very proper and psycho babble. I just throw my arms out. It seems the only answer, and Mariah comes trotting over.

"This is me, embracing," I say into her lush black hair. Then, on a whim, I pick up her left arm, the one that was in a cast for over a year and had caused her so much angst as a teenager. I start to sniff it and make a funny face like it stinks. Mariah jerks back and shoves me hard on the shoulders, then apologizes immediately, realizing I'm in a hospital bed, but I'm just laughing.

"Yep, still you," I say, and Mariah pulls her arm back to snug it across her chest, but something catches my eye, so I snatch her arm back. I'm turning it over and around before my eyes because I kind of can't believe it.

It's the friendship bracelet I made Mariah for her fourteenth birthday, out of the discarded curtains from her bedroom. The fabric isn't as sheer anymore, much more beige and worn, but I can still see the little green seashells. I look up and meet Mariah's eyes. She grins and shrugs.

"I told you you were the best friend I'd ever had, up until that moment," Mariah says.

"You didn't throw it away," I ask, dumbly, childlike, because the answer is staring me in the face.

"I didn't throw it away," Mariah confirms.

We're interrupted by a thumping knock on the door.

"It's Detective Carter," his voice thundered through. "We've got some new evidence, Ms. Avalero. I need to speak with you."

Mariah clears her throat and gets all business. "Give me five minutes, Mike," she says. I mouth the word *Mike* to her, my eyebrows raised. She rolls her eyes. We wait for his response.

"Five minutes," Detective Carter says gruffly. "I'll be in the waiting room." Mariah and I stare at the door and wait until we hear his footsteps retreating.

"Mariah, please, just tell me everything you know. Don't hide anything from me. Please," I beg her.

So she doesn't.

"Okay, here's what we're dealing with. You know you were in a motor vehicle accident," I nod. Of course. "The accident took place at the corner of Rowling Street and Ninth. There were two cars involved." I perk up at this new fact.

"The other driver—thankfully, he was alone in the car—was a ... fatality," Mariah gives me a look that I'm not sure how to read. It either means *'Don't freak out yet,'* or *'This is where you freak out.'* Both seem equally possible.

"Now, he, the other driver, was obnoxiously drunk. Way over the limit. Like point-one-four or something." I keep listening. "But you're no saint there either, Callie. You were point-oh-eight." I nod—no sense in hiding from it. But now there's a death involved. This could be manslaughter. If I'm convicted of a felony, I could lose my license. My heart starts beating faster, and the beep of my machines betrays me.

Mariah looks up at them, takes in the numbers briefly, then picks back up, knowing she doesn't have much time.

"The tire mark evidence shows your vehicle, the SUV, rolled off the embankment after the collision and into the ditch where it landed. You landed in the backseat, but the other occupant was thrown when your vehicle rolled."

She's giving me so much information, my mind is clicking and smoking. But something stuck.

"SUV?" I ask. "We weren't in my car?"

Mariah looks at me a little bewildered.

"I don't remember a thing after ordering my second gin and tonic. … Double," I tell her. "I drove my Corolla to the bar. I do remember that. But I can't recall whether I left Nick's in my car or not."

Mariah nods slowly, seemingly taking this in for the first time. "You weren't in *your* car, Callie," she confirms, but I don't like her tone. It feels like a half-truth.

"Mariah," I push on her. She heaves a great sigh and releases it.

"You were in a Nissan Pathfinder," she says and drops my gaze.

"Pathfinder …" the word slips out of my mouth like oil. Mariah nods.

"A blue Pathfinder?" I ask. Mariah nods again. Her eyes are on my blanket, where mine have spent so much time over the last few days. I know she won't find any answers or help there. I've tried.

"Mariah …" I start slowly. "What was I doing driving *his* Pathfinder?"

Mariah shakes her head solemnly and raises her shoulders, indicating she doesn't know.

"And so … the '*other guy?*'" I step timidly into this space because I'm terrified of what she's going to tell me. The clock on the wall ticks twice as Mariah pulls a long breath into her lungs.

"Was Braden," she says, her voice soft as a whisper.

CHAPTER TWENTY-SIX
LUCY

"I think I might have met someone."

The room fills with crickets. A dog barks somewhere. I chew my lip.

"Think?" Levi says.

"*Might?*" Jude seconds. "You either met the person or you didn't, that's easy to answer. But whether the person is … *someone* or not is what I'm guessing called for the 'think' and the 'might.'"

As I eased into my second year of law school, Jude and Levi found a little house they wanted to rent together with a much bigger kitchen and an open floor plan. It also had a nice fenced-in backyard, which the boys fell in love with. "Maybe we could get a dog," Levi had said dreamily. They also chose a place, again, with two bedrooms, so that I would have one there. While it may have seemed strange or unorthodox to others—for two gay men to always keep a spare bedroom open for their sister ("natural and adopted," Levi claimed)—it just felt right and comfortable to us. I was helping them move in when I'd sprung the news on them.

Jude and Levi both put down their moving boxes. As an unspoken team, they scooted a little camping chair next to my rump and pushed me down into it with a flop. Jude scooted a coffee table right in front of me and Levi. They both sat down on it, crossed their right legs over their lefts in surprising unison, laid their chins on their propped-up hands, and cocked their heads at me, batting lashes while they waited for the juicy story, although I didn't feel it was all that juicy. But with all the hell they were giving me, I felt I deserved to have a little fun with this, too.

I wiped my sweaty hands on my jeans, took a deep breath, and started.

"Her name is Lucy," I said.

Jude narrowed an eye at me from behind Levi's shoulder, and I struggled to hide the smile it ignited as he knew what I was doing. But Levi didn't, so I ran with it for as long as I could, describing her glossy hair and contagious smile, the sway of her hips as she walked, yadda, yadda. As Levi's brows rose, Jude bit his lips and just nodded along, enjoying the ruse.

———

I found it while walking home one Thursday after Dead Law class. "Animal Shelter," said the little sign. The first time I saw it, I just stopped, dead in my tracks, and stared at it. I saw Pepper, sitting by Dad's boot near his trailer back in Clovis, laying happily on the dirt with her front paws crossed. Something tugged at my heart, and I turned and started walking toward the shelter without really thinking about it.

I almost toppled at the scent of wet dog when I opened the door, bringing back so many of my childhood memories with Pepper. *You don't have time for this,* my law school brain told me. *It's just a couple of hours a week; they're puppies!* My little girl brain shrieked back. The minute they led me into the back and I saw her—shivering in the corner of her cage, her nose turned toward the back wall and her fur growing in little tufts and patches—I knew why I had done this.

"I need to volunteer," I said out loud, to really no one in particular, as my eyes were still locked on the shaking dog in the corner.

"You *need* to?" he asked, an eyebrow cocked, rising slowly from his plastic chair. He was probably five inches taller than me, slim build, with wavy, sandy blonde hair he tried unsuccessfully to push back away from his face. Both in hoodies, we looked like an instant pair. Next to my worn-out UT number, his hoodie sported that famous photo of the four Beatles walking across whatever famous street that was, in London, I assumed.

"Maybe I *do* need to," I challenged him and raised a brow to match his, but then I smiled, and something in his demeanor shifted. It was hard to put a finger on it—a relaxation of his shoulders, a curl of a grin beginning on his face.

"I believe you do ..." Beatles paused, extending a hand to me: my cue.

"Callie," I said, shaking his hand firmly.

"Braden," he replied, matching my firm grip.

"I'm no one important here, Callie. Sorry. But, I'm happy to talk to Chuck—the director here—for you, if you'd like. Great guy, and he needs all the help he can get. I don't think they'll have any problem helping you fulfill your ... *need*," he said with that same dimple-laden smile. *Nope. We're not doing that, Callie.*

"Thank you," I said. "I don't need anything else, though." *Nice, Callie*, I scolded myself. *Your hoodie should have a mean-looking cat on it and say, 'Doesn't play well with others.'*

But Braden's smile didn't fade. If anything, it only grew and sparkled a little, which irked me for some reason. I turned sheepishly away to talk to this Chuck guy about volunteering here.

———

After a big meaty handshake from Chuck, who did turn out to be a great guy, and a "Come anytime you'd like," I made my way hesitantly back toward the pens, not sure I wanted to see Beatles Braden again. When I peeked my head around the corner, I was simultaneously relieved but also just the slightest bit saddened to see he was gone.

"Hi Lucy," I said softly to her as I approached her cage. "I'm Callie," as I eased the latch open and slipped inside. Lucy started to shake when I entered, and she jammed her nose deeper into the concrete walls forming the corner of her cell. My heart dove down in my chest at the sad sight of her. I just wanted to scoop her up in a warm blanket and spend the evening petting and soothing her, but I knew this would take time, and I only had so much to give. But I was determined to have some kind of impact on this poor animal. I didn't care if it took me months.

I sat cross-legged by Lucy in her cage, moving slowly and not looking at her, just sitting beside her, looking out of her pen like she was usually doing. Not knowing exactly what to do, I decided to just start talking to Lucy like she was a friend, something I didn't really have in Austin anyway.

"I'm just going to talk to you, Lucy," I told her, very proper and forthright, like she was a human. "Just talk and you can just listen, or don't if you don't want to, that's fine. But I'll just sit here and talk to you to see if it makes any kind of difference. I hope it does," I ventured a side glance at her, but she was still shivering and shaking vigorously with her nose buried in the corner. "I don't care if it takes months," I said. Then I proceeded to talk.

I told Lucy about my Law and Religion class that afternoon and how Mr. Strichman would sometimes spit when he got excited during his lecture. I mentioned the lilies I had just noticed by the law library that were probably going to split and bloom in a few days, and mused about what color she would probably like them best to be, eventually settling on orange. I told her some silly stories from my shifts at Cracker Barrel.

"The Lindens like hot corn bread and strawberry jelly brought to their table the minute they sit down. With at least five butters, no less than five." I realized I had been unknowingly talking with my hands. Worried that might spook Lucy, I immediately tucked them down. But, when I looked over at her—forgetting, as I had been at it for more than an hour, it was supposed to be a side glance and not a full neck move—Lucy wasn't shaking anymore. She was just laying there, still with her snout in the corner, but there was no more shivering. I didn't know whether Lucy had simply become too exhausted to keep her shaking up or whether she had felt enough at ease around me to forego it. Either way, I melted a little right there on the concrete floor of that pen.

"Alright, Miss Lucy, I'll see you next week, okay?" I phrased it as a question, as if she could reply back. "I'm just going to come and talk to you, alright? And see if that makes a difference. I don't care if it takes months," I repeated.

In the parking lot, I saw a dinged-up blue Nissan Pathfinder with a sticker near the back bumper with what looked like a simplified graphic sketch of John Lennon with block letters underneath it that read: IMAGINE.

I shook my head side to side, making the connection. *Beatles Braden*. Had to be.

———

"That's how it started anyway," I tell the boys. The two of them were still sitting perfectly poised and cross-legged on the coffee table in front of me, listening intently. Levi gave a "go on" wave of his hand, so I continued.

"Turns out," I told the boys, "that Braden was listening the entire time I was talking to Lucy, and—over the course of many weeks—I told her just about everything," I give Jude a knowing look. "Clovis, Mom, Dad, LEGOS, Biscuit Donuts, Janessa, Calliope, you name it."

Jude and Levi both straightened up and leaned back in unison, like watching a dramatic moment in a movie. "Not like spying," I defended. "Braden volunteers there, too. But, he's also a graphic design artist who helps put together marketing campaigns, digital flyers, social media content, stuff like that for small, local businesses, and he was working with Chuck at the shelter, helping him to promote their upcoming adoption drive."

"How did you find out he was listening?" Levi asked—ever the professor.

"He told me," I admitted, not liking the sound of how upfront and valiant it made Braden sound.

"He *told* you?" Levi pried. I huffed. The boys weren't focusing on the right thing. Braden's betrayal!

"A couple of months ago, Braden and I started walking to a nearby coffee shop together after our volunteering. He kept leaving these little lady's fingers from Starbucks at the front desk that he somehow found out I like." Jude bit a nail, and I scowled at him. "After it kept happening for a while, I told Braden he had to stop because I didn't want to owe him anything, and I demanded he let me get him a coffee after our shift until we were even. It was just to work off my debt," I said defensively.

Levi leaned back in his chair, like a detective piecing it all together, while Jude just remained laser-focused on me. I didn't like his penetrating stare, so I focused on Levi.

"How long has this been going on … the …" Levi searched for the right word, something that was always important to all of us, "cookie-coffee transaction," he finally decided on. Out of the corner of my eye, I saw Jude put a hand to his mouth, trying to hide a laugh. I huffed again.

"They are not just your random cookie, Levi," I nitpicked. "Have you ever eaten a ladyfinger? It's a delicate, cloud-like, life-changing experience," I attempted to hold ground. Levi just blinked and blinked until my faux charm dropped to a scowl.

"Three months," I answered, then quibbled. "Well, three months of the ladies' fingers and now I'm working toward three months of the coffees so that … we're even," I blushed.

"And, he's never tried to …" Levi let it drift off and made a little hand gesture in the air.

"Oh, he wanted to, trust me. But I told him no. Absolutely not. I'm focused on law school right now. It was a firm no," I made that clear to the boys. For some reason that was very important to me, that the boys not sense I was trying to add a fourth. At least not yet.

"We just talk. We're just friends," I finally ventured a glance at Jude, who still had his lips bit. "Braden's really interesting. He's from Germany. He's an orphan, actually. His parents both died in a pretty horrific car accident, the three of them were in when he was like ten. He suffered a torn spleen, broken ribs, and a fractured pelvis. Thankfully, he eventually healed up just fine, but his parents didn't make it. Can you imagine that? Losing both your parents so suddenly like that?" I still felt like I was defending Braden, and I didn't know why. "He had to live with an uncle after that who was pretty grim and probably borderline verbally abusive, but he was in Hamburg, where the Beatles played for, like ever, and he loved being immersed in their history and the music scene there. His uncle moved them to the States right before high school. Braden loves vinyl records. Says he has a whole collection of them. He likes to draw, too, and design. Well, obviously, that's his career. He's into dogs. Well, obviously …" I realized I'd been rambling.

"What does he look like?" Levi asked, without a tone or implication. It seemed like a straightforward question, but I should have known.

"He's tall-ish," I started, holding my hand above my head. "Dresses kind of nerdy," I giggled. "All band t-shirts and blue jeans. He's got sandy blonde hair that he's always tucking behind his ears. Green eyes.

This stupid dimple." I looked up just in time to see both boys leaning their heads to one side simultaneously.

"And you have no desire to ..." Levi did the same hand wave thing again.

"No, absolutely not." I turned to Jude.

"I was firm," I wanted Jude to know that, although I wasn't entirely sure why.

Jude finally released his lips. His shoulders softened as he leaned toward me and put his hands on my knees.

"Lil' Bit," he started, and I dove into his eyes looking for answers. "You deserve friends, your own friends, outside of me and Levi. And Tammy," he laughed. It was like Jude took a knife and expertly sliced off my gruff exterior the way only Jude could.

"You deserve far more than that, actually," Jude said, and I shook my head 'no.' Jude shook his head 'yes' and we stayed locked like that for a while. But then Jude broke first.

"*Assuming*," Jude leaned back and hooked an arm in Levi's, which Levi accepted affectionately, "we approve of this sexy, softhearted Beatles fan, you need to explore this."

Jude eyed me. "You need to let someone in, Callie. It's time," he squeezed my knee gently.

"We can't know joy," Jude said.

I squinted my eyes at Jude in protest. It was downright criminal what he was doing and using Dad's words. Although he was right, I hated the fact that I knew I was being played. Just as Braden had played me a little, too. I decided enough was enough. It was my turn.

"Okay, I'll make you boys a deal," I started, my eyes sparkling. Jude threw a brow up in response. The boys waited, always eager to engage in a juicy negotiation, as we often did over what we were going to make for dinner, who got to pick the movie this time, and where we were going to grab coffee. "If the goal is to let someone in," I glanced at Levi to let him know he was going to be implicated here, too, as it had been too long since the two of them had ganged up on me.

"I'll bring Braden somewhere to meet you two on one condition. This is an offer," I made eyes with the Professor. "And, if you *accept,* you realize we'll have a contract," I added with a wink, which set Levi into a peal of laughter that bounced off the walls like a ringing bell, making their new place feel like home.

"What's the condition?" the boys asked in unison. I smiled because I knew it. *Softies.* I had them.

CHAPTER TWENTY-SEVEN
PAWS FOR A CAUSE

"Paws for a Cause!" I practically shouted at Braden when I got to the shelter that afternoon after my classes, just a few weeks ahead of the upcoming adoption drive we had all been working toward. It had been twelve and a half weeks of lady fingers with Braden, and there was definitely something more than coffee brewing there. I couldn't quite explain it, but the animal shelter—and Lucy, really—had opened a crack in my armor. Rather than the typical drone of law school outlines that I typically recited through my head as I walked to class, dropped sweet tea off at tables, and nibbled out of a peanut butter jar in my house, I found I had started thinking *creatively* about things other than school and the law.

Braden perked up at my voice, his head popping up just as it had the first day I had come into the shelter. He was working on the official flyer for the drive, and we had all been batting around different catchy names and themes. The minute it slipped into my mind, the idea exploded like a cannon because it was such a perfect fit! After two very disheartening student suicides that year, the University of Texas had been promoting May as Mental Health Month pretty heavily, doubling down on their suicide hotline, offering psychology majors credits for a certain number of free therapy sessions, and posting flyers around campus suggesting different ways to connect with fellow students, diversify interests, and stay physically active.

"We team up with UT on this for an … *annual* May Mental Health Month pet drive, encouraging students, teachers, admin, and alumni to take time—*pause,* get it—to connect with an animal who can offer a … listening ear," I pointed to Lucy's cage. She pushed her snout into the gate on her pen as if she knew I was talking about her. *Smart girl,* I thought.

"A reason to get out for a walk, or jog," I pointed at Tigger, a rambunctious collie.

"A laugh," I pointed at Chester, a black, orange, and white Calico cat who would sit back on his haunches to play with toys and make a face that was so human—like an irritated old man—it always made Braden and me bust out laughing.

"A helping hand," I pointed to Bernie the St. Bernard Braden we'd put to use many times pulling a heavy wagon full of whatever kind of equipment we needed for the day, including the occasional kid who came to visit. Pepper had been the same. Work made Bernie thrive.

"A coffee mate," I pointed at Sassy, a perfectly groomed silky grey cat who loved to eat a "cataccino" we would make him out of steamed milk by dipping his paw in and licking it.

Braden had risen as I walked around, pointing at the different animals. "We can label each of their pens at the event with the mental health benefit they can provide, encouraging people to simultaneously take a moment—a *pause*—to focus on things that ease their mind and improve their mood and mental health while offering the animals themselves—the *paws*—a moment of empathy and joy. The hope would be that people see value in it long-term and think seriously about adopting an animal in need to help both themselves and the animal. Am I explaining it right?" I turned to look at Braden, a little out of breath.

Braden looked stunned, at a loss for words. I worried I had blown it out of proportion in my mind and that maybe it wasn't really that great of an idea at all.

"What … what do you think?" I asked, feeling that sickening, exposed feeling I always felt around Braden again.

"Braden?"

"I really like you," he said, leaving his mouth just slightly ajar afterward as if the words had just poured out. It appeared he wasn't breathing, like he was just frozen.

"You mean *it*," I corrected. "The idea. You really like it?"

Braden nodded his head 'no.' Still frozen.

"You don't like it?" I shot back, knowing I sounded a little whiny as I had really, really liked this idea.

"I meant what I said," it seemed Braden had finally recovered, his typical confident, suave demeanor returning as he closed the gap between us with three graceful steps and took a deep breath in, his chest rising with it.

"I really like you," he said again, his eyes darting left to right, looking at mine, begging—it seemed—for some kind of response. He swallowed hard. "And I love this idea, Callie. It's unbelievably perfect. I can't wait to design it. You're so …"

I got nervous and cut him off, because I wasn't sure how I would react to whatever other nonsense he was about to spout out. "Good! I hoped you would love the idea. You're going to make it phenomenal. You can design all of the little mental health benefits with graphics on their pens," I said, twirling around in place, waving at the pens. I turned to face him again and saw in his eyes that same burning need for something from me. I knew what it was. But it was my turn to play.

"And," I met Braden's eyes. "I think I like you, too. We'll find out if I *really* do at the drive," I told him, relishing in the mystery of my answer, the delicious vagueness. "Here's my number, you know, for planning and stuff."

I couldn't believe it myself. I'd just handed that over, after only thirteen lattes. *God, I was a pushover.*

———

I was nervous to text you,

I read on my screen later that night, after I got home from my shift at the Barrel. It was the first text Braden ever sent me. I had to admit I was a little nervous, too, texting back.

> I actually believe that, seeing as it took you seven months to do it.

Haha. Fair point, but I had to get creative. You know you don't give off the most … welcoming vibe, Callie.

> Valid. I don't welcome a lot of people into my little world.

Why do you call it little?

> I mean my actual friends and family. My circle. It's pretty small.

Do you like that it's little?

> I can manage little. My focus right now is school and work. As you know, relationships can get messy, … and complicated.

Life's messy and complicated.

> Not if you stay focused and on track.

I think to myself as I see my outlines scattered on my kitchen table, as well as my resume and writing samples, that I need to polish up and send them to local firms for my summer clerkship. The brochure for Goldman Carr—the crème de la crème of defense firms in Austin—is sitting on top.

Hmmmm ...

Your answer is hmmm?

No. That wasn't an answer. That was my
bullshit detector. Who else have you let into
your 'little world' this year?

Lucy.

——

On the day of the drive, we all woke to a gorgeous sunny May Day, seventy-eight degrees, and just delicious. We have brought seven dogs total and twelve cats. Braden has done a fantastic job putting together the Paws for a Cause flyer, yard signs, t-shirts, and little placards for each of the animals' pens. He really has a natural eye for graphics.

Braden has been playing things pretty suave and cool all morning, but I caught him watching me more than once. I would scrunch up my nose at him and make a face, and he would smile and look away. Having this big, consuming crush reminded me of Roddie. I'm equal parts excited and terrified by it. *What the hell am I doing?* I keep asking myself. On the cusp of my first summer working as a law clerk and going into my third year of law school, and this is the time—*now, Callie?!*—that I decide to start a relationship. It's nonsense!

Then I look over and see Lucy in her pen. Although she has made great strides in the comfort of the shelter, particularly with me—licking me the minute I walk into her pen, wagging her tail, even playing a little with toys—this new environment on the UT quad has her feeling a little spooked, so she's reverted to her old coping mechanism of jamming her nose into the corner and staying curled up. The irony of her actions is not lost on me. My 'little world' is also a pen. I make a decision.

I walk up to Braden, turn him around by the shoulder, and press my body into his. I look into his green eyes. His body is warm and comforting. I like that he's tall. I can feel his breath increasing and his heart beating, but he calmly circles his arms around me, although it's the first time, like he's done it a thousand times. His hands on my back feel like they hold me up.

I swallow my fear and kiss him. It's one of those Hallmark movie kisses at first. Time slows, and some magic camera circles around us while Brandi Carlisle sings a powerful, tear-jerking ballad. At least, that's what I heard. Braden's lips are as stupidly soft as his dimple, and we somehow know how to do all the right things with our hands and mouths. My heart is thumping. I could be peeing and I wouldn't even know it. I don't think I have any control over my body anymore. I don't think I have control over anything. But being in Braden's arms feels right. I wonder if I'm really hearing a ballad or if I've lost my hearing altogether when an all too familiar voice breaks through.

"Well, well, well."

It's Jude. A laugh bubbles out of me, and I kind of snort into Braden's lips, very romantic like. But I will never tire of hearing that voice. Jude's words have taught me, comforted me, scolded me, and guided me. I'm actually so glad he's here, but not glad at all that he caught me in this state.

I sweep a hand through Braden's blonde, wavy hair, pushing it back the way he always does—a hundred times a day—and I tuck it behind his ear.

"No matter what happens today, I've decided I like you. But, don't blow it, okay?" I raise an eyebrow at him. Braden licks his lips, and I think he might swoon. He nods his head as I turn around to introduce him.

"Braden," I start as I slip out of his embrace, already lamenting the coolness on my body that replaces his absence. I turn around and see Jude and Levi standing together, looking particularly dapper in ironed shorts and crisp pastel polos. Levi is sporting his perfect beard and a smart fedora, and I think Jude has new sunglasses that are really working for him. They must have gotten on the road before coffee to get here this early, looking that fabulous. I knew they were excited to meet Braden, but getting two gay guys primped, polished, and on the road before 8:00 a.m. is a feat.

"This is my brother, Jude, and his partner, Levi," I tell Braden, and I feel a tremendous amount of pride in being able to introduce my brother and his partner to people.

Braden's eyes pop wide for a minute, as I did not tell him he would be meeting my brother today. But from his listening in on all my conversations with Lucy, he knows far more about Jude than Jude knows about him, and that impressing Jude will earn him multiple years' worth of points with me. He clears his throat and practically shoves me aside in his effort to extend a hand, first to Jude, then to Levi.

"I'm Braden," he says. "I have no idea what Callie might have told you about me," he chuckles nervously, "but it's an honor to meet you both. Thank you for coming to our drive. Callie came up with the name: Paws for a Cause. Isn't it great?" he looks to me then, and I realize I'm blushing. Just a little. And that Braden is rattling on like a nerd—just a little. Jude is watching us too closely. I narrow my eyes at him, and I see him narrow his eyes behind his new fancy shades. Then he smiles broadly and grips Braden's hand.

"The pleasure is ours, I can assure you," he tells Braden with a wink. "We're just thrilled to see Callie playing nicely with others. She hasn't let her claws come out yet, has she?" Jude asks him.

"Only when warranted," Braden replies coolly. "She's definitely capable of taking care of herself."

Then they're all three looking at me, and I curse this entire idea. It was too soon. I've only known Braden for a few months. Okay ... *seven,* but we're just friends. *Friends who kiss?* My mind torments me. *But we only kissed just now?!* Then I realize I'm arguing with myself internally and that I probably look like a closet psychopath on the outside. Like I'm going to lock Braden in a windowless pantry tonight and skin him. Just a regular Saturday night for this crazy lady.

"Jude, I hear you're studying architecture," Braden starts, and I'm immensely grateful for the segue.

"Yeah, I've only got two more years of classes before I start studying for my ARE. My registration examination," Jude explains to Braden. "It's like the Bar Exam for Callie."

Braden nods. "Nice, congratulations. Have you designed any buildings yet?"

Jude perks up. Levi and I catch each other's eye and share a *Here we go* eye roll.

"Now *that's* the right question." Jude's smile is dazzling. Levi grabs my arm and pulls me to the side as Jude begins describing the house he's been designing since he was nineteen.

———

"Jesus, you didn't say he was gorgeous," Levi hisses at me.

"I didn't? I mentioned the blonde hair and green eyes," I feign ignorance.

Levi slaps my shoulder. "Girl, please. But way more importantly, what the hell was going on when we walked up? Who initiated that? And, is he a good kisser?"

I laugh out loud because this feels too incredibly good. So good it almost scares me. At the thought, I look over to Lucy's cage and see her with her soft little nose jammed into the corner of her pen, her body a tight curl of fear. I let out an exasperated sigh because I know what I'm going to do. She and I are going to be brave and do it together.

"Levi," I start to walk him toward Lucy's pen. "Remember that condition I told you about?"

Levi gives me a weary look. "Wait, did we officially accept your offer?" he asks.

"Now *that's* the right question," I say, mimicking Jude. "Because yes, Levi. Yes, you both did. You two verbally accepted when I presented the offer, thus forming our contract. And," I point to Jude and Braden, who are now deeply immersed, with animated hand gestures and nods, "I've now performed my end of the bargain, so …" I trail off.

"Okay," Levi concedes, holding his hands up in the air. "We were supposed to meet someone else, right?" Levi is trying to recall. "A woman? Someone close to Braden, you said. Isn't that right?"

"That's right," I confirm, but offer no more details as Levi eyes me suspiciously. I call Lucy's name from the door to her pen and enter. She immediately picks up her head, and Levi sees her big brown eyes. She looks at him, and I see something in Levi unfold. His shoulders drop, and he swallows. Lucy walks carefully toward me, her tail wagging just the tiniest bit. I sit down cross-legged near her, like I always have during the many hours we've talked. Well, I've talked and Lucy has listened. And, she curls up next to me like she's always done and lays her head in my lap. I begin petting her and talking in my usually slow and steady tone.

"Lucy, this is a really good friend of mine," I tell her. "I've told you about him many times. You remember my brother Jude. This is his partner, Levi, whom I've told you about. Remember, I said he was handsome and kind." I look briefly up at Levi, and his expression is one of extreme hope. "He also loves to read and write. He's working to become a professor. I bet he'd love to read books and essays to you and tell you stories," I tell her. As if on cue, Lucy's eyebrows go up as she looks cautiously over at Levi, but she keeps her head in my lap. "I've told Levi you are …" I pause to tap on the cute card Braden made for her pen:

> *Hi! My name is Lucy. I'm a little shy, but I can offer a:*
> LISTENING EAR

Braden has drawn a Precious Moments worthy graphic of a brown lab laying her head in a little blonde girl's lap, listening intently as she talks on and on, little letters and words floating above her head and popping. "An exceptional listener," I say.

I motion for Levi to sit down in front of me so he can reach Lucy as I continue to talk to her in my usual tone and rhythm. I take Levi's hand and place it on Lucy's neck and shoulders, encouraging him to pet her. Levi's eyes meet mine when he feels how soft Lucy's fur is. I nod and chuckle at his expression because I know the feeling. Lucy's like a dog made out of cashmere. *Perfect for two gay men,* I think.

Something inside of me unsnaps. I feel warm liquid oozing through my rib cage at the thought. *Family.* Although it's been almost three years since Dad's death, it still feels too fresh when I think about him, so I swallow the memory down and inhale sharply to control myself.

"Lucy," Levi begins nervously. "I'm so much more handsome and kind … and neater … than Jude. You'll see," Levi says, and I laugh out loud at his comment and what it means.

———

"So, this is 'the woman' we agreed to meet?" Jude says, sidling up next to me beside Lucy's pen, both of us watching Levi swoon over her. Jude is scraping a hand down his face like *Here we go.*

I don't waste this alone time with him.

"So, should I let him in?" I ask bluntly.

"Yes," Jude replies curtly, like he didn't even think about it.

Jude finally breaks his gaze away from Levi and Lucy and turns to me.

"Because that man loves you, Callie," Jude says point-blank, which takes my breath away. No one was talking love here. This was all just fun and banter, a cookie-coffee transaction. Lady fingers and lattes. I shake my head 'no' and Jude shakes his head 'yes.' I'm dumbfounded.

"I don't know when he'll work up the nerve to tell you, Lil' Bit, but I can hear it in everything he says about you—which is just about everything he says," Jude chuckles. "I can see it in the way he looks at you."

I swallow down the discomfort Jude has created.

"But what do *you* think about him?" I ask Jude.

"Callie, he's perfect. Funny, intelligent, emotionally aware. His design work is great. I wonder if he would ever get into interior design, wallpapers, or backsplashes, something. He's got a lot of talent. It also seems he's independent and motivated. He's not a scrub," which makes me laugh. "Fucking sexy as hell, too. You never mentioned that," Jude points out.

"Levi said the same," I note, to which Jude nods.

"We'll need to see his place and how he keeps it. That'll tell me and Levi everything else we need to know," which makes me laugh, realizing I'm now going to have to cajole Braden into opening up his apartment—which *I* haven't even been to yet—for a full-on Queer-Eye inspection—poor bloke.

I'm watching Braden gently put Chester back in his cage when Jude gives me his final thought.

"He's definitely a little two percent, though," Jude says.

Two percent? I wonder.

CHAPTER TWENTY-EIGHT
THE GOLDEN YEARS

"Levi, look. He's got the Eagles, Elvis, CCR, Donna Summer, and even Madonna!" Jude practically shouts.

I had been right. Braden hadn't hesitated for a second. He had eagerly invited Levi and Jude over after the drive, unabashedly. We are all mesmerized when we step into the living room of his small apartment and bask in the entire wall, floor-to-ceiling shelves, that is dedicated to Braden's record collection with a vintage Victrola in the center.

"She's brilliant," Braden says, taking the Madonna record from Jude to put on. "Really ahead of her time in the production department. But, I mean, nobody's got anything on Dolly as far as a business head goes." Braden's eyes were down on his record player, so he didn't get to see Jude and Levi mouth a silent, over-acted *Dolllly* to one another.

Braden's apartment is in immaculate shape. Strange as it might sound, it meant a lot to me that he was obviously tidy, as my spaces had always had the same "mise en place" look. I like that Braden has a particular cup for his coffee with a saucer that he uses every day. He liked teas, too, and has a pretty impressive assortment. The fronts of his cabinets are glass so that I can see everything inside: healthy foods, snacks, and neatly organized dishes. He also has an easel set up in the corner of the living room, where he was working on different sketches of the Paws for a Cause poster.

"Hey," Braden says, sidling up behind me in the kitchen as I'm looking at the frame of what appears to be a young Braden with, I presume, his dad on the counter. "That's him," he says.

"Your dad?" I ask, and Braden nods, but then I notice something familiar in the photo. "Wait? Is that?"

"It is," Braden says with a smile, looking at the photo like it takes him back fifteen years.

"That record player was your father's?" I ask. Braden takes the frame from me gently and looks at it.

"Yep," he says. "Dad called her Vicky," Braden says nostalgically. "Mom always joked he was having an affair."

Our faces are inches apart, but it feels natural.

"I hope you don't mind, I just invited them over here," he says.

"Of course not," I laugh, "but you certainly didn't have to. You know they're going to pick this place apart later and judge *everything*, right?"

Braden smiles. That stupid dimple. "They'd better, if they're looking for the person who's good enough to be with you, Callie," he says, and I feel my backstabbing knees go weak. I don't like this out-of-control feeling. It's delicious but dangerous, too.

"Pretty sure I've been falling for you since you curled up on the floor and started talking to Lucy," Braden says, putting words to my thoughts. "Everything you told her—all the stories of you growing up, with Jude, and everything you've been through. Everything you've accomplished, and yet you still have the biggest heart I've ever known."

Braden leans down then, tips my chin up to his, and places a gentle kiss on my lips that I think might completely undo me.

"Lord, Jesus, you two get a room, would you?" Jude says laughing, and I go completely pink.

"Come on, Levi, let's go make out in Braden's bedroom," to which Levi quickly puts down a record, does a pretend spray into his mouth, and follows Jude to the back. I'm giving Jude the evil eye as he saunters by. My little world is definitely growing.

I break out of Braden's makeshift hold and begin following the boys down the hall, but I turn back to Braden, and I see he is doing a little dance in the kitchen—a very nerdy one at that.

"We figured if you two were okay with a little PDA," Levi says, smiling at me. He rushes over to me quickly, before Braden comes in. "Callie, just yes. Yes, yes, yes. The whole thing. Nothing has ever felt more right. Braden. Lucy. That record collection?! A thousand times, yes."

Levi's shaking my shoulders with the goofiest grin on his face, making me giggle. I see Jude over his shoulder, looking at us wistfully, and I realize the best part about potentially meeting someone new is that I now have friends to share it with.

———

Over the next few months, the four of us fell into an easy pattern of visiting and staying at each other's places—Braden's or the boys'— every other weekend or so. We learned to cook together, listened to every record in Braden's collection, caught new movies and restaurant openings, and just slowly got to know one another. We all became fiercely competitive players of Scrabble, Taboo, Cards Against Humanity, and even putt-putt golf. "Come here, pretty boy," Jude would growl, chasing Levi around the course with his club.

Our absolute favorite, however, was tug of war. Lucy was the hands-down champion, ruthless in her refusal to let go of the tattered little rope toy the boys had picked up for her the Sunday after the drive—along with just about everything in the store that said "dog" on it. Anything with feathers. Anything pink. The gal went from sad and lonely in her pen to the best kind of pampered princess.

As soon as Braden or I came through the front door, she would do this whole body wiggle toward us with something jammed in her mouth—usually one of her million pink toys but occasionally a shoe, a Kleenex box, a sock, anything she could find. And, Lucy smiled! A real dog smile. It looks like bared teeth with her eyes all squinty, like the Cheshire cat, and she breaths kind of raspy through her teeth when she's doing it, but her full-on butt wiggle tells you she means no harm. Watching Lucy blossom was one of the greatest joys of my life during those years. And they were some pretty amazing, exceptionally golden years.

The four of us dubbed them that for all the obvious reasons, but also because I got the clerkship position with the prestigious insurance defense firm in Austin—Goldman Carr. I was told that if I worked hard enough and proved myself, they might offer me an official associate position after I graduated *If I worked hard enough.* The phrase had actually made me laugh.

I dove headfirst into it, only researching and writing at first, but it wasn't long before several partners had me tagging along for site inspections, hearings, and even depositions. The firm primarily repre-sented insurance companies, defending against claims from home and business owners with property damage or people injured in accidents who had sued for liability. Desperate to please and prove myself, I came in early every morning at Goldman Carr and stayed late while Braden started with a local design firm in downtown Austin.

It wasn't long before he and I had moved into Braden's little apartment, as I had no space suitable for his staggering record collection in my rental. On nights that we weren't hanging out with Jude and Levi, Braden and I would both come home from work and school tired and strung out, but we would pile up on the plush rug in his living room, put on a record, pour a glass of wine, and share our days with one another. I'd even started eating out of peanut butter jars, singing off-key, and watching true crime with popcorn late at night in front of Braden, thinking of Jude and how he found he could finally be his "complete self" around Levi.

Braden and I had carried the Paws for a Cause theme—which, Chuck was right, was the inaugural of many and helped dozens of animals in need get adopted each year—through our texts. If one of us were having a moment and needed to unleash, share, or just vent, we would reach out to the other for a mental health break.

Paws for a cause?

Braden might text.

UT Shelter at your service, where listening is our passion.

We always threw in some cheesy tag line.

What type of service do you need?

Was our standard response.

A partner in crime.

What type of crime are you looking to commit, Sir?

I'm going to kill Luke. Again.

While Braden loved his job, he occasionally hated his boss, Luke.

Ahh, what method will you be using this time, Sir?

Electrocution.

One of our specialties! We can certainly help you with that.

I was an equally frequent user of Paws for a Cause.

Paws for a cause?

UT Shelter at your service, where bullies come to cry. What type of service do you need?

I need a sketch artist.

I want to get really drunk tonight and draw
ugly caricatures of Wesley.

We can certainly help with that. What
should your partner Wesley be doing in
these caricatures?

I giggle because I know Braden will immediately start the sketch and present it to me—along with some elegant handmade cocktail that he probably named The Death of Wesley with ingredients to match—when I get home. We'll spend the evening sprawled out on the plush rug in the living room, bashing Wesley and cheering our immensely better life decisions.

Eating pencils.

Vile. We specialize in vile.

Then shitting them out bloody and
half-digested.

Wicked. And graphic. Have I told you yet
today, how much I love you?

After that request? You must be joking.

———

"This joker? Sure, I'll take him," I told the chaplain when—three years after moving in together—Braden and I got married at City Hall. Jude and Levi, and even Lucy as the flower girl, had been there. Afterward, we all went out to eat at this hole-in-the-wall dim sum place we had all gushed over in downtown Austin. I found this really trashy, poofy thrift store prom dress number that I wore for the ceremony, while Braden rocked a purple velvet ruffle-collar disco suit and Jude and Levi donned bell-bottoms, too-tight shirts, and rose-colored John Lennon glasses. We piled into the dim sum place in our seventies getups and laughed until we cried at the sight of me in all my taffeta, trying to sit down cross-legged on the floor and spilling saki all over Levi in the process.

Levi was thriving, having graduated and obtained his teaching certificate, he had taken his first job teaching English at a community college in Houston, finding his passion in sharing literature with curious minds. Jude had graduated from Houston's architectural program and was working toward the ARE exam. And—after months pacing our apartment, eating peanut butter, and alarming Braden with my robotic recitation of legal causes of action, I passed the Bar. I accepted the associate position with Goldman Carr.

———

I found the work thrilling at first, although—after a couple of years at the firm—I had started to sense some of the lines of questioning and legal arguments my partners were training me to make felt unfair, a little like we were playing games with the law.

"Are you happy?" Jude had asked me one night, when he and I had settled onto the boys' back porch after dinner with a bottle of wine.

The question had almost made me laugh out loud because my knee-jerk, completely honest reaction would have been: "No, because I'm not even here." What I didn't want to tell Jude was that Calliope had come back.

Somehow, when I wasn't looking, she'd slipped in, slinking her arms into mine, craning my head up, and possessing me to run myself to the bone trying to please everyone and perform perfectly at the firm as the pressure mounted. I wasn't sure how and when all these financial obligations had stacked on me. My purchase of what I would have called a "fancy house" growing up—only because it was a split-level with a wall of shelves for Braden's records—had come with a mortgage, insurance, HOA, and upkeep payments larger than I had anticipated. My agreement, at the firm's prompting, to sign up for life insurance,

LTD insurance, a 401k, and IRA contributions—all very prudent, but expensive things—had meant I came home with only a fraction of my salary and very little leftover time. I wanted to tell Jude I was beginning to sense the weight of the structure being built around me, containing me in a cell doing work I was beginning to think I did not love, and that I was starting to wonder if my big fat salary was truly better than what our parents had done, living paycheck to paycheck. Emphasis, however, on *living*.

I remember Mom baking in the sun in the back yard on one of our worn-out tri-fold lawn chairs, drinking beer, and thinking not one thought about work. I never saw her reading work papers at night at the kitchen table. I remember Dad singing and joking while loading up Blackie for a long-haul run, without one nauseous worry—like I had daily—about making a mistake that could sink our case, disappoint my partners, embarrass the firm, cost my clients millions.

"Am I happy? I'm tired," I had responded to Jude, only half joking. "And stressed," not joking at all.

Lucy had curled up next to Jude on the porch swing, and he was lazily stroking her glossy chocolate head.

"I know you are," Jude said. "We all know."

"You *all*? Is this something you guys talk about often?" I bristled.

Jude gave me a look. *Calm down.*

"I'm just asking, now that you've accomplished the big, huge dream—you got out of Clovis, you went to college, became a professional with a big salary, a house, a husband—are you happy? What else do you want in life, Callie? Kids?"

"Kids!" I just about spit up my wine. The thought of trying to work, caring for a screaming, pooping infant, into my sixty-hour work weeks at Goldman Carr literally seemed laughable. But then the question really seeped in. And, because this was Jude, I gave him my honest, knee-jerk answer.

"I don't think I should, Jude. Considering my torturous relationship with Mom, I'm not sure I want to perpetuate that cycle."

"And that's all Mom's fault?" Jude asked, pushing as hard as I could ever remember. My defenses went up.

"Oh, you're going to take her side? Mom's not some angelic little six-year-old with an innocent heart and big Precious Moments eyes. She's like one of the bad gremlins, after you pour water all over it."

Jude laughed, a sound like bells tumbling out over the lawn.

My body calmed.

"I'm just saying," after he recovered. "You've climbed the hill, Callie. You're at the top. You got your law degree. You can keep working for that firm, make partner, make a million, whatever, and that's all great, if it's what you *want*. All I'm saying is it's time for you to start asking yourself the tough questions. What kind of home—*life* do you want to build up here on this hill? Who and what is important to you? This is the hard part, Lil' Bit."

Jude's questions had been haunting me for months because I knew he was right. I knew I wasn't spending enough quality time with Braden, often giving him only a half hour of time in the evenings, outside of reading depo transcripts or medical records at the table over dinner. He'd wanted us to get a dog, and I had initially loved the idea, reminiscing on my fond memories with Pepper. I'd told him we would when "things settled down at the office." That had been over a year ago. It had been even longer since Braden and I had lain on the rug and listened to his records all evening.

I also had not been back to Clovis since I left over nine years ago, and I only talked to my mom two or three times a year. Was that a terrible thing? Did I miss her? Did she miss me? Would I regret not having tried harder with her? I honestly could not answer those questions, and I didn't have time to ponder them.

I knew, with the stress and pace at Goldman Carr, that I was starting to question whether my life was *balanced*. But I couldn't let myself believe all that work—those millions of rolled silverwares, hundreds of bowls of Cream of Wheat in the dark, and hours spent reciting and pacing—may have been directed at the wrong goal. Nonsense. I pushed the scary thought aside.

But, my life—currently consumed by work—was beginning to feel like a washing machine out of balance, spinning wonky, squealing out, threatening to break.

Then it did.

CHAPTER TWENTY-NINE
DOORSTEP

The doorbell surprises us both—Braden and me—on a rare evening where I am thankfully not imprisoned to the kitchen table poring over documents, and we are watching a show together, eating pizza on the couch. Someone ringing the doorbell at night was a pretty rare occurrence in the gated community in Austin where we lived.

When I first peer through the little peephole, I almost don't recognize him. He's just a disheveled guy on our doorstep, his hands shoved in his jean pockets, ripped and greased around the edges like he'd been wearing them for years. His appearance scares me a little at first. I worry this drifter could be trouble. Then he raises his head, and we make eye contact. He'd grown so much. Even overlooking the black eye and bandage on his left cheek that had soaked through with dried blood, his face looks ten years older than mine. But his eyes haven't changed. They are moist and blinking rapidly, seeming to plead with the door, but they are the same. I know those eyes. Those eyes know me.

Jay.

I fling the door open. "Jay, oh my God! How did you? What happened? What … Are you okay?" I flip on the porch light, revealing his sad reality—the trash bag of clothes on the porch next to his feet, the lack of any car he'd driven here, his greasy hair, and musty scent.

I look back at Braden to gauge his reaction to this living piece of my dirty past, standing right here on our doorstep. He just stands there breathlessly watching us, his mouth open.

"I need you," is all Jay says.

For some reason, I know in that moment, I need him, too. I need a second chance with Jay to right the wrong I did back in Clovis. He is my cousin. If he needs me, I need to help him. I've never been more sure of anything.

———

"I'm not so sure about this, Callie. Is it a good idea?" Braden whispers, as I'm rustling around in our dresser drawers, trying to find some pajama bottoms and a shirt of Braden's that Jay can borrow after he gets out of the shower, where I had forced him immediately without a word.

I set the t-shirt I'm holding down to turn around and face Braden, disbelieving for a moment that I heard him correctly.

"A good idea?" I repeat, feeling some creature inside me stand to the full height of the room and pop her knuckles.

Braden immediately puts his hands up.

"I know Jay's your cousin, Callie. I know. You've told me a lot about him. But, we have no idea what he's been doing for what, the last ten years?"

Although I feel the temperature of my blood rise, I wait—because he didn't ask me a question.

"I just," Braden shoves his hands forcefully through his hair. "I know this sounds completely heartless of me. Trust me, I know. If it were anyone but you, I wouldn't even put words to these thoughts. But I'm being honest in telling you he scares me a little, Callie. Something about him feels … disruptive."

I slam the drawer.

"I'm afraid of what he might bring into our home. I'm just telling you what I'm feeling, Callie."

"Yeah? Imagine what *he's* feeling," I realize I'm cutting Braden no slack here, but I can't stop myself. It's Jay. And, a second chance for me to undo what I did before. Not many people get those.

Braden is silent, his eyes swimming in worry.

"Jay's always felt like he was tossed away, because he was. I saw it happen time and again. I will not be just another person in his life who does that to him." What I don't say is *Again,* although it's true. "Jay's not trash," I fume.

"I never said that," Braden defends.

"You said he's not a good idea."

"I just told you this worries me. I mean, are you going to just let him move in? Live here with us? For the foreseeable future?" Braden's hands are flinging with every phrase.

"If he needs to," I say, stone cold.

"I'm your husband, Callie. I know you bought this house, but I live here, too. All I'm asking is that we talk about this first, and that you listen to what I'm feeling. What I'm worried about."

It angers me that Braden sounds so fucking rational.

"What are you so worried about?"

Braden bites down on his lips.

"I'm worried the lengths you might go to here because you see him as family, and you're the most loyal person I've ever met."

My cheek twitches as I cringe internally, thinking how utterly and totally wrong he is on that one.

"I don't want to see you bend over backwards. Give too much of yourself. Loan him a bunch of money, or let him take, I don't know, other things from you. I'm worried he might take advantage of you somehow, Callie, is all I'm saying. Is that such a bad instinct to have?"

We stand in a stalemate, and I'm pierced with the realization that this is our first big fight. I look away.

"Well, my instinct right now is to help my cousin," I pick up the clothes for Jay and start walking out of the room. "I'm at least going to find out what he needs."

———

I step into the guest bedroom that now feels entirely too small and forever changed with Jay's presence in it. I click the door shut for Jay's privacy. Jay is standing by the bed. He does look better, pinker after the hot shower and freshened up in a clean long sleeve and pajama pants of Braden's, rather than the dingy plaid and jeans I'd found in his duffel, which I'll simply be throwing out. I had insisted on the fresh clothes. Jay combed his hair after the shower, giving him a schoolboy look, but the image immediately shatters. I inhale sharply when Jay turns toward me, and I see the deep, open gash on his left cheek.

"I know," Jay says, trying to lighten the mood. His eyes meet mine for a second. They are the same deep brown but somehow so much older. They still have a little twinkle, though, like when he would do his voices and make up stories for our toys. "I'm not going to win any beauty pageants," Jay says, which surprisingly does make me chuckle just a little, and I am amazed he can still make me do that. Jay was still funny.

"Will you help me dress it?" he asks.

The wound is deep. I can see just a sliver of bone, pearly and wet. Mostly it's just pushed-away flesh, but the wound is now clean. It seems it might have been made by a blunt strike. The corner of a piece of furniture—I know first-hand—or perhaps a fall to the street, if I had to guess.

"The folks who were renting Grandma Peggy's place up and left last year, so I moved back in. I don't know if your mom told you. I know you two don't talk much."

The bluntness of it hurts me, but I know Jay isn't trying to hurt me. It's just the truth. We don't.

I squirt some Neosporin onto a piece of gauze and begin dabbing it onto the wound. Jay grimaces but holds firm.

"It wasn't good for me to be there alone," Jay says, which tells me far more than those few words. I keep quiet, letting Jay fill the space.

"I know you probably hadn't heard about me and Katie." I had, albeit extremely briefly.

Mom had mentioned her in one of our couple-of-times-a-year calls. "Jay married a girl in Portales," she'd said. "Katie's her name. We think she's pregnant." I hadn't asked for many more details, and Mom hadn't seemed interested in providing more.

"I heard you got married," I said, not making eye contact. "Congrats," I said as I met his eyes.

I startle as a loud cackle erupts from him. It isn't the reaction I had expected. His laugh starts genuine, but it turns, twisting like a knife, halfway through until it morphs into something sinister before fizzling. His eyes cloud, turning a dark mahogany.

"We had to get married. Shotgun, ya know," he chuckles, but his eyes are on his lap. "Can you see Grandma Peggy with a shotgun?" Jay asks, which brings a smile to my face as I imagine her poofy old lady hair behind the scope.

"She had Amber just a few weeks after our wedding in Debbie's backyard," Jay's hands do something awkward in his lap, as if he's trying to hold—or drop—something. "Stinky little thing," Jay looks up at me, trying to smile, but it seems he couldn't manage it (from the pain of his wound or emotion, I'm not sure), so he just looks back down. "But she was cute, Callie. She was." *Was.* My breath catches in my throat.

Jay swallows. "A few months later, Katie told me Amber wasn't mine and left."

I gasp. Mom hadn't told me that part yet.

"She just. Left."

I'm not sure I'm still breathing.

"It's stupid that I miss that little girl when I am nothing to her. She will probably never even know I existed. She'll never know I was the one who pinned her little diapers all wrong and tried to sing little lullabies to her. You know what a bad singer I am." Jay's attempt at humor fails completely. He just keeps staring at his hands.

"I started drinking myself away and just … never stopped." Jay takes in a deep breath and lets it out. "A few years passed that way. Vodka in the morning. Slogging my way through work at Guthals—you know, that landscaping outfit on Prince Street. Beer and whiskey in the evening till I passed out. Wake up. Do it again. Pass out. Wake up. Do it again." Jay fiddles with the cuff of Braden's shirt, then clasps his hands in his lap.

"I woke up in my front yard two days ago. My truck was parked in the yard, and the front door was open. Still running," Jay shakes his head at that. "I must have busted my face on the porch steps on the way down and walked away with this prize," Jay motions toward his cheek.

He surprises me, then slips down to the floor, like he has no spine. Jay puts his hands on my knees, buries his head into them. I can see his shoulders shaking as I feel hot tears I didn't know had been forming spill onto my cheeks.

"I'm not sure I should even still be alive. I don't deserve to be, but I do want to be," Jay says. "Here," he says, staring into my eyes. "I knew I had to get out of Clovis. You were the only person I could think of who might help me, but I won't be a burden, Callie. I promise," he insists. "I promise," he says again, pulling my hands into his and mashing them together in a sad little snotty temple of fingers. "I'm going to check myself into this rehab center I found here in Austin tomorrow. I just need help paying for it, at first. But I'll pay you back. Every cent. I promise."

Braden's words slip through my mind, making me take a moment longer than I would have liked to answer, and I blame him for it.

"Of course you will," I say, in a tone even I don't recognize. Braden's got me all mixed up. "I know you will," I repeat.

Jay raises his head to look at me. There's something in his eyes.

"I really need something more than the money, though, Callie. Because I know—*I know*—I will pay you back. That's not the important part. What I really need right now is to know there's someone out there who cares about me. Who *wants* me to get better? Someone who knew me before I … gave up. If I have that, I know I can do this. I can turn my life around if I have you in my corner, Callie," Jay says, rendering me both captive and speechless with his piercing stare, framed by the gruesome wound on his cheek.

"I think everyone deserves a second chance, don't you?" Jay lets the question linger.

I flinch at that phrase and match Jay's piercing stare. *Does he know?*

He knows.

"I do," I respond. "I'm here for you this time, Jay."

———

Back in my bedroom, I slip into the cool sheets of my bed with Braden—my brain racing through the emails and deadlines I need to tackle tomorrow, my hearing at 11:00 a.m., my agreement to take Jay first thing to the rehab center and visit every week, and what this really all means for me, expanding my family and obligations at a time when they are only increasing daily at work. Then there's Braden and what I seemingly just did to him—opening *our* world up against his will.

"So what does he need, Callie?" Braden finally asks.

"You'll be happy to know he won't be living here with us," I say, curtly.

"Callie, come on, don't …" but I cut him off.

"But, don't worry. You were right, Braden."

Braden holds his breath.

"He needs money," I say as I shut off the light and we go to bed.

———

Immediately after dropping Jay off at the rehab center the next morning—which is a nice sprawling campus with an impressive staff and mission that gives me hope for Jay—I call Jude. He's the only other person who could understand the gravity of what went down on my doorstep last night. After I share the details, including Braden's surprising reaction, I have to ask him.

"What would you have done, Jude?"

Jude is quiet for a bit.

"I'm not the right person to ask, Callie," Jude says, which shocks me.

"That's stupid, why not you? You're the only other person in the world who knows Jay as well as I do."

"Yes, but I'm not you, Callie. I don't fall in with the Levis and Callies of the world. I'm a taker," Jude says.

"So, me? I'm the giver?" I ask, although I know the answer.

"You know you are," Jude calls me out. "You give your time, your energy, even your body if it's required. Do you know how many times you let Jay and me launch you over a fence so you could 'clear the area' for us? All the silly, but impossibly cute, cards you made me for my birthdays? The times you came over to visit Dad, even when he ignored you to go out drinking, and you didn't even react? You would just come back the next weekend, full of hope again, like it had never happened. You and Mom clash because you're so much alike—you're stubborn, disciplined, but you're both deeply loyal to family. You two would never be able to do to people what Dad and I sometimes can." This unique comparison to Mom stings me.

"I wasn't always loyal." I tell Jude about my lie to Jay back in junior high, my betrayal of him, which elicits a slow whistle out of Jude.

"Jesus, Callie. Lifetime movie much?"

"I was fourteen," I defend weakly.

"I'm not saying what is right or the best, safest choice for you and Braden, Callie, but I know what you're going to do. It's programmed into you like DNA. This is why family flocks to you. Like Mom, you're the big beating heart, the provider, the comforting net. Thankfully, you're just not nearly as mean. Yet," Jude says, trying to lighten things.

I'm quiet, confused whether these are compliments or just unfortunate truths.

"You're asking me," he picks back up, "but you already know what you're going to do. Both because you want to right your past wrong. You want this second chance. And because Jay is family—I agree. At least until he proves he's not, but I believe he will be loyal to you till the day he dies for what you're doing for him now. You'll probably save him, Callie. But, even considering how I feel about Jay, I'm a bit with Braden on this one. I would have been more hesitant to open my home, my wallet, my life immediately to Jay. I," Jude searches for the right word, "would have been more protective of my little world, my happiness, than agreeing so readily to expose it to this entirely new person."

"But he's not entirely new," I interrupt. "It's our cousin, Jay."

"Whom you haven't seen in ten years. I'm not saying I wouldn't have done it, Lil' Bit. I'm just saying I can understand Braden's feelings."

"But you were there yourself, Jude! You stood on Levi's doorstep in almost the same condition, asking for help, too!" I find Jude's taking of Braden's side blindsides me. Again.

"I know that, Callie. But that's my whole point. That is the reason *I* was the person on the doorstep, and *Levi* was the person answering the door. Think about it, Callie. No matter how far down the hole you might fall, what kind of trouble you might get into, or how—oh, perfect example—how much *help* you needed during college and law school and just how many family members' doors did you go knocking on to ask for it?"

I know the answer. But Jude's bullshit precision logic is irritating me.

"That's different," I try to fight him.

"Oh, is it?" Jude clucks.

"Just don't let your impervious—yes, that's your word today, Counselor—*impervious* desire to help Jay, for reasons both selfish and noble, harm your relationship with Braden. That man will do anything for you, Callie. Don't abuse that."

I hang up with Jude feeling irritated, worried, and motivated all in one. But, Jude's right. I've already decided to pay for Jude's rehab and help support him through it. Truth is, in the long run, whether Jay pays me back or not, I can afford it, and I couldn't live with myself if I had turned my back on him again. The rest I'll have to figure out after I visit Jay next week, and the week after that, and the week after that, to see if he's truly committed to this change. I can only hope Braden will come with me and start to see what I see in Jay.

CHAPTER THIRTY
OUR PROTE-JAY

I'm stunned out of words. Of all the mess and problems I had just caused, I didn't know I had dragged Braden's beautiful mind and body down into this hell with me. Bricks in walls that once stood firm around me begin to crumble and fall to the ground. I taste bile.

"Is Braden?" I ask Mariah shakily.

"He's in the ICU, Callie," Mariah tells me, laying her hands on my forearms, trying to calm me down. "He's alive."

I feel my body deflate into an empty sack of skin on the mattress.

"He had a lacerated spleen and a collapsed lung, among other injuries," Mariah carries on. "Then he developed a really bad infection. He's fighting for his life," she grabs my hand and squeezes hard. "We don't know exactly whose fault it was, or who was even driving your … the Pathfinder," she corrects herself. "So, just …"

I turn my head to the window as my breathing betrays me, coming in and out in short rasps that don't fill my lungs. My body starts sweating again, immediately and profusely. Tears fill my eyes and spill over, but I have no words—my *handsome, kindhearted Braden.*

"I've gotta go, Callie," Mariah tells me. "Detective Carter is waiting for me. I'll be back as soon as I know anything new, okay? You know everything I know now, I promise." Her voice sounds like it's gone underwater as a buzzing tone fills my ears. The window and blinds go blurry before my tear-brimmed eyes.

"I'll be back, okay, Callie," I hear her say forcefully as she exits my room.

As soon as I hear my door click shut, I sob. I just let it rack my body and fill my eyes and pour out of me, and I swim in this sense of feeling impossibly guilty. *What have I done?*

Whatever little ounce of strength I had somehow mustered to get through this feels like it has just been blown away. One gust and it disintegrated into thin air, leaving me tumbling back down to my murky depths. My hands slide down the walls, and my nails catch on one last cliff, but I look at the digital clock, and the numbers displayed there do it. Two. Three. Four. Like a haunting, they reach out and pluck each finger to send me plummeting again.

———

2:34 in the morning. 2:34 in the morning. I will never, for the rest of my life, forget 2:34 in the morning. The problem was that the years and months leading up to 2:34 in the morning felt like some of the best of my life.

———

The day after Jay knocked on our door and came back into my life, I went to visit him at the rehab center, even skipping two hours from work to do it, making me feel both nauseous for neglecting work and simultaneously proud for putting family first. Jay's crash into our lives also showed me how much time Braden had been spending at the house alone, as he worked remotely most of the time now, and I left early and came home late, day after day after day.

Braden and I had been stiff but polite to one another in the initial days of Jay's entry into the rehab. But, I'd eventually caved and told him Jude had agreed with him, in part—a concession Braden did not take lightly, as he knew any opposition from Jude would weigh more heavily on me than opposition from him. It was just a fact. Braden did not boast about it, though, or get defensive, a testament to his wisdom and love for me.

"I just want what's best for you, Callie," he'd reiterated, and I believed him.

"I know you do, and I'm grateful for it. But, you know, I have to do this. He's family."

"I know. I knew you would. The minute he showed up. That's why I worried. I don't know him at all, Callie—but you, I most certainly do—and I know how much you can give. I just. I don't want you to give up too much of yourself for someone who may not deserve it."

Braden could say that because Jay wasn't in the room. He was in rehab, working hard to get better. He was doing everything I'd made him promise me when I dropped him off that first morning.

"Do this, Jay. Commit. Stay sober and contribute to our family, and you are welcome in it."

"I will, Cousin," he'd said. "You have given me my second chance. I won't waste it."

"And, you gave me mine," I'd told him.

Feeling there was no clear 'right or wrong' when it came to Jay— just difficult decisions and emotions as essential as blood on either side—I decided to give Braden an offering to help us work around our most contentious disagreement yet: Jay.

"I do work too much. You're right about that, Braden," I told him over dinner the second week of Jay's rehab. While I had seen Jay multiple times, Braden had yet to visit him—with me or without— and we'd been circling the issue like cats at home, both flinching and hissing when the issue of Jay came up. Enduring a stalemate with my own husband was making me nauseous.

"How about this. I promise to try to work on it. I'll see if I can work some hours remotely, or transition out of litigation to a different department at the firm, like wills and estates, or something that requires less hours, I don't know, but I promise you I will try … if,"

Braden looked up at me, then, his eyebrows raised.

"If you'll promise to just give Jay a chance. He's really making strides in rehab. Hasn't had a drink in weeks, obviously, but he's also joined activities. He's reading and participating in all the group sessions. He's even taken up carpentry, building shelves and things. I think you two would really hit it off," I told him. Braden had remained quiet about it the rest of the evening, so I picked it back up the following morning. If anything, I am persistent.

"Bring some playing cards or, hell, even LEGOs. You guys would have fun. Channel your inner kid," I told Braden sprightly, firing off the idea while in my work suit, headed out the door to the office at 5:45 in the morning.

"Says the adult," Braden responded, smashing his face into the pillow, waiting for me to leave so he could go back to sleep.

———

Braden proved to be much better at channeling his inner kid than I, especially on weekdays. While Braden kept his right under the surface, all fed, groomed, and happy, I often felt like I had drowned my inner kid in vats of coffee and run her over on my way to work. I was thrilled to see Braden finally start visiting Jay and the two of them growing as friends. Although Braden would usually come home afterward, invigorated and trying to get me to play Uno or a board game with him in the evening, I was just too beat. He and I had also talked about renting a van or RV and going on a road trip, but I had yet to take a vacation.

We had flirted with the idea of renovating the loft above our two-car garage as a studio for Braden or a rental space, but I couldn't find the time to focus on it. We still had no dog. I still worked most weekends. Even I was ready to admit it. Calliope was getting tired.

For this reason, the most exciting thing coming up on my calendar was not my big summary judgment hearing before Judge Duncan, as it likely should have been, but the day I'd planned to bring the boys to the rehab center to reunite with Jay.

———

"Bring Lucy, too," I'd told the boys. "She's just as much family as you two are," which was met with snorts and a "Honey, please," from Levi.

"Might I point out, *we* are human. *She* is canine," Levi said in his proper professor voice.

"My point exactly. Makes her better than you two combined," I said, dismissing him outright. But Levi just looked down at Lucy, "the second love of my life," he would always say to her, petted her soft brown head, and agreed with me. "True," he said to her and nuzzled her neck. Lucy thumped her tail all over and licked Levi mightily.

Jay had asked during our frequent visits if I had heard anything about Jude, and—although I felt bad lying to him—I had been very vague and told him I thought Jude might be in California or Houston but that I was still trying to find him. This time it was a well-intentioned little while lie because I wanted to surprise Jay.

"Oh no. This isn't some kind of pitiful Make-a-Wish visit, is it? Please tell me you guys didn't do that to me?" Jay looked genuinely worried, which had Braden and me rolling.

"Make-a-Wish?" I cackled at Jay. "You're not dying!"

"That's like for kids with terminal cancer," Braden was laughing just as hard as I was. "I don't know that they do that for adults who just

… drink too much." I laughed even harder. It was nice that we could have a little fun with this. It showed me how far Jay had come.

"Besides, who would we get for you?" I was having too much fun with this to just let it go. "Sylvester Stallone?"

Immediately, Jay went into impersonation mode, throwing on a sloppy, thick-tongued Italian accent. "I dunno, Adrian. I-uh thought jews would, you know, reach for da stars for me."

Braden and I are doubled over.

"What about Eddie Murphy? Should we have gotten him for you?" Braden asks through a snicker, and I love to see him loving this so much.

Instantly, Jay transforms into Eddie before our eyes. "But then I'd come walk up here, looking all fly in my head-to-toe red pleather, doing my thang, and all these fools here would want to party with me. And, start drinking. And, I … I just think that might be a problem for this, uh, you know, facility and all."

"Stop it, STOP!" I interject because my sides are hurting. We could do this all day. But I'm too excited for this reunion. "Jay, I need you to promise me something, okay?"

Jay is recovering from his own laughter. He clears his throat and looks at me with too much seriousness, but I know he means it.

"Anything, Callie. I would do anything for you," he says. I can feel Braden's eyes cut over to me in the moment.

"It's nothing big … yet," I tease. "Just close your eyes, okay?"

"Oh, please let it be Scarlett Johansson," Jay says as he closes his eyes and makes boob-grabbing motions with his hands. "Or I'd settle for … what's that chick's name in Gossip Girl?" He opens one eye to Braden.

"Blake Lively," Braden responds, and I'm thrown.

"You guys watch Gossip Girl?" I ask incredulously, but then

immediately decide we're getting off track. "Wait, I don't care. It's not a girl," I tell Jay. "Just close your damn eyes and roll with this, okay?"

"Okay," Jay says, smiling, and he closes his eyes again. "But I don't get to control what's on the TV here, just for the record. You have to watch whatever is on." Braden is shaking his head 'no' at me. He mouths the words *Not true* and I giggle, then hop up to jog around the corner and let Jude and Levi know it's time for them—and Lucy—to come around and see Jay.

———

"I smell cologne," Jay says as the boys and I approach, which causes a bubble of laughter to erupt out of Levi. He pokes Jude in the rib and whispers, "I told you, you wear too much." Jude rolls his eyes.

Jay has rearranged his face—eyes still closed—into a funny expression. He has turned his blind, funny face toward me as if he's directing this question-of-an-expression at me. However, I wonder how he knows where I'm standing in this lineup. I sniff under my arms to check, but then decide I can't stand it any longer.

"Okay, Jay, open your eyes," I tell him, and so Jay does. He blinks a few times, seeming somewhat confused. He looks at Levi, briefly down at Lucy, who is sitting patiently before him, then Jay's eyes fall on Jude, and he leaps out of his seat.

"Holy shit, JUDE!" Jay screams. Jude pops up and they grab one another in a bear hug that starts to spin in a circle. Lucy's up and thumping. Levi's brows are knitted in awe.

"Hey, Jay," Jude says. "It's good to see you."

"Good to see *me*?" Jay asks, and he puts a hand instinctively to the wound on his cheek, which hasn't yet healed completely, then drops it. "It's good to see *you*, Jude. You look like a million bucks!" Jay is practically shouting. He has his hands on Jude's shoulders as he takes him in.

I have to admit Jude is looking rather snappy in a fitted polo tucked into khaki pants with a woven belt, but Jude always looks snappy. Jude is the king of snappy.

"I want you to meet my partner, Levi," Jude says, motioning for Levi to stand. Jay doesn't seem surprised at all to see that Jude is gay and has a partner. I'm guessing he always knew. Jay stands and extends a hand to Levi, who slaps it away.

"That's not how we greet family," Levi says as he pulls Jay into a big, warm hug. Jay meets my eyes, and I feel like I can see them overflowing. Like he has too many blessings to count, which I have to believe must feel true because they've just tripled before his eyes. *Family.*

The five of us talk amicably for a bit, with Lucy enjoying the frequent head scratches from Levi and Jay, catching up on what's been going on in everyone's lives over the past ten years. Both Jude and Jay skim over the rough parts.

Levi asks Jay what it's "really like in there," he says, pointing to the facility with a bit of a scary face. "Are there like people drooling in corners or drawing on the walls with crayons?" Levi asks, which makes us all laugh.

"It's not an insane asylum," Jay answers, chuckling. "I mean, people here are dealing with some very dark shit, though," he admits. "It's actually given me a lot of perspective. My story is, well, just my story. I can seem sad, sure, but it's not nearly as tragic as some I've heard in here. I feel really lucky that I have so much life ahead of me, and I'm still healthy and have friends and family who care about me. I'm not in jail for DUI or manslaughter or anything. All I have to do is make good choices, work hard, and be good to my family," he looks first to me, then Braden, then Jude, then even Levi and Lucy.

"We're going to get you through this, cousin," Jude says after an hour of us chatting, and I see something pass briefly over Jay's face. A muscle pulls at the edge of his wound.

"Cousin," Jay repeats the word in awe. "I'll be the best one you've ever had," he tells Jude, and it doesn't sound cheesy at all. "I'm …" Jay is searching for the right word. "More grateful than words could ever convey," he finally decides on.

"Good," Jude says. "Not everyone gets second chances," Jude looks up at me briefly, then over to Levi.

"Trust me, Cousin. Don't squander it."

Jay looks at me again, and I'm unnerved.

"This is way better than Sylvester Stallone," he says, holding one hand up to hide his finger pointing at Jude. This sends Jude into a peal of laughter that ignites us all.

———

After our initial visit, Jude and Levi made a habit of visiting Jay on the weekends while he was finishing out his three months at the facility. With the help of his steadfast rehab team, his regimented program, AA meetings, and family support, Jay was able to go cold turkey and get sober. He excelled in carpentry, even building the facility a rock-climbing wall, and new shelves for books and other media at their library. When Jay "graduated" from the program, all five of us were there cheering him on. Braden had drawn a little sketch on fabric that I hot-glued to the top of his graduation cap. It was Jay standing on a pile of broken bottles—all with XXX on them to symbolize liquor—like King Kong smashing each one to the ground.

In support of his growing carpentry hobby, Jude and Levi had made a T-square out of LEGOs for Jay for his graduation gift. The boys had stuck the LEGOs together with paint, like we had done at times as kids, so they would never come apart. Our little Arnie Armstrong had grey paint on his boots for years from us plopping him down on wet moonscape paint, from which we'd had to pry him with a steak knife. They had painted "Jay the Invincible" on the T-square and even wrapped a little satchel of carpenter's pencils in ribbon around Lucy's neck.

"Showoff," I'd told Jude when I saw what they'd put together.

"Please, child. I'm not the giver," Jude had snapped back, knowing what I was planning for Jay.

"Open mine later," I told Jay when I gave it to him, a small envelope, and he obliged, slipping it into his pocket.

"Dis better not be money, Adrian," he said in his Stallone voice when I handed it to him.

"Psssshhh no," I told him. "You owe me a shit ton, remember?" I teased him. Jay smiled and nodded eagerly.

What was in the envelope was a handwritten letter from me telling Jay many of the things my Dad had told me in one of our last deep conversations about life being messy and the beauty of not knowing who it would bring to you or take away. I told Jay I would never regret him coming back into my life and that he had opened me up in ways I could never properly thank him for.

Tucked into the envelope was also a key. To mine and Braden's house, in particular, to our guest bedroom where Braden had painted a mural replica of King Kong on Jay's graduation cap—that spanned, floor-to-ceiling, on the back wall. I had stocked the shelves and closet with clothes for Jay, books I thought he might like, even a CD player and a little TV/DVD player that Braden stocked with all the Gossip Girl series. Braden and I also included a pair of climbing shoes and a chalk bag in Jay's closet with a note telling him to build us all a rock wall on the side of our garage.

Our work on Jay's room—a project Braden had lovingly dubbed "Prote-Jay, because we're indoctrinating him into our family, get it?" and laughed at his own joke like a complete nerd—had unknowingly finally given Braden and me a project we both looked forward to working together on. Recently, the evenings and weekends found us often singing and dancing, eating pizza or some other handheld dinner in Jay's room, while we painted, organized, and let Braden's records croon us from the living room.

It was as if Jay was the light that needed to be turned on to expose my dark study. There I'd sat for years, the mold and cobwebs growing up my ankles to my desk, and Prote-Jay was the gust of wind that blew it all away—the desk, my laptop, all my books and papers. Just poof. Out the window. It was amazing how quickly I got used to having two boisterous men to come home to who would ask me about my day, wanting to hear every story. Bottom line was Jay made me want to come home more.

———

"I'm going to build something else for you two first," Jay said, startling us both, after we showed him his new King Kong room. I looked to Braden to see if he knew anything about this, as he and Jay had started spending more time together, as Braden's work made it easier. Braden shook his head *no*.

"I'm going to convert that empty storage and HVAC space above your garage into a carriage house where I can stay while I finish it and keep working and saving to pay you back," Jay explained, noting the job he'd just taken at Home Depot after coming out of rehab. "I'll have to learn how to do the sheetrock and appliance installation. Carpet, whatever, all that, but I'm looking forward to it. Maybe it could be a new skill, a new trade for me. I could take classes and get certifications and stuff," Jay said, his brown eyes sparkling with excitement.

"And, the best part," Jay can't contain himself. He's all fidgety and wiggling. "After I finish and move out to my own place, then you guys can rent it out for extra income. I've been doing some research, and I think you could get like two grand a month for it, if I make it nice enough, which I will!" he exclaims.

"But mainly, I thought, maybe, with that extra income, you could work less, Callie, and have more time off." I feel like Jay just put a heat lamp underneath me.

I look to Braden immediately, thinking this has to have been his plan. He just shrugs, and I'm embarrassed even Jay knows I work too much, but also uplifted knowing this was all his idea to help.

—

A year into the project, Jay had almost completed "the loft" we'd begun calling it. Jay and Braden had spent many hours working together on the sheetrock, flooring, and installing the appliances, while Jay and I had bonded over tiny home concepts and ways to dream up creative uses for every inch of the space, including a fold-down Murphy bed with swinging shelves and a convertible couch/desk area. All the living I did in mobile homes and trailers—even Dad's sleeper in his big rig—felt like I had just been training for this lifestyle. Braden had also designed some wallpaper that was Avant Garde, but understated, elegant splashes of color and texture.

"Jude inspired me," Braden had said.

"As he has done for me my entire life," I answered.

The boys had a great time getting all Queer Eye with the décor, bringing the hints of color from Braden's pastel abstracts to life and helping us with the final design touches: throw pillows, art pieces, and plants.

"Just two," though, Levi said. "Three would be too many thirsty bitches in here."

And, true to form, Jay really did use the LEGOs T-square the entire time he worked on the loft. When he had his tool belt on, the square never left his side. He'd also finished the rock-climbing wall on the side of the garage, and the three of us enjoyed hanging out in the evenings or weekends, challenging one another on "the wall."

Jude had finally finished his ARE exam and started working as an apprentice at a pretty prestigious architecture firm in downtown Houston. After he finalized his own dream house sketch, he helped Jay design a beautiful archway in the loft as well as vaulted ceilings, a kitchen island, and custom cabinetry. Jude's designs were functional but magnificent. After it started to come together, I told the boys, Jay, and Braden many times that *I* wanted to live in the loft. It was that cool.

———

One Saturday in April, as we were all putting the finishing touches on the loft, Jude and I found ourselves in a shady corner sharing a moment. Levi and Jay are toting some wood and materials out to the loft, with Levi serenading everyone in a half-mile radius with "You make me feel like dancing. I want to dance the night away!"

Jay is shaking his head from side to side with the beat, but I can see he's smiling. Braden, bringing up their rear, shuffles over to me and Jude and hands us each an ice-cold soda, then picks up as Levi's off-key harmony. "I feel like dan-cing—whoo!—dan-cing—whoo!" Jude and I open our cans and share a look, savoring our crazy ensemble and the warm, musical moment we have found ourselves in.

"Maybe it's like three and a half percent," Jude says as we watch Braden do a few turns and jerky finger points. Dancing was never his strong suit, I'm reminded. But then my eyes fall on Jay, who has grown tan and toned over the year he has spent living in our home and working on the loft. It's been humbling and thrilling to watch his confidence and sense of humor come back.

"What percent is Jay?" I ask Jude. He stops mid-sip and makes a thoughtful face.

"Good question," Jude says, watching him closely. Jay is instructing Levi on where to lay the two-by-fours they are carrying. To me, nothing in Jay's gait or manner or speech ever leaned toward the Richard Simmons side of the spectrum. But I do remember Jude telling me about the two of them … experimenting when they were younger.

"Well, to be fair, I didn't know *you* were gay until you told me. And you were twenty-seven years old at the time. I don't think my gaydar is properly calibrated," I tell him.

Jude clucks. "Sometimes it can be harder than you think. Often, the bisexual guys are these brooding, mysterious types that like to really … dominate behind closed doors."

"Yuck! Grody. Stop." I slap him. I don't like picturing Jay *dominating* anywhere. "Forget I asked. It makes no difference."

"No, it doesn't," Jude confirms. "But now we'll all be watching a little more closely, won't we?" He and I cheers conspiratorially.

"Do you ever worry, Jude, that this is all too good to be true?" I ask the question that has been weighing on me for months. I had worked so hard, been so isolated for so many years, that when I finally started letting people back in—first Jude, then Levi, Lucy, then Braden—it seemed like I didn't know when to stop when Jay crashed into our orbit. But I had been feeling like it was all stacking up to some dangerous point, where it might all topple over. I wanted Jude to tell me this golden era wasn't finite.

"What?" Jude asks. "Levi and I? You and Braden? This house, Jay, our family? Do you feel like it's too good to be true? Or just too good for us?" His precision pierces me, as it always does.

I think about it.

"The latter," I finally decide.

Jude is silent for a bit.

"It isn't too good for you, Callie," he finally says. "You deserve all this and more."

———

324 days after Jay started working on the loft—and exactly six months after he finished paying me back for the rehab—he completed the project. May 27, 2012. It was a Thursday evening, and I had finally made it home just after 6:00 p.m. when Jay planned the big reveal.

"I think you've turned this space right around, mate," Braden says to Jay in a fun British accent, spinning around in the open living/bedroom, which feels quite spacious with the Murphy bed folded up.

"Frankly, I'm just gobsmacked," I say, mimicking Braden's accent. "You've gone from pure rubbish to … a space fit for the Queen. I tell you this calls for bubbles, it does," I tell the guys as I make my way over to the fridge to pull out some non-alcoholic sparkling wine I've been saving for the occasion. Jay and Braden put a little distance between themselves as I walk over, and I get a funny feeling.

"What is it with you two?" I ask, with no accent. They turn to look at one another as if they're asking each other a question. "Any day now. What's going on, guys?"

Jay tells Braden, "Good a time as any," and Braden turns to me. A wave of relief washes over me when I realize whatever it is the two of them have been conspiring on, it's something for me. I can be the third wheel—in exchange for a cool surprise—I assure myself.

"Paws for a cause?" Braden asks. I look briefly at Jay, who is aware of mine and Braden's silly little language. He nods for me to … take the call, so to speak.

"UT animal shelter at your service," I respond trepidatiously, as I have no clue where this is going. "Where we make depression eat dirt and die. What kind of service do you need?"

"A life coach," Braden blurts out, and I'm confused. Our Paws for a Cause needs are usually quite dark and often involve gruesomely murdering someone we're merely irritated with. This request is way too 'actual mental health' for me. I make a funny face.

"I've been waiting for the right time to talk to you about this, Callie, and now seems like as good as any," Braden breaks. "We know this has been a problem for you for a while. You are so driven, Callie. You're committed and disciplined and smart, but it's sucking you dry. No one should have to work as hard as you do. And, I don't have the answer. I would never ask you to give up everything you've worked so hard for." I let out a huge breath I didn't know I was holding, and I fall back on the trust I have always felt with Braden. "But I think there is an answer out there that we all need to search for and work out together."

At Braden's use of the phrase "we all," I look to Jay.

"Yes, Callie, Jay, and I have been talking about this," Braden confesses. "We want to … solve this problem together as a team, that's all. Jay and I have found a life coach for you, Callie. All I'm asking is that you be willing to talk to her. That you take it seriously and talk honestly with her. You're going to be completely blown away by who we found."

I can feel Braden's excitement. It's thick in the room. He's practically giddy. And, the look on Jay's face tells me he's been in on this and that he's excited, too. The scar on his cheek betrays him any time he's trying to hide a smile. I can't help but smile at these two—my *guys*.

I mouth an uneasy *okay* at them, and Jay leaps off the floor, his LEGOs T-square clattering to the ground. He picks it up and high-fives Braden as they both turn back toward me.

"Good, because you're never going to guess who we found," Braden grins, and I know I'm not, because I have never met a life coach in my life. I picture this gorgeous, jet-setting Middle Eastern woman with a thick Syrian accent telling me. "You not listen when I tell you, you must feeeeel your priorities here, in your chest, your heart, Mizz

Callie." My imaginary life coach is kind of terrifying, but also exotic and titillating. I kind of like her.

"It's Mariah!" Braden shouts, and Jay is standing next to him, nodding like a fool.

"Mariah?" I ask dumbly. I've only known one Mariah in my entire life. "You can't mean …" I start, and both Braden and Jay now start nodding in unison. They look like two adult bobblehead dolls.

"Mariah Avalero?"

———

I looked up Mariah's website after dinner and was blown away to find she had become a lawyer, too. Mariah went to Texas A&M School of Law and got her law degree the year after me. It seemed she had started her own firm right after graduating and passing the Bar—Avalero and Associates—and began handling a good bit of wills, trusts, estate planning, and some litigation, on the plaintiff's side.

Mariah included a little paragraph about herself and how watching her family go through such an intense, disruptive life transition when she was just a teenager encouraged her to want to help others tackle big life challenges and see that things could always be better on the other side, as long as you could trust and embrace change and control your attitude. *Change gon' come*, Mariah tells her potential clients, a quote she attributes to Sam Cooke, and I admire the reference as it reminds me of my dad and his 'life is a river' mentality.

For the first time in a long time that evening, I felt hope for my legal future, my career. Maybe Mariah could help me navigate some different work situation with Goldman Carr, or maybe she could help me start out with a different firm, or start my own firm like hers—I had no clue—but I knew the thought of something different ignited me. Something more balanced and fulfilling.

I felt like a lamp that had just been collecting dust, but suddenly someone had plugged me in.

In hindsight, I should have been worried. Feeling so impossibly airy and happy and untouchable, with my life looking so impeccably perfect.

Because that was never our fate.

Then it was May 28th.

A Friday.

And my phone buzzed at 2:34 a.m.

CHAPTER THIRTY-ONE
CHANGE GON' COME

I scramble out from under the covers to get to my phone. "Levi," my voice is husky and doesn't sound like my own. At the sound of it, Braden turns on the lamp on his bedside table and turns to face me, his face ashen.

"Levi," I repeat because I didn't hear any words from him, only muffles and what I think was him sobbing. My terrified mind senses the worst and takes me back to a sunny day on the UT campus. I'm staring at a red brick building with my hair in a ponytail. I'm wearing my UT Rec Center polo. The bricks have a pattern: little divots and crosses, staggered.

"Callie," I finally hear Levi's voice. He takes a big, rattling, wet breath in, and my world stops.

"It's Jude, Callie. He's been shot. Oh God," Levi falls apart on the other end of the line.

Shot?! At first, I thought I didn't hear him right. I couldn't have heard him right. My brain must have filled in something incorrectly.

"Wait, Levi. Shot? Did you say Jude was shot?!" I'm shouting now in our bedroom. Braden puts a hand to his mouth; he's breathing heavily through it. "Oh, Callie," I hear him whisper.

I find I'm squeezing the covers in rapid succession in my left hand and that I'm suddenly sweating all over.

"Yes, Callie. I'm sorry. He was … he was …" Levi tries to choke his emotions back. "Protecting me." I hear Levi's phone clatter and more sobbing.

I throw the covers off of me and start pacing my and Braden's bedroom. Braden is pacing with me, searching my face and eyes for answers. My throat has tightened and I feel like I'm going to choke. I'm surprised to find my face is wet as I bring my fist to my mouth to cough.

"Callie, is he?" Braden starts.

"I don't know!" I snap at him. "I don't know yet. I don't know anything!"

"Levi! LEVI!" I shout again into the phone. "LEEEVVVIII!" I give it my all. Braden and I both look up to see a light come on in the loft. I've woken Jay.

I hear clatter and movement at the end of the line. "Callie, come," is all I hear Levi say. "You gotta come now. The doctors are coming to talk to me now, and they don't know if he'll make it. Callie, hurry. We're at Sacred Heart ER."

I hear Levi hang up, and I shout uselessly into my phone. "Levi! LEVI!"

Braden brings me into his arms, but I try to fight him. I push and shove and claw at him until I finally fall into his chest, beating on him and screaming through tears. "Jude! Fuck! Fuck!"

I hear Jay's voice in the house now.

"Callie, CALLIE?!" he shouts.

"In here," Braden shouts back, and Jay comes running into our room, his face a mask of terror.

"It's Jude," I tell him. "He's been," I hiccup, trying to get it out. "Shot, he's been shot. He's in the hospital in Houston."

"Shit, we gotta go," Jay says, snapping immediately into action, and I'm grateful for Jay's practical roots because I've felt too stupefied the last minute to do anything right. Jay flings open a drawer and throws a pair of jeans and a t-shirt at Braden. I wonder for a second how he knows where Braden's clothes are, but I shake the thought as I see him clamber through several of my drawers until he finds some pants and a sweatshirt that he throws at me.

"C'mon!" Jay screams. "We gotta GO! I'll bring my truck around to the front." With that, Jay runs out, a full sprint. His quick, executive movements snap Braden and me into action, and we start throwing on our clothes.

"Levi didn't say anything about how it happened?" Braden asks me.

I put my sweatshirt on inside-out, but I don't care. My throat feels so dry, I'm not sure I can swallow or even make a sound. Even though my mouth feels chalky, I realize I'm drooling as I'm putting my socks on, and I wipe my mouth with my sleeve. Suddenly, I can't see my shoelaces, and I hear an animal-like sound ricocheting through the room. Then I realize it's me. I'm sobbing into my sneakers, and Braden is hunched over me, holding my shoulders.

"Callie, it's gonna be okay," Braden says. "I promise. It's gonna be okay."

I shove his hands off of me. "Don't make promises you can't keep. We don't yet know if it's going to be okay! My fucking brother has been shot!"

I grab my phone and computer bag and bust out of our bedroom. Work flits briefly through my mind as I think about the motion to dismiss hearing I have before Jude Kitchel in about seven hours, but I can't deal with that right now. I've got to get to Jude.

Jay has his truck parked in our front yard right by the front door when Braden and I come out. We jump in, and Jay takes off, squealing a little rubber on the road. Houston is two and a half hours away from Austin. Jay's radio is playing, but no one is really paying attention until I hear a word that catches my ear.

Shooting.

"Turn that up," I tell Jay. Nerves of fire, he immediately reaches for the knob and increases the volume. A news anchor's voice fills the car, with the sound of police sirens and voices in the background.

"All we know, Joan, is that at 11:30 this evening, a gunman entered P.L.A.Y., a local gay club here in Houston, with a loaded AR-15," the reporter says.

I roll down the window of Jay's truck and throw up out the side. The smell is putrid, and I watch my vomit splatter the side of Jay's truck and the road. Jay tries to pull me back in, and I shove him forcefully back. I suddenly hate that I had that conversation with Jude about things being too good. What the hell was I thinking jinxing us with that? I find I'm beating the side of Jay's truck, screaming and crying, shouting and spitting into the wind.

Levi called us halfway there and relayed what we all feared. He and Jude had been at P.L.A.Y. that night. "It was date night," Levi had said through sobs. "We were both feeling a little punchy after dinner, so we decided to go to the club for a bit. Just to, ya know, have a couple more drinks and dance. It'd been months since we've been to the club, Callie, then this happens? What the ever-loving fuck?!" Levi is talking a mile a minute, rattling out words in a slurry.

"I know," I try to control my breathing. "We heard it on the radio. How many times? Where was Jude shot?" It feels like three minutes pass before Levi responds.

"Oh God, Callie. The face! His goddam perfect face. Jude had pushed me behind him. He was protecting me, Callie, I'm so sorry!"

Levi says, and I can hear the shake in his voice. "But that psychopath shot him in the stomach, too, and the chest. Jesus! I can't believe this!"

It feels like a bullet tears through me each time Levi mentions one. I feel it in my teeth, in my lungs, my ribs. I close my eyes and see Jude's angelic body getting hit. One time. Two times. Three.

———

Levi, Braden, Jay, and I sit, pace, sprawl, tap our feet, and basically torment one another in the waiting room over the next hour, which Levi called 'the purgatory,' and it's already stuck. I ask Levi if he's let our mom know, and he shakes his head 'no.' I feel like he wants to apologize, but he just doesn't have any apologies left. I just nod, knowing it's what I have to do. None of us has seen Jude yet, as the doctors and nurses are working feverishly on him. Jude is in surgery when I call Mom and tell her.

"Shot?" Mom hisses, just waking up as she's an hour behind us in Clovis. "Jude, shot?" She's trying to make sense of it. "How? When? Why? Not Jude. Not my son," I hear her voice crack, and I lose it, too, knowing she vocalized the exact thought I'd just had. *Not Jude.*

"Stop yer' crying," I tell her, which gets her attention. "Jude was shot, Mom. It doesn't matter how right now. Who did it, or why? Just get here—the Sacred Heart ER in Houston. Leave now," I tell her.

Next, I call my partner, Justin, at the firm to tell him what's going on and brief him on the motion to dismiss hearing I'll need him to cover for me this morning. I surprise myself at the firmness of my own voice as I explain my brother has been shot, is critically injured, and I'll be by his side in the hospital all day. I hang up with Justin right as the doctor finally approaches us.

"The bullet that entered his abdomen did some extensive damage, piercing his intestines in multiple places," the doctor tells us. "We had to remove a portion of his lower intestines, but we couldn't salvage his tattered colon. So, he's on a colostomy bag. That should all heal just fine, though. I know it's not ideal, but it's also not life-threatening for now. We're going to get him stabilized from this surgery before we get the rest of his imaging and other diagnostics working, before we schedule him for the next surgery to remove the bone shards in his face and chest, and do what repairs we need to do in there. He might be ready for visitors in an hour or so."

I turn to Levi, who feels closer to Jude than I do. But Levi turns to me. "Callie, you're his sister. We don't know how long he's going to live. And, he's in this state because of …"

"Because he wanted to protect you," I correct Levi adamantly, bluntly, with a tone louder than I intended. I soften it. "Because you are his *person*, Levi. He chose you as his family because of the man you are and the connection you two have. I don't give a rat's ass what they say about blood and kin. You're going in there first, Levi. I'll be right behind you, okay? Jude will hang on for us."

———

Jude comes to in the early afternoon, and we all send Levi back to Jude's room to see him. It's the first time, since Braden, Jay, and I got to the hospital, that we've had a moment just the three of us to process this together.

"Callie, babe, is there anything I can do for you?" Braden asks. "Did you get everything squared away at the office? Do you need me to go … talk to any of your partners or get any files for you or your other laptop?" Although my eyes are so dry I don't believe they will ever form tears again, they start to prick at the sincerity of Braden's offer. But it only makes me feel guiltier because it reveals my truth. Work consumes me. I just shake my head 'no' and plop down.

Jay sits down next to me and lays his hand on my forearm. Braden follows suit and sits on my opposite side and lays his hand on my other forearm. I look at the two hands on me—Jay's more tan and calloused from the work he's been doing on the loft, Braden's a lighter shade and softer from all the computer and design work he does. But they are both equally filled with love for me, and for Jude, and for each other—I hope—as we've all been working to build this family together over the last year. I take both of their hands and mash them together in this little homemade-looking mangle, then I wrap my own around them and lean my head down onto it.

"I love you guys," is all I say.

Jay puts a hand on my back. Braden does the same.

"Callie," we hear Levi's voice, frail and scratchy. "He asked for you," Levi says. His eyes are red-rimmed, and his expression gives me zero comfort. Jude must look awful. I brace myself and rise, Braden and Jay's hands slowly cascading off me.

———

Walking toward Jude's room feels like walking in the Alice in Wonderland hallway, where everything is shrinking toward the door at the end. Though I feel like I'm trying to walk quicker, the hallway is stretching out before me, and I'm actually going slower. I hear the beeps of machines before I stick my head in his door. I take one deep breath and enter.

I'm relieved when I see him. Jude actually looks better than I thought he would. My imagination is pretty robust—it must be more gruesome than Levi's—because I had marred him significantly in my mind, with jagged, gnarly wounds and tubes going in and out of him like a science project. In reality, Jude's entire body is covered by a sheet, so whatever gaping holes or tubes may lie underneath, I can't see them, and I'm grateful for it. The right half of Jude's face is bandaged from below his eye down to his neck. The left side of his face is puffy and blotchy, but you can still see the beautiful man that he is. A thousand bandages couldn't hide that.

His eyes travel over toward me, and a wave of relief washes over me when I realize he recognizes me. *Jude. You're still there.* The unbandaged corner of his mouth tries to turn up, and I remember what the doctor told us about his jaw. I'm sure the simple act of trying to smile causes tremendous pain.

"I'll smile for the both of us," I tell Jude, through a big phony smile.

"Lil' Bit," Jude says through clenched teeth, and I choke back a sob.

"Don't," I tell him. "Not that name. I can't take it."

"Callie," Jude starts again. "Come here." His voice is a little slurred, and he has to suck up saliva every five to ten seconds, but I can understand him perfectly.

I see a little rolling stool near his bed, so I roll it over next to him and sit down on the left side of his bed. Jude offers me his hand. When I take it, it feels too cold. I blow on it and try to start warming it between my own.

"Are you … in a lot of pain?" I ask. Jude shakes his head 'no' then changes his mind and makes a *so-so* face.

"Do you remember what happened?"

"I remember enough," he starts slowly. Jude's words are pained and slow coming, but it seems it doesn't pain him to talk to the point that he doesn't want to do it. I'm grateful Jude still has a voice, as there is so much I need to tell him, for him to tell me, as selfish as that sounds.

"I know I was put there in that moment to save Levi. But don't you ever let him feel like he wasn't worth it, promise me that, Callie. Selfish as I am, you know me," Jude gives me a look, and I try to fight a smile because smiles feel all wrong here, "I would do it again."

Jude's concession causes a Rolodex of memories to cascade through my mind: Levi, Jude, and I sitting on the back patio of their old apartment playing rummy; Levi and Jude cooking in that kitchen, swatting each other's asses with wooden spoons; Levi and Lucy rolling around on the living room floor of their new house in complete bliss. I try to imagine myself in Levi's position and how I would feel if this were Braden under the sheet. *Would that be worse than Jude?* I hate where this situation has taken my brain—to dark places, where I'm negotiating with some evil force about the pieces of my life I might get to keep. I put my focus back on Jude.

"But, please tell me—whatever happens with any of this—you will always be one hundred percent honest with me," Jude's eyes are pleading with me.

"Of course. I would demand the same of you," I tell him.

"Okay, good, then I need you to do something for me," he says. Immediately, I get a little scared thinking Jude's going to ask me to wheel him out of here like a bandit, but I don't think I can with all the tubes and wires and stuff leading to his body under the sheet. Then I worry he's going to ask me to end his life, and I don't think I can do that either.

"What?" I eventually ask him.

"First, confirm that I will, in fact, be shitting into a bag attached to my body for the rest of my life. That wasn't just some nightmare that's going to go away, is it? It's real?" Jude asks.

I take a deep breath in and shake my head 'yes', trying to keep my eyes from looking down toward his abdomen to find it. Then I'm left wondering, is this how Jude will feel for the rest of his life anytime he meets someone new, wondering if they can see … or smell it? I swallow back the agony of that reality for Jude.

Jude closes his eyes and seems to absorb this slowly. He pulls his hands up closer to his chest and chin as if he doesn't want them to graze his bag. To find something attached to your own body so repulsive has to be a nightmare, I think.

"Okay," Jude says, determined. "I have to see what this looks like. My face," he points to his right cheek, and I instantly start shaking my head 'no.' The whole right half of his face is bandaged. I'm afraid that if I pull any of the tape around the edge of the gauze, I'll open the wound or allow infection in, or do something medically that I am unaware of, that will put Jude at risk.

"No, I can't, I'll cause more damage. It'll expose …" Jude cuts me off.

"They're going to redress it when they come back in here, they told me," Jude is pushing on me. "Some nurse is just going to come in and pull that tape off just like you would do, but she won't let me see it. They've told me many times they won't let me see it yet. But, Callie, this is my face. I am a gay man. It means … more to me than most people. However shallow that sounds, I don't care. It's you and you know me. I need you to do this for me, okay?"

I'm still shaking my head 'no.'

"God dammit, Callie. I'm lying in a hospital bed, completely mangled." Jude is getting angry, and I hear his machines start to beep more rapidly. He winces in pain, then takes a calming breath.

"Okay," he re-strategizes. "There's something I want you to know."

I wait.

"Remember when Mom drove over to Lubbock, where we were staying with Dad and Sissy?"

I nod. Of course, I remember. That was also the day Mom ripped us apart and drove away with Jude.

"Well, I got us back together," Jude says. This surprises me. I never knew what made Mom get over her rage and let Dad drive me back to her. I figured she had just cooled down … if you could call ripping your children apart a mere heated moment. I wouldn't.

"What do you mean?" I ask him.

"I don't know how long Mom was planning to keep us separate,"

Jude says. "Maybe she was just going to be a bitch for a week and then reunite us. But, heck, I was, what? Only nine at the time? I was scared to be all on my own with Mom, and I was worried Dad wouldn't know how to feed and look after you or protect you from Sissy's wild pack of kids. I wanted you back."

I realize I'm breathing hard through my open mouth, so I close it and try to moisten my mouth again. It's hard to hear these truths coming from Jude's mangled, saliva-leaking face.

"I stopped eating, Callie," Jude tells me, and I cock my head towards him.

"Stopped eating?" I ask dumbly, although I heard him just fine.

"Yeah," Jude confirms. "I refused to eat any food until Mom brought you back. That was my plan. I wouldn't talk to her, and I refused to eat. I only left my room to go to the bathroom or get water. Mom was furious at me. Said I was betraying her, but I held firm, Callie. She let me go about a day and a half, then I refused to drink water."

My eyes grow livid.

"She didn't do that to me, Callie," Jude says, sensing my mom's rage. "I did it to myself."

"After she tore us apart!" I object.

"Lil' Bit, you can't blame her for making mistakes. She was a young mom. And, Dad—much as you love him, I know he's your cowboy hero." Jude's tone is a bit mocking. "But he could be a real selfish asshole a lot of the time. Where do you think I get it?" Jude asks. I refuse to laugh.

"I don't think you realize how much Mom did for us, thanklessly, daily. Maybe she didn't do it with a chipper smile and a song, like Dad, but she did for us, Callie. And Dad had really hurt her, threatening to steal us away. Try to imagine what that would feel like for a mother. You've got to cut her some slack."

I just huff. *I'm not cutting Mom anything,* I think stubbornly to myself.

"Anyway," I can sense Jude's growing impatience. "I told you all of that because it hurt like hell not eating, Callie. I thought my little nine-year-old stomach was going to suck back to my spine and never be able to accept food again. I literally thought at the time that I was destroying my anatomy. I did that for you," Jude says, and I suddenly see through his … workings.

"Oh, c'mon, you did that for *you* so you could have me back as protection from Mom," I say, with more force than I intended.

"Are we really going to have a fight right here, with me on my deathbed?" Jude asks.

"Shut up, it's not your deathbed," but the feeling of Jude and me fighting gives me so much hope.

"I'm asking you for a very small favor here, Callie. Nothing like forced starvation. Just pull some tape back and give me a mirror. Or, hell, just get me a mirror and I'll do it myself. I know I'm being a complete bitch about this right now, but it's what I need. And, you're the only person I trust would understand me enough to give this to me."

I huff, hating myself for doing this, but simultaneously knowing I'm going to do this. I start to look around the room, thinking they probably don't have a countertop mirror. It could be dangerous if it were knocked over or whatever. I realize my phone is in my back pocket, and I pull it out and wave it at Jude. He understands. The selfie function of my phone will do the trick.

"You're still gonna owe me for this one," I tell him. "Hospital bed or not." He nods. Jude looks eager but also terrified. I'm nervous, but I'm still feeling a thousand times better now that I know Jude is lucid and still concerned with his looks. As shallow as that sounds, it tells me he's definitely not on his deathbed. At least not knowingly.

I ease the tape back just slightly, trying to control my breathing and my reaction. I keep working it around the edge by Jude's nose and under his eye until I have about seventy-five percent of it lifted, so I can lay it down on his shoulder to expose the wound. I gasp when I see it and curse myself. I close my eyes and turn away for a second, holding a finger up to Jude to give me a minute, angry in the moment that I'm turning away from him, but finding myself incapable of doing anything else.

When I turn back to Jude, I can take it in more clearly. The right side of his face is a crater, like a firework went off inside his mouth. The jagged edges of his cheek are held together by fat black stitches, and I can see pieces of teeth underneath, but they're in the wrong place and turned around the wrong way. It looks as if the stitches weren't there; the whole bottom half of Jude's cheek would just lie down on his neck, exposing his jaw and a round hole where his teeth used to be. The whole side of his face looks like a slab of raw meat, thirty shades of red and crimson, with silvery slivers of tendon snaking throughout. Jude looks like something out of a Terminator or Marvel movie, half beauty, half beast.

I don't want him to see it. This I know as I start to bring my phone up for Jude to see.

Jude gasps. He makes animal-like sounds. His breathing starts to increase, and his machines start beeping louder and more frequently.

He starts wailing so loud that I know the nurses are going to come. Drool and spittle are starting to ooze out of the right side of his mouth. I try to console him, but it's no use. Jude has seen his future, and it's worse than he could have ever imagined, with his face half blown off and his bag of shit on his hip.

I shove my phone back into my pocket and push the bandage back up and tape it in place right before the nurses rush in. They look at me accusingly, and I hold my hands in the air. They lay Jude's bed down flat and start tapping his IVs and checking his instruments. One nurse grabs me by the arm and starts escorting me out.

The last thing I see as they walk me out the door is Jude's hand clenched on the blanket, his knuckles white.

CHAPTER THIRTY-TWO
HONEY, I AM FAMILY

"Honey, I *am* family!" I hear through the closed door of my hospital room, snapping me back to the present. My hand, white-knuckled on my blanket, reliving that horrific moment with Jude—over two hundred miles away in Houston, and two months ago, although it felt like yesterday—finally uncurls at the sound of his voice. I release. *Levi.* Instantly, my body floods with joy. Mom, curled in a chair by my bed, rouses, too. *Still with me, huh?* I think.

"Callie!" I hear Levi shout. "Counselor!" he yells louder.

"In here!" I shout.

"Oh, thank God," Levi comes busting through the door with Tammy in tow. He's holding her hand and, I'm confident, he has dragged her all the way from San Antonio to this hospital and then all over it with his hand in hers, not letting her wriggle away at any moment. Tammy is flustered and panting, but she looks excited. I wonder briefly how Mom will react, but Levi is so excited, his enthusiasm washes any fear away.

"I hope you didn't think you were going to go through another tragedy, alone, did you?" Levi asks impetuously. "I told you once, and I meant it forever. We are family, little lady. Next time, *you* call me yourself or you're in real big hot trouble, you got that?" Levi says to me with an eyebrow raised. I can't help it, but I'm giggling. Levi's presence here only reinforces my recent revelation. I love this man. Not in the traditional sense, in a way—freaking better one.

"Jude's watching over Lucy," he says and gives me a wink.

"Hi," Tammy says meekly to Mom, and I'm a little embarrassed realizing they are just now meeting for the first time. Levi looks to me and gives me a *Whoops* look, which has me giggling more. What else can we do?

"I've heard so much about you, Charlene. I hope you don't mind that I'm here," Tammy says to Mom, sheepishly.

Mom is looking at Tammy like she's some kind of circus animal. As much fun as it is to watch, I want to help Mom out. I'm sure this is a really weird moment for her.

"Tammy, this is my stubborn, indomitable Mom. She's harmless, I promise. Just give her a smoke and she'll be your friend," I say, hoping this lighthearted approach will work. Tammy is usually so good at welcoming new people from all walks of life.

"Oh, that's perfect, because I picked some up on the way," Tammy says, reaching into her handbag.

Levi looks conspiratorially at me, then Mom, then back at me. He holds a hand up to his mouth. "It's true. She made me stop. But I told her what kind to get," Levi whispers, his eyebrows wiggling.

Tammy pulls a pack of Capri menthols out of her purse just enough to show Mom, then tucks it back in as a nurse comes swooping through the door. Tammy winks at Mom, and I swear I see Mom try to hide a smile.

Levi turns to me in bed and strokes the hair from my face. "It's going to be okay, I promise," Levi tells me. "I've got a whole line of designer shoes coming out for your prosthetic."

"Well, that's good," I say. "I can't wait to get back in high heels."

Levi chuckles and lowers his tone. "Seriously, Callie, you going to be alright?" he asks.

"I will be," I tell him in earnest.

"Praise Jesus, finally," he says again, in a Southern drawl, Baptist church accent. "Because I can't tell you how many times …" but he's interrupted by Mariah charging through the door.

"Callie." She pauses when she sees all the people in my room. "We need to talk," she tells me.

"C'mon, girls," Levi says, hustling up Tammy and Mom. "I think someone needs a smoke." Mom is nodding her head vigorously, and I give the three of them a little wave and mouth *Thank you* as they file out.

"You've got quite the fan club," Mariah says, approaching me with a smile.

I just shrug, relishing in the warmth Levi's presence has brought me.

"What was Detective Carter's new evidence?" I ask her as I can't wait any longer.

"They got an accident reconstruction guy on their team to look at the site," Mariah tells me as she eases onto the corner of my bed and imitates the accident, making vehicles out of her flat-palmed hands in the air.

"The collision sent the Pathfinder back into the ditch, where it rolled several times. The Ford careened out of control for a bit, then hit a tree on the opposite side of the road, killing the driver instantly."

I'm nodding, listening. It feels very strange to hear things that happened to me that I cannot remember at all. I wonder what the vehicle rolling must have felt and sounded like. But a huge part of me hopes I never remember.

"We're trying to get more proof of what happened via CCTV cameras that were positioned along the way and might have snagged some footage of you and Braden," Mariah continues. "I don't have that many resources, but the 'DUI Specialist' guy your firm hired sure does. Much as I hate the blood-sucking insurance bastards you work for, I was glad your firm brought this ace in. He's got his minions scouring for any photos or footage we can find of you two right before the accident. We're on it, Callie, I promise."

I swallow at the fact that my firm was forced to hire some DUI guy to try and get me out of this mess, and that I will probably become the one embarrassing exception to their 'work is work' philosophy—where everything personal is left at the door—because everyone in the office is undoubtedly gossiping about me now. But I can't deny that I need a 'DUI guy.'

"I'll spend the rest of my life owing you," I feel I have to tell Mariah first.

"Bitch, please," Mariah starts. "You think I'm going to give you that much time to pay my whopping legal bill. Think again! I'm getting Avalero and Associates off the ground, see. We collect promptly." She slaps my good leg.

"Is Braden …" I find I can't finish the sentence because I feel guilty. While I wish and hope he'll wake up with a crystal-clear memory of the accident so he can help save me, really, all I want is for him to live. Even if it means I was driving and have to go to jail.

"He's still unconscious, Callie. His infection has caused a serious fever and a spike in his blood pressure. His white blood count is dangerously low at the moment. They're trying to get him stable first."

My head drops onto my chest with the weight of this. *You did this, Callie.*

"Hey," Mariah says. "We are going. To get. To the bottom of this. Just like I told you, okay? And, whatever we find, we will deal with it together. You, me, and your entire—she waves a hand around the room, indicating the people who were just here—family. You've got people," she says forcefully.

"Say it, Callie," Mariah says, pressing hard on my legs.

"I don't deserve you," I tell her.

"That's not what I told you to say," Mariah holds firm.

We stare at each other.

"I have people," I finally admit.

"I never deserved you," she responds and walks out.

CHAPTER THIRTY-THREE
THE PROMISE

"Jude wants to see you," I hear a nurse behind me say, and I immediately follow her, thankful I'll get to see Jude again before Mom comes. I haven't seen Mom in over nine years, and I'm nervous. Though he is lying mangled and weak in a hospital bed, I need Jude's strength.

"Hey Lil' Bit," he says as I make my way to his bed, the steady beep of his machines our accompaniment.

"Hey," I tell him. I can see he tries a smile, but then stops. I'm sure any movement of any muscle on his face is painful. I'm glad the big white bandage is once again covering the monstrosity that I know lies beneath. It's easier to talk to Jude without having to look at that, then I immediately feel guilty for having that feeling, as I know that's exactly what Jude is fearing will be everyone's reality for the rest of his life.

"How are you feeling?" I ask him, then immediately regret that choice as well. *He's feeling like he just got shot multiple times, Callie, duh.* I curse the fact that I don't have any guidelines for this. Jude just shakes his head side to side.

"I need you to promise you will do something for me, Callie." His curtness bothers me.

"I can't marry you and Levi. And, this is Texas," I tell him, trying humor. It falls flat.

"We're more married than most married couples," Jude dismisses me.

"I promised I would reconcile with Mom, and I will. Must be my lucky day," I breathe out, dreading more than anything my reunion with Mom today.

"Good. That's been long overdue. This will be harder than you realize for her, Callie," Jude says, and it surprises me. *Like this is easy for me?* I bristle internally and give Jude a hard stare.

"You just …" he sighs. "Seeing her kid all tubed up in a bed like this will set her off. There are things about Mom you just don't understand, Lil' Bit."

Selfishly, I'm angered by this constant feeling of my family hiding truths from me.

"But what I'm asking for now has nothing to do with Mom. And, I need to get this out before anyone else comes in, okay? Just listen, please, Callie."

I swallow back my mounting anger. Jude is scaring me.

"I need you to promise you'll do this before I tell you, Callie. You're the only one I can trust to do this because it's going to be very hard. But you *can* do it. I know you can, and I'm trusting that you will. Have I ever told you you could do something that you couldn't?"

I don't like this at all. Suddenly I feel nauseous.

"Can I say no, before I hear it?" I ask, my voice shaky.

"No," Jude is firm.

"I'm sorry I'm asking, but I am. I am your brother. Asking. Say you will, Callie," Jude waits for me. I look into his beautiful hazel eyes, and I know. I know what he's going to ask from me. I feel like my spine goes soft and my body sinks down several inches. I keep staring at Jude. I shake my head 'no' and he shakes his head 'yes,' then winces in pain, and I know there is only one answer.

"I will," I whisper.

"Thank you, Lil' Bit."

———

"Calliope!" I hear and I know immediately that it's her. She's not shouting, but she's being too loud for a hospital wing. I can hear the anxiety in her tone. "Callie, where is he? Where's Jude?!"

I try to make my way quickly toward the sound of her voice so I can quiet her, but when I turn a corner and finally see her, it takes my breath away. She's so much frailer than I remember. Her frizzy, dirty blonde hair is more grey than blonde, and the mascara under her eyes has smeared. She's got one of her "grungie" flannels on with the sleeves cut off and a long-sleeve black long john underneath that says Sonny's BBQ, paired with tattered green cargo pants. I can see she has a slight limp, favoring her left knee, when she walks.

Ten years, almost. I can't believe how much time has changed her, and that I let this much time go by without seeing my own Mom. I have to imagine I look pretty different from Mom, too, though. Ten years. The last time we saw each other, I was eighteen, leaving Clovis. Mom was forty-nine, staying put.

"Mom, keep your voice down," I hiss at her when I get close enough to her for her to hear me, but I instantly regret it. Ten years, and the first thing I do is snap at her?

"Sorry, I mean, hi Mom. I'm glad you're here."

"Well, I'm not. How the hell did Jude get shot?" she asks me, and I notice her head is bobbing a little on her shoulders. I sniff indiscreetly and smell gin, but it doesn't surprise me, and I really don't care. Mom's son has been shot. She can do whatever the hell she wants to cope.

"Mom, come over here, let's sit down, and I can explain," I try to steer her down the hall to our purgatory area, but she's fighting me.

"I want to see him, right now, Callie. I want to see my boy." I look at her. I can see she's trembling slightly. For a brief moment, I wonder if I can do to Mom the thing Jude has made me promise to do. Then I close my eyes and see Jude lying in that bed, his face half blown off, and I know I can. I have to. I promised.

"I'm going to take you in, now, Mom. But remember, we have to talk in soothing tones and keep everything easy and gentle to keep Jude calm. We can't upset him. He's ... well, he's fragile, Mom."

Mom looks at me, then. She has tried to wipe the mascara from under her eyes, but she's only smeared it out to the sides like a raccoon. I take the edge of my sweatshirt and wipe it off for her. I always hated it when she wore black eyeliner and mascara anyway. I thought she was so much prettier natural, without it.

"Callie, is he going to be okay?" she asks me, through eyes that are pleading for me to say 'yes.' But, that's the one thing I cannot do, because—no matter what happens—I know Jude will never be the same, and I honestly don't know if he will be 'okay.' Frankly, I don't know if he will even 'be.'

"I don't know, Mom. I just don't know. None of us knows. It's ... it's pretty bad."

I find my hand is shaking as I'm leading Mom into Jude's room. I can feel her ribs and spine as I place my hand on her back to guide her inside and smell the light whiff of cigarette smoke on her, and I can only imagine what the last eight hours have been like for her.

"Jude, I've got Mom with me," I tell him as we make our way in, but when Mom sees Jude in the bed, she turns around immediately, puts her hand to her mouth, and starts sobbing. She crashes into me, and I try to hold her up as I lock eyes with Jude, who looks utterly defeated, seeing his mother break down simply at the sight of him.

"Mom, Mom, shhhhh ... it's okay," I'm trying to calm her. "Remember what I said about staying calm, for Jude? We've got to be strong for Jude, okay? Now, stop it," I tell her softly and wipe under her eyes again with my sweatshirt, wanting this feeling of mothering my mother to go away. I don't like it. I need Mom to be stronger because I want to break down, too.

"Hi, Mom," Jude says through his clenched teeth just as I get her set up on the stool I'd been using, but the strangeness of his raspy, wet voice sets Mom off again on another sob.

I give Jude a *What can I do?* Look and shrug one shoulder.

"Mom," Jude tries to soothe her. "Mom, it's okay," but she continues to sob.

"My boy, my boy. Who would do this to my boy?" she says, picking at Jude's hospital blanket, and I'm starting to think she might be having a mental breakdown or going into shock. Jude, through a mighty effort, raises his left hand to lay on top of hers on his right forearm. I've got my hands on her shoulders and cradle her like that, a makeshift human temple, for a while as her sobs finally start to slow.

Then a nurse knocks on the door and tells us they have to take Jude for his MRI. The nurse starts to unplug his bed and machines to make him mobile as Mom just watches the nurse's hands flutter all over Jude. Jude squeezes Mom's hands, and I can see the pain it causes him, and tells her, "I'll be back, okay, Mom?"

Somehow this seems to snap Mom out of her daze, and for the first time she looks into Jude's eyes. Jude meets her gaze and waits patiently.

"I love you, son," Mom says.

"I love you, too, Mom," Jude replies.

———

Mom's introductions to the group are a mix of heartwarming and unbearably awkward.

"I can't tell you what an honor it is to meet you, Charlene. You've raised an incredible daughter," Braden says.

"You're the husband?" is Mom's response.

"Jude didn't tell me you are a downright beauty queen, Charlene," Levi tries between meltdowns.

"You're *Jude's* … husband?" is all she could muster.

"Mrs. Charlene," Jay is the only one who feels at ease. "I finally kicked Katie. Oh, and the booze," he says proudly.

"That bitch," Mom replies through a sneer. "She doesn't deserve your time and money. Neither does the vodka. Steve and I are proud of you, Jay."

"I couldn't have done it without Callie, Mrs. Charlene," Jay says, looking to me.

"I know," Mom does not.

I decide to leave the four of them for a bit so I can make my calls before the close of business. I want to see how the motion to dismiss hearing went for Justin and discuss some things on my calendar for Monday, as I imagine I'll be here until Jude recovers. *Until.*

My next call is to Mariah. The excitement Jay and Braden shared when they introduced her to me as a life coach feels like it happened a month ago, although it was just yesterday. But Mariah is also an estates and probate attorney, which is just what I need right now, for both Jude's current state and his future care. I find a quiet corner and sit down to make the call.

After two rings, I get an answer, well, a sound of fumbling keys and a door opening, I think. Then an answer. "Avalero and Associates," she says.

"Uhhh, yes. I'd like to speak to Mariah Avalero, please," I notice I've donned my formal lawyer voice that I use day in, day out at Goldman Carr.

"She," Mariah says, and it catches me off guard. First, that I didn't recognize her grown-up voice. Second, that she answers her own phone, but I guess when your name is on the door, that's how it goes.

I fumble a bit. "Mariah, hi. This is. It's Callie," I just let it drop.

"Callie?!" Mariah says, sounding shocked. "What the heck? I'm so glad you called. How are you? *Where* are you?" she asks, and I hate that she's so bubbly and fun and happy to hear from me, especially when I'm about to dump all over her exuberance.

But I do it because it has to be done. I explain everything that's going on to Mariah and what I need from her to help Jude.

"I'll be there in an hour," she tells me. "I'll bring the paperwork you need. It's best to get these things signed as soon as you can if the person is still … lucid. I'm on my way."

——

Later, I find Mom on a bench outside the emergency room, puffing on a cigarette.

"Mom, Jude's back in his room if you want to come visit again." She immediately smashes her cigarette onto the pavement, pinches the burnt tip, puts it in her pocket, and gets up to follow me.

"I like Braden," she says. "And Levi."

"Yeah, they're pretty amazing." I find I don't know whether to brag about my little incredible family or hold back, as I definitely haven't been including Mom in it. We walk for a bit in silence back into the building and toward the elevators.

"You know, I always knew about Jude," Mom tells me, and I decide to just listen. Whatever little shards of memories and Jude facts she has still rattling around in there, I want them.

"He just, as a little boy, always had such a gentle way about him.

He was soft, ya know? I mean, tender-hearted. He really saw other people, other kids. He often tried to help other boys by teaching them or sharing, but they were just so rough, always shoving and blowing stuff up and sticking disgusting things in their mouths," this makes me laugh, "that, after a while, Jude just decided he wanted nothing to do with them. I knew he was different in some way, and then as the years passed, all signs just kept pointing toward … he's gay." The word sounds really strange in her mouth, like an awkward shape that was hard for her to work out.

"I knew he was different, he was special," I add, finding it more comforting than I could have imagined to talk to someone who has known Jude for as long as I have—even longer—someone who was there with us through it all. "It seems unbelievable in hindsight, but I swear, Mom, I didn't know until he told me. The minute he did, though, it all clicked. But, he's so incredibly happy, Mom. The happiest I've ever seen him. I want you to know that. After everything he's been through, he's really built an amazing life for himself."

Mom puts her hand to her chest as the elevators take us up.

"That's what worries me," she whispers.

I want to ask her more, but when the doors ding open, Mariah is there.

CHAPTER THIRTY-FOUR
THIS RIGHT HERE

"Avalero and Associates, huh?" I ask her as I rush out of the elevator and hook Mariah's elbow, shuffling her immediately away from Mom. The last thing I need today is Mom figuring out what I'm doing.

Mariah is short but slender and moves with grace. She has her long, thick black hair braided neatly into a long braid that she's twirled around up on her head. There's no Aqua Net cemented wall of hair hiding her beautiful face anymore. Her outfit surprises me—for a lawyer—as it's not my daily getup for the firm, but Mariah looks very comfortable in some sleek athletic casual pants, with a white, loose button-down tucked into them. Her belt looks like something handmade in Santa Fe, and she's got an interesting coral necklace and matching bracelet on. Then boots! These REI-looking, hike-up-Everest things. She's also sporting a leather satchel that I'm sure qualifies for a briefcase at Avalero and Associates, with a colorful woven strap. Mariah looks like the Bear Grylls version of a lawyer, and I immediately decide I like her version better than my pantyhose and hair-sprayed bun type. I look down at my oversized sweatshirt that has Mom's mascara still smeared across it and try to smooth it down out of habit.

"Well, there's actually no associates ... *yet*," Mariah chuckles. "It's just me right now, but the name gives me room to grow. Someday. But,

I'm happy on my own right now. I like the one-armed paper hanger pace of it," Mariah says, and I realize how much I've missed her.

Mariah and I talk earnestly, but hurriedly, about what needs to be taken care of as we make our way to Jude's room. I hear Braden's voice coming out from the door as we approach.

"Callie doesn't even know about that part, yet," I hear Braden say as I come in. He winks at Jude, and Jude gives an awkward wink back. I narrow my eyes at Braden, and he just puts a finger to his mouth and smiles at me. I look to Jay to be on my side here, but he just shrugs his shoulders.

"That's how it's going to be, huh?" I say to him and I rap him lightly on the shoulder. Braden slips back by Jay as I come around to Jude's good side with Mariah alongside.

"Mariah!" Jay and Braden both say and high-five one another. Mariah looks at them strangely, then she cocks her head to one side.

"Jason Lawler, as I live and breathe, is that you?"

Jay smiles, his scar pulling tight, and blushes. He nods. "Hi Mariah, thanks for coming."

"Of course," she says, and they hug.

"This must be Braden," she says, extending a hand, which Braden slaps away—just like Levi did when they first met, I'm remembering— and pulls her in for a hug.

"For the record, I'm the one who found you," he tells her. Jay gives a monstrous eye roll but remains quiet.

"You're a smart man," she tells Braden. "We'll talk more later, okay?" she tells my guys. "I've got to deal with my client here." Mariah turns and gives Jude a warm smile. She must have seen a lot of injuries and hospitals and death in the ten years we've been apart, I think, because Mariah moves around the hospital room like she's comfortable here. She didn't even flinch at seeing Jude's condition in the bed. It was nothing like Mom's reaction, or even mine.

"Hi Jude," she says to him softly. "It's been a long time."

Jude nods, tries to smile, but it fails, and then reaches, with some effort, a hand out to Mariah, who instantly takes it and wraps it in both of hers.

"You're doing alright, buddy," she tells him. "I'm here to help."

Watching the two of them, I feel my throat try to close up again. For the first time since I got that terrible call, I don't feel like I have to be entirely in control and know every step to take. Mariah's confidence and ease in this situation bring me immense comfort. She feels like a cool salve on this hot wound.

Although Mariah is talking to him, Jude is looking past me at Jay and Braden. There's something in his expression I can't read, but then again, he has a bandage covering half of his face, and his jaw is wired shut. I chalk it up to his condition and fall back in with Jay and Braden as Mariah is explaining everything to Jude.

"Listen, guys. My mom doesn't know what's going on here with Mariah, okay?" I tell Jay and Braden.

"What's going on?" Braden asks, now sounding concerned. "I thought she was just here to visit, to help you through this?"

I shake my head 'no.' "Well, she is. But, not in the way you're thinking. I'll definitely need a life coach after we survive all this. But Mariah is here for Jude now. I'll explain when I can. You'll just have to trust me, right now, because we need to move quickly." Jay and Braden don't even look at each other. They keep their eyes on me and say in unison.

"We trust you."

"Okay," Mariah says when she finishes with Jude's signatures, taking command of the situation. "I want to get the doctor in here to talk about it, and Callie, please call the chaplain up to act as a witness."

———

Hours later, I wake from a fitful sleep in the purgatory area. I quietly ease myself from my chair, look around to see Mom gone—probably outside for another smoke—and Jay and Braden tucked up in positions that look as uncomfortable as I was, trying to sleep. But, I don't see Levi.

On a whim, I tiptoe down to Jude's room. It's around three in the morning.

As I get closer to Jude's door, I hear hushed voices. Levi is sitting by Jude's bed holding his hand. Jude is awake and calm. They're talking. It sounds like they're reliving a memory, and a pang of love and sorrow runs through my heart.

"Sorry," I tell them as the door creaks, betraying my presence.

"Don't be," Levi says immediately. "We were just talking about you, Callie. We need you. Get in here."

I make my way over and pull up another chair next to Levi.

"I need to thank you," Levi says.

"Thank me? For what?" I ask.

"For what you've done for Jude."

I settle myself down next to Levi and lay my hands on both of theirs. It reminds me that I just did this earlier today with Jay and Braden. My shoulders feel like they're being pulled to the ceiling with the gift Levi has just given me, thanking me for what I've done.

"I love you two," Jude says, squeezing our hands. "You both loved me even when I didn't know who I was, or what I wanted, or what was right for me. You loved me when I messed up and made mistakes. You loved me when I left my disgusting socks all over the floor."

A snotty laugh gurgles out of Levi. "They were so grody," he whispers to me.

"You loved me when I lied to you about the rules of Monopoly so I could win."

An equally wet laugh erupts out of me.

"You loved me when I tried to pair my salmon shorts with that striped blazer." Levi shakes his head and clucks. "Just no. Fifty shades of no," Levi breathes.

"You loved me even when I pushed you off our fence back in Clovis, and it knocked the wind out of you."

"Wait, you *pushed* me?" I ask incredulously. I see in my periphery Jude gives a little *maybe, maybe not* shrug. Levi and I still have our eyes on our hands because I think we're afraid to look anywhere else. But, Jude pushes on.

"This, right here," Jude squeezes our sad, wet little hand temple. "This is what you have to keep pursuing. And what you have to protect. Family, in any form. You two are family, now. Do you understand me?"

"Jude, stop," I beg. This conversation hurts too much. Levi puts a hand around my shoulder.

"You'll need him, trust me," Jude says. "You've got big changes coming, Callie," I wince, thinking he's talking about his own passing. "Not me, not this, Callie," he reassures me. "I don't know what's going to happen with me. I'm talking about other things in your life. We'll talk about that another time." I glance at Levi, and he nods. This both relieves me and scares me a little. But all I care about right now is Jude. Whatever further change comes in my life after we get Jude past this travesty, I can handle.

"But—listen to me," Jude picks back up, but waits until I can gather the strength to raise my eyes and look at him. When I lift my eyes and see, again, the reality that Jude has found himself in, all I can think is I want to claw off that big white bandage from his face and tear it to shreds. I want to scream until my lungs are raw. I want to punch the walls and throw everything that's not bolted down, and then run. Run, run, run, just like I did when I left Clovis.

"You're going to get through it, with your family surrounding you, and have an amazing life on the other side. I see it, Callie. I do. And, you're going to do that because you're strong. And, you have Levi. Keep Levi close."

Suddenly, Jude's head slams back against his pillow. He looks like he's having a seizure. I hear what sounds like sirens in his room. Levi and I jump up and back as nurses come rushing in.

"Oh God, oh God, oh God!" I hear Levi shout.

"Room 418 is coding!" A booming voice echoes through the room.

———

"We're not sure exactly yet what threw his heart into tachycardia," the doctor explains to the five of us after the dust has settled. "It may have been a bone or bullet fragment that moved around in his chest. On the imaging, we did see some troublesome spots and blotches in his mediastinum that were hard to decipher and had us concerned, but— because he was hemodynamically stable—the surgical team was going to address them tomorrow morning during his scheduled surgery. But, they're bumping that surgery up to 6:00 a.m. now in light of what just happened. He's okay for the moment. We intubated, sedated, and stabilized him."

Jay, Braden, Mom, Levi, and I all look at each other as if there are answers there. They're not. Not a one of us knows if Jude will be okay.

Then a word the doctor said hits me. *Intubated.*

I look to Levi and whisper. "They intubated him."

Levi matches my stern gaze, knowing what this means. I look down at my watch. It's 4:14 a.m. Jude's going into surgery at 6:00 a.m.

My organs feel like they've turned to lead and all lumped together, and now they're making it hard for my heart to beat. My mouth tastes bitter. I look at Mom because I see what Jude knew was coming. This is going to eviscerate her.

Mom senses my panic like electricity in the air, and I curse the unspoken, unseen bond we have.

"What, Callie?" she asks. Her voice is no longer soft or forgiving. It sounds like the mom from my childhood. The one I'm afraid of.

Levi squeezes my shoulder. "It's what Jude wanted," he whispers. His words form some tiny thread, spiderweb thin, that somehow holds my spine together and keeps me upright. *For Jude*, I tell myself.

"Mom," I start shakily. "Jude signed a DNR. Do you know what that is?"

Mom's face looks horrified, contorted.

"That's why Mariah was here," I breathe out. "Jude didn't want any life-saving measures taken in case he … well, did what he just did. Coded."

Mom is starting to shake, looking at me, so I try to explain.

"Mom, he didn't want to end up worse off if the surgery didn't go well, paralyzed or in a coma or, ya know? He's already not sure he wants to even live like this anyway. A gay man with a fucked-up face and a bag of shit he carries around with him every day. You have to understand, Mom, who Jude is. What makes Jude, Jude? He wanted me to help him get all his affairs in order so he could … make his own decisions. Or, well, give me the power, to be more accurate, to enforce his wishes if he couldn't. But I'm only doing what Jude wants. This gives him control and dignity. You have to understand that, Mom."

"You wanted to take away any chance he might have of surviving. That's what I understand," Mom hisses at me. Cold and steely. The fear I used to feel as a child when Mom turned like this is flattened by the anger I have for this situation and the deep-seated commitment I have made to Jude. Mom's venom scares me none in this moment. I unleash.

"No, Mom. Fuck! I didn't *want* any of this. I only did what *Jude* wanted," I can hear my voice rising, and I'm afraid all of this anger welling inside of me is about to blow like a volcano, rushing out of me so forcefully, it will singe Mom to the ground and erase her, and this entire hospital, from existence.

"But *you* made it so they could take my boy off life support?" Her chest is heaving now, and she's shaking all over. As much as I'm worried she's going to cause herself a stroke or heart attack, I can't stop the anger I have right now, and how much of it is directed at her. If she accuses me one more time of doing something Jude didn't want, I don't know what I might do.

"Jude was trying to make it so they would never put him on life support in the first place, Mom. *Jude* wanted this," I repeat.

"Until you have a child, you will never understand," Mom growls at me, her eyes piercing, her finger in my chest. "You will want every possible thing done to save them if they're hurt because you … feel like it's your fault. You feel like a failure because you couldn't save your own child."

I see something flash in Mom's eyes then—something else she wants to tell me. The two of us—mother and daughter—stare at each other with matching blue eyes. Mom bows her chest up. I bow mine.

"Jude. Wanted. This." I snarl at her, feeling so mad I almost want to grab a wad of her hair and slam her head into the wall, which frightens even me.

Mom shakes her head 'no' at me and turns to walk down the hall toward Jude's room. Levi and I jump up immediately, seeing her head that direction. She's not shouting or running. She's walking calmly, so we simply follow behind her, trying to coax her with words to come back, but we're having no impact on her. Mom keeps walking.

When she makes it to Jude's door, we try to stop her. Levi puts a hand on her shoulder. I try to stop her from opening the door, but she's stronger than I ever imagined. It feels like some demon has slipped into her skin and he's moving her arms and legs with unworldly, evil strength.

"Mom, NO!" I shout forcefully, trying to prevent her from opening the door. Mom elbows me in the face. I don't know whether it was intentional or not, but it stuns me for a moment, enough for her to get the door open. I wrap my arms around her as she tries to lunge into Jude's room.

"Levi, get the doctors and nurses!" I shout. "Give them the DNR!"

Mom and I crash to the floor in Jude's room. I look up to see Jude is sedated, and I pray, however deep he is buried in his own subconscious, that he can't hear or see us because I'm afraid of what I am about to do to my own mother. But, if it means protecting Jude's wishes, I will kill anything moving.

"Mom, stop!" I'm screaming at her.

"I am his MOTHER!" She shrieks. She is fighting me with inhuman strength, but I finally get her pinned down enough to be able to form words that I hurl at her.

"Then, for once in your goddam life, act like it! Stop torturing him with your demons and just support him! If you can't do that, then leave!" I can't comprehend my own anger at her.

"Not my boy! My child! Not again!" Mom has become feral now, clawing the floor, grunting, making sounds humans should not be able to hear as I press my body weight onto her.

"I WILL NOT LET ANOTHER CHILD OF MINE DIE LIKE THIS!" Her voice is becoming hoarse. I can see veins in her throat bulging as she turns over on her back and kicks me squarely in the stomach, with strength I can't even comprehend. Pain explodes inside my left shoulder as I'm thrown back against the cabinet, and I land hard on its corner. But I see Mom is starting to scramble up, and I can't let her reach Jude. He has a chance of surviving this on his own if this surgery goes well, and I'm not going to let Mom try to touch or move him in a fit of maternal stupidity and ruin whatever shot Jude has. I feel anger I've harbored since I was a child rise inside of me like a tsunami—for her poor decisions, her overreactions, her selfish rage.

I leap off the floor.

A bloody scream rips through the room before I realize it's me as I crash into her body, tackling my own mother to the cold tile floor. We land hard, and my shoulder bursts into fire. I hear Mom groan as the sound of nurses' and doctors' shoes and shouts begin to fill the room. I realize I have my arms wrapped around Mom's torso with my wrists locked, and I've even wrapped my legs around her legs and crossed them tight. My shoulder feels like someone is ripping it from my body, but I push into the pain, gritting and drooling, seeing red. I will not let go of her. *I will not let go, Jude. I will not let go;* I drill myself.

Mom is sobbing into the floor, her mascara leaving streaks on the tile. She is still screaming, although her voice sounds like it's coming through broken sticks in her throat.

"My son!" she shouts. "Not my child! Not again! NOT AGAIN!"

I realize I'm sobbing now, too, as her pain is palpable. It fills the room, fills my mouth and nostrils. It tastes like blood and hasn't left any air in the room to breathe. There is only Mom's unthinkable sorrow pulsing and bending the walls.

"Not Jude! Not Jude!" she screams as I start to feel hands on us, simultaneously helping and manhandling us. I feel my arms being taken behind my back, and I cry out in pain as they rotate my left shoulder. I see them scooping Mom up off the floor and bringing her hands behind her back, too. She's not fighting as hard anymore.

"You!" She hisses as they traipse her past me toward the door.

"I hate you for this," are her last words to me as two burly nurses force her out of the room.

CHAPTER THIRTY-FIVE
MOM

I almost told her this time. There have been many times I thought about it. But then I can only wonder what god damn good that would do. Jude and Callie knowing. None is the answer.

When they were little, they worshipped their Dad. Hell, I did, too. Once. Bill. He was an easy man to fall for: handsome, clever, smooth, and just busting with joy and light. That is, until he started drinking anything brown. Then he shape-shifted right in front of you and turned into a nasty, mean drunk, ready to avenge his honor if any comment—he thought—challenged it. None did. But you couldn't tell him that. Once the switch was flipped, Bill could never be stopped.

I can't put my finger exactly on when Bill started to turn into an angry drunk. But, not long after we married and moved into the house in Clovis, I believe he felt trapped. A wife, a mortgage, a baby on the way. Things like that weigh on men. He tried to drink away his fears, but that never works, especially when the weights just keep coming. By the time Callie and Jude had come, and Callie was almost two, Bill was drinking himself into a stupor every night.

I had wanted to leave him for a long time, but I remember the day I knew I had to. The day the choice was taken away from me. It wasn't the first time he'd hit me. He was three sheets, but I wasn't far behind him that day. We'd been fighting nasty, like we did often back then. I felt like the first few times he smacked me, that I'd caused it, asked for it even. But, after they continued, and I couldn't dole out the blows he could, I realized they would never stop. I had rolled the idea of leaving around in my mind for a while, but I wasn't sure Bill would leave us alone in the house. Not without a fight. And, the only plan I could come up with was to pack Callie and Jude up and stay with my friend, Joellen, until I could find a place for us. But I drove a damn school bus. I didn't make enough on my own to support all three of us. And Joellen lived in a tiny trailer with her own kids and spotty air conditioning. That wasn't a real option. It's easy to see men hit women in the movies and say, "I'd never let a man do that to me." But, in real life, exit plans are harder. Resources are scarce. Reality is just different.

But resources be damned, the minute I saw Bill hurt Jude—and saw the hurt, even in his four-year-old eyes, saw the *understanding*—I knew. I had to leave. Bill had come home early from a long-haul cattle run and had already had a few; I could smell it on him. He was itching for a fight. Jude had drawn him this cute little picture of Bill and his big rig, even got the naked ladies on the mud flaps right. Made me wonder if Jude knew what the hell he was drawing. I hoped not. But, he'd been so excited to show it to his dad that I couldn't convince Jude it wasn't a good time. After he realized his dad was home, I couldn't keep him distracted anymore.

He burst into the kitchen shouting, "Daddy, Daddy, I made this for you!" waving his little piece of construction paper for Bill to see, he was circling Bill, tugging on his pant leg. He accidentally spilled a little of Bill's drink, and Bill lost it. Grabbed Jude by his little t-shirt collar and threw him and his little paper drawing against the wall. Jude slammed against it and slid down, his drawing fluttering in the air.

"Goddamm it, Jude!" Bill shouted. "Watch what you're doing, Son!" Bill was brushing some of the whiskey off of him, but when he looked up and saw Jude crumpled against the wall, the neck of his shirt torn open, a red welt forming on his face, something inside Bill shifted. He set his glass down gently on the table and just walked right out. I think Bill knew what a danger he was to his family in that moment. I told him the next day I wanted a divorce and would be leaving. To Bill's credit, he agreed to move out of the house and keep paying the mortgage for the time being, although that didn't last.

As old as I am now, I know it will be—till my dying day—the hardest thing I ever had to do in my life. To look down and know those two little kids, just babies really, were looking to me for everything. I tried to sing songs like Bill in the beginning. To make fun nicknames for them. I tried to make a game out of the bad situations—like when they cut our heat off that one winter, when I lost my cashier job, and all I could feed them was ketchup soup for a month, when I had to steal toothbrushes for them from Walgreens. But I just didn't have the joy Bill had. I was too angry to sing a damn song. But I fed and cleaned them and made them go to school. I did my best.

That's why it would kill me when something would happen—something that happens to all parents, nobody's perfect—and Jude would look at me like I'd failed. Like that time Callie rolled through the railing when we went to the Balloon Fiesta and stayed at that Motel 6. I heard a loud crack and looked out to see the railing all busted up, Callie gone, and Jude looking over the edge, screaming. Nothing can prepare you for a moment like that.

But then, I have to watch Jude lean back and then jump right off the balcony after her! Now, that?! *That.* That's something a mother should never have to endure. I run to the edge, though, and look over at what I think will be my children cracked wide open, and I see they're safe, thank fucking God. But I look down, and you know what I see? There's Jude, cradling Callie, looking up at me like … like, it was somehow *my fault.* Mine?

Jude would do that at times. Look at me like I wasn't fit to be a mom. And, hell, half the time I agreed with him. I never knew what the hell I was doing, and there were times when I wanted to give up. Just lie down on the floor with them and pitch an even bigger fit. Let them figure it out. Callie and Jude always did anyhow. And, I was proud of them for it. I was. Because that's how it was for me growing up. After my mom left, I had to keep the house clean, feed my brothers and sisters, and get everyone ready for school. I had to cook dinner and get groceries—shit like that. Kids *should* know what it takes, what the world is really like.

But what made it all really hard, so incredibly hard, was Bill. He would always swoop in as the fun dad, the rodeo cowboy who drove a really cool big truck, and he could just scoop them up and take them on an adventure, feed them kappercinos, and take them horseback riding. It was all fun and games. Then they would come home, and I would have to discipline them. I was the mean parent who had to make them brush their teeth, cut their hair, and stop their crying. And, it was like they always stood up for one another—each other, Bill, even Jay—but never me.

They made me feel like I was never welcome in their club. And, I get it. I'm not funny. I don't sing songs like Bill. I don't make jokes. But I gave up everything for those kids. And, I'd do it again. I put a roof over their heads. Fed them and got them to school just like I did my siblings. And, I taught them the hard life lessons: how to work hard, earn a dollar, have a plan, expect pain and loss, and keep moving forward. I made them strong. I do know that. It wasn't a rose-colored, privileged childhood. I know that, too. But Callie and Jude grew up knowing how to take on the world and hold onto one another. Because together they were always happy and capable. Always. I'm proud of that.

I think that's the reason I could never tell them the entire truth about Cadence. I was afraid they wouldn't believe me and would think I was just trying to badmouth Bill … again. I did that more than I'm proud of, but that man just unnerved me, and I always felt so alone in my battle with him. It was as if the three of them were against me when I was the only one trying to do what was actually best for Callie and Jude. I feared that if they believed I was lying about something that awful, it would impact our relationship forever. That's the reason I didn't tell them.

I also worried it might make them hate their dad and—as much as I hated Bill—I didn't want them to. Then there was the thought that if they had to know *that* about their own family, if they had to come to terms with a toxic fact, that it would poison them from within like it has me. I didn't want that for them either. That, well … those are the reasons—I guess—that I never told Jude and Callie the truth about Cadence.

The truth was, Bill and I had started fighting pretty nasty by then, about a year and a half into our marriage. We were both feeling trapped and edgy, both unhappy and not sure our marriage was a good decision, so we snarled and scratched at each other because we had nowhere else to turn. I was drinking some, but I had cut back immediately when I found out I was pregnant, down to just a drink or two a day, and I had stopped smoking entirely. I had done my part. But Bill wasn't supportive at all, coming home every day, pounding them back right in front of me. I hated him for that.

So, one afternoon, during my last term, Bill and I really got into it at the house. I was in what was going to be the nursery—it later became Callie's room—painting. Little butterflies and hearts. It looked silly, but I was a first-time mom. I used to want to do all those cute parent things. A long time ago. But Bill came barging in after work, picking a fight. I was pissed at him for a thousand different things, so I started shoving him and putting my finger in his chest. It was stupid. We were both stupid. And, so young. Bill was so drunk he couldn't see straight. I could tell when his pupils got too big and two different sizes that I was in trouble.

I tried to get into the bathroom so I could push him out and lock the door, but I'd gone too far, saying really hurtful things to him, telling Bill he was going to be a terrible father and that I'd never wanted to have a family with him in the first place. I even told him I would kill our baby if he laid a finger on me. Stupid, childish stuff. But, it set Bill off. He chased me into the bathroom. I don't know what he was going to do. Maybe just grab me by the shoulders and yell at me. I could have taken that. I should have taken that. But I did not stand there. I kept fighting back, and Bill shoved me so hard I stumbled back and fell into the bathtub, bringing the shower curtain and rod down with me.

I landed hard on my stomach. The minute I hit, I knew we'd done something terrible. A nausea swept through me. I lost my bladder, but then my water soon followed. And, when my vision cleared, I felt my contractions start. Bill's shoving me had induced premature labor. We found out at the hospital later that the fall had caused my placenta to detach from my uterine wall, throwing Cadence into distress.

Even though she wasn't fully developed, my little girl, my brave little child, came out into this world and tried to breathe on her own. They plugged her up to all these machines and tubes—like Jude is now—and she kept fighting and trying, just as much as I know Callie would if it had been her. Or Jude. We do breed fighters in this family, I know that. But, it wasn't enough. I had to watch until Cadence stopped breathing. She turned a sickening shade of blue, and her hands grew so cold I swear they burned me. My heart emptied itself into the hole she left behind.

Callie and Jude know we lost her, but they don't know about that fight between me and Bill that happened before, and I've decided I don't ever want them to. Bill and I said things to each other afterward that can never be unheard or unsaid. "Your drinking killed our baby." "Your throwing me to the ground killed Cadence." "You were never fit to be a mother anyway." "You'll never be anything but a washed-up cowboy and a violent alcoholic." "I hate you." "I never loved you." If I told Callie and Jude the truth about how Cadence died, they would start thinking those things, too. Even though Bill is dead, a fact like that changes you. It is a fact that changed me. A huge piece of me—the naïve, hopeful, happy woman that I was when I first got pregnant— died along with that struggling little blue body in the hospital.

But the day Bill threw Jude across the room, I knew. I knew where we were headed. Again. One more shove or punch or lost temper, and we would have another dead child on our hands. As scared as I was to leave Bill and be a single mom, I was more scared of losing Jude or Callie to Bill's brute hands and what I might do to him or myself if that happened. Deep down—and this is a fear I have never told anyone about—I was afraid if he killed one of them that I would not be strong enough to pick up and continue as a mother of one living, but two dead children. Those are the deep thoughts I was wrestling with, while Bill was singing his songs, telling his jokes.

But, hell, that's probably a better way to deal with pain: by pelting it with joy. I could just never do that. I couldn't smother mine like Bill could. For that reason, I was actually glad Jude and Callie had Bill as a different role model. I'm afraid what kids raised entirely by me might turn out like. Depressed little serial killers? Angry goth thieves? See? I can make jokes. Sometimes. They're just a bit darker.

But I don't think I can forgive Callie for this. Helping Jude leave me and helping him turn me into the thing that I feared most in this world of becoming: the mother of two dead children. How could she do that to me?

Then I think back on what I did to her. I'm pretty sure I kicked and clawed and elbowed my own daughter just now, which is hard to believe. The image of us wrestling flies through my brain in flashes and blips. But it always hurt the most when Callie and Jude ganged up on me and never acknowledged everything I did simply to try and save them, to protect them. The look Callie gave me before I went into Jude's room at the hospital was the same look Jude gave me after she fell into the dumpster. She looked at me like I wasn't fit to be his mom. Like everything I had ever done for him and for her, it counted for nothing. *Nothing?!*

But then I sit here. On this old back porch, in my rickety chair, with my beer and peanuts—that I know Callie makes fun of me for—and I think.

I smoke and drink and think.

Then I drink some more. And I think some more until the cigarettes run out.

And, I know, after hours of it, that I am already regretting the things I said to her. No one gives you a manual for mother-daughter relationships. Sometimes I see her as an ungrateful, vile child. But I know she sometimes—or maybe most of the time—sees me as a hateful, heavy-handed influence on her life, someone who was so mean, she had to run away from me. And, as much as that hurt me, I'm glad I was strong enough to let her think that and go. So Callie could shake out her glorious wings and fly. And that's just what she did—one hundred percent without me.

That's the reason I wouldn't send her that back child support. I knew she would be so much stronger, resourceful, and capable if she did it all on her own. And, I was right. One hundred percent. Knowing what her dad may have done to Cadence won't help Callie in any way. So, I will continue to carry this secret for Callie as she's already been fed enough misery and hurt for one life. And I will sit here and drink and think and hope someday my daughter will forgive me because she's going to need me with what's coming.

I already know it's happened. I feel it in my motherly bones.

CHAPTER THIRTY-SIX
THE CRATER

"We need security in 418!" I hear overhead as I look around the room, trying to get my bearings. I am overwhelmed with gratitude as I see that Jude is still safe in his bed. Mom didn't get to him—to do what, I have no idea—but at least I did that. He's still sedated, but his machines are beeping normally. I see scuff marks on the floor, Mom's mascara on the tile, and a rolling cart that I have to assume we crashed, but never even realized it. *I just tackled my Mom.* I can't really get my head wrapped around what just happened in here.

"But, you can't," I start to protest weakly to the nurses as they're picking me up off the floor. "He doesn't want," but they cut me off.

"Not now, Mrs. Potts. We've got to get this room secure and make sure this patient is still stable before we can talk about any of this. You have to leave now," they tell me.

"But, but …" I can feel I'm losing strength, or resolve, I'm not sure.

"Now, Mrs. Potts," she's pushing me, and I understand why. I see Levi standing outside of Jude's room, looking horrified, but he has some papers in his hand.

"Levi, you have to tell them he's DNR," I tell him, pleading with my eyes.

"I did, Callie," he responds. "They know. They're just. He's so close to surgery now. He's going back in like thirty minutes. They said they would honor it going forward, but this surgery will probably save his life." Levi's face is wan. Big, black bags have taken up residence under his eyes, and his cheeks look like they've caved in. He doesn't even look like himself anymore, and I wonder briefly what I must look like. A mad woman? An insane but loyal sister? A child who would fight her own mother?

A warrior, I finally decide as I'm cleaning myself up in the hospital bathroom ten minutes later. I've got a black eye forming that I don't know where it came from. Probably when Mom elbowed me, my shoulder was in a lot of pain, and I couldn't lift my left arm above a certain point, but I've decided not to tell anyone about that because I don't want them to send me away for treatment or surgery or whatever I might need when I need to be here, standing guard for Jude. Hospital security took Mom away. I don't even know where, yet, and I really have no desire to find out at the moment. I'm absolutely furious with her.

I swiped a roll of gauze from the nurse's station and had Braden sneak into the women's bathroom with me to help me secure my left arm against my body like a sling underneath my sweatshirt. I put his jacket on over and had him tuck the left arm of it into the left side pocket so it's not immediately noticeable that my arm is incapacitated. As Braden was circling around my torso with the gauze, I was pierced by the memory of Jude doing that with toilet paper when I fell from the tree in Mom's backyard, and we wanted to hide my mangled tummy from Mom to stay out of trouble.

I think cruelly in the moment that I should have asked Jay to help me with this, because people who have come from broken homes, fighting parents, crimes, drugs, fistfights, they just understand these situations better. I'm guessing—as an orphan and someone who misses his mother every moment of every day—Braden can't comprehend how either Mom or I could come to blows. But that's exactly what we did. In front of everyone, like the white trash I have to assume we are.

Because it's not the first time I've felt angry enough in my life to hit my mother hard enough to hurt her. Not by a long shot.

But, with each pass of the gauze around my bruised body—as he's done a thousand times in our relationship, reminding me, time and again, the man he is—Braden changes my mind.

"Callie, I … do you want to talk about what happened with your Mom?" Braden asks timidly.

"No," I say, so clipped I practically cut him off.

"Are you okay?" he asks, which I shouldn't have let irritate me, but I did because it's such a dumb question in a situation like this. Of course I'm okay. I mean, my life has turned to shit, my brother's hanging on by a thread, I'm losing control, and my own mother hates me and blames me for this mess, but that's been pretty par for the course of my life, so, yeah, I'm fine, and that's what I tell him.

"Yeah, I'm fine."

"I just," Braden tries to start, and it happens before I can stop it, like a seam on my side just opened and she slipped out. The Mom I carry inside of me answers him.

"But you don't, Braden. I'm sorry, you just don't. You don't know what this situation is like. You've never fought with your parents over something like this. You've never tackled your mother to the ground. You've never had to help your brother get his affairs in order or, God forbid, kill himself if he feels the time has come. You don't even have a sibling." The minute the words leave my mouth, I want to snatch and claw them back—because they were so impossibly mean, they were Mom mean—but I can't. They're out.

Braden takes a deep breath before responding, and I see his patience for me open up and enclose us both like a shield.

"You're right, Callie," Braden says. "I've never fought with my parents as an adult, because they died when I was a kid, and that's something you don't know anything about. And, I don't have a brother.

I'm an only child. Again, something you know nothing about. And the things you said just now hurt me. But you know what? I won't do anything now to make this harder for you. I will absorb whatever you need to release. Whether I am capable or not, of doing these very hard things you think I cannot handle, I will not leave your side. Do you understand me?"

At that, I crumple into him and sob into Braden's shoulder. "I don't want to lose Jude," I tell him through tears and snot, drool and terror, my fear flowing out of me and squeezing Braden like a vice.

"I know, babe," Braden says as he hugs me tighter than he ever has. "I don't either. But, mainly, I can't lose you, and I want you to know you will never lose me. I mean, unless I die before you. I'll try everything I can not to, but you're pretty damn tough, Callie. The odds are against me." A small laugh wriggles out of me, and I realize I have been wrong, again, about Braden's resilience. In this moment, right now, that was the exact right thing to say, and that's saying a lot, considering the moment. I give Braden a sturdy nod afterward and thank him before we shuffle out with my makeshift arm sling secure.

Jude is in surgery for three painful hours as the four of us—me, Braden, Jay, and Levi—wait in the purgatory area. I haven't seen Mom since our fight, and I have no desire to find her. When the surgeon comes walking toward us, we rise and each grab a hand.

The time it takes the doctor to get to us feels like an eternity. He's taking steps. I can hear them reverberating off the walls, but it doesn't seem like he's getting any closer. The hallway is stretching before me, and he's getting further away. I am so sick of the shades of cream and the too-bright lights and the cold of this place. It feels like a cold, sterile hell.

I see the doctor's chest rise in a big breath and fall right before he makes it to us.

My brain starts to loop.

Not Jude. Not Jude. Not Jude.

"I'm sorry" are his first words, and my knees give way. I crash hard to the floor and start sobbing. I hear more words.

Bullet embolism. Small fragment. Pericardial window. Projectile. Right ventricle. Aortic dissection. Sudden. Traumatic. DNR.

None of them made much sense to me, other than the last few. I knew what it meant. Some piece of a bullet had moved around in Jude's chest and caused his aorta to dissect, suddenly and traumatically to the extent that they couldn't stop the bleeding, and they couldn't resuscitate Jude because of his wishes, which I implemented—so, because of me.

I don't know what else the doctor might have said or when the doctor leaves. I am only aware of Levi, wadded up next to me on the floor, sobbing as hard as I am. Jay and Braden are kneeling around us, crying as well. It makes me think of the little mashed-up temple of our hands. I feel like the four of us are the same, each forming a leg of this wayward, leaning-over temple, now without the center pole that held us all together.

I try desperately to remember the very last thing I said to Jude. *Did I tell him I love him and how much he meant to me? How much he did for me, and how I will never ever be able to repay him? How much has he made me the person I am today? Did I?*

Fuck! I can't breathe. My chest feels like I have one of those lead X-ray vests on. My mouth tastes like copper. I feel fluids running out of my nose and mouth, but I can't do anything but cry onto the floor.

I hear feet moving around me. I hear people saying my name. But I can't react to anything. I'm not sure I can stand up and keep living without him.

Jude's face flashes before me, perfect and whole, his smile dazzling. I see him running around with Lucy, playing tug-of-war. I see Jude as a child, teaching me how to build with LEGOs. His voice whispers through me—*Lil' Bit.* I can feel him giving my foot a lift to sling me over a crumbling cinderblock fence. I smell biscuit donuts. I hear Jude land in a dumpster beside me. I see the sandbox. I sense a thread running through my entire life being tugged and giving way, and the whole thing being yanked out. His spindly little sandcastle washes away in the rain. I don't know when I will find the strength to get off this tile floor and continue living.

I see Levi in my periphery, and I worry—from this, he may never recover. Through my own tears, I can see his face is mutated, red and twisted in pain, and he's drooling onto the floor, a deep, soulful wail coming out of him. I have an instinct to try to be strong for him right now. To try to lift Levi up, encircle my arms around him, and say something Jude would. But I find I can't. My arms won't move, and I realize I can't help anyone right now. I can't do anything else for anyone, not even myself, because I don't want to do anything. I don't want to cry or talk or even breathe. I want to die on this cold fucking floor so that I don't have to feel what life is going to feel like without Jude in it.

Jude.

Levi's beautiful, creative, intelligent partner.

Jay's cousin and confidante.

Braden's inspiration and friend.

My guide, leader, soulmate, companion, comrade.

Mom's son.

Jude.

My brother. At only 32. Is gone.

As I lay crying on the hospital floor, a massive crater opens next to me, and my heart starts pouring into it. It's deep navy blue and so cold I swear I can feel it.

CHAPTER THIRTY-SEVEN
JUDE

She did tell me. Every time Callie looks at me—with those liquid blue eyes, like I'm the most important thing in the world to her—she tells me. I hate this for Callie. Losing me is going to be one of the hardest things she's ever faced, harder than leaving Clovis, and harder than losing Dad. But Callie was born to endure things like this. She hates that fact, but it's true. She's a Potts. Plus, something about my time here always felt finite, too delicate and thin to stay attached. I sense Callie always felt—or feared—that, too. But, Callie's time here? That's been reinforced with rebar. She will survive, just fine, but I want her hope and love and wonder to survive, too. Callie sometimes buries her warrior heart too deep.

The person I really hate this for is Levi, because I feel like I pulled him in selfishly, knowing I was probably only going to hurt him in the end, either through something I did or just the person I am. My actions toward Callie aside, I'm a selfish person. Always have been. But Levi's love was so pure and selfless, it was impossible to turn away from. He wanted so much for me. I probably would have finished my architecture classes and gotten my degree and become an architect on my own—mind you, before Calavetti, I, too, was a Potts—but doing it with Levi by my side, with the joy and laughter and fun he brought to my home and my life, made it all a different experience entirely.

I can't say I know for sure whether the love between two gay men is different than that between a man and a woman, but there's something to be said about the adversity it must overcome, like a rose fighting to the surface. Surely it comes out stronger, dewier, redder if it had to fight harder to get there. I can't say that I know, because I did love Rachel—as a person, a woman, a friend—but it was nothing like the love I have for Levi. That love is a rich, maroon river that pumps the very blood through my body. My love for Levi was the cornerstone of everything I became. I hope he will come to learn and understand that and know that my passing had nothing to do with him—it was a chain of events set into motion a long time ago.

What I do know will happen is that Callie will hold all of these men together. What she is about to learn about Braden will be crushing. She will mourn and falter and fall apart, but she will pick herself back up and carry on, eventually. What I have always loved—and admired—about Callie is her unparalleled tenacity. I would watch her as a child try to match a drawing of mine, and she would try, again and again and again, tracing every stroke, matching every color, until I couldn't tell the difference between hers and mine. Callie would sit and memorize what she needed to for school tests and exams until she could read the entire chapter back to me pretty much. She would spend hours making homemade birthday and Christmas cards for us all with her tongue sticking out and a pipe cleaner accidentally glued in her hair. If you've ever seen a child have to get up and stretch her body because she's had it folded over for so long, she got sore—at age five—you know that kid is committed.

Callie never quits.

She never gives up on anyone who never gave up on her. That is the reason she will patch things with Mom. I know it. I see it. Even considering what they just did to one another. I saw that, too. *White trash is right, Callie. Let's not do that again.* But Callie will also carry Levi through this. She will pull him under her broken wing and hold him until her body is sore from it. She will also forgive Braden and work through all of that mess. I know she will, and I know she will come out on the other side with all the love these men can offer.

Especially Jay. Although they have their history, Jay would walk through fire for Callie. I see it in the way he looks at her. *You're a good man, Cousin. Watch over her for me.* Those two will prop one another up as they've been through hard times together. They know this is just a part of life. All Callie has to do is be open-minded. Choose love. And see that my time here was always meant to be fixed. I was meant to be a torch for her, to get her through the dark tunnel we emerged from.

But I cannot exist on this earth broken, scarred, and mutilated. I don't have the strength to face something like that every day and carry on. That's something Callie could do, but I could never. I'm actually glad my aorta dissected mid-surgery, and I passed away gently under anesthesia, so I didn't have to deal with the pain of facing my own hideous appearance every day and pretending like I was okay with it, or living life as a disabled, disgusting science project. I also didn't want to have to put Callie through more than I did by making her perform her own brother's euthanasia. But she would have done it just like she would have defended me every day of her childhood if I had come out to her sooner. For me, she would have. I know that.

As I would have done this favor, any favor, for her, if she asked, although I sense deep in my bones that Callie is going to live a very, very long time. She's all grit and guile. And rebar. And—in addition to Mom, Tammy, Levi, and the guys, her family—she has Mariah. I see them rekindling what I think was already a lifelong friendship. And, I will be forever grateful for the hoops Mariah jumped through, last minute, to get a few things in place for me, for Levi, and Callie.

I can feel them crying now. Wailing. I can almost hear it in the distance. I can see Callie and Levi crumpled on the floor, their distorted faces screaming into the tile. I see Jay and Braden crouched over them, standing guard, not letting anyone touch or move them. I see my family in incredible pain, but I see them together. Holding onto one another in their worst moment. That's what matters. I turn away from the scene because it's too gut-wrenching, and I know it is temporary. The four of them will eventually stand themselves up and dust themselves off. They will persevere. They will remember me and mourn me, but they will all carry on. And, they will laugh and love again. This I know.

My presence is starting to wane. It feels like I'm being erased and redrawn somewhere else. I want desperately to do more, to say more things to Levi and Callie, even Mom, but I know I can't. I have to trust everything has already been said. I wish I could have spoken to Mom again one last time, but I did tell Callie the things she needed to know to see Mom as she never has. Callie will understand Mom better after she endures this. Losing someone this close to you, who was too young to die, changes you. For Mom, it was for the worse. I hope for Callie that it will be for the better. But Callie will absorb what I told her about Mom in her own time, and eventually, she will reach out to her. I know this, and that is my gift to Mom.

It is a weird state to simply *know* things that will happen in the future, as much as I know my middle name is Herbert—*gross*—and the sky is blue. I just know them, but I can't tell you how. Maybe it's one of the perks.

The image of my family on the hospital floor looks like it's getting further away. That or I'm getting further from it. Their sobs are now just a faint howl in the wind.

This is it. I have to wonder if I did enough with my time here? Did I touch people? Did I make them feel loved? Should I have broken my promise to Rachel and reached out? Should I have tried to be a father to that little girl? And, did I not because I was scared or because I thought it was the right thing to do? Did I show Levi enough love, the amount he deserved? Did I make Callie strong enough? Did I teach her enough? I'll never know, as my time is over. I have to make peace with it all, or haunt them like a raging queen for the rest of my spirit life.

As fun as that might be, I choose peace. For them, and me.

Callie, Levi, Mom, Dad, Rachel—wherever you are—I love you all. I know you tried, and I know I wasn't perfect. I do wish I could have spent more years happy, but I'm grateful for the ones I got. They were more than I ever thought I would have, and more than I deserved.

Mostly, I'm going to miss you, Lil' Bit. For most of my life, you were the most important thing in it. You were always this bubbly, adventurous, tough-as-nails sidekick I could always depend on. It meant more to me than you'll ever know that you looked up to me and stood up for me. You and Jay both. But you were the first person in my life to see me as valuable. Not a burden, or a problem, an odd, ill-fitting person you simply had to take care of because society expected you to. You, Callie, *chose* me as your mentor. You accepted me exactly as I was—your confused, nonconforming, fragile, finite gay brother—and I will never forget that.

I need you to keep your mind open. Be flexible and creative with your life. Let it get messy if need be. And, keep loving people because, despite the pain, it is always worth it.

I love you, Callie. I know you won't believe it for a long time, but you've got this. And, you've got an incredible life ahead, with an amazing, unconventional family. It is one of the things I just know. All you have to do is open your heart to it and be the person I've always known you to be. I'll be there with you for all of it. Like I said: Keep Levi close.

It's not goodbye, because I'm always with you.

CHAPTER THIRTY-EIGHT
FROM JUDE

Everything just feels so jagged and torn apart. Like a bomb went off in my life. I felt the searing burn from the gun powder, my body and soul are battered from the blast, and now there is a curtain of ash that has covered everything, turning my entire world a chalky grey and making it hard to breathe and see. I keep coughing as if there really is ash in the air, but it's just my ravaged throat. My eyes are swollen and spent from crying, and one is black.

I don't know how much time passed as I was curled up on the floor, watching my heart pour into a hole, but Mariah arrived at some point and gave me a confused look when she tried to raise and hug me, only to find my arm in a sling.

"I just … we," I try to start, but words fail me. "Jude died," is all I can get out, and it crushes me anew. I crumple into Mariah and sob again, although no tears will come. In a few broken sentences, I am able, at least, to explain to her that the DNR worked and that we were able to honor Jude's wishes for the most part, but that he died in surgery. I thank her, but it's all I can really do. Unbidden, Jude's words have now risen to the surface—*"You've got big changes coming, Callie"*—and I fear I cannot handle any more change in my life.

I've got to face this head-on, whatever it is, and cut it out, so I can start to put everything back together and find out whether a life without Jude is worth living. As much as I hate to do it, I don't have any capacity to be polite right now.

"I have to find Levi," I tell Mariah as I leave her with a face full of worry and a million questions to begin roaming the halls looking for Levi.

———

"You'll need him, trust me," Jude's words haunt me as I jog the sickening cream halls and check the nurse's station and bathrooms. I finally find Levi crumpled in a corner, and a pang of guilt runs through me as I realize I don't even know when he left our circle. My memory of the last half hour—hell, the last twenty-four hours—is so fragmented and fuzzy, it all feels indecipherable.

"Levi," I say as I fold myself and my good arm around him. He just remains sitting with his knees up against his chest and his arms wrapped around them. Levi is staring at the floor, with no affect, and I wonder if humor and laughter will ever come back to us.

"Levi, I'm so sorry," I start, but immediately decide it's a stupid start.

"*You're* sorry," he looks up at me then. His face is ashen and streaked with salty rivulets, but his focus is clear. "Callie, he was your brother. *I'm* sorry for you." Levi says.

"Jude always told me he felt something like this was going to happen," Levi picks back up, in a voice I'm not sure is even his. "Some sudden, tragic end to his life because he felt things were too good to be true, but I didn't believe him. I just thought he'd never been part of a loving, healthy family before. It was new to him. That's why the feeling scared him. But I should have told you, Callie. If you had known something like this was going to happen, maybe we could have prevented it. We should have never gone to P.L.A.Y. that night," Levi scolds himself.

I take his hands in mine and look him in the eye. "Levi, I already knew."

Levi looks at me, perplexed.

"I know what Jude felt, because I felt it, too. I've felt it my whole life. Like Jude was too … " I can feel myself struggling for the right words as I've never really said this to anyone out loud before. "Too … pristine for this world. Too smart, too bright," they are the only words I can find, but even they are not right.

I couldn't stand up and be strong for Levi earlier, when we were both pouring our hearts into the floor, but I feel I can—or at least I have to try—now for Jude. *We do the hard things others can't,* my mom's words whisper to me.

Levi absorbs that and remains silent for a moment. The Professor, taking it all in. He finally sighs and responds. "You've really felt that way, since you were little, Callie? You're not just saying that to me to try to make me feel better right now?" Levi asks, and his face looks like a child's.

"I swear to you, Levi. What Jude told you he felt, I felt, too. This I promise you, Levi. Because if we're going to get through this together." I squeeze his hands and hear Jude again: *This right here.* "If we're going to protect this right here, I promise right now to be completely honest with you, all the time. I won't hide or sugarcoat anything. Not when it comes to you. And you damn well better do the same for me. Deal?"

Levi nods as a tear drips off his nose. He and I stay huddled up together like that for a while, sharing Jude memories, crying some more, talking about the dreams they had—to redo their kitchen, to get Lucy a playmate, to maybe even eventually move to Austin, closer to me and Jay and Braden, and build the dream house Jude designed. It hurts to talk through these things, but it also helps a little, too, to know what an incredible life they had together, and the incredible man Jude was. It also gives me hope for the incredible life I know Levi can build again with my help.

"We just … have to stick together like Jude said. You, me, Braden, Jay, even Tammy, Lucy, and my mom. We are a family."

At this comment, Levi's head falls down between his knees again.

"What?" I ask him. "What did I say? Lucy counts," I protest, which elicits the tiniest chuckle out of Levi, and however small it is in the measure of chuckles, it gives me reciprocal-sized hope that Levi is going to survive this. It was merely the tip of his chuckle iceberg.

But Levi recovers quickly and resumes his somber, sad face. Now I'm really getting worried.

"Callie, I don't want to do this here. Not now. Please don't make me," Levi says, and I stop breathing.

It's a secret. I can sense it. Janessa taught me how to smell them in the air like a campfire. I ease back away from Levi and pull my own knees to my chest because something tells me this—whatever this secret is—is really going to devastate me.

"Callie," Levi warns, but I curl back further. I'm shaking my head 'no.'

"Callie, just not now, okay?" Levi begs, but I lose it.

"Not *now*?! Levi, I just promised to be one hundred percent, brutally honest with you all the time, and I told you a secret feeling I've had since I was a child, something I have never told anyone but Jude that I felt." I look at him fiercely. I know I'm pushing on Levi right now, but I can't let this go. "Do me. The same. Courtesy." I tell him, as calmly as I can, through gritted teeth. "Just. Spit. It. Out."

"I don't want to," Levi whispers. "I don't have any strength left to help you through it."

A feeling snakes down the back of my throat and settles deep in my stomach, telling me whatever secret Levi is holding, it's really bad, like another bomb in my life, bad. I try to speak, but my mouth is dry and chalky. Must be the ash.

"Levi," I start slowly. "Just say whatever it is. Say it."

Levi's eyes are still on the floor. He takes a big breath in and heaves it out.

"Okay, first, I do promise to be honest with you all the time." I nod. This is a start.

"That said, know that this is true. Don't ask me a hundred questions, or say you can't believe it's true, please, because this came *from Jude*. He figured it out," Levi is giving me a look. I nod. If Jude said this is true. It's true. I will not question it.

"Callie."

I take a breath in.

"It's Braden and Jay."

Time stops. Air stands still. My heart sits down in its chamber and slumps over.

"Braden, my husband? And, Jay, my cousin?" My voice doesn't sound like my own. It's airy and two octaves too high, but I have to confirm.

Levi brings those exhausted, gorgeous green eyes up to meet mine. He nods.

"They … they're … there's something going on between them."

I hear my heart pump once. Twice. Three times, because I'm not sure I can comprehend what Levi just told me. *Something is going on.* My hands fall off my knees and thump onto the floor.

This came from Jude, I tell myself. *It is true.*

"Jude said he could tell by the way they interacted," Levi says. "And, once he told me, I could too, Callie. You probably will now as well, if you haven't picked up on something already." My mind flits back to a time or two in the last few weeks where something felt strange around Braden and Jay. *Something is going on,* I repeat to myself.

"We don't know if they've actually been together," Levi continues, "or just developed feelings for each other, or what. Shit, I'm not saying any of this right. Why did you make me do this now?" Levi snaps.

Something is going on... is all I can think as I rise slowly. I'm catatonic, like a zombie, as I walk away from Levi. I can hear him slapping the tile floor, saying, "Dammit, Jude!" as I turn my back and begin to run.

CHAPTER THIRTY-NINE
JAY

I didn't. Couldn't. I would never do that to Callie. Ever. She's the only family I have ever been able to count on. Callie saved my life. There is nothing I wouldn't do for her. Even if it means turning my back on someone I believe I could love for the rest of my life. And that's exactly what I did.

I told Braden no.

I told him no, even though it wrecked him, and it crippled me.

I just wish he hadn't. I wish *I* hadn't. We didn't mean to. But that's the thing I've come to learn about love. Rarely is it convenient. It doesn't happen like in the movies—when the star has been single most of their young adult life, just waiting for the right, gorgeous person to walk in and sweep them off their feet—and then that person comes and does just that, and it's all so well-timed and perfect, and music plays and fireworks explode. It doesn't happen like that in real life. Often, people are married when they fall in love. Or their lover dies, and then they're alone, and they never fall in love again. Or they fall in love with someone they can't be with—star-crossed and all that.

I believe just as often as love works out, it doesn't.

Love fucking hurts. I'll tell you that. I can kind of understand why Mrs. Charlene just gave up on it altogether. Because my Uncle Steve is fine, he's bland, wouldn't hurt a fly, he's a reliable husband, but she doesn't *love* him, not like that. I don't know if she ever loved Callie and Jude's dad. Probably. But I can see what she chose. To just cut herself off from all of that pain and mess. I see that. And, I can see Callie choosing that, too, if this burns her too badly.

And that's what kills me. *That right there.* That was me. Braden and I—a man who would put Callie on his back and crawl through burning coals if it would save her—we're the two people who have caused her pain that just might be equivalent to what she just endured. We did this. Me. And Braden. We hurt Callie.

Fuck!

I wish I could take it all back. Not that there's anything to take other than emotion in the air, shared glances, long conversations, a brush of the hand. There was something that happened the night he and I first … saw one another. Something about Braden felt like it might change everything in my life. I know now it was an attraction—like cosmic level, deeper than the surface—but in the moment, it was unsettling, terrifying—a feeling like something I should have run away from. Braden and I have talked about that night several times.

He even admitted to me that he was opposed to my moving in because he had the same reaction to me. "Disruptive" was the word he used, and I agreed it fit. But I didn't tell Braden it had made me even a little prouder knowing that Callie had fought for me then, even pitting herself against her own husband. I don't care what she did back when we were teenagers. That one took my breath away.

What I hate about it, though, is that Braden and I were both right that night. Because look at us now. We've disrupted everything. The thing that has scared me the most about Braden, though, is that I've never felt this for anyone. This consuming, intoxicating, mind-numbing feeling. No wonder they make so many movies about it. It's the airiest, happiest feeling in the world, until it's not. Then it's the most devastating, soul-wrenching feeling a human can endure.

But we ignored it for almost a year. Braden would come visit me in the rehab center and bring Uno cards and LEGOs and stuff—all things Callie told him to bring, I know, which was really cute. He didn't even know how to play Uno, so I taught him. We talked a lot during those times. He helped me process my emotions about Katie the Bitch—it appears that will be her official name for the time being—and Amber and my own mom. We talked about his parents and the accident, and his cold-shouldered uncle who sounded a good bit like Mrs. Charlene. Like Jude, I encouraged Braden to pursue other creative outlets, like designing the wallpaper and tile backsplash, and other things in the loft. Braden's eye for graphics is unreal. He's incredibly talented.

But then I moved into the house after rehab, and there he was. Every morning, it was Braden and me making coffee together—as Callie always left for the office before sunrise—talking about our day's agenda. Then we were often together for lunch. Then the evenings with Callie. The weekends with the boys. Then Braden and I started working on the loft together, and all that did was shine a bright spotlight on our compatibility. We worked so well together, and enjoyed it even. I have never been happier than when I was working on that loft with everyone involved: Callie, Levi, Jude, and Braden. We were perfect.

And we would have remained perfect had it not been for this … this thing that kept growing between me and Braden. I hate this more for him because Braden didn't really know he was bisexual before me. He had never been around someone who was, and it just changes the chemistry in the air. I've seen it many times. Smart, established men, thinking they were completely heterosexual, then they let their eyes linger for a minute. They let their curiosity unfold. You can feel it. They want to know. And I know what Braden will do to me there. I want to know, too. And, I know, once we both find out, neither of us will ever be able to turn it off or ignore it again. He ignites me, and I can tell the feeling is mutual, if not stronger on his end.

That's why we haven't acted on it, as hard as it's been. I've been afraid this entire time that I would cave and take Braden the way I want to. There have been a million opportunities when we've been alone, but neither of us could do that to Callie. As twisted and weird as it sounds, it felt like—if we were going to pursue this—it had to be a decision the three of us made together. So, for months and months, we ignored it. Pushed it away. Didn't talk about it. Even though the air between us was electric, we did that for Callie. And, I even hate saying it like that. Like I'm justifying it. Look how good we were by waiting for months and months before we broke Callie's heart.

Godammit!

I am so mad we hurt her, but I can't figure out who I'm mad at. Myself, I guess? Braden? No. He just finally put words to what we both were feeling. He was actually the bigger man about it, which only makes me feel worse about it. A few weeks back, Braden finally caved and did what I hadn't been man enough yet to do.

"What are we going to do about this?" he'd asked, plopping a pile of carpet samples down in the loft.

"What do you mean? I thought you liked the champagne color?"

"Not the stupid carpet, Jay, *this*?!" Braden said, waving a hand, indicating what was happening between us. "What the heck *is this??* I'm not gay, at least I didn't think that I was. But I fucking love you, and I don't know why. I shouldn't, but I do. I want to be with you *that way,* and I don't know why. But, God, I do. What do we do?" Braden was exasperated, hot and fuming, pacing. This was eating him up. I knew because it was feasting on me, too.

At the moment, I was spooked at how similar his reaction was to mine when I first acted on my feelings for Jude. Braden was so confused, scared, and irritated by the weird feelings he was having. I remember that place. But I wished he hadn't developed those feelings for *me.*

"I can't do this to Callie," I told him, forcefully, and I meant it. As much as I would miss her, miss them all, I would move to a different state and just send her postcards if it meant sparing her from any more pain.

"I know. I can't either," Braden replied, with equal force. I'm confident he would even pack my bags if that's what Callie said needed to happen, although the thought terrifies me. I've never had a family before, so the threat of losing this incredible one—the best one I've ever been welcomed into—makes my body turn cold. But if anyone stands to be cut out first, it's me. I know that. It's always been that way for me.

But they changed me—Callie and Jude. For only the second time in my life, I felt included, loved, and *needed*. I have felt valuable, and I'm honestly not sure if I'm strong enough to stay sober and build a solid life for myself without the love and support of this family. Callie picked me up off the ground when I had thrown myself out like the sad sack of trash that I was. She gave me a home, help, and hope. She turned me into the man I am today. Looking into Braden's eyes, standing across from me in the loft that day, I knew he felt the same way. He's told me that many times during our long conversations. Braden felt isolated and scared when he first started branching out from under his uncle's wing, and Callie felt like a plug right into his socket, lighting his entire world with her ideas, gumption, and chatter. She's a life force. I know how Braden feels about Callie, because it's exactly how I feel.

I just don't have answers. I hate that this has to be so hard. There's no hate here. Only love. Shouldn't we be able to find space for it?

On one hand, I feel like Braden and I deserve a chance, because I think it could be a relationship they would write epic biopic movies about. We would be that couple who crossed the stars. I can feel it. Braden's heart is so huge and giving. When he looks at me, I feel seen and wanted. And, I know that's a once-in-a-lifetime feeling, to both give and receive.

But, then there's the other hand. There's Callie. The center of my universe. The woman who brought us all together. She is the bright red leather tie that binds us all. And, she just lost Jude.

So, the answer is no.

It has to be no.

It has to.

That's where Braden and I were. Constantly reaffirming our decision—the answer is no, the answer is no—trying to avoid one another and trying, like hell, not to touch one another. But, Jesus, the past couple of days haven't made that easy. Dealing with something this devastating, Jude's injuries, his suffering, his death—it's an event that makes you want to grab the people you love, in whatever way you love them, and hold on, clutch them so hard they can never leave you. At least that's the hope. That your terrified, white-knuckled grip can keep them here, on earth with you. But if Callie's jaws-of-life hold couldn't do it, no one could.

I remember her as a gritty little kid. She was so intense sometimes, trying so hard to create or fix something, her tongue sticking out of the side of her mouth, pushing, pulling, usually grunting. I remember her the night she socked Tyler Beck in the throat, her dress ripping with it, her fist exploding into his fleshy neck. She was so fearless at times. Running out of the house that time when the boys were picking on Jude in her front yard. Three years his junior and three feet shorter, but she was ready to ball her little fists to defend Jude. She always was.

And I cannot believe she just lost him. My brain just can't yet process it. The two of them together is how I will forever see them in my mind—sticking up for one another, looking out after each other. They included me in their childhood games, sure, but no nail could ever be driven between those two. I cannot say the same for Callie and Mrs. Charlene, though. Those two have been crackling lightning rods since as far back as I remember, often popping and zapping one another. They were never meant to exist under the same roof. They're too much alike.

Callie doesn't see that now, but she will. She's just as stubborn and bull-headed as Mrs. Charlene, but she is softer in the center. Jude made sure of that, always teaching her, being patient with her, and making her feel important to him. Those things shape a child. I should know, because I didn't have them. I also know because it showed on Callie. Even in my darkest moments—when I was drinking myself into oblivion—I always held onto that little LEGO man. Arnie Armstrong. Because Callie gave it to me at Grandma Peggy's funeral, she was like ten, and it was her favorite, but she gave it to *me*.

I'll never forget her standing there, her dirty little fingers wrapping it in my hand. Jude was behind her, watching. And, Mariah even came—completely alone—simply to be there for Callie. They were a little misfit kid army right there, all the way back then. But they weren't mine, and that's what I hated. They had each other, but I didn't have anybody. I ran away because it was too much emptiness to bear, but I never forgot Callie's gesture.

Then again, when she scooped me off her doorstep almost twenty years later, it was the biggest sacrifice I can remember anyone making for me—outside of Grandma Peggy taking me in when she could barely afford it. I know it strained her to make my meals and keep me clothed. I've still got the letter Callie gave me when I graduated from the rehab program, the one she put the key to her house in. I know a lot of them—Jude, Levi, Braden, and Callie—are all wordy and English majors and whatnot, and they write nice notes and letters to each other often, but before Callie, I never had anyone write me such a nice letter. Katie the Bitch never wrote me anything, I can tell you that.

But, after we reconnected as adults, Callie passed everything Jude taught her—about forgiveness, fighting for people, believing in love— on to me. Callie changed me when she scooped me up off her front porch step and took me in. During the whole drive to her place, I feared it was just as likely she would have thrown some money at me for a hotel and closed the door. That's what most people would have done. But, not Callie. And, now her prize for that sacrifice is the potential loss of her husband, right after the loss of her brother. *Jude.*

I will miss Jude more than anyone I've ever missed in my life, more than Grandma Peggy, more than my dad, I think, wherever he might be. *It's good to see you, Cousin.* I remember his words from the day he and Levi first came to rehab. Jude looked out for me as a kid, taught me so much about how things worked—math, science, cooking, building. He always pushed us to be creative, too. Callie and I. To create things that did not conform.

I sensed early on that he was gay, and I actually admired him for it. Not the difficult road that lay ahead for him, but the certainty he felt for who he was, even though it was a very difficult thing to be. Being bisexual can sometimes feel more difficult because you have one foot on either side. For me, making a meaningful connection—with a man or woman—is one-hundred percent person-specific. There are many women I'm just not emotionally attracted to, same with men. And, it's the same with physical attraction. It's all person-specific, which means I can't predict it. That's the rub.

I was attracted to Jude, as was most of the gay male population. He was a brilliant light, dazzling, beautiful, charismatic. Too fucking perfect to exist in Clovis, New Mexico, in the early nineties, or even now. Everyone knew that. He was magnetic, and I'll never regret the years I got to spend with him growing up. Looking back, that section of my life looks sparkling and golden, much like the last year, when I reconnected with Jude and Callie. They are the shiny highlights on the timeline of my life. The rest is greasy, dark shades of grey.

That's why I tried to make a move on Jude so long ago. He was fifteen, maybe sixteen? I was only thirteen, but I had this deep desire for him. Jude was definitely the first man who intrigued me that way. Jude had seen it coming, though. He had my number. He was always three steps ahead like that. But when I think back on what he said to me then, it still gives me goosebumps.

"You sure about this?" Jude had asked as I had leaned in to try to kiss him. We were in his room with the door locked. Callie was at

Mariah's as she often was then. Mrs. Charlene and Uncle Steve wouldn't be home for an hour. There was no one there to stop us.

But Jude.

"I'm sure," I'd told him, because all of my thirteen-year-old self was sure. "I have feelings for you."

"You have hormones for me, that's different," Jude had said dismissively. But I had to know what Jude felt like, what he tasted like. I had dreamed about it for so many months, and I truly believed I couldn't carry on without knowing. It was a burning teenage thing.

"I am sure," I told him.

"I'm sure you are sure. But, do you even know if you're gay, Jay? Have you … tried with any other boy?" Jude asked, and I was both embarrassed that he used the word 'boy' and that my answer had to be 'no.'

Jude nodded. I could see the wheels in his gorgeous head turning. "Well, everyone needs to try something for the first time, because that's all this is going to be, you understand? We can't do that to Callie. Team up and leave her out as a third wheel. Plus, I'm getting the hell out of Clovis, so I don't think striking up a relationship with my local … cousin-in-law? … would be the best choice for that plan, wouldn't you agree?"

I was nodding along with everything. Whatever Jude said, as long as he would give me a taste.

"But I know this stuff can be hard. The first one is so awkward and bumbling and …" Jude shuddered. "And, you may find you don't even like kissing a guy. But, let's find out. To experimenting?" Jude held out a hand for me to shake.

I shook it.

It was a pretty amazing kiss. To this day, especially now with Jude gone, I feel honored that he was my first. What a first?! I wonder if he's ever told Levi, although I know them well enough, they would have just laughed and joked about it. Those two were tied together so deeply that nothing could shake them. I envied Jude and Levi that open, genuine, impenetrable love. And, Jude must have known he was destined for a love that great, even if it would only be brilliant and brief. He also knew it wasn't going to be me.

"Okay," he said, pulling away after the kiss. "You definitely like kissing guys, but you don't really like me that way … do you?"

I started to protest just because I wanted to kiss him again, but then I sensed what Jude was doing. He held my gaze to reinforce it. It was really *he* who didn't like me that way. And, we couldn't do that to Callie. Jude was giving me the upper hand. Classy.

"You're right," I treaded in lightly. "I don't. *And*, we can't do that to Callie," I threw in for good measure, although I had felt a little heartbroken at the time. Remember what I said about love being inconvenient. At thirteen, it is both inconvenient and consuming.

Jude nodded. "But someday you will kiss a man you love, Jay. Then the choice will be much harder."

To this day, I have yet to kiss a man I *love*, but because of Jude, I look forward to it.

He was always like that. People probably think we're painting Jude in a grander light than he was, but we're not. Jude was perceptive, aware. He often said things that sounded like Confucius. That's just who he was—had been since he was a child. I think growing up, battling an identity crisis every day like Jude did—where he was always watching, learning, listening, trying to find answers for himself—made him that way. While the rest of us were bickering and gnawing through our normal lives, Jude quietly watched and grew wise.

I think we all knew Jude was too good to last. But, damn, none of us were ready for him to leave now, right when everything had gotten this impossibly good. Maybe that's the point, though. End on a high note. Leave while you're on top. I don't know. I haven't figured out all the answers to Jude's death, and I'm not sure I ever will, because I miss him.

Every day I miss him. *Cousin.* And, if I miss him this much, I can only imagine what Callie and Levi are feeling. Jude was just so damn smart.

The minute Braden and I walked into his room at the hospital, it was like Jude knew. When Braden first had a moment to process Jude, all bandaged and beeping, he turned toward me and placed his hand on my forearm. He didn't mean it as any kind of romantic gesture. It was just a visceral reaction. And, I had laid my hand on the back of his head, only to comfort him. It was a knee-jerk reaction. Then we both realized where we were, and we threw our hands down in unison, like they would sting us. Mariah was explaining things to Jude at the moment, and Callie was facing him, but Jude's eyes were on us. Jude looked at me so intensely that he practically told me out loud.

I know. Followed by. *You can't do this to Callie.*

I gave him a look back that I hoped conveyed: *I know. We haven't.*

I never did get a moment alone with Jude after that to talk to him about it. For the life of me, I wish I could have talked to him about it because Jude knew us all, he knew what was at stake—on both sides. He could have been our guiding light through this tangled mess.

All I have is *"Your decisions will get much harder."*

Jude was always right. I hated that about him. I loved that about him.

I miss him. Every day. As I sit in this hotel and stare at the walls.

I'm so tangled up and confused right now. I don't want to hurt Callie, and I don't want to hurt Braden. And, I've really hurt myself in all of this. I didn't want any of this.

Love sucks sometimes—most of the time.

But, we can't. We just can't do that to Callie.

It's the only answer I know.

As much as I cannot bear to witness the hurt and betrayal in Callie's eyes when—not if—she finds out, more than that, I fear everything wonderful in my life that had just started to take root will be trampled and ruined forever.

This is paralyzing.

I don't want to hurt Callie, but I don't want to go back to Clovis.

I don't want anything to do with Debbie and whatever crappy boyfriend she's shacked up with now, especially if it's god damn Christoph-her. He touches me again, I'm afraid I'll kill him, because the boy he abused deserves it, so does he, and I would want—too badly—not to.

But my life as I knew it in Austin will be over. That's what's coming. I know it.

And, it's not Callie's fault, but it's not fair that I always have to play the role of the outsider who's cast off.

CHAPTER FORTY

LEVI

This? The role of the gay grieving widow. The sad-faced "he was too young to die" guy. No. I never signed up for this.

Because I don't know how to do this. Any of it. I'm supposed to be able to dig deep and find this inner strength, be inspiring, and parse out little glowing things Jude said to me over the years that are going to light all of our paths forward. I'm supposed to pick up and move on, somehow coming out the other side of this carnage more what? Brave? Wise?

I'm neither of those things and never will be. I know Jay and Braden and Callie are tangled up in their love drama right now, but I'm standing here, and I cannot breathe. I feel like my heart sawed its way out of my chest and left this world with Jude. When I breathe out, my ribs seem to collapse inward because nothing is there. I just curl over like my spine doesn't work anymore. I know Callie needs me right now, but Jesus, I need her more.

I need her to crumple to the floor with me and just melt away because I don't want to be here anymore. In this cruel, grey world, where my bright, bedazzled sun has been snuffed out. Jude was the smartest, most creative, resilient man I have ever known. No one can ever understand the richness he brought to my life, the joy and fun that will never, ever, come back. Without him here, it's all too grey.

It feels like I turned my back for one second and his brilliant, blinding light went out, leaving me groping for him in the dark. Hardly a day passed from the time Jude and I were laughing in our bedroom—feeling light and giddy, getting dressed to go out for dinner—before he was lying, mangled and destroyed in that ghostly beeping bed that he never rose from. I can close my eyes and still see us.

"You'll turn Oompa Loompa orange," I'd told him, vetoing his sunless tanning lotion idea. "And who will love you then, looking like a washed-up game show host?"

"You," Jude had said matter-of-factly, rumpling my hair, which, thankfully, had not yet been styled. "You will always love me," Jude had said, seemingly in jest, tossing shirts onto the bed to try on. And, just like that. His flippant comment stopped my heart, because he was—too often—irritatingly right.

I will always love him.

I knew it the minute Jude sauntered into my living room in response to my ad for a room to rent. He gave a vibe that he was a little lost, but there was an undertone there, too. That maybe—just maybe—he was actually in the exact perfect spot because he was also the most gorgeous man I'd ever laid eyes on in my twenty-three years. I also sensed maybe—just maybe—a little part of him knew that. Jude immediately intrigued me.

"Just need a place to lay my head," Jude had said, and I'd recognized his attempt to lower his voice a bit, sound more macho. I know the tone well. We all do. I didn't match it when we spoke, and he eventually broke out of it, although we didn't get to talk as much as I would have liked in those first few months Jude stayed with me.

When Jude left for California with Rachel, I thought he had walked out of my life forever, killing my hopes that things might blossom between me and this handsome new stranger. It stung, but the truth was I'd never really had him. I hadn't yet experienced *having* Jude as my partner, which is an emotion I don't even have words for. But just that initial short brush with Jude was enough to change me. He was that potent. While I had not been *hiding* who I was, I also hadn't been really putting myself out there either. Really *trying*.

In truth, I was scared to find the right man. Because what if I did, but he didn't love me back? Or he left? Jude leaving for California made me wonder if that had just happened—I'd found the right man, then he left. The possible reality of that made me want to try harder. So, I did. Surprising myself even. In the nearly two years that Jude was gone, I went out on more meaningful dates—like not just coffee and walking the dogs at the park. I went out for dinner in highly visible restaurants. Bought guys steaks and wine and went to see movies, went out dancing and stuff. Nothing felt quite right, but for the first time in my life, I had tried, and that was because of Jude.

Then it was like someone took my world and popped it like a sheet because there he was. Jude. Suddenly. Standing on my doorstep, disheveled and mortified, a sad Hefty bag at his feet. I didn't know what had happened between him and Rachel—or what he'd been through in California (had to have been a shitshow from the way he looked)—but I didn't care. He was back. *My Jude came back.*

"I don't want you to ever leave me again," I'd told him right there on the porch. I didn't even think it through. I just said it. But it's proven true every single day. I wouldn't trade the last eight years with Jude for anything. Millions of dollars. Mansions on the beach. Even tenure at Harvard. He was worth more.

Watching Jude slowly heal, regroup, and blossom into this successful, confident man will forever be the single greatest thing I have witnessed in my entire life. My stars, he was a sight to see. It was like a spotlight came on when he entered a room. You could hear it, click on, and buzz. And, to know Jude felt—for the first time in *his* life—safe to be completely himself, to anyone and everyone, made me deeply proud. As if I had, in a small way, provided that space for him, and when Callie forgave him after their dad's funeral, it only expanded Jude's world further. But I had not hesitated.

I had welcomed Jude to me completely, encouraging him to tell me absolutely everything, because I wanted to know every single thing that had ever happened to him. His story broke my heart. His troubled years in Clovis. Facing rejection from both his mom and dad, and the torturous spiral he fell into after leaving home. I vowed to make sure Jude knew every day how much love he deserved to receive, and how much he was capable of giving.

I felt the same about Lucy, too. She couldn't tell me her story, but I had to imagine it had similar threads of rejection and hurt like Jude's did. It was a privilege watching both of them come out of their shells: my dazzling Jude and our glossy little princess.

Poor thing has hardly eaten since Jude passed. Or smiled. She greets me at the door, sadly, with a limp sock in her mouth and sets those chocolate eyes on me like I need to answer her question. *Where's Jude?* "I don't know, sweet girl," I tell her because I don't. Not really. He's just gone. *My Jude is gone.* Being with Jude had felt like being coated in warm honey. I could close my eyes and feel it roll down me, thick and viscous. I used to be able to feel it anyway.

Now …

Grey.

Chalk.

Nothing.

I can't even begin to imagine what this has been like for Callie. I don't know what happened after we'd all crumpled to the floor at the hospital with the news. Time warped and slid around underneath my feet. I just know she came up to me at some point in the hours after, trying to console me, and I was so angry. So, unbelievably angry—that Jude had left, that the world took him from me, that this had wrecked the first family I ever felt I truly fit in, and that I was left behind to shatter Callie even further on my own? It wasn't fair. Jude and I had talked about breaking the news to her together.

The fact that Callie's cousin and her husband have developed feelings for one another is really a revelation that would be best coming from your brother. From blood, not the boyfriend. Anyone would agree. But there we were, with Callie probing into me, knowing the news wasn't good. And me, in no condition to console her or help her through it at the time, assuming I even can now. I honestly don't know what the answer is there. It's a hotbed of love, betrayal, and hurt that none of us has a roadmap for.

I know Callie too well, though. Jude, too. They always felt, growing up, that they were the only two people in the world who could understand what they had been through and wanted to embrace them *because of* their struggle, their truth, not feel repulsed by it and reject them. It's not true, but you could never convince either of them of it. That's why Jude never felt he was worthy of my love, in the beginning. It took me many long, patient months of telling Jude, "I love the very person you are, every single amazing, stupid, irritating thing about you," to convince him otherwise. Now, if Callie thinks her husband could just … *unlove* her, decide she wasn't good enough—is how she will take it anyway, I know—it would only reinforce that deep fear. That someone she thought loved her has now fully seen her and will decide she is expendable. And that's exactly the feeling I saw on Callie's face when I told her.

I am expendable.

I finally found her locked alone in a bathroom afterward. I pounded and shouted at the door. Callie didn't want to let me in at first, but once she did, I saw the sight of the room. The paper towel holder smashed to the ground, a sink corner jagged and broken off, the mirror fractured, streaks of black and red and wads of hair on the floor, Callie's bloodied knuckles. I can't explain it, but suddenly there was no Jude or even a hospital. There was just a young girl who had suffered two losses so great that she felt she didn't matter anymore to anyone. My fear of what Callie might do to herself took over. I just reacted.

I cradled Callie to me, busted shoulder and all, and hustled her out toward the elevators so I could get her out of there. Jay and Braden came running toward us in the hall, but I mustered my anger over losing Jude and shouted at them both with a voice I only hoped could protect her.

"Don't you dare come near her! Either of you!" I thundered down the hall at them, one hand outstretched, the other curling Callie to my chest.

My last image of them is Braden standing back, looking hollow, his mouth dangling open, and Jay on his knees in the hall, his head on the floor, his shoulders shaking. I'm glad Callie didn't have to see that. Those men love her almost as much as I do.

We got her shoulder popped back into place in the ER. Stone Cold Miss Austin barely flinched. I have to admit I was a bit scared of her in that moment. It felt like she was rewiring her own brain. Callie was making a plan, as Callie always does. But then she turned to me immediately after and said, "First, I just want to lie in a pile of blankets and cry about Jude." So, I put her in the car, and that's what we did. I wasn't sure taking her to mine and Jude's place was the right thing to do, but in all honesty, we had nowhere else to go in Houston, and I had not wanted to go there for the first time alone. Selfishly, I took Callie there—busted and broken open as she was—as *my* shield to the devastating time capsule our home proved to be. But, I know, in any condition, on her deathbed even, Callie is ten times stronger than me.

It proved to be the right decision because there was evidence of Jude everywhere. His keys are by the door. His mug is in the sink. His fleece was over the dining room chair. I couldn't decide whether to gather it all up and bring it under the blankets with us or rope it all off with police tape so no one could ever move any of it ever again. Instead, Callie and I just curled up on the couches, smothered ourselves in covers, and lay there all night, crying, talking, laughing, blowing our noses, sharing a can of Pringles with Diet Cokes, and sleeping on and off. We talked about Jude the entire time, and I couldn't have imagined a better way to mourn him, paying homage with the only person on earth who knew him better than I did. The girl who had taught, shaped, and motivated Jude since he was a child.

But I have his recent memories. His everyday silly adult things. The Pringles can on the coffee table reminded me of Jude's asinine desire, more like an obsession, really, with getting all the paper from the seal off the rim of the can. This applied to anything with a paper seal—peanut butter, spices, toiletries, medications. "He wouldn't stop picking if the house was on fire," I'd imitated his fiendish obsession to Callie's tearful laughter.

The Diet Coke spoke to me, too. "They cancel each other out," Callie had said it for me, knowing it's what Jude would always say when he indulged in a greasy cheeseburger—always pairing it with a zero-calorie Coke.

Then I think about the time he tried to sneak a big Styrofoam cup filled with Coke into the movie theatre by hiding it under his jacket, but I accidentally let the door swing back on him, crushing the Styrofoam cup and all of its contents to his chest—the look on Jude's face. And the waterfall of Coke was soaking his entire front. My word, did we laugh. We laughed and laughed and eventually just ran out of that theatre trying to hide what had happened. "No, everything's fine, Sir. We just realized we had already seen that one. Gwyneth Paltrow is amazing!" We were practically falling all over ourselves, tumbling into the parking lot, Jude soaked and starting to get sticky.

But then the image morphs into my open, bloody chest with my heart missing, and I wonder if I will ever look at anything again and not feel sad if it reminds me of Jude.

Part of me envies Callie's unshakeable strength, because I know she will recover from this. She will mourn Jude, but she will figure out the best solution for her, Braden, Jay, and she will continue to hold some form of family together. It's in her blood. Callie is like the oak tree we all live in. She supports us, holds us up, and provides shelter. Without Callie, none of us would feel we had a real home. That is why I know—in the face of this tragedy—she will rise. I watched her do it just over the course of twelve hours at my house.

She spent the first half of the night sobbing, snotting onto her sleeve, and reminiscing with me about Jude. The next few hours, she spent starting to take action because she didn't know how to operate any other way. She sent Mariah an unsolicited online payment for her time spent helping Jude get his DNR, and a nice thank-you note, although I know it was really a "don't try to console me" note. I speak fluent Callie, and I knew she was already receding into her warrior armor, pushing everyone out and plotting the lonely path she believes lies ahead so that she can somehow fix all of this.

While she broke down during the night a few times when our conversation turned to Braden and Jay, I could feel her hardening to it as we approached dawn. Where her questions had begun with "Why would they have even let those feelings develop, Levi?" and "How could they do this to me, to us?" to "I don't want to hate them for it, but what else am I supposed to feel?" until she finally landed on "I don't hate them. It's fine, really. I hope they're happy together. I just should have seen it coming. I should have never let them in, right, Levi?"

My answer to each of them had been "Child, I don't know." I was angry at Jay and Braden for whatever they'd let cook up, but honestly, I could see it, too. The minute Jude pointed it out to me, it felt like one of those digital pictures that you stare at cross-eyed until a hidden image comes to life. Once you've seen it, you can't *unsee* it. It was undeniably there. But I didn't have the capacity to even think about any of that drama when I had just lost Jude, drowning in the tsunami of my own emotions. But I didn't have to. In true Callie fashion, she handled that shit all on her own.

After checking her Mariah box, she then left a voice note for Braden, and she did it all in one take, no redos, no rehearsals. Callie told him not to reach out to her right now and for her and Jay to be out of her house the following afternoon so she could collect her things and decide her next moves. I hate to say it, but her stoicism in handling all of it spooked me a little. I was starting to understand what Jude had meant by "Clovis people" and "we've been through things."

The last hours around sunrise, Callie spent showering, cleaning up our mess in the living room, taking Lucy on a walk, then making all of three of us eggs and toast for breakfast. And, she did all of that with a displaced shoulder, mind you.

Then, her next mission was to look after me, asking me if I had to teach that week, where Jude and I had left my car, if I needed her to get me some groceries, yadda, yadda. Annoyed and in awe of how practical she was being, I had to ask.

"How are you able to just … get on with it?"

"This is just what we do," Callie had told me. "Jude, Jay, my mom, and I are Clovis people. We pick up and carry on. I know this sounds unforgivably harsh, but we've seen tragedy before. It doesn't make the sun stop coming up. It doesn't pay the bills. I love you, Levi. I'll be back Tuesday."

And, then she was gone. My back support. Without her, I just sank down to the living room floor with Lucy and melted away.

CHAPTER FORTY-ONE
EMPTY NEST

I pull up to my house back in Austin at 2:34 p.m. The irony of it singes my insides, and in a weird, robotic motion, I pull out the mascara tube from my purse and swipe it over the clock display until I can no longer read the numbers. I feel like a live wire ready to pop, and I'm grateful Jay and Braden are nowhere in sight. But there's a note stuck to the front door.

Callie:

This home is yours. It's no home without you. We are not a family without you. I know you feel betrayed and hurt, and we both hate that. We hate ourselves for the feelings that developed, but that's all that developed—just feelings. I put Jay up at the Holiday Inn. I'll be in the loft, but I won't approach or bother you at all, I promise. Neither of us will contact you unless and until you want us to.

But, Callie, please want us to. Someday.

We will give you as much space and time as you need. I'll pursue you another seven months if that's what it takes, and another seven months after that. I know it doesn't feel like it, but we both love you more than you can ever know. Please don't give up on us, or this family, Callie. We can figure this out. I promise. You are, and will forever be, my wife.

I wish I could help you work through the loss of Jude. It's wrecked us all. But I'm glad you have Levi, and I understand you two need each other now. You're the tie that binds us all, Callie. You are the center of this family. Always have been.

We all love you so much. I've said that already. I can't say it enough.

I love you. Still. Always. Forever. Please never forget that.

-Braden

He drew a little caricature sketch of all my men—Jay, himself, Levi, even Jude as an angel with his hand on Levi's shoulder—squished together and clutched tight in my muscular cartoon arms. Little hearts are floating up and popping above my head, like I'm giving them all the love that I can possibly push out from my body. *Because I always did!* I think.

At the sight of Jay with his telling cheek scar, Levi's meticulously trimmed beard, Braden's unruly hair looking on fire, and Jude with his stupid long lashes and—now—a stylishly cocked halo and wings, the five of us reunited for the last time, I feel knocked flat. I rush into the house, slam the door, and crash to the floor, where I curl up and cry and scream and cry, slapping my tears into the carpet. Visions of Jude—smiling at me in front of Mom's Oldsmobile, drizzling wet sand, his hand in the limelight of the TV, adult Jude dazzling in shades, chasing Levi with a putt-putt club, petting Lucy and telling me '*It's not too good for you, Lil' Bit*'—gut me. I cry for so long I fall asleep right there, on the foyer floor, my keys and Braden's drawing beside me.

When I finally roll onto my back and start to look around, I see similar hand-drawn notes everywhere. Stuck to the TV screen, the couch, the mirror in the hall, the ceiling fan pull above my face. I rise and make the mistake of glancing at that one.

We're your biggest fans!

Braden wrote, with a little sketch of him and Jay in cheerleading outfits, jumping up and down with pompoms in their hands. I vow not to look at another one. They hurt too much.

The house is spotless as I walk through, passing an elaborate bouquet of orange lilies in the hall. I notice it is stocked and clean, but incredibly empty—immersed in the scent and presence of the men who used to occupy this house with me—as I try to process my emotions.

Am I supposed to fight for Braden?

Why should I? He doesn't love me that way anymore.

Can I refuse Jay this?

Why would I? Jay deserves this. I won't deny him his happiness again.

I glance out at the loft—a habit from the many evenings I would come home and look out to see Jay's progress out there—only to see the light on illuminating a big "We love you Callie" written on the windows in shoe polish. I pull the curtains shut.

It's Sunday.

Work will be the most distracting, productive thing I can do right now, I decide. It is the only thing I can see doing right now that might hold the last shards of my tattered life together.

I revert back to old instincts. Head down. Work hard. Failure is not an option.

I'll make partner early, I tell myself.

I set to it.

———

At Goldman Carr, work is work. It's separate from family. This is just how it is at big firms. Aside from one question from my partner Justin about Jude, no one says a thing, and I hide under the shelter of stacks of work that I have to do, immensely grateful.

It's after 1:00 p.m. before I get a text back from Levi in response to my check-in on him this morning.

I'm okay, Callie. I'll eat and shower, and take
care of Lucy and all that. I'm just not going
to be happy or fun for years.
I'm worried about you burying yourself
over there. How many people outside of
work have you talked to today?

The cashier at the gas station.

I'm not even trying to be funny. That's just the answer.

Well surprise. I thought the number
would be zero.

It will be until I have to fill up again.

The rest of the day passes like an accordion—some moments feel impossibly slow, like I'm moving in molasses, while others feel like they zipped by in a blur—but I make it, finally, to 6:00 p.m., an hour I feel I can respectably shut down and go home.

On my drive home, I make the mistake of letting the radio play. *Africa* by Toto comes on, and my throat closes. Jude and I loved this song. We used to sing it into hairbrushes in his bedroom in front of the mirror. If there was any sign when I was younger that Jude was gay, that should have been it. But, then—during the Golden Years—when the song would come on, Jude and I would belt it out, wherever we were, customers, onlookers, fellow drivers be damned, and he would always say, after the "hundred men or more" line: "I think a hundred men might change my mind." Levi would then swat him, and we'd all laugh.

My vision starts swimming as the song plays, and I see the gas station I stopped at this morning. On a really weird whim, as it seems I've been doing a lot of things recently I cannot explain—including my mascaraed-out clock in the car that I'm now noticing—I pull in and go inside. I walk up to the cashier. It's the same little Indian guy from this morning, the same one I've seen in here often, I realize.

"Hi, I …" I suddenly become aware of how super weird this is, and totally awkward, but a hundred men can't stop me.

"I came in this morning to fill up," I tell him. The man nods.

"Yes, I remember you," he says, in his thick Indian accent. He reminds me of Rami at the Dairy Queen, where Jude and I used to play Simon and win Blizzards. The memory is so sharp it almost takes my breath away, but I push forward. Thankfully, the man's expression is one of patience and sympathy. Then I realize he can tell I've been crying. "Did you lose something?" he asks me.

I sniff. "No, well, yes. I did. But, not here. I … My brother just died. This past Saturday. And, he was amazing," I'm really starting to tear up now, but my words are coming. They're strong and true.

"He was funny and kind and smart. And stupidly handsome. Like ridiculously good-looking." I say that because I know Jude would want me to include that. "He was gay, and it made him the best person I've ever known."

The attendant blinks and swallows. *Poor man*, I think. I stand there awkwardly. "I just … wanted to tell someone that," I tell him.

The man fidgets with something by his register, but then he clears his throat and says, "I'm sorry for your loss. You've been filling up here for years. Always right when we open in the morning or around sunset at night. I've seen you many times," he says. "You work very hard. Your brother must have been very proud."

A wet sob escapes me as I never knew I was seen by this man. And, he just said words to me that I know to be true, although I often forget them, and I know to be heartfelt. And that was the perfect thing to say. I clean up my face, as best I can, take a big breath in as I hear the door chime with another customer.

"I'm Callie," I tell him, and I extend a hand to shake his. The man fumbles a bit, trying to wipe his hands on his pants, but then he extends one to me as well.

"I am Sunil," he tells me. "It is an honor to meet you. I hope you will talk more when you come."

I'm looking into his dark, dark brown eyes, almost black. I see genuine sympathy, wells of it, and I wonder what or who this man has lost. It's probably much more than a single brother. And knowing this likely fact somehow helps me.

"I will," I tell Sunil. "I'll talk to you soon."

——

Back home, the house is ridiculously quiet. I wait for Braden to say, "Hey, babe, in here. How was your day?"

It never comes.

I wait for Jay to come stomping up the stairs to the back porch, a carpenter's pencil tucked behind his ear, saying, "Ahh, Counselor Callie," always said in a British accent, "did you leave them shaking in their knickers?"

It never comes. Then I think meanly, *they must be together, having dinner, laughing, listening to records, having a wonderful time.* In a catatonic state, I pull one of the white wine bottles Braden stocked for me in the fridge and the lady fingers and start drinking straight from the bottle on the couch, making sure the curtains are closed so I cannot see the loft.

——

When I get to Levi's on Tuesday, Levi and Lucy answer the door together—Lucy with nothing in her mouth and Levi looking five pounds thinner. He is clean and upright, as promised, but he looks like hell. Deep bags reside under his eyes. His skin is grey and waxy-looking. His beard is unruly. Suddenly, I feel terrible for having ever gone home.

We spend the evening curled around bowls of carryout in the living room, playing rummy just to keep our hands busy.

"So, I started talking to the gas station guy," I tell Levi, trying to perk him up.

"Talking? Like *talking,* talking? I didn't say start dating him, Callie. How old is he?" I am glad to see it worked. I laugh.

"Just talking. I introduced myself. Told him about Jude. He's the first stranger I told."

Levi is quiet for a minute.

"I told one of the baristas at Starbucks yesterday, when I started crying at the creamer station thinking of the kappercinos you and Jude used to make, making the most awkward moment for this little gal who was just trying to restock the Splendas. Poor thing."

I nod and pat his shoulder.

"Besides, it's way too soon for you to start dating," he starts lightly, but then picks back up more seriously with "I can't share you with anyone else right now." I know he means it, because I feel the same.

I tell Levi my decision. It's one of the main reasons I came over tonight.

"I've decided to get out of Braden and Jay's way. If it really is love, they deserve to pursue it, and I only have myself to blame. I brought Jay into our world, even over Braden's initial resistance. Jude's too. Did I ever tell you that? They both worried Jay would be too … disruptive," I try to chuckle. It doesn't work. "I just never thought it would cost me my marriage, my family, maybe my home," I tell Levi, in a whisper, trying to hold back the fear that is clenching my throat, squeezing the back of my eyeballs.

"What do you think?" I ask him, feeling impossibly vulnerable.

Levi is quiet for a long time, then he comes over and drapes his arm around my shoulder.

"I think—*know*—you have not lost your family. Where Jude once stood, I will always be. By your side, Callie. We'll get through this together."

I curl into his shoulder and break down, leaving a disgusting snot and mascara trail on his shirt.

"But, damn lady, you don't have to give them the house. This ain't Jerry Springer or Judge Judy, and I'm pretty sure you bought it, right?" Levi says, which surprisingly makes me laugh. I wipe my face, letting a big belly laugh roll through me.

And, just then, it hits me like a bolt. It is my house, dammit, and Levi can teach anywhere. I need him. I don't know what Jay and Braden are going to do. I won't deny them the loft, but Levi is right. The house is mine.

Keep Levi close, Jude's words come to me. I say it before I can ruin it with any logistics.

"Move in with me, Levi."

CHAPTER FORTY-TWO
MAKE IT A DOUBLE

"Hey Jim," I say as I shuffle in. The bar is dimly lit and grimy, a place you can escape for a few hours if you pay your tab and don't make eye contact with anyone. After several weeks of this, the bartender at Nick's has learned my pattern.

"Yeah, the usual."

He pours me up a gin and tonic—my mom's specialty.

I've fallen into a bad routine over the last few weeks. Levi isn't moving in until mid-July to get settled into his new teaching job at UT, and I seem to be using the isolation to drive myself further underground. I say seem because I find I'm not often in control. It's not Calliope this time. It's her black sheep cousin, Autopilot.

Sometimes I wake up on the living room floor, and I have no memory of when I had laid down there. Sometimes I spill wine and find it the next day. Sometimes I get into a jar of peanut butter and find it in the fridge the next morning.

In my drinking spirals, I've managed, unintentionally, to see just a few more of Braden's little love notes scattered all over. The one by Braden's record collection says:

> *Break as many as you want because our love for you is record-breaking!*

The little sketch below it is of Braden at a DJ table, spinning records, while Jay is dancing with little hearts floating up and popping above both of them.

They're adorable and sweet and such a freaking betrayal because Jay and Braden hurt me. They're in love. Fucking fantastic. Get it out of my life.

For three weeks now, I have stopped at Nick's after work every day to get plastered before I go home so I can ignore the notes. This also means I drive home drunk more than I would care to admit, even a few times completely on autopilot, which really scares me. The last time I woke up in my bed not remembering how I got there, I made a snap decision. I don't know whether it's right or not. There is no rule book for this. But, it's the one that I believe lets me and Levi heal and move forward. I just have to have the courage to see it through.

——

"Do you love Jay?" I ask before Braden can even slide down into the booth at the coffee shop on the UT campus, where our relationship first sparked, the place I told him to meet me this afternoon at four so we could finally talk. He looks a little gaunt, having lost pounds he couldn't really afford to lose, and his hands flutter nervously. But his sandy blonde hair is still unruly, and his stupid dimple is still there. Braden stops sitting midway down and just hovers there for a moment. Eventually, he eases into his seat and leans back.

"Like you do? Of course. He's a part of our family." I can't stop the eye roll then.

"Not like *I do*," I can hear the anger rising in my voice. "Like Jude figured out you did." I play a harsh card.

Braden looks at me. "We haven't done anything, Callie. Nothing, seriously. The most physical touch we've ever had has been in your presence."

"You didn't answer my question."

"I don't know that I can," Braden fumbles. He starts twisting a napkin on the table. "I think I do, or did, or could. But I don't want to find out if it means losing you. I won't pursue it. Neither of us will. You have to believe that. Remember, Callie, the night I first laid eyes on Jay, I told you the feeling he gave me. I chose you then, and I'm choosing you now." Braden tries to reach for my hand, but I keep them in my lap. I can feel sweat dripping down the sides of my body. He pulls his hands back.

"I think you've already lost me, though," I say to him. And, I can hear my tone is softer now, as if we're trying to solve this problem together. "I don't see how we can go back to being married and happy, knowing this about you. Knowing this is something you need to explore and may find that you want …" I pull the muscles behind my eyes as hard as I can to hide the hurt that statement causes me. "It may be the best thing you'll ever experience in your life, Braden. What if that's true and I'm just standing in the way?" I bite down on my cheek so hard it starts bleeding, but I just suck at it so I can keep my expression stable.

"Callie, no, no," I can hear desperation creeping into Braden's voice. "You can be a lot of things, Callie, but never 'in the way.' You and I, we're so good together. I want you in my life. We have such a great home and so much to look forward to. I want you to get your dog. I want you to change your career. I want us to travel together like we talked about. Cross-country by van. Around Europe with a camera. I want … everything for you, and I want to be there, right by your side," he says. "We were so happy."

"I know," I reply, then break his gaze before I lose it.

"Listen, Callie, I don't know how to explain what happened. Jay and I never wanted it or asked for it. You have to believe that. You know us. It just happened. And, we didn't do anything about it. Nothing. And, we weren't going to. We had decided not to—together. I can't even believe Jude picked up on …" I cut him off.

"Don't bring him into this."

Braden's entire demeanor drops. "Callie, don't be like that. I'm the same guy who loved him just like all of us did. I know he was your brother, and it's been killing me to not be able to be there for you right now, but nothing about how I feel about you, Jude, or Levi has changed. I know this … these *emotions* … Jay and I have felt have blown everything up, but it doesn't change the past. It doesn't change the amazing family we had built."

"But it does, Braden. You and I, as a married couple, were in the center. And, we can't be married anymore. What part of that don't you understand?" I'm struggling to keep my composure because I feel so kicked out of their little gay club. I never dreamed a relationship *I chose* to create could hurt so much. Maybe that's why I'd spent all those years alone and would go forward, with just Levi, never letting anyone else in.

But the problem is, I *had* opened my heart to Braden. I did bring those walls down. I had trusted him and let him—and Jay, too—in, and this is what happened.

"Here's what I understand. This joker needs you," Braden says, his eyes brimming. "I know that I love you more than anything. More than this new feeling and wherever it might lead, because I'm not sure I entirely trust it yet, Callie. But I trust you, us, our love for each other. I love our home and our life and everything you bring to it. I know it will hurt Jay if we send him away, but he and I talked about that, and he's ready to go if you say the word. He has flat-out refused to do anything that will hurt you more than we already have."

This stings me as I think about Jay and how it would feel to him to be cast off. Again.

"Jay matters," I say, even though I know it's a strange thing to say and not really a response to Braden.

"What?" The word falls out of Braden's mouth.

"I said Jay matters. Out of the three of us, the person who really deserves a chance at this is Jay. You're an incredible man, Braden. Anyone—man or woman—would be lucky to call you their partner."

Braden is shaking his head 'no.'

"I've made my decision."

Braden sits in complete silence. "Now I ask that you both honor it. Can you make that promise to me on both your and Jay's behalf?"

"The answer is yes, but not if you say what I think you're going to say." Braden looks like he's stopped breathing.

"I am going to say what you think I'm going to say, because I think deep down you knew this was going to be my decision. But," I reach across and grab Braden's arms forcefully. "I need you to both do what I ask, okay? This has been hard enough, Braden. No more notes around the house, no more flowers, or any lady fingers or other kind gestures." I drop his arms.

"I want you and Jay to go and be together. Figure out what you have. If it's real, if it's love, you both deserve it. Especially Jay. Pursue it. And go live a happy life together. But I can't let either of you … 'choose me,'" cruelly I mock Braden's own words. "And then I have to live with the feeling that I stood in your way for the rest of my life. I will forever feel that you chose me out of pity, and you two weren't brave enough to see where this might take you. I can't do that. I won't."

Braden is crying into his hands now.

"I hadn't told you yet, but Levi will be moving in later in July," I continue. "He needs help financially, and he and I need each other right now. I just need to focus on work and him and heal. You and Jay go off and do what you need to do."

I start to ease out of the booth because I don't feel there is anything more to say.

"Callie, you can't mean this," Braden starts, his eyes red. "We can find a way to fix this. I know we can."

"We can't, Braden. I'm not angry with you. I'm hurt," I bite my lips to stop tears, "but not angry. I understand they were just emotions that you never asked for and couldn't control. I get all that, and it's exciting. Jay is an amazing man. I hope you two are very happy together. But, you and I?" I make a hand gesture between us and see that my hand is trembling, so I put it back down immediately. "We will never be the same. We can't, Braden. I don't know what we can be, if anything, because I …" Braden raises his face to look at me. I see genuine, deep hurt there, but I also see the man I am losing. I see the man who broke my heart, and it fucking hurts, so I tell him:

"I don't think I can ever forgive you for doing this to us," and I walk out.

My chest is heaving as I bust out through the doors of the coffee shop. Each time this happens, I'm not sure my body will be able to pull air in, but—in a panicked response to my fear—it gulps it. I put my hand over my mouth so strangers in the parking lot don't hear my sobs. I'm so shaky and strung out that I'm not sure I can drive in this condition. So, I pop my trunk, throw my heels in the back, put my tennis shoes on, and I start walking. I walk and cry and walk and cry for hours.

Then I get in my car, and I drive to Nick's.

"I'll have a gin and tonic," I hear a raspy voice say as I sit down, before I realize it's my own.

"Make it a double."

CHAPTER FORTY-THREE
COWBOY WISDOM

"So, this best friend of yours, Levi," Mariah pauses briefly, looking around my hospital room, but Levi is nowhere in sight. "You're sure he's gay?"

"Insufferably so," I tell her again. Mariah harrumphs.

"Always the super-hot ones," she clucks, commiserating. "What gives?"

"I know," I shrug.

"So, I've gone to every store on your route," Mariah is animated, talking a mile a minute, telling me about her efforts to find some footage of Braden and me in his Pathfinder on the night of the accident. "Callie, we scored at a jewelry store. It's this little mom-and-pop operation. Your DUI guy's team tried to come in all brute force and stiff lips, and that didn't work. Never works," Mariah rolls her eyes and makes a face.

"That bully tactic only rubbed them the wrong way. But I brought some lunch in yesterday and sat down with one of the owners, Mrs. Kittery, and just talked to her. Asked her about when she first set up shop there and why she chose that location. How she got into jewelry, etc. It's amazing what you can learn when you just talk to people and, here's the kicker, *listen*. Remember that, Callie." I give Mariah a bit of a funny look because it feels like she's trying to groom me.

"Anyway, we keep chatting, and guess what I find out. Mrs. Kittery went to high school in San Antonio, Texas, which, in and of itself, is a pretty big city, right? They have several high schools. But, guess which school she went to."

Mariah is pacing the room now, and I can see she's loving this. I can feel the joy she has for her job—for snooping and doing real street work, putting clues together. I think about the mountains of documents that are sitting on my desk—the angry emails and unfair tactics, and I envy her.

"That's right," Mariah answers our thoughts. "Mrs. Kittery—formerly Ms. Dillon—went to Thomas Jefferson High School. Class of 1972."

My hand goes to my mouth because I know. I just know. I'm shaking my head from side to side now because I just can't believe it. Dad tried to tell me it's impossible to predict how life will twist and turn, but this. Is. Just. Unreal!

"Yep!" Mariah confirms.

"Anyway, the insufferably gay Levi put it together. Your mom-and-pop jewelry store owner—who has a camera pointed directly at the intersection of Rowling Street and Ninth and who, don't tell your DUI guy, keeps backups of the footage in a cloud—went to high school with none other than ..." she does an overly-dramatic fake drumroll. "Tammy!"

Mariah is looking at me like I should applaud. She bows.

"Tammy is coming with me to the jewelry store today to speak with Mrs. Kittery, well, Fran is her name, and, hopefully, get the footage. Tammy even remembers her, if you can believe it. Said they were in the Spanish Club together," Mariah is beaming. "That's why I had Levi bring her in today."

Had Levi brought her in? Mariah speaks like she's been a part of this family from the jump, and a huge part of me feels like maybe she has—at least for the really meaningful parts.

"Oh, and I've got a few things for you," Mariah says, reaching into her braided satchel.

"Jay was adamant about this," she says, bringing out a little box, not much bigger than an envelope. I look up at her as I take it in my hands.

"Oh, you better believe I'm waiting for you to open it. If I have to be a courier, I at least get to satisfy my own curiosity," she says, crossing her arms over her chest. "It's from him and Braden."

At the sound of his name, I pull a trepidatious breath in from Jay *and Braden*.

I find courage and lift the lid.

Inside, on a soft bed of foam, sit two items. One is a letter. I recognize the scrawl on it immediately. *Callie,* it says, in my dad's handwriting. I smell Copenhagen and swell inside.

Next to it is a little LEGO man. Arnie Armstrong. And, not just any Arnie. It is *the* Arnie. The one Jay, Jude, and I used to play with because he still has the little swipe of grey moon paint on his foot. "We'll need Astro-glue to put him back together," I remember Jude saying when we'd tried to pull him off the quickly drying moon-landing site. His little Astro-body had separated from his Astro-legs, and the three of us peeled out in laughter.

"Jay said when Braden first woke yesterday, the first thing he did was make Jay promise he would go get this letter from your house and bring it here to you." Mariah glances at it and lets out a sigh. "I see now. Braden said this would probably be the perfect time for some 'cowboy wisdom,'" she says with air quotes.

I melt. These last few weeks, I've been harboring such intense anger at Braden—the man who knows me so well, that he sends me this. Right now.

"Mariah, there's so much I have to tell you about … what happened in my life, since Jude. It's all such a mess," I say, defeated.

"I know you do," she responds. Always three steps ahead. Reminds me of Jude.

"Maybe a lot happened in my life, too. Maybe it involves you," Mariah says resolutely, and I'm reminded how bold she is. Mariah has been one of the defining forces of this period of my life—pulling and clawing me through this with her legal and street savvy. Her and Mom both, even Tammy, and I'm humbled by the strength of the women who surround me—myself included.

A thought strikes me, and I do something completely out of character.

"Mariah," she gives me her full attention. "Could it be time for a little coaching now? I need some advice," I start.

Mariah puts her satchel to the side and clasps her hands together. "Of course. Start talking."

So, I unload on her. I tell Mariah everything that's been going on with Jay and Braden—the big, devastating discovery that my husband is no longer in love with me, that he's fallen for my cousin, a wonderful man I brought into our lives to save him, although it ended up wrecking me. I tell her about my plans to have Levi move in with me, and maybe he and I stay in the loft together and rent out the house so I can make ends meet. I'm worried about all the debt the firm has saddled me with, not to mention the medical and other bills I have surely generated with this accident that will only continue to mount, all the out-of-pocket cost co-pays, and modifications we may need to make to the house for my new disability. I feel more lost than I ever have—romantically, logistically, financially.

Mariah listens captive the entire time I spilled my frantic, jagged thoughts out onto the bed. The telling of my fears feels kind of like passing my emotions over to her to hold for a minute. Mariah takes a slow, calming breath before responding.

"Let's start with the heart—always the right place. No one said Braden doesn't love you anymore. Or Jay, for that matter. And, that's not the sense I've got from either of them over the last couple of days. Anything but, Callie."

I just frown. None of that sounded like what the hell I should do.

"You always give so much of yourself, Callie. From what I can see, you are the linchpin that is holding your family together. Do I want to get angry, scorch the earth in your honor, and tell the two of them to go fuck themselves because they hurt you? Of course," I smile a tiny smile at this. "But, how would you feel about me doing that? How would you feel afterward if *you* did that?" My smile fades.

"The problem I see is, I can't see you doing anything here other than what is your nature, Callie. No matter what I say. Or anyone says. You will fall on your instincts. All I find here is love and respect, among all of you. Isn't it possible to just rearrange things? Absorb the blow but flow with the change?"

I let this seep in. I had been flirting with something so bold myself, but I was afraid to put it into words. It seemed strange thinking I had fought and scraped and worked so hard to obtain this so-called perfect normal life—a job with a big salary, a nice house, money for vacations, a husband, a loving family—and here I was leaning toward the most unconventional outcome I could have anticipated.

"Hell, maybe your answer's right there," Mariah says, pointing to the box in my lap. "I'll give you some time to read it. I've got to get to the jewelry store with Levi and Tammy."

I just nod, my thoughts and brain a million miles away. But something pricks me.

"What about work and my debt? Finances, career, don't life coaches typically focus on those things?"

"We'll get to that," Mariah snaps back. "In another session," with a wink.

"Oh, hey, they recovered your phone from near the scene," she says, pulling it out. "It was completely dead, but I charged it for you. I gotta run," Mariah says, scooping up her satchel and hustling out.

I turn my phone on and wait as the little progress bar appears.

I gasp audibly when I see it, the last text notification right at the top—received twenty minutes ago. My heart starts thumping like a dog's tail because he reached out first to me.

The words can mean only one thing.

Paws for a cause?

I can't wait to respond. But, first things first.

CHAPTER FORTY-FOUR
DAD

Babes:

I don't know when you'll read this. A long time from now, I hope, because I hope you live a long time. Longer than me. I know you won't make near as many mistakes as I did. You're smarter than I am. But I know you are going to make plenty, and you need to know it's okay if you do. Just make amends after, do what you feel you need to do to clear your heart, and then pick up and be more kind and selfless the next time. That's all you can do.

The main thing I wanted to get on paper, Callie, just because you never know what's going to happen, was my biggest mistake. My biggest mistake, Callie, was with you kids. I didn't say these things to you and Jude when you were growing up because, to be honest, it's a scary thing to do. I didn't want you or Jude to think less of me, mainly you, because you always held me up so high. You, in particular. But you should know these things. I should have told you these things because they shape who you are, which affects who you will become.

Your Mom and I were never meant to stay together. We would have killed each other eventually. Our love was so passionate and strong that it crept over to the other side at times. It crossed the line. Intense love can do that. But I should have made sure you and Jude knew the sacrifices your Mom made for you two. I was the one who screwed it up, and she was the one who worked hard, stayed focused, and did the very hard things that made her the villain. But she did those things because she loves you two, and she has more of a backbone than I do. That's just the truth, Callie, and I want you to know it, because you're so much like Charlene some days it scares me.

If you haven't already—knowing you, you have—but forgive her, Callie. Reconnect. Remember what Charlene's been through, and how much life experience she can share with you. And, forgiveness is one of the most graceful, selfless gifts you can give someone, my girl. If my letter accomplishes that, I will know it was worth it. But I still want to ask for more. I am your dad, so I get to.

Callie, don't let bad things that happen to you—because Callie, know that bad things will happen to you as they do to everyone—taint you inside like they did Charlene. That's the lesson. Even when it hurts, you have to keep letting love in. As I've told you before, people will slip into your stubborn heart, Callie, and love will grow in ways you never dreamed possible. I only know these things because with age comes experience, which brings wisdom.

It's actually a peaceful feeling growing older, I have found. It calms you, gives you footing, and makes you see outcomes developing early on. Bad decisions and bad people become easier to spot. Age also makes you aware that things are always, constantly changing, and that that's okay. Necessary even. Life flows like a river. Which means it will split apart, circle back, pool up, and come crashing back together again, in ways you could have never predicted, but when you can take a moment to appreciate the current state you're in—and be sure to do that every chance you get—you'll feel like everything is just how it was meant to be from the start. It's a strange but humbling and comforting feeling. You're not nearly as in control as you would like to be, Babes.

And, that's okay.

You will always work hard. You will always give more of yourself than you should. You get that from Charlene. But you will also bring joy and laughter. You will lean on humor to get you through emotions that try to tear you down. You get that from me. And, mainly, you're smart. You can thank Jude for that. I've never seen a young child so intent on teaching and developing another. You were like Jude's own personal project. In the worst situations, he would always shelter and shield you and keep you distracted with education. It was amazing to watch.

I know you two will reconnect, Babes, because I know how much not having Jude in your life has been hurting you. If I had to guess, Jude is just going through his twenties right now—making mistakes and trying to figure himself out. Some people never finish that phase. He will. And you two will then find each other again. I know it. You're destined.

When you do, please tell Jude I'm sorry, Callie. I've known from the beginning who he was, and my fear for the terrible, very difficult life I felt it would cause him made me angry at him for his choice. I just wanted an easier life for him, but it took me years to realize that was never going to be possible for Jude, because there is no choice for Jude. Jude is Jude. He's the most unique, clever, compassionate person I've ever met. My son. It feels so strange saying that. But he is. And it's damn sure not because of me. He deserved more from me, but I didn't give it, and I have regretted it ever since. Please promise you will do whatever it takes not to live with regret. Be brave and do the hard things that I didn't do.

I'm not a person who can live with those kinds of feelings, Callie. Charlene would hold onto those things. Let them fuel her. But I let them go. I make amends with it, find a way to clear my heart, and I carry on, with songs and jokes and a happy voice. I don't know which method is right out of those, Callie. Maybe it's in between—right about where you fall. I sense you'll find a deeper, more meaningful happiness than I did, even in these later years with Tammy and you, which have been some of the best of my life. I mean, I had a helluva lot of fun, and you should, too, but I was chasing something during my rodeo days that I don't think I ever found there. Fulfillment? Happiness? I'm not sure. But I know you'll find it.

You'll do better than I did, Babes, because you have an incredible life ahead of you, my girl. You have people around you who will fight and stand up for you, because they know you'll do it for them. You'll be the oak tree of your own family, just like Charlene. I know it. And, trust me—to Tammy's dying day—she will be there for you, my girl. Call on her. And your Mom, much as y'all fight, would still scorch the earth for you. You are getting an education, which is critical, and you are smart and driven, but also compassionate and aware, like Jude. Nothing can stop you. So, I'll send you these:

Learn from your mistakes and losses, but don't let them paralyze you.

Remember, pain is a necessity. We can't know joy …

Embrace the tangled, unpredictable messes. They're the best part.

I love you, Babes. Know that I'm always right there with you, in your heart.

CHAPTER FORTY-FIVE
FAMILY, IN ANY FORM

I smell tobacco. I see him sitting atop Little Man, smiling in the sunshine. I hear his melodic baritone—*Jude Boy, Jude Boy, where you been?* His words resonate through me.

Forgiveness is the most graceful, selfless gift you can give.

Be brave and do the hard things I didn't.

My hands are shaking as I fold the letter back gently and start my reply to Braden. Can I live with Braden and Jay being together and happy? *Can I?* I ask myself as my fingers hover over the phone. The longer I think about it—and when the alternative is another member of our tribe dead from an accident—then the answer is yes. Yes, I absolutely can. Not only that, but I *want* to. I would rather have both Jay and Braden alive and a part of my life in a different way than not a part of my life at all. If there's a choice to have or not, I'll take family, in any form.

I wiggle the shake out of my hands, pop my neck, and wipe them on my hospital blanket to get the sweat off.

I'm doing this.

UT Shelter at your service.
Where forgiveness blooms.
What type of service do you need?

With a shaky thumb, I hit send and put the phone down on my bed. I feel like I've been on a mental roller coaster—ups, downs, anger, hope, past, present, all colliding like fireworks, then spinning like one of those round apparatuses at the playground—all while I was just holding on, fighting the centrifugal force. Braden's response buzzes back in seconds.

I need my best friend. She's funny and clever and so incredibly strong. I need to spend the rest of my life showing her what she means to me.

A kaleidoscope of memories crashes through my brain—Braden and I laying on the rug listening to his records, the five of us playing Monopoly in my living room, Jay and Braden hollering at, and heckling, me on the rock climbing wall, Braden buying me my first latte at the coffee shop—as I keep deciding, with more and more clarity, what a wasteful, foolish thing it would be to cut Braden, and Jay, out of my life simply because they are happy together.

Well, I recently gave the best friend designation to Levi, but you are still my husband. We'll have to get inventive. And unconventional. Luckily, creative solutions are our specialty here at UT Shelter.

While my heart does feel bruised—hurt, and sore from everything that has happened in the last months—I can feel it taking on a stronger beat. It reminds me of my dad's horse, Kip. After running him hard, his coat all lathered and foamy from it, I could put my hand on his chest and feel his massive heart beating, like a leather tribal drum compared to my little snare. My heart is starting to feel like that: a deep, rhythmic, healing thump. It tells me this is the right decision. Then something else tells me, too.

Jay comes crashing through my door. He looks like a five-year-old at Christmas. His face is so lit up. I see teeth I've never seen before. He's smiling so big, his scar pulled taut and pink from it. Jay knocks over a plastic water pitcher and some cups near the counter by the door, and he fumbles to catch them and put them back in place. They eventually clatter to the floor, and he just throws his hands up and comes racing over to me. Jay leaps on top of the bed so he's straddling me. He's even landed perfectly around my mismatched legs. The move is so sudden and surprising that a yelp escapes me, although he didn't hurt me at all.

"I don't care who's your best friend, or your husband, or whatever else. I. Am. Your. Cousin," he pounces a little, making the bed bounce with each word. I give him a sly little smile and whisper.

"Damn right you are. Don't make me regret this. This is your third chance."

Jay shakes his head side to side in long, meaningful passes.

"Here on out," he says. "I've got you." We share a knowing look as I see Mom peek her head into the room. She must have heard the commotion from Jay and came to check on me.

Seeing her, something inside me shifts. Gears turn. I straighten up. *I have so much to do.*

"Mom, come in," I tell her, ushering Jay off my bed. He dutifully retreats to the corner and extends a hand to guide Mom's way.

"Mrs. Charlene," he says with a respectful nod.

And, there she is. My mom, a wounded woman herself, who has absorbed the entirety of my fury, as I have hers, but we both unleashed in the name of protecting our family, and I realize: *She is not my enemy here.* Whatever I think of her and her choices in the past, which is where they should stay, and what she did or didn't do for me and Jude when we were growing up, she's here now. I have a mother, and she's here for me right now, at a time when I need her, a time when I seem to need everyone.

There is no way I can walk out of this hospital, considering I can't even walk, and start my life over without the help of every single person who is here for me right now. And then, I see my path. It stretches out behind Mom's shoulders, busting through the walls of this prison-like hospital room, and extending out into a brilliant horizon. It is right there before me, just waiting for me to take the first step, which is good because one step is all I can take right now. It's so blinding, I swear I can feel rays from it on my face as I blink and smile in this strange, exalted moment.

My chest inhales with the revelation. What I can control here is my response, my attitude and outlook, and what I do with the life I still have.

"Mom, I'm sorry for never taking your side."

The room takes a breath in and holds it. The clock ticks. Once. Twice. Mom's brow knits the slightest bit, skeptical at first—a protective instinct I know all too well. Then I see it release as she exhales, and her shoulders drop slowly. I continue.

"I … I want to work on us. I promised Jude I would, which you know means I will." We share a knowing look. "We've all lost enough. And I think we—you and I," I motion between us, "can learn to understand one another."

Mom is still standing there awkwardly at the foot of my bed with her arms hanging by her sides. Jay is silent, watching us. Mom bites down on her lips, and I can see her jaw muscles working feverishly. She swallows and blinks, her lips trembling.

"Stop yer' crying," I say, gently, with a little smile, which makes Mom laugh, a snotty little bubble of a laugh. She just nods.

"Do something for me," I tell her. Mom nods, wipes her hands on the front of her jeans, and mashes some grey hair away from her face. She's clear and committed to me. I can see it. That snake is in my corner. I smile.

"Anything," Mom says, and I one hundred percent believe it.

I instruct her to take the framed photo of me and Dad and open it up in the back. Mom looks confused, but does it anyway without a word. When she pulls the back of the frame off, she finds the picture Dad gave me of him and her when they were both so young, and I wonder what it will feel like for me—when I'm fifty-nine—to be looking back at a photo of myself at an equally young age. Before the amputation, when both my legs were strong and whole, and my entire life ahead was an unknown.

"My God," she says. "We were so young. It's hard for me to even remember what this girl was like." I find I can relate to that feeling, as I find it hard to remember the girl I was just a few short months ago, when my life felt gilded and too perfect to be true.

"I know she was adventurous, and fun—a bit too disciplined—but very, very brave," I tell Mom, because I know it's true, and I feel like it describes me, too.

I hold my hand out to her. Although we've never been very affectionate, she takes it. Mom's hands are cold, bony, and weathered, and I'm reminded how much more life she has lived than I have, how much experience she has that I—in my self-absorbed, righteous mindset—simply dismissed because I thought she had made poor decisions. But here I am in this sad hospital bed—the undisputed Queen of Poor Decisions.

"I'm sorry for what Dad did and what happened to our family. I should have taken your side more," I repeat. Mom opens her mouth but immediately closes it tight, just a little puckered bit scrunched over to the left. She finally takes a big breath in and lets it out.

"Me too," she whispers.

I look in her crystal blue eyes, and I see mine and Jude's childhood. I see Mom plopping a dented metal salad bowl on my head and blowing hair off my face. I see her tiptoeing through LEGOs all over the shag carpet. I see Mom's butthole mouth as she's giving us a much-deserved whooping. I see the yellow swoops on the linoleum floor in our bathroom. I see my Mom's hands, tucking us in, making us Cream of Wheat, wiping our dirt-streaked cheeks with a thumb she licked, rubbing our chests with Vicks VapoRub.

"Mom, I love you," I tell her, and I mean it more than I ever have. I can feel Jude in me when I squeeze her hand. "I'm sorry, Jude, and I didn't tell you or show you enough."

She bows her head in tears, her shoulders shaking as Jay comes and cradles her.

—

I have so much to do, churns through my brain again. While we are all aware of the steep climb I have ahead, dealing with my medical recovery and workload at the firm, I haven't told anyone yet, but I've also come up with something else to motivate me through this recovery: My Completely Crazy Idea.

"Jay, get me up out of this bed." Jay makes sure Mom is settled and then complies immediately, standing me up next to my bed, holding his arm for support.

"I need to start strengthening my 'good leg,'" I tell them both. It feels strange saying that, but I've yet to come up with a better name, so that's it. She'll need to bear the brunt of my standing, walking, and balance for the time being, until I figure out what life is going to feel like on a leg and a peg. I have a brief fear that maybe they'll take my prosthetic away from me in jail, if I go. I wouldn't think so, but I don't know. Mainly, I hope they let me keep it on so I can take it off when I'm cornered and need a weapon. Having a bionic bat permanently attached to your body could be pretty cool.

I grip Jay's arm with one hand and the bed rail with the other as I start to dip down a little on my good leg and push back up to standing. Jay and Mom watch as I do a couple, their faces a mix of awe and bewilderment.

"Someone's motivated," Jay says through a grin.

"You're damn right," I confirm. "I've got a hell of a lot of living to do." I ease down another time and push back up to standing to look Jay in the eye. I see Mom shaking her head in my periphery, but I keep at it as we start to hear muffled voices out in the hall.

"Woman, un*hand* me!" Joy unfolds like an octopus filling my chest. *Levi.* My best friend.

The three of them clatter into the room—Mariah, Levi, and Tammy.

Levi is tossing Mariah's hand off his shoulder as he comes in. "You will not steal my moment, you hussy! I cracked this case!" Mariah is playfully swatting at him, and I'm happy to see the two of them have become fast friends.

"But, wait, didn't *I* …" Levi pulls Tammy close and puts a finger on *her* lips, which makes me laugh. Tammy's got a funny look of confusion on her face, but she just holds it. She's used to our particular brand of crazy by now. Levi gives one look at my off-kilter quad presses, nods in approval, and continues.

"You may have assisted, yes, thank you, Tammy," Levi says, still enjoying the spotlight, "but the record will reflect, Counselor." Levi takes a breath in, and we all presume to begin a lengthy diatribe.

"Oh, wait," Jay holds up a finger to everyone and pulls his phone out of his back pocket. I watch him curiously. We all hear ringing and then … Braden's voice. It feels like honey in my mouth.

"Hey," he says, and I think my heart stops. I forgot exactly what he sounds like, his rich baritone, his comforting presence, even just by phone.

"Hey, Bray," Levi says loudly into the phone. "You're looking much better this morning, Sir."

"Hi Braden, I'm glad they finally gave you your phone," Mariah says.

Jay looks to me, so I chime in, surprisingly a little nervous at first.

"Hi Braden," I say, about as brave as a mouse. The room goes quiet for a beat before Braden explodes on the other end of the line.

"Callie, thank God you're okay. You're okay! Never hang up. Never! I love you so much!" I nod and start to tear up.

"Oh, puke!" Levi starts in. "We can deal with all this love stuff later, Chief. You saps are ruining my moment. Mariah, can you please show Counselor Exhibit A?" Levi says, sounding ever the Professor. Mariah starts to pull a manila folder out of her satchel and make her way toward me when Braden says boldly and loudly over the phone.

"I was driving."

Mariah lets the envelope drop down to her side while Levi lets out a monstrous, audible eye-roll.

"Braden, your timing," he says, looking to the ceiling aghast.

"I'm sorry, but I was!" Braden says over the line. "I remember up to the point of impact, Callie. Jay and I had been … we were only talking by phone, I swear … but we had been keeping a close eye on you and we knew you'd been going to Nick's often in the evenings."

I look down at my blanket, fresh blooms of blush forming on my cheeks.

"Every other night, one of us had been following you home to make sure you made it okay, because we knew you didn't want us contacting you." Jay gives me a slight nod, saying it's true, and I'm humbled into further silence.

"But that night, Callie, you were just too far gone. Stumble down drunk. I didn't want you getting behind the wheel. Even to drive just those few blocks home."

I look around the room feeling embarrassed, but I don't see disappointment in anyone's eyes. I guess it wasn't the worst thing in the world to do, but I'm still mortified as Braden continues.

"You were livid, Callie. You wanted nothing to do with me. But I finally got you in my Pathfinder and buckled in, and you passed out pretty quickly, which I was grateful for. But there was this drunk driver on the way home, on Ninth Avenue."

The entire room is keyed into this, listening intently. You could hear a mouse fart.

"He swerved off the road, then came back on aggressively into our lane. So, I swerved off to avoid him, but the embankment was too rough. I was afraid we were going to flip or hit something really hard and stop too abruptly. I was trying to ease back onto the road just to slow down and get us safely on the shoulder when the other guy came careening into our lane again. Then he hit us on the back driver's side. That's the last thing I remember. I don't think there was anything else I could do to avoid it, Callie. I'm so sorry. I was just trying to get you home safe," Braden's voice leaves the room, and we all look at each other.

"Well, that's more detail than I was going to be able to provide," Mariah starts. "But we are able to prove Braden was driving that night, see?" Mariah pulls an eight-by-ten photo from the manila folder. It feels like everyone in the room tiptoes toward me or arches their neck to see it.

"And, exactly how much alcohol had you consumed that night, Mr. Bauer?" Mariah asks, in her stealthy cross-examination voice as she begins pacing the room with the photo in her hand.

"Zero. I had no alcohol. Not a drop," Braden says.

"It's true. The blood test proves it," Mariah says to me with a wink.

"And if the driver of Vehicle No. 1 was not drinking—'not a drop' I quote," Mariah is having fun with this, I can tell, "what does that mean for our potential charges of DUI and manslaughter, Counselor?" Mariah turns to me. My hand goes to my mouth because I just can't believe this. I asked, prayed, begged for just one break here, and dammit if I didn't get it. And, it came right after I decided to forgive and open myself up again? It's all too coincidental. *Jude,* I think. *And Dad. You sneaky angelic bastards.*

"No charges," I say, my voice strange and small in the room.

"PRECISELY!" Mariah's booms around me. "The other guy, now he was hammered. God rest his soul," Mariah makes a cross over her chest. "And, you were three sheets to the wind. Trust me, we have proof," she taps the photo, and my curiosity is burning. I want to see it. "But the driver of Vehicle No. 1, ladies and gentlemen, was stone cold sober. And, if they try to fight us on it, which I don't think they will—I've given Detective Carter many reasons to choose not to go to battle with me—your slick DUI lawyer's accident reconstruction guy can piece together what Braden is willing to testify happened with the tire tracks and vehicle evidence and all. So, there you have it, folks. My friend, Callie, is not in any legal trouble," Mariah takes a bow before she makes her way over to me to hand me the photo.

And there it is. In full color. Clear as day.

I am passed out, leaning against the passenger window of Braden's Pathfinder. We're both buckled in. Braden has one hand on the wheel. His face is clear and focused. His eyes are on the road. But, his other hand. His other hand … closes my throat.

In the photo, you can see Braden has reached over to my side of the car and taken my hand in his. He—the man I told I could never forgive and never wanted to see again—is holding my hand as I'm passed out against the window.

I look up at Mariah, wide-eyed.

"You did it," I tell her. "You got to the bottom of it."

"Did I not just say who cracked the case?" Levi asks with a huff. "Kidding," he puts both hands on Tammy's shoulders. "It was really this lovely lady, here, sweet-talking her way in."

"Oh, stop," Tammy says. "Everyone loves my rum butter almond cookies," she waves a little hand. "I can't believe Frannie even remembered me from Spanish Club, though. That was a lifetime ago. I will say, she looked amazing. Well, unique, I'll go with that. Must have had some work done," Tammy giggles.

"Oh, definitely," Levi agrees, pulling his face back in a mock facelift.

When Mariah does the same, I lose it laughing.

"Frannie found the footage in five minutes flat and happily gifted the screenshot to us," Mariah adds when she finally recovers.

I look around the room in complete awe. There's Tammy, Levi, Mom, Mariah, Jay, and Braden on the phone. Here they all are. My army. My misfit, pieced-together family.

"Wait, what's that?" I ask, pointing to the photo. "It looks like there's a …"

In the photo, it is hard to make out, but it looks like a cardboard box in the back of Braden's Pathfinder with holes cut in it, and a puppy is poking its head out of the box. Her tongue is lolling out like she's on a big grand adventure.

"Is that a *dog* in the backseat?" I ask.

"Oh, that," I hear Braden's voice over the phone, and Jay laughs.

CHAPTER FORTY-SIX

MARIAH

I don't know how she does it. Looks like she's all meek and humble when she is, but she's also the strongest force I've ever felt in my life. From the moment I met her, Callie was fire. Considering the typical Clovis track, she was disruptive: creative and smart, always pushing herself to learn more, memorize more, excel. She got that from Jude, I know.

Roddie told me about him back when we were younger. They were kind of secret, star-crossed friends. Roddie told me he had been pretty sure Jude was gay, even back then, but Roddie didn't do the typical "Not that there's anything wrong with that" line, like most people do. Roddie told me he felt it made Jude a more aware person, more sentient, empathetic. And, I can totally see that.

While I wouldn't say the path Callie and Roddie and I had to walk, being straight teenagers and doing the normal thing was *easy*, I can't imagine what life must have been like for Jude—in the early nineties in *Clovis, New Mexico*, of all not-so-gay-friendly places—growing up trying to sort that out, with no role models. No one to really talk to about it? It just reinforces what I've learned on my own: gay people are often far more experienced, more grounded. They're resilient and tested. And, they're usually wildly hilarious, including this sexy Levi character. Hate we lost him to the dark side. But I keep thinking maybe I can convert him. Like Callie, I do love a challenge.

Speaking of, Callie is my next one.

Some days, I find it surreal to believe Callie really did endure all of this. Losing her brother, then her husband, almost. Her leg, the lower half at least. And, almost her job and law license. She was on the brink of being arrested for manslaughter, and we somehow pulled her back. Although I know they all have some tough adjustments and new truths to work through, Jay and Braden were instrumental. They both did everything I asked of them to help us get the evidence I needed to prove Callie's innocence. I'll be honest, in my first interviews with those two, I felt they would say and do whatever was required to save her. I suspected Braden was just falling on Callie's sword, claiming he had been driving, until I saw the photo. That's love there. Throw Levi, Tammy, and her mother, Mrs. Charlene, in, and Callie has a pretty impressive army.

Above all that, she's also the breadwinner—a truth that came out rather quickly when I started to ask some tough questions about their finances and Callie's mounting medical bills. Callie really did climb her way right to the top. Goldman Carr is one of the fiercest firms in the state, and she's their new golden female litigator. Word travels in the legal world.

Once she crashed back into my life and I started asking around about her, I wasn't surprised to find Callie had climbed even faster than most associates, earning her right to make partner this coming year. The only problem is she's representing the bad guys—huge corporations and insurance companies that have no soul. They harm and hurt people every day, and just argue their way out of the millions they owe. I should know because I'm about to sue several, one in particular is a huge international pharmaceutical company, like many, Callie has represented over the years, that has hidden the truth about their product and the thousands of consumers they have injured. I want Callie on my side for this fight. I need her. And, in all honesty—I'm biased, but that doesn't necessarily make me wrong—I know Callie needs a more fulfilling fight.

I'm just going to have to convince her to leave her firm. Now that I've saved her law license, I think she'll listen. I would never say she owes me this, but I am moving pieces and planting seeds in Callie's best interest. Once she sees she's fighting on the wrong side, she'll come to Avalero and Associates.

Her partner, Justin, came by the hospital on her third day here, and I pulled him aside to talk for a while. Of all the stuffy white guys at Goldman Carr, he's pretty approachable. Justin told me he lost his own brother in a hiking accident a couple of years back, and he wanted to make sure Callie was doing okay. He told me he could see her spiraling at the firm recently, but the office culture just didn't provide a good space for him to check in on her. After a while chatting, I sensed Justin was also unhappy at Goldman Carr, too. That's when I began to hatch my plan.

I started to think about how great it would be to bring in *two* new attorneys to my firm. I could make them both partners right out of the gate. Callie was on the verge anyway. She deserves it. But the two of them, she and Justin, will have to invest in my firm. Bring some money and put some skin and faith into what I'm building—a brave, cunning David to take down the greedy Goliaths of the world. The good news is they will be able to work remotely. Oh, and the better news. Justin is a total hottie, and he's single. Did I mention that? You see? I'm always plotting.

I've got a plan for Callie. She'll just have to take a leap and trust me and know that I'm setting all of this up for her. Well, for us both. I do love watching Callie's eyes twinkle.

That's why I've saved the best surprise for last.

EPILOGUE
ONE YEAR LATER

"Maxi pads?" I ask, perplexed, when I pull them out of the glove compartment at Levi's insistence. I've called the boys back at home about an hour out from Mariah's in Houston in my freshly rented sprinter van.

"Extra plus, plus," Levi snickers as the three of them laugh. "For … roadside emergencies."

I warm at the memory, realizing it was the story I told the day Levi and I met. Not surprisingly, he remembered. One year since Jude's passing, and Levi and I have grown closer than I believe even Jude and I were as kids. In the grey, stretched out months after Jude's passing, Levi and I leaned on one another in my house together, picking the other up off the floor often or—when it seemed right—just laying a blanket over and curling up alongside.

We never keep Pringles in the house. We both fall apart if *Africa* by Toto comes on. Lucy still has the pink elephant Jude got her just before the shooting. Neither Levi nor I has been on a date. We love each other, but I'm afraid we have worked ourselves into a kind of an unhealthy rut, living in the time capsule that has become my house together, while Jay and Braden—living in the loft—have flourished. Braden started his own design firm and has snagged a few high-end Austin clients, while

Jay started his own handyman/construction company doing jobs for Mariah's property damage clients.

"You might have kept Levi a little too close," Braden's been saying during our weekly coffee-cookie dates at the now infamous coffee shop.

"I know what you both need. *Launch projects*," Jay had said with a wink, during our weekly taco date at the strip mall by Home Depot.

While others find our arrangement quite strange, I now know I was put on this earth to bring Jay and Braden together. Outside of Jude and Levi, I've never seen a better fit—my smart, gentle Braden with tawny, good-natured Jay. Both are creators, congenially competitive, and full of fun and love for each other *and* me. When Jay takes Braden's hand and curls him up on the couch next to me for movie night, it all just feels right. I can't explain it any other way, and I don't feel I have to.

Our arrangement is strange, for sure, but others can bite me. I'll take strange any day of the week. I'll say this: the four of us have a lot of fun introducing one another to new company.

But, Jay's 'launch projects' idea had singed a hole in me because I knew he was right. It wasn't long after he'd said that our new pet project—Jude's House—was born. Braden found the plot of land on the outskirts of Austin. I scraped together the down payment of $50,000 so we could buy it and begin building the house Jude had been sketching since he was nineteen, with its sweeping open floor plan, sunken living room, and up near the widow's walk, "Callie's Room"—it says in Jude's handwriting on his original sketch, which I framed. Unbeknownst to us all, however, Jude later modified the living room to add a whole wall of rectangular, recessed shelves perfect to display art, antiques, or … a record collection. Braden had to leave the room when the four of us first found it.

Jay, Braden, and I are planning to spring the "Jude's House" project on Levi when I get back from this soul-cleansing trip, the goal being for the four of us to work together—well, with Prote-Jay in charge, naturally—getting the house built. Then Levi is going to move out of my house and into Jude's, giving us both a chance to start new chapters. It's time.

I don't yet know how Levi is going to take it. He puts on his flamboyant, bubbly persona every time he leaves the house, but he often hangs it on the coat rack when he gets home to me. I'm a little nervous to share this plan with him, but I've got weeks to think about it while I'm driving out west. As well as how I'm going to break the other news to him.

The other reason I'm on this trip.

I did want to go back to Clovis to visit Mom—we have a date to play backgammon out on the back porch—and Uncle Steve and others from my past. Again, it was time. And, I did want to try out this van lifestyle that I'd started dreaming about in rehab, fueling my growing muscles through extra sets of exercises by imagining myself in a badass sprinter van—all tricked out with tiny home hacks thanks to Jay's handiwork—cruising across the U.S., free as a bird. But I also had another highly motivating factor: My Completely Crazy Idea.

Levi was not on board with this.

The first time I tried to talk to Levi about my idea to find Rachel, he was adamantly opposed, probably still feeling a bit of the deep-seated jealousy he initially harbored for Rachel. But, I explained, I just wanted to see if Rachel would be open to the idea of us meeting Jude's daughter, offering her only the love of five times more family than she had before.

"I just want to let her know she has an army—an outfit of aunts and ... uncles, guncles? —who will love and support her. If Rachel shuts me down, she shuts me down. I will let it be her decision, Levi," I'd pressed him, wanting this more than anything I could remember.

"Oh, *will you?*" he'd asked, flanking my armor and false logic just like Jude always did. "Because you're really good at just backing down, Callie. That's your specialty. And, persuasion isn't like ... your *career* or anything."

But I knew Levi was secretly scared to let someone else in. He was afraid of being hurt and gutted like he was last time. I know because it's exactly how I felt before I forgave Jude and opened myself up to a world of gutting and hurt as well as love and overwhelming joy. I guess my dad taught me well. Because I've decided to pursue this with or without Levi's blessing, and with whatever resulting joy or pain it might bring.

I'm going to California.

—

After my five weeks in rehab—where Tammy, Mariah, Mom, Braden, Jay, Levi, even Lucy, and hell, even Freeze-Face Frannie (Jay dubbed her) visited me often—I really settled nicely into my prosthetic. I even have a little flipper one for swimming, and I'm working toward one of those scoop-shaped, space-age looking ones for running and more vigorous activities. I also became the first attorney at Goldman Carr to structure a reduced hours, remote work position during my recovery. At the time of my accident, I was on too many cases for them to just let me go, particularly right after a tragic injury, so we—as in Mariah— negotiated. Mariah was instrumental in the first few months during my recovery and transition back to full-time. Then she was surgical and went too far, catapulting us into a fight last week that I'm pretty sure was worse than the Stupid Fucking Party.

"I can't believe you talked to my partners behind my back, Mariah!" I'd shouted at her. "Pretty much telegraphing to them that I want to leave the firm. Who would want to put me on a big case, now? Thinking my heart's not in it."

"It's not," Mariah held firm.

"But that's not for you to decide, Jesus! This is *my* life, Mariah! Not yours," I'd been livid. "Everything I've worked so hard for here.

And, you take it upon yourself to sabotage it, let them think I'm going to leave?"

"You are," she'd said, quietly, resolutely. I met her eyes. Fire to fire.

"Look, Justin is the only one I talked to, okay?" Mariah broke first. "And, he's looking to leave, too, so he's not going to tell anyone. It's in his best interest for the two of you to remain quiet and then leave together. It's the perfect situation."

I hated to admit the news about Justin was so surprising that it temporarily curtailed my rage. Justin and I had never talked about anything as scandalous as this, but I guess who would? At the office. It was intriguing, but I didn't feel I had the breathing room to even ask myself whether I was happy at Goldman Carr—because deep down I also knew the answer. Bottom line was, the boys and I needed the money. Between Levi's meager income teaching part-time at UT, and Jay and Braden both trying to nurture new, fledgling businesses, I was by far our breadwinner, and we still owed a ton on the mortgage. Yet, Mariah wanted me to leave a six-figure salary to both invest *and* join her small-time solo firm? It was ludicrous. Frivolous. Insane!

"Callie, I've given this a lot of thought," Mariah had pushed, methodically, persistently, like she always does. "I have valuable cases I want to pursue, that I *need* a team to pursue. I'm having a CPA draw everything up. I want to offer you both ownership in the firm. We all invest a little in ourselves, in … the fight for justice, and it all comes back to us threefold in the future. When you meet some of my clients, Callie, you'll see. What they've been through," she points to my leg. "Yet, what they're still striving toward," she taps my head, then my heart. "It will revive you."

I couldn't deny intrigue. I wondered briefly who these clients were, what they had endured. Then Mariah took one step too far.

"And you need a change, Callie. Working sixty hours a week with you and Levi holed up in that house together for over a year now, constantly cycling through your grief over Jude. Five years there, and this van trip you're planning is your *first ever* vacation. Pssh! With me, you can work remotely. You'll be free! And, both you *and* Levi need exciting, independent solo projects to pursue and encourage each other on."

Mariah knew the Levi/Jude card was a bold move, one that would either sway me or backfire royally.

Right before I hung up on her, Mariah spat out, "We'll talk about it when you come on Friday."

Click.

———

It's now Friday.

On the road, heading to Mariah's place, having cooled and contemplated her offer for days, I make a snap decision and punch in her number. I've got an offer of my own to make her.

"Callie, my girl, you on the road?" Mariah asks after the second ring.

"Yep," I confirm. "I'm about an hour out. Hey, I've got an idea. How you can make it up to me—you're snooping around at Goldman Carr trying to get me ousted."

"While I object to that gross mischaracterization of events," Mariah paused, always loving a good negotiation, "what's your idea?"

I smiled, knowing I had her.

"Write this name down. I need you to do some digging for me. Find Rachel Kohl. Sacramento, California."

I glance at the clock as I hang up, and my hands fall off the wheel. It's 2:34 p.m. I'm feeling a little strange setting off on this trip, alive, crackling. I glance at the photos I've slipped under the visor—me and Dad on our horses, me and Jude with our silly little kid shades, Mom and Dad by the lake. I'd even added a shot of Jude, Levi, Braden, and me on my wedding day, all dressed up in seventies disco, with my taffeta filling the frame. Next to it, I'd saved Braden's first drawing of Jude as an angel, me hugging the life out of all four of them. On my rearview mirror dangles Mariah's seashell friendship bracelet, which she'd lent me "as good luck" for the trip, and on my dash, I hot-glued Arnie Armstrong with one arm outstretched, and one leg kicked back, leading this crazy charge.

I am a single, one-footed, thirty-year-old woman setting off on her own to travel in a van, eventually to California to try and find my late brother's lost daughter. If that doesn't sound like a made-for-TV movie script, I don't know what does. *Jesus, Callie. Lifetime movie, much?* I can hear him agree. It may seem a little bit crazy for a gal to do alone. But, that's just it.

I'm not alone.

"Am I a girl?" I ask and reach over and pat her silky soft head.

That piercing crystal blue eye—the other is a deep honey brown—that looks out at me from the black spot that covers her left eye tells me she gets me. And, this little herding dog really crawled through the abyss to be mine. Jay and Braden had secretly adopted this adorable little puppy from Chuck at the shelter and meant it as a gift for me to help me slow down at work—right before Jude's accident. She mangled her right leg in the crash but survived, roaming the woods by the accident scene for days until she finally approached a woman on her back porch, still with the stuffed monkey "Cheeky" Braden had given her in her mouth. In a wild twist of fate, the woman ended up being a UT Alum familiar with Paws for a Cause. She'd called Chuck at the shelter, and he was able to bring this brave little soul back to our family.

She had to undergo an amputation all the way up to her shoulder. But I tell you, it hasn't slowed her down at all. I honestly don't think my dog even remembers what it was like to have a right leg; she runs and jumps and does twenty tricks like it was never there. "Scars make good stories," I tell her when I pet the little white nub of a scar on her chest. Needless to say, we make quite the matching pair for it.

"Ain't that right, Clovis?" I ask her.

I tuck Cheeky by her in the seat and give Clovis the little "click-click" cluck of my tongue. She responds with her little "Whoof" of a bark. Like Pepper, she never barks without reason, and only whines when it's really important—when she has to pee or when I've put Cheeky in the wash and she goes nuts by the machine, acting like he's undergoing open heart surgery.

She loves to play fetch, terrorize squirrels, bake in the sun like Mom, and Lucy just dotes on her. Thinks the world of her. Clovis is easily the brains, but Lucy is the tumble around goofball willing to do any of Clovis's bidding. The more I watch them, the more I see Jude and me recast as dogs.

—

"Hey, pretty girl," Mariah calls out as Clovis comes running to her after I park my van in front of Mariah's little southwest-style bungalow on the edge of a ranch outside of Houston, decorated to the hilt with chili peppers, tumbleweeds, and dreamcatchers. Her place feels like an old Indian's teepee, minus the teepee.

"So, I found Rachel," Mariah tells me as she's closing the door to my van after her thorough inspection, and we're making our way up to her house.

"You did?" I exhale as we make our way inside.

"If you can believe it, she's still at that same P.F. Chang's where she and Jude used to work together. For now. But they're transferring her this fall."

I raise an eyebrow.

"She's actually moving *here*, Callie. To Houston."

My eyes fly open, but Mariah holds up a finger.

"Gets even crazier. Sit. Trust me." Mariah motions me toward her little round kitchen table, where we plop down and she starts pouring us a Coke.

"Once I found Rachel, it didn't take much more effort to identify her … dependent. I know her name."

I find I'm no longer breathing. I can feel my pulse whooshing in my neck. I don't want to get overly excited as Rachel may put the kibosh on all this, but—*fuck it*—I'm already excited. This is my niece.

I have a niece!

I meet Mariah's eyes and give her the nod.

"Cadence," Mariah says, and my stomach drops to my pelvis with a thud—the clock ticks.

"I know," Mariah nods. "I have many theories. Selfishly, I'm going to need you to go to California and get me the answer to that one. But first," Mariah takes an abrupt turn, and I swear I hear gravel crunch on the driveway. I start to turn in my chair to look, but Mariah snaps, literally, right in my face.

"Take this," she's setting a manila folder on the table. "All I'm asking is that you read it carefully and give it some real thought. You know my motives are always pure with you, my friend. This could be the most rewarding challenge of your stubborn life, Callie Potts."

I take the folder as we both hear a truck door outside slam. Mariah grabs my chin.

"Look, I'm a pusher. I know it. It's what I do. And, you're a giver, Callie. You've given your heart, your mind, everything you've got to those incredible guys. Your family. And, your career, not to mention the soul-sucking clients you work for, who don't deserve it. But, at this juncture, you've got to think about you. What do *you* want to do with your life, lady?"

I make the mistake of opening the folder and peeking at the top page. It's a proposed Avalero and Associates partnership agreement between Mariah, me, and Justin for a buy-in of $50,000.

Fifty thousand, I think—my *Jude House money*. I look at Mariah like she knew.

I glance down again and see another tab in the folder titled "Funding?" *Question mark?* I can't help it. I peek. It's a life insurance policy for Jude. For a pretty hefty sum. $200,000.

I gasp.

"I know, Callie. Can you believe it? I found it while digging around for Rachel because they worked there together for a time. It was included in his employment package because Jude was management. But someone converted it to a private policy and has been paying the premiums."

"Rachel," I say.

"Well, blow the lid off it," Mariah tuts.

"No, I wasn't answering you," my eyes are racing across the page. "I just saw she's listed as the beneficiary. Well … one of. Jude made Rachel and me both equal primary beneficiaries?" I ask Mariah, although it's not really a question posed to her. It's right there in black and white.

"But, Rachel's been paying it," I protest. "This policy wouldn't even exist otherwise. I can't take any of that money from her. Or Cadence. I won't. They should use it for Cadence's college fund."

Mariah lifts a shoulder. "Sounds like you two will have a lot to discuss when you get to California."

I fall back into my chair in a huff. It's just so overwhelming. But my eyes start darting around the room. I can't sit still. My back and thighs tingle where the chair touches them. I don't want to tell Mariah, but it feels like someone just plugged me in.

Launch projects, I think. I can still see Jay's wink when he said it, and I have to chuckle.

"Is this what most life coaches do?" I ask her. "Needle and pry. Plant Easter eggs and dangle carrots?"

"You bought the life coach bundle," Mariah quips.

"I haven't paid you for any coaching yet."

"All the more reason. What a bargain!" She smiles.

"I'm not doing this," I tap the folder.

"Okay," she says.

"It's not the right time."

"It never is—for change."

Then we both hear it. The back door opens, and a man's voice booms through the house.

"Mariah, where are you?" I hear. "Who's driving that cool van out back?"

It sounds familiar, but not. Distant but very close. It's almost as if it's traveled through time to reach me. I don't know if I can handle any more jolting revelations today.

"Surpriiiiissseee," Mariah says to me, imitating a little surprise-party-welcome with jazz hands, her dark eyes sparkling.

And then he comes around the corner and sets his keys on the counter. And, he's tall and handsome and perfect. Jesus, he's chiseled and tan and blinding. I almost don't believe I'm seeing him at all, like he's some kind of angel that descended. I hear harps.

It's Roddie in all his adult glory. He's got that same athletic build, broad shoulders, now more muscled than I remember; his thick, wavy hair is glossy and falls right behind his ears. And, he still has those stupid supermodel good looks when he lifts his lashes and meets my eyes.

"Oh, Callie, hi," his arms fall down by his sides as he takes me in.

Part of me wishes I had worn jeans that day to hide my bionic leg, but the other part of me wants him to see it. This is me. The same Callie you once knew, minus a left foot, well, and pimple craters.

"Roddie just got back this week—my big brother. Honorably discharged and ready to enter the civilian world," Mariah says as she makes her way over to him and hooks an arm through, but Roddie's gaze is still on me when I realize, dumbly, that I haven't even responded to him yet.

But, it's like I can't. He's this pulsing force in the room. He has sucked all the air out and made it fifteen degrees hotter. He's like Heman or a demigod. Roddie can't be that perfect and standing here and be human. But I realize he hasn't said anything either, and it dawns on me that I was a surprise to him, too.

"Hi Roddie," is all I can get out. And, the sound of his name in my mouth feels like Pop Rocks. I feel like I have them all through my body, tingling and bursting all over. I'm sure my neck has turned completely red, and it's entirely possible I'm drooling.

"He's going to stay with me for a few weeks until he figures out where he wants to live before he starts classes. As you know, there are some great options near the UT campus," Mariah says. I'm in too much of a daze to fully appreciate how much she is enjoying this, but I know I will get a complete reenactment from her when we settle with our wine glasses after dinner on her back porch, like we always do.

"UT?" I ask dumbly. "You're going to go to UT?" *God, Callie, be cooler!* I scold myself.

"Yeah," he says. "Assuming I can get in." It seems Roddie has recovered a little better than I have.

"That means you'll live in Austin?" It's all I can do. Ask stupid questions with obvious answers.

"It would make going to UT easier," he chuckles, and my heart grows little fairy wings.

"He's going to do paralegal work for my firm while he's in school. I'm grooming him to join Avalero and Associates," Mariah stretches up to her full height to try to reach and ruffle Roddie's hair, but he dodges her.

Roddie brings a hand up to sweep through his hair, and I see he's missing a pinkie and half of his ring finger on his left hand. Roddie notices my eyes on his hand, and he pulls it back and holds it out in front of us.

"Oh, this. Happened when we were trying to diffuse an IED. My buddy Jack took the brunt of it. He has a leg like yours now, but it hasn't stopped him one bit. He's training for marathons, desert runs, and all sorts of extreme outdoors stuff. They almost amputated this hand of mine, but I got lucky and they had an exceptional ortho on base when I came to the infirmary. He saved what he could, and I at least can use my three fingers and thumb well enough. Seriously, this is nothing compared ..." he drifts off.

I find I'm mesmerized by Roddie's altered hand moving and waving in front of me. It reminds me of my lady stump and Betty, my bionic leg, and I find myself, as I often am when I look at my own leg, mesmerized by what the human body can endure, overcome, and adapt to. The human heart and spirit as well.

"They were some tough years, but I'm glad I served," Roddie continues. "They claim I'm traumatized, though." The way he says it sounds like Roddie is almost apologizing for himself, as if he may not be a suitable mate for anyone anymore, and his impulse—for whatever weird reason—pricks me, so I respond in kind.

"I'm married, but my husband is gay," I say, and Mariah spits out a swig of Coke she had just taken.

"Wow, what an intro. This is going even better than I expected. Wait till I tell Levi," she chuckles. "You two sound perfect for each other. Come on, help me set up the table out back for dinner." She claps us both on the shoulder as we make our way onto Mariah's expansive back patio, overlooking a gorgeous mesa scene.

Clovis is stretched out on her belly in the back yard, and she starts army crawling toward me, her hind legs dragging behind and tail wagging, as we make our way out—her version of acknowledging me but making sure I know just how much she enjoys the feel of sunny grass on her tummy. I find I agree and want to join her.

"Clovis?" Roddie asks, smiling at her. I nod.

"The one and only," I'm smiling too, as I keep my eyes on her—the furry, sun-soaked jewel of my life.

Roddie pulls a chair out for me, which surprises me. My guys love me, to the moon and back, but gay men don't have that chivalrous instinct like … *knights in shining armor do,* my brain finishes for me, as I close my mouth to make sure I'm not drooling. Again.

"I was really sorry to hear about your brother, Jude, Callie. He was a really good person. We grew closer than I think you know when we were younger. Jude had a real impact on me. I want to tell you more about our time together," Roddie tells me, and it takes my breath away.

The entire purpose of this trip—for me—has been to rebuild myself, grow my confidence in being and doing things alone, and to find more pieces of Jude in the world to savor. I never dreamed this huge, living, breathing, hunk of a piece was waiting for me here when I arrived.

But Mariah did. *Surprise,* I laugh to myself. *I'll say.*

I look to Mariah to see if she can possibly understand the gravity of what I'm feeling. She grabs my hand and gives me a knowing nod.

"Someone really wise once told me good friends are like magic. Rare and hard to explain, but wondrous all the same."

I'm speechless, looking at her, thinking vaguely somewhere back to my fourteen-year-old brain that those words are mine. And, for just a small sliver of a second, I think I might be able to see myself through Mariah's eyes. Shimmering and splintered. A bright pulsing oak tree.

It's quite a sight.

———

Later that night, when Mariah and I are curled up on her back porch swing with Clovis between us, sharing a bottle of Merlot, I find it's the perfect time.

"Mariah, I've got a story for you."

"Oh?"

"I know you remember Tyler Beck."

Mariah starts imitating Tyler groping around on her carpet for his busted-out tooth. I join her, our laughter rising and hanging gingerly from the trees above us.

"That's the one. Well, I don't know if you know this, but he and I went to prom together."

Mariah raises her eyebrows.

The End